COLD
PURSUIT

COLD
PURSUIT

Toni Anderson

ALSO BY TONI ANDERSON

For my sisters,
Julie and Eileen.

CHAPTER ONE

THE ROLLER COASTER thundered high above them in the mall and people screamed. Vivi Vincent's son's blue eyes widened with wonder as he watched with obvious delight. He grabbed her sleeve and grinned like any normal eight-year-old boy.

The bright colors of the rides and glaring sunshine through the glass roof made her eyes water. That's what she told herself. It had nothing to do with the disastrous meeting they'd had first thing this morning with Dr. Hinkle.

She patted Michael's hand, and he caught her gaze. The intelligence that shone in his eyes took her breath; as if all the secrets of the universe were locked up inside that bright, young mind.

He kept tugging her arm, trying to get her to go on the ride, but her stomach was too jumbled to even think about going on a roller coaster right now. And no way would she let him go alone—if something went wrong who knew what could happen? She'd never forgive herself if he got hurt just because she was too chicken to go on an amusement park ride.

"Want to visit the toy store?" she suggested instead.

He nodded and smiled, but she knew he was disappointed from the look of yearning he sent to the seventy foot monstrosity behind them. They headed past old-fashioned carousels and giant mushroom-shaped swings—much more her speed. The Minneapolis Mall, a smaller cousin to the Mall of America a few miles across the city, was a kid's paradise.

She straightened her shoulders. Michael *would* enjoy this outing today, even if she had to subject herself to the terror of going on that thing. It would hopefully make up for his being poked and prodded by Dr. Hinkle this morning, then patronized within an inch of sanity by a local TV reporter doing a feature on the famous psychiatric neuroscientist's research program. The woman had interviewed them about Michael's "issues" and drawing ability. Hopefully it wasn't a slow news day in the twin cities.

Michael spotted the intricate green serpent who guarded the entrance of the toy store and any lingering disappointment in his expression vanished. They stood in silent fascination for several long minutes as they took in the display that clambered up and over the shop. There was a teddy bear in cowboy gear riding a horse, a dinosaur on a motorcycle, and above it all a giant clown that made Vivi distinctly uneasy. What was it about clowns?

"OK, let's go inside. You can choose one thing from the store, and then we'll go find something to eat. Later we'll hit the rides."

He grinned and ran inside. Vivi hid a smile. She took a step after him only to collide with someone massive and bulky who knocked her on her ass. She ended up sprawled on the floor as the man kept on walking. Her jaw dropped at his rudeness, and she climbed awkwardly to her knees, cradling her wrist, which hurt from the unexpected impact with the floor.

"Need some help?" A man crouched beside her. He had

short, black hair and rich, brown eyes that crinkled attractively at the outer edges. His fingers were strong and firm as he eased her to her feet, holding onto her good arm.

"Thank you."

She gripped him for balance as she slipped her shoe back on. He had a straight nose, full bottom lip and a cleft in his chin. Those dark eyes ran over her critically as if assessing her injuries, then something changed and they warmed with frank male approval. She let go of his hand, and her knees wobbled. She blamed it on the high heels she so rarely wore.

Another round of screams from the people on the roller coaster broke through her reverie.

"Thank you, again. I'd better go find my son." She nodded toward the toy store. It had become automatic to use Michael as a barrier, and the habit was starting to wear on her nerves. Maybe one day she'd get over the trust issues her ex had instilled in her.

Maybe.

One day.

"Good luck getting him out of there." The handsome stranger held up a plastic bag with the distinctive logo on the side. It looked incongruous against his smart business clothes—a black suit, blue shirt, purple tie. How someone carried themselves revealed a lot about a person—his posture suggested a military background—and maybe some sort of law enforcement. He also exuded an air of competence and authority she recognized from her days working at the UN. The last guy who'd affected her this way had taught her that a handsome face and commanding manner were no substitute for compassion or morals. Still, it was nice to look at.

"I got my fix buying for a friend's kid." For a split-second a shadow passed across his features then disappeared. Maybe she imagined it. He took a step away. "If you're sure you're OK?"

She nodded and he smiled back and then strode away.

Gone. Vivi blinked.

It had been a long time since a man had looked at her like she was anything except a frazzled, single mom over thirty. The sensation of being a flesh and blood woman slid over her body like a skintight dress, rekindling a part of herself she'd forgotten existed. *Great,* another thing to add to her list of frustrations.

Walking toward the store she fingered her sore wrist and decided it was nothing more than a mild sprain. She'd ice it when they got back to the hotel later tonight.

A loud boom erupted from the center of the atrium. She jumped and spun around. Screams grew louder and for a moment she thought the roller coaster was malfunctioning. Then a weird noise peppered the air, one that sounded familiar but she couldn't identify at first. Then she did. *Gunfire.* People started running. A man standing beside the candy store dropped to the floor, and the glass from the window shattered and rained down on him as a wide pool of blood spread around his body.

Oh, dear God.

There was a shooter in the mall.

Michael!

She spun and ran inside the toy store, searching frantically. People were rushing around desperately looking for children and loved ones. A display crashed to the floor, and a model disintegrated into a thousand pieces. She skidded on the tiny bits, but righted herself before she fell. A woman rammed a stroller into Vivi's ankles in her determination to get to her toddler, who was wandering off to the front entrance. Vivi grabbed the kid and thrust him back into his mother's arms.

"Thank you." The woman's face was white with terror. She had a baby and a toddler to deal with, along with masses of shopping bags.

"Leave the stroller. Grab the children and get out of the mall as fast as possible," Vivi told her. That's what she intended to do. She scanned the store for the carrot-topped head of the most important person in her world. *There.* She pushed her way through people milling around in confusion.

Michael was starting to get agitated and stood silent and shaking. She got to him and cradled his precious face with one hand, pushed back his hair with the other. She had to calm him down if they hoped to get out of there alive. "I'm here, Michael. I'll look after you, but you have to listen to me and you have to concentrate, OK?" *Please don't freak out.*

Blue eyes cleared and focused. Her incredibly brave son squared his shoulders and nodded, taking her hand and squeezing tight. He knew they were in danger. Love for him swelled inside her so enormous it wanted to burst through her skin. The terror was bigger. It wanted to crawl through her veins and eat her alive.

She would do anything to protect this child. Anything.

One of the cashiers was on the phone, presumably talking to security. Another cashier yelled, "Cops are telling us to sit tight while they assess the situation."

Sit tight? No way in hell.

The sound of gunfire was getting louder now; bullets blasted glass and concrete. Metal hit metal and she could hear the ricochets whizzing around the structure, turning the mall into a deadly pinball machine. Gunpowder was growing thicker in the air, clogging her throat. Then more shots, but these sounded much closer, on the other side of the store. Her mouth went dry.

Two shooters.

And she and Michael, and all the other customers and employees, were trapped between them.

She walked quickly to one of the doors at the back of the shop and peered out cautiously. A man at the far end of the corridor stood holding a large automatic weapon. The same man who'd knocked her to the ground earlier. Thank God he hadn't stopped. He was facing the other direction, scanning the area, then pausing and squeezing off rapid bursts of gunfire. Screams rose, some of which were cut horrifically short.

Bullets rained down from the balconies above and the over-sized model creations on the roof of the store shattered.

The sweat on her skin went cold. There were at least three shooters. They were in the middle of a war zone.

Vivi looked back over her shoulder and froze. A gunman was winding through the rides toward the stores. His face was covered, but his gait was relaxed, almost indolent. This was a man who'd killed before and would show no mercy. She'd worked with this sort of man, at the White House, at the UN.

What the hell could she do? The second gunman was too close in the corridor behind the store and they were trapped. Others spotted the approaching danger and started pouring out the back of the shop screaming, including the woman with her two children, still pushing the stroller and clutching her shopping bags. Michael tried to follow them but Vivi pulled him back and pressed his face into her stomach as the people who'd run were mowed down.

Bodies fell. Contorted in agony. Blood smeared the floor. The woman with the stroller crashed atop the toddler, but the little boy's leg kept twisting as if he were trying to get free.

Stay still!

Her gut twisted and bile rose up her throat. The bright, white halls of the shopping mall were being turned into a butcher's shop.

Michael shook in her arms. She hugged him closer. "I won't let them hurt you," she whispered. But she had no clue how to stop them. She kept one eye on the man approaching through the amusement park rides and peeked out to see where the other shooter was. He was about six stores down, looking into the store windows. Unless he turned around and moved off, he'd spot them as soon as they made a run for it. If it was just her she could maybe slip past him, but dragging an eight-year-old through a rain of bullets? Was it even worth making a break for it in that direction or should they head toward the bus and metro station? But looking at how organized these terrorists were—and what else could they be except terrorists?—she figured they'd have the main entrances covered. The shops then? Some of them must connect to the outside world through back exits but she didn't know which ones.

She spotted the cupboard beneath the cashier's stand and an idea took hold. "Michael," she whispered in his ear. "We're going to play a game of hide and seek. Only this is a very serious game because these people want to hurt us, so you mustn't give yourself away. Understand?" He nodded, those blue eyes of his wide with fear, but also total understanding.

He wasn't stupid the way some people assumed, but his intelligence wouldn't matter a damn if one of these monsters put a bullet in him.

If anything happened to him, she'd die too.

She hugged him fiercely, then sank to her haunches and made him follow her as she crawled to the register. She slid one cupboard door quietly open. It was full of supplies. Staplers, receipt rolls, plastic bags. She shoved it all to one end of the cupboard and urged him inside. He lay there, curled up, shaking, eyes wide and frightened.

"You have to stay here and not make a sound." She laughed a little hysterically at that. "Don't thump your head or hands and feet against the sides, or else they'll hear you, understand?"

He nodded but grabbed her hand in a desperate plea.

"I'm going to run to those two shops over there." He rapidly shook his head. He'd seen what had happened to the others who'd tried to run. "I'll wait for the bad men to look the other way before I go. I'm a fast runner." She slipped off her heels, squeezed his fingers. "I swear I will come back for you, but whatever happens you have to promise not to move from here. Not to make a sound. Promise?" She held him so tight he winced, but he nodded even as tears started to roll. She held his fingers to her lips and then kissed his warm cheek. "I'll be back, Michael. I won't let them hurt you. You trust me, right?"

He nodded.

"And I trust you because I *know* how smart you are." Tears blurred her vision but she blinked them away and a solid wave of determination moved through her. She kissed him again. "No moving from here until I come get you. No matter how long it takes." She held his gaze. "I'll be back as soon as I can. I promise."

———————————

FBI SPECIAL AGENT Jed Brennan did not spend a lot of time hanging around malls—especially not during the run up to Christmas. He'd rather have a root canal.

Officially he was off duty from the FBI's Behavioral Analysis Unit-4, taking some long-overdue vacation days. Unofficially things were a little more complicated.

His boss had insisted he take some time after using excessive force on a suspect. That's what you got for punching a wealthy serial killer in the face when you arrested the fucker. No matter Miles Brandon had smacked him so hard his skull still buzzed, or that the guy had tried to slip a slender blade between his ribs. Let alone what he'd done to his unsuspecting pick-ups from DC gay bars. Didn't matter. Breaking the asshole's nose was against the rules.

It was a fine line he'd crossed and he doubted ASAC Lincoln Frazer—newly promoted after the old unit leader had unexpectedly retired last week—would have done things different.

Thankfully, he and Frazer were old friends, going back more than a decade to when Jed had been stationed at the Kandahar Air Force Base and had called in the FBI to investigate a suspected serial murderer. The young soldier, together with the inexperienced FBI Special Agent, had caught the killer, but Jed had been too late to save Mia, the woman he loved. The case had made Frazer a media superstar, but the guy was a solid investigator who'd devoted his entire life to the BAU.

Friend or no friend, Frazer had the power to not only bench him, but to put him out of the game permanently if he wanted.

There were plenty other federal agents eager to fill Jed's size eleven boots. So, he'd wait his boss out.

He had cases to work on his own time. He'd make the most of his enforced vacation and visit his family during the festive season. The holidays made humanity's general bat-shit craziness worse so it was usually hard to take a break then. The world was full of whackos and sadists with nothing better to do than figure out new ways to hurt people. It was his job to keep a lid on the insanity although some days he thought his own head would burst from the horror of it all.

Hell, maybe his boss was right. Maybe he could use some downtime in one of the quietest, most peaceful places on earth—the Northwoods of Wisconsin. The fact he'd have to visit Bobby's widow and young son was beside the point. He should have done it months ago.

Last night he'd visited an old Army buddy he hadn't seen in a couple of years—Jack Donovan—who was a homicide detective with Minneapolis PD. Today he was hitting the road for the much shorter drive to America's Dairyland. It was close enough to Christmas he could nail all his family holiday obligations in one relatively painless swoop. Hence, the mall.

Root canal. Maybe even a flesh wound.

The woman with the bright red hair and intriguing eyes was an unexpected bonus. The asshole who'd knocked her over was oblivious to the damage he'd left in his wake. Jed had been torn between going after him and helping the woman up off the floor. The protective streak he and his brothers had inherited from their father was too ingrained to just abandon her.

He'd been knocked off balance, too, by her beauty. Plus, she had that innate poise and confidence that totally did it for him. He shrugged off a moment of regret that he'd never see her again. He loved women. It was relationships he avoided at all costs. His job wasn't exactly nine-to-five, and since losing Mia in Afghanistan all those years ago he'd put a firm guard around his heart. Which was exactly how he liked it.

Still, it didn't hurt to look.

A hunting store caught his eye. Thousands of knives of every size and color. *Oh, yeah.* He went inside and started looking for new knives for his dad and two brothers and a pocket knife with lots of handy gadgets for his mom. Two shops and he'd be done.

Happy Christmas.

BOOM!

An explosion reverberated from the amusement park rides. *What the...?* Then the sound of shots being fired. Terrorists or heist? Jed reached for his gun, swore when he realized he wasn't wearing it. He'd left the SIG locked in the car because he'd wanted to take a whirl on the roller coaster for old times' sake—something him and Bobby and Liam had always done as teenagers. He hadn't wanted to be armed with a deadly weapon while experiencing g-force.

He flashed his shield at the store's security guy. "Call 911 and mall security. Any way out back there?" He pointed to the hidden door at the rear of the shop.

The guy nodded even as he held his cell to his ear. They made their way toward the back of the store. A woman in a black suit, probably the manager, put a key in the lock.

"Hang on. Got any hunting knives behind the counter?"

Who knew what lay behind that door? He wanted a weapon. Jed's car was in the parking lot on the opposite side of the mall, otherwise he'd have gone for his SIG. He eyed the glass cases on the walls. He could smash one open but didn't want to draw that much attention to himself or the other people hiding here.

The security guy looked at him uncertainly.

Jed thrust his badge closer to the guy's face. "Off duty FBI Agent. Get me a damn knife...now!" A blade wasn't much against a sub-machine-gun but it beat the hell out of the plastic toy he currently held. He placed the box on the floor. He'd pick it up later. Hopefully.

Bullets sprayed along the corridor outside, and more sounded from levels above them. People crouched in terrified silence. Piercing screams told him civilians were dying and he was ill-prepared to save any of them until he could get a gun. The security guard hustled behind the desk and handed Jed a knife with a six-inch blade. *Better*.

"What do you want me to do?" the guy asked.

"The mall has its own security, correct?"

The guy nodded but looked uncertain. "Security Center is on this floor. Over near where that first explosion came from. No one answered when I tried to call them."

Crap. If these guys took out the security nerve center before they attacked they were highly organized and deadly serious about doing as much damage as possible. Or stealing a massive amount of money with total disregard for public safety.

Jed ran his eyes over the ten or so people milling around uncertainly. "Get them out of here and tell the cops outside what you know. Which other stores along this block have rear exits?"

"Just us and the restaurant at the end of the row. Once you're in the corridor, there are exits to the parking garages and the loading bays used for deliveries."

Jed nodded. "Leave the premises ASAP but watch for shooters on the outside. Tell cops there's an—" he tested the point of the knife with his thumb "—almost unarmed FBI agent inside."

He pulled out his cell phone and dialed the local FBI office. Busy signal. He texted his boss instead and shoved the cell back in his pocket. So much for R&R.

They cautiously unlocked the door at the back of the shop and checked the corridor—clear. The security guard took the lead. Civilians started to pour out, hopefully on their way to safety.

A black shadow passed the front of the store and Jed held his breath. It was the asshole who'd knocked over the pretty redhead. Everyone in the shop froze and then started hustling faster as the guy slowly turned toward them, shouldering an assault rifle and aiming it right between Jed's eyes. Jed had no choice. He threw himself through the door after the others. He slammed it shut as bullets tore through the walls beside him.

"Run." He waved the others frantically in the opposite direction. Held his position as he listened closely for footsteps. He'd switched into attack mode and he'd done this sort of drill a million times over. He'd just never done it armed with nothing except a blade, and surrounded by potentially thousands of innocent civilians who could get caught in the crossfire.

CHAPTER TWO

V IVI QUIETLY CLOSED the sliding door of the cupboard, leaving it slightly ajar so Michael wouldn't be in complete darkness. Satisfied no one would see him unless they actually opened the cupboard door, she peered up over the service desk.

The mall had gone eerily quiet as if everyone was holding their breath, hiding. No sign of the shooters. She had a horrible vision of the gunmen lying in wait for the unsuspecting shoppers trying to escape. The rides still flashed with bright lights and garish displays, but they'd all stopped moving. Her eyes rose to the roller coaster in the distance. If they'd been on that ride there was a good chance they'd already be dead. Her legs trembled at the awfulness of this moment. She'd seen this stuff on the news, but had never expected to get caught up in it herself. Especially not with her child in tow.

Small pockets of people crouched and hid around the store. She met the terrified eyes of a middle-aged man who clutched a little girl to his side. His eyes seemed to beg her for help but what was she supposed to do? She had no training, no weapons. She nodded to him anyway. She'd do whatever she could to get them out.

At the back door of the shop she used the reflection in

some of the windows opposite to look for the bad guys. She stilled when she saw the shooter prowling some distance away down the corridor. The toddler on the floor in front of her started writhing and trying to get free of his mother's unresponsive arm. Vivi's eyes flashed back to the shooter. He went into one of the shops and she braced herself to move. Gunshots rang out from inside the store he'd entered. *Don't think about it.* She ran across to the little boy, dragged him from beneath his mother and picked him up. But a glance in the stroller showed the baby, all pretty in a pink bonnet, eyes wide open, and smiling.

Oh, hell. She couldn't leave a baby.

Vivi placed the kid on the floor and he grabbed onto her leg. She pulled away the blankets to undo the straps on the baby harness. Her fingers shook and couldn't manipulate the hard plastic snaps. She kept looking at the shop where the bad guy had disappeared. More shots. Her blood pounded through her ears so loudly she was deafened to everything but her own erratic heartbeat. Finally she got the catch free and eased the baby onto her shoulder. Then she took the toddler's hand and urged him to run to the clothes shop immediately in front of them.

She quickly scanned the interior of the store. It was empty of people which gave her hope for escape. She headed through to the changing rooms at the back. The door to the storeroom was firmly locked. She knocked gently and whispered, "Is anyone in there? I have a baby out here. Can you let me in?"

No sound came from behind the door, but the weight of fear hit her in a wave. *Dammit.* She couldn't blame people for not putting themselves at risk but...

The baby snuggled against her shoulder and started gurgling. Her heart twisted with grief for the mother and for the others who'd already died, for the cruel needless waste of human life. Who were these monsters? What did they want?

She was torn about her decision to leave Michael. So torn she could barely function, but she had to. He was hidden and hopefully safe until she found a way out of here. Being in small compressed spaces comforted him, the tighter the better. But what if something happened to him? Or to her? Doubt and uncertainty whirled inside her brain until her heart raced as if she was about to have a heart attack. She forced herself to calm down. Yoga breaths. *Don't let these bastards scare you to death.*

She opened every unlocked door in the store, but found only small storage spaces. No escape. She went back into the main entrance, crouched low behind the clothes rails. The little tyke held onto her leg in an unbreakable grip and moved like a third leg. She stroked a hand over his curly hair. He was going to be traumatized for life.

Using the reflections in the glass, she once again scanned the corridor. No one was visible. She ran into a restaurant next door and ducked inside. It was dimly lit with lots of alcoves. Probably a good spot to hide, but she didn't see anyone, which gave her more hope that there was a back way out of this hellhole. If there was, she'd run to get Michael.

She cradled the baby carefully against her shoulder, darting looks around every corner before rushing forward. She reached the kitchen and was hit by a weird combination of smells. Food cooking on the gas burners, mixed with the stench of violent death.

Three bodies lay twisted on the ground. *Oh, no.*

She spun around, hoisted the toddler into her other arm as she stepped over the corpses to check out the back of the kitchen near two massive walk-in freezers.

Where the hell were the cops?

The sensation of sticky blood on her stockinged feet made her want to throw up. Her arms ached from the weight of the children, but she gritted her teeth and kept moving. She spotted a door with a fire exit sign. That was it!

The metallic click of a weapon had her freezing and turning around slowly. The man who'd knocked her over earlier was pointing a matte-black assault rifle at her face. She clutched the baby tighter, put the little boy on the floor, and tried to push him behind her leg.

The gunman was tall, over six feet four; Arabic features, small, hard ebony eyes in a round face that couldn't have been over thirty. His olive skin was free of sweat. No visible sign of remorse.

"Why are you doing this?" she asked.

His nostrils flared.

She asked him again in Arabic.

His eyes widened and then swept over her uncovered hair. She saw him draw in a deep breath and knew he'd fire on the exhale, so she threw herself to the floor behind the kitchen counter. She tried to shelter the baby who started to cry at the sudden jarring movement and blast of noise as bullets ripped into the wall behind where she'd been standing just seconds ago. The direction of the bullets followed as he started walking toward them and she scrambled and dragged the boy and the baby along the floor by their padded jackets as she tried to escape. Her nylons made her slip on the bloody floor. She sprawled and scrambled, clawing for purchase. The gunman came around the corner of the kitchen bench and she closed her eyes and braced herself for a bullet. Instead she heard a grunt and more deafening gunfire pelting the metal in the kitchen. Then silence punctuated by heavy breathing. She opened her eyes but no one was there.

She held still, unsure what had happened.

"He's dead. Come on out," said an oddly familiar voice.

She climbed to her feet and there stood the guy who'd helped her earlier in the mall. A knife in his hand dripped crimson droplets of blood onto the tile floor. The terrorist lay twitching at his feet. Her stomach turned, relief competing with horror. Her rescuer grabbed the bad guy's rifle, searching through the man's pockets for more weapons and ammunition which he shoved in his jacket pockets.

"Thank you. *Again*." Her voice was rough as crushed gravel. If it hadn't been for him she and the children would be dead.

He nodded. "FBI Special Agent Jed Brennan at your service, ma'am."

He wasn't just handsome; he'd just taken on superhero status.

"Very happy to make your acquaintance, Special Agent Brennan. You saved our lives." The baby started crying, and she joggled her gently in her arms and kissed her sweet forehead. She walked toward the FBI agent. Now she could go get Michael, and they could get out of here. She handed him the baby. He handed her straight back.

"You don't understand," she told him. "I need to go get my son. I left him hiding in the cupboard beneath the cash registers in the toy store."

He frowned in confusion. "So who're these guys?" He pointed to the toddler and baby.

"I found them outside. Their mother was shot." Her voice

caught. She tried to hand him the baby again, but he took a step away. OK, less superhero, more federal law enforcement officer—another brand of male she'd dealt with in the past. She dared not raise her voice in case she attracted the attention of more bad guys, but she was desperate. *"Please.* I need to get my son out of there. Other people too."

"How many others?"

"At least fifteen, maybe twenty in that store alone, many children."

The sound of footsteps rushing toward them had the FBI guy pushing her and the children behind him and them both crouching behind the kitchen counters. The middle-aged man who'd caught her eye in the toy store came tearing into the kitchen with a whole swathe of people running behind him. They crashed to a halt when they saw Special Agent Brennan holding a gun.

"He's OK. He's with the FBI," she assured them.

The faces of the scared shoppers relaxed slightly, but the terror at the situation remained. They were far from safe.

She scanned the crowd, then frowned. "Where's my son?"

The gray-haired man stepped forward. "I tried to get him to come but he wouldn't budge."

Her heart sank. *Oh, no.* She'd made him promise not to move.

"We need to get out of here." Agent Brennan spoke quietly but made it an order. He eased open the fire exit door and peered down the corridor. "This way. Quickly. Keep your hands in the air in case you meet cops who think you're part of this terrorist gang. Keep your eyes peeled for shooters."

Vivi tried to pass the baby to another woman, but the kid wouldn't let go of her and started crying even louder.

"What are you doing?" the fed asked impatiently. Those chocolate eyes were now as black and cold as obsidian.

"I *need* to get my son. I *promised* him I wouldn't be long."

"If that baby keeps crying you're putting all these people's lives at risk." The sharp gleam of intelligence in those eyes reminded her of Michael. "Let's get everyone here out and then we'll come back and get your son, OK?" He tried to put a little warmth into his voice.

The fed was manipulating her and right now she hated him for it. She didn't buy it, but the idea one of the bad guys might find them all because the baby was crying wasn't something she could live with. "You don't understand, my son won't go anywhere without me." She soothed the baby, who quieted. "So if you're lying to me…"

"I never lie to beautiful women." The brief flash of smile was not a compliment. It was a *move-your-ass-now-before-I-make-you* smile.

She wasn't intimidated. The only thing she cared about was getting Michael out safely. She opened her mouth to argue, but was swept along by the crowd. The little boy grabbed her leg again, and she scooped him up even though he was heavy as hell. Her biceps burned. She found herself tucked between all the other terrified people as they ran down the long corridor toward the parking garage. *Damn it.* She gritted her teeth. OK. She'd get these kids out and go back for her own baby. Five minutes, tops. Please God keep him safe until she got back. Her body shook from shock and exertion, but she concentrated on getting the kids out. Then she'd go back. Then she'd save her son.

A wave of fresh, cold air hit when they got to the parking garage; her bare feet immediately frozen against the unforgiving concrete. Jed Brennan dangled the weapon he'd taken from the bad guy by the strap and held his gold shield in the other hand.

Her arms felt like they were about to drop off. Shouts rose, and men in black uniforms herded them toward a cordoned off area. The cops held them at gunpoint and made them put their hands on their heads. Didn't they understand they were victims here? The babies both started screaming when someone took them from her. They were safe now so it didn't really matter how much noise they made, though it tugged at her heartstrings. She hoped they had a loving family to take care of them.

She whirled toward Jed Brennan, and he was watching her with those keen eyes as black as midnight.

"Let's go get my son," she urged him.

A police officer pushed her toward the others but she stood firm and argued. "That FBI agent said I could bring out those two children and then go back for my own son."

"The fed isn't in charge and no one is going into that mall who ain't law enforcement, ma'am. You're staying here until we can verify your identity."

"Special Agent Brennan!" she started shouting. He was talking to someone who looked like they were in charge. His expression went carefully blank and then he turned his back on her. He wasn't handsome any longer. He was just another guy who'd lied to get what he wanted, and then walked away on his vows.

She shouted louder. "You *promised* I could go back for my son!" Rage filled her and she tried to dodge the cop on guard duty. Next moment she was on the ground, chin grazing the wet, dirty pavement as her wrists were cuffed. "You lied to me.

If anything happens to my son, I'll... Stop. Stop!" she hissed at the cop who was manhandling her. "There's something you need to know about Michael!" She broke off because nothing would matter if anything happened to her beautiful son. Brennan looked at her again as the cop hauled her off the ground and started pushing her away from the mall. She didn't let go of the FBI agent's gaze, not even when she tripped and fell. "Get him out of there, please, or so help me God..."

———————————

JED COULDN'T FILTER the guilt or the hysterical redhead out of his brain even as he tried to concentrate on the update from the commander of the SWAT team. The fact he'd lied to her to get her out of the mall shouldn't bother him, but she'd left her son behind and the kid was in extreme danger. That made his insides ache.

Push it aside. Don't let empathy for the victims cloud your judgment—his boss's words were good advice. Hell, he *was* trying.

The terrorists had taken out the Security Center first and all cameras were down so they had no eyes inside the mall except for a couple of armed security guards who were pinned down in the northwest corner, and trapped shoppers who were tweeting the cops for help. Police had advised them to stay off social media in case the bad guys were also monitoring it. Not a good idea to state your exact location to the world when someone with a loaded gun wanted to kill you. There were reports of multiple casualties and at least seven gunmen, probably more. Two on each floor and one hosing down the transit center with an assault rifle; waiting for people to try and escape that way, or for the cops to move in. Many people had gotten out. Many more were still trapped inside—like the redhead's son. His name was Michael, apparently, because she wasn't done yelling at Jed yet.

The fact he'd killed one of these assholes was starting to make him feel better about what was rapidly morphing into one of the worst days of his life—and he'd had some humdingers. The redhead screamed at him again and a cop tackled her. He opened his mouth to get the guy to ease up when he caught her gaze.

Hatred and desperation poured off her. He'd lied to get her out of there, but now her kid was stuck smack bang in the middle of a gun battle that was about to get a hell of a lot worse. *Shit.*

He could deal with the hatred; it was the desperation in her dark blue gaze that twisted his gut. And the certainty that if the other police officer wasn't forcibly restraining her, she'd have run back into that death zone, armed with nothing more than her sharp tongue and a pair of brass balls, and tried to rescue her kid herself.

"Because that's what real parents did." The voice inside his head was his father's.

"Get him out of there, *please*! Brennan, please!" she shouted louder.

He swallowed the knot in his throat. Nodded.

The SWAT guy eyed him like he was an idiot.

"I need to get back in there."

"We don't need any dead heroes, son."

"You didn't see the bodies of all the civilians these guys have already killed. They don't want hostages. They want blood." He rubbed the back of his neck. "I *am* going back in

23

there."

"Not on your own you're not." The commander eyed him the same way his boss did when he thought he was about to do something stupid. The guy said something into his mike.

Jed stood taller and braced his legs apart. "I'm SWAT trained. Seven years in the bureau and Army before that—sniper school. Give me some men and we can start evening the odds, protecting civilians."

The captain's eyes flicked to the woman being cuffed. "What's going on with her?"

"She left her son hiding in a cupboard in the toy store while she searched for a way out. I promised her we'd go back for him together. She just realized I lied."

The guy let out a heavy sigh. "You did what you had to do to get her out of there."

"And now I'm going back to get her son like I told her I would." Jed held the man's steady gaze. "Give me a couple guys otherwise I'm going in alone."

The man's expression turned amused. "I'll give you two guys, but only because that was already my plan. You're the backup. Let's try and get that kid out alive."

Jed nodded. He knew he shouldn't make promises he might not be able to keep, but he couldn't witness the fierce maternal passion on the woman's face without at least trying. "Thanks."

The captain's gaze went back to the furious redhead who was glaring at them both. "Don't fancy your chances with that one, son."

Jed huffed out a laugh. "No kidding. I've got more chance of helping the Packers win the Super Bowl."

Two heavily-armed officers approached him. One handed

him tactical body armor, comms, a fully loaded assault weapon and Glock. He geared up, put spare ammo in his jacket pockets, checked both weapons and nodded. "Let's do it."

The other guys, Wright and Marcos, led the way back into the mall. Jed felt a hell of a lot more comfortable going back in with these guys than he had leaving with all those unarmed civilians. Didn't mean it wasn't about to get a lot more dangerous though.

He directed them to the restaurant kitchen fire exit. Paused long enough to photograph the face of the guy he'd taken down earlier. Emailed it to his boss. A team from the Critical Incident Response Unit would be on the way ASAP.

Wright cleared the kitchen area and radioed in to the commander who could see and hear everything via an onboard camera.

They moved slowly toward the front of the restaurant. Jed counted bodies along the way. Three so far, not counting the terrorist scumbag he'd helped meet his maker. They got to the open front of the restaurant and squatted behind a fake rock facade. *Shit.* The carnage was gut churning. Men and women lay strewn across the glittering mall, and broken glass sprinkled like diamonds across ruby-red blood.

Not everyone who lay there was dead. He could see some movement. The odd, shallow breath, the flicker of an eyelid. But they were injured and vulnerable and goddamned they were hurt. Fury rose inside but he pushed it down. Emotion wouldn't help. Tactical training and well-placed bullets would.

He eyed the toy store, which looked empty. The white cabinet beneath the cashier's register was still closed and not riddled with bullets. A good sign.

They were about to move when a gunman came into view

inside the toy store, pacing back and forth. They all froze. The guy wore a balaclava rolled up his forehead. Aviator sunglasses and a black-trimmed beard. His features were hard to make out. Wright lined up a shot.

"Hold fire," Jed murmured as he saw something else re-flected in the glass at the other side of the store. Another gunman, then another figure—that looked like a woman under some bulky clothing and a headscarf. One of the notorious black widows? She was talking rapidly to the others though he couldn't see her face. They were all heavily armed, no doubt conferring about their sadistic battle plans.

The cupboard door moved a fraction.

"Hell, kid, don't come out now." It was terrorist central, and the last thing he wanted was a firefight with a child slap bang in the middle.

CHAPTER THREE

"ANY CHANCE WE can get someone to create a distraction on the other side of the plaza so we can get in there and extract the kid?" He looked at Marcos.

Marcos kept low and moved back into the depths of the restaurant to talk to his boss.

Jed scanned the mall and spotted several shooters in the wings, all watching and waiting. For what? Victims? Cops? Santa?

"Think they're Islamists?" Wright asked him softly.

"Beats the fuck out of me. Could be Islamist, could be domestic pretending to be foreign to stir up trouble. We'll know more when we get an ID on the dead guy. All I really know for sure is my mother sometimes shops at this mall and that could be her lying there dead. The idea they'd shoot her as easily as they'd shoot anyone else pisses me off."

Marcos hunkered down behind Jed's shoulder as they watched the terrorists. "Boss has a team about to do a hard entry from the north side. They're trying to get to the security guards who're holed up, and hopefully get better intel on what went down earlier." The guy stared at his watch. "Ten seconds."

Jed counted down in his head. It felt like an eternity.

A flash bang went off, and the terrorists jerked to attention. Three of them ran in the direction of the firefight, a fourth came out of the store and started patrolling the corridor in front of them with his weapon raised. As soon as he turned his back, Marcos drew his knife, ran up behind the guy, and cut his throat. Wright moved out to cover him, sweeping his gaze and his gun over the upper levels. Jed was sprinting to the toy store before the terrorist hit the deck. He slid to a halt and opened the cupboard door. A pair of big, blue eyes locked onto him, huge with fear.

"I've come to get you out…"

The kid shrank to the back of the cupboard. Then he closed his eyes and started to rock, which was about to make a lot of noise in the enclosed space.

There's something you need to know… The redhead *had* tried to tell him. He was an asshole for not listening to her.

He spoke quietly but firmly "Michael. Your mom sent me to get you out."

The kid stopped rocking.

"You don't believe me?"

The kid opened his eyes. Jed wished he'd say something. They had to move fast and get out before the bad guys came back and started shooting. He fished out his badge and showed it to him.

"Your mom is a redhead just like you, right? But prettier." He joked. "And she's loud when she's angry, really loud, and she was angry with me for not letting her come back in here to get you like she promised." Jed swallowed the saliva that pooled in his mouth. "She yelled at me a lot. So I guess she's got a redheaded temperament too, huh? Fiery?" *Passionate.* He mentally kicked himself for his thoughts wandering in that direction when people were dying and he was trying to save her son. Still, he was a guy and adrenaline was pumping, amping up his idiot quota by a factor of a thousand.

The kid's eyes locked on him. Connected. Concentrated. Jed had him, and he wasn't about to let him go. "I don't think she likes me very much, but if I get you out of here like I promised, I think we can get her to stop yelling at me. You think you can help me with that, Michael?"

Something weird was going on inside that kid's brain, but clearly he wasn't dumb. Maybe he was traumatized. Jed got it. This was not how he'd wanted to spend his day either. He offered his hand and dragged the kid out, giving him a quick squeeze of reassurance. The boy leaned down and picked up a pair of high-heeled shoes from the floor.

"Brennan, let's go," Marcos said. He and Wright scanned constantly for shooters. Jed held tight to Michael's hand as they ran toward the restaurant. A woman who lay curled up on the floor groaned. Wright and Marcos didn't break stride as they each took an arm and dragged her along too. Gunshots peppered the floor behind them, blasting out of nowhere. Jed grabbed Michael and picked up the pace. He ran inside the restaurant and turned, saw Wright stop and take aim high above them. Two seconds later came a cry and a whoosh of noise as the shooter fell and landed not ten feet from where they all stood. Jed covered Michael's eyes and forced him to keep moving.

They sprinted fast through the kitchen and along the exit corridor, Jed taking the lead, Wright covering their asses and Marcos carrying the severely injured woman in his arms.

Wright radioed ahead that they were coming out. Fresh air hit them with a blast and they held up their hands for as long as it took to be ID'd as good guys. Another team passed them on the way back inside. Marcos handed the wounded woman off to a paramedic and Jed heard a shriek that pierced his brain.

"Michael!"

The sound of running had him bracing himself for impact.

The redhead had escaped her police babysitter and launched herself at her son like a rocket. Thankfully they'd uncuffed her. She grabbed her kid in her arms and swung him around in a tight circle, kissing him and squeezing so hard Jed winced.

"He's fine." Jed holstered the Glock.

The blue eyes told him to fuck off. Apparently rescuing her son wasn't enough to win back any good points. Too bad. Michael passed his mother the shoes and Jed noticed for the first time her feet were bloody and bare.

"Thank you, Special Agent Brennan." She surprised him. The words were tight and angry, but she got them out without choking. She closed her eyes for a moment before slipping the shoes back on.

"You're welcome. And I'm sorry I lied to you about letting you back in there…"

"Don't worry." Her lips curled. "You're not the first man to lie to me."

Ouch. Back with the glare again. He raised his hands in surrender. Another time and he'd have tried to get into her good graces, but people were trapped and bad guys were running amok in this city, killing innocents.

The redhead glanced at the woman being put on the stretcher. "Oh lord, I thought she was dead." She whirled and waved over the cop who was supposed to be in charge of her. Jed didn't know who this woman was, but she was certainly not cowed by authority. "That's the mother of the baby and toddler." She pointed to the kids she'd carried out of the mall, reminding Jed she'd done some pretty brave things herself today and didn't need to thank him for a damned thing. "They should stay together."

The cop nodded and went off to arrange it. She turned back to him. Michael pulled away from his mother's grasp and grinned. Despite his ordeal the kid looked remarkably OK.

Press bulbs started flashing. Jed put up a hand to shield his eyes. "What the hell are they doing so close? Get them away from here." A couple of beat cops moved the offending press back to a safer distance.

Jed glanced at the woman. She and her son looked very alike though her face was so pale he could see the occasional blue of a vein beneath her skin. "He was exactly where you left him." He ruffled the boy's hair. "He was great. Never made a sound even when we were shot at."

The kid lit up like a flame, but the woman's eyes narrowed and she opened her mouth as if to lay into him. *Crap. Wrong thing to say.*

Jed held up a finger to intercept a barrage of censure. "I promised your super-brave son that you'd stop yelling at me if he came out of there with me."

She closed her mouth again. Then looked down at the carrot-topped boy and swallowed whatever she'd been going to say. "He did?"

Michael nodded rapidly, but his shoulders started to shake, shock finally setting in. Kids bounced back with ridiculous speed although they'd probably all need therapy for this one. There'd be fallout in the short-term to deal with first.

"Right." She looked drained. "I'll stop yelling then. Can we go?"

The idea of never seeing her again felt wrong, but they were in an ongoing terrorist situation. It wasn't time to ask for her number or make plans to meet for coffee.

"We need to interview both you and Michael about what he saw or overheard in the mall. What's your name?"

"Veronica Vincent—but everyone calls me 'Vivi' because of my initials." Her eyes misted, and the kid looked at the floor and scuffed his shoes. "We won't be able to tell you anything you don't already know."

"You don't understand." He lowered his voice. "Michael spent time in that store with some of the terrorists. He could have seen something or overheard a conversation that might seem like nothing to him, but could be vital to the investigation."

"No, *you* don't understand." She lifted her son in her arms, and he buried his face in her neck. "I tried to tell you earlier, but it was a little difficult from my position handcuffed on the ground." Those eyes of hers were spitting mad with recrimination. "Michael doesn't speak, Special Agent Brennan. He doesn't write and he doesn't sign. So I'm afraid he can't help you, and I've already given my statement to that nice police officer over there." She jerked her head to the guy who'd cuffed her. "Can we go now? I want to get him checked out at the hospital."

Jed's mouth went dry. He nodded. She turned away, but not before he spotted the anguish on both their faces.

Perplexed and frustrated, he didn't have time to ask what the hell was up with that. Her son didn't talk? Ever?

Shit. He rubbed his brow and went over to the command center. It was time to get the rest of these people to safety. The redhead and her kid weren't his problem.

———————————

PILAH'S FELLOW ATTACKERS rushed toward the flash bang the authorities had thrown into the mall. The cops were beginning their assault. She hung back from the others and then spun around and watched as Jamal was shot and tumbled from the upper balcony.

Three, no, four running figures headed toward the restaurant that had a fire exit to the outside world. She glanced at the weapon in her hand and made her decision. Now or never, and she wasn't ready to die. She ran toward where Jamal had landed, quickly wiped down the weapon they'd given her for prints, then dropped it beside the twisted wreckage of the man's body.

Such horrific injuries—it turned her stomach. But she'd seen so much violent death and destruction over the past few years it barely registered. It wasn't as if Jamal was someone she loved. She didn't even like him very much.

The feds could track the burner cell she'd used, so she wiped it clean against her thigh and slipped it into Jamal's jeans pocket.

Renewed gunfire made her hurry. She ran inside a clothing store next to the restaurant and found her size in pants, a blouse, sweater and a jacket. She took everything behind the counter and removed the security tags and price labels, then took off her boots and stripped down to her underwear. The sound of movement and the battle was getting louder. It wouldn't be long until the cops stormed the mall. Quickly she pulled on the new clothes, stuffing her old ones and headscarf under the counter. Hand sanitizer sat on the countertop and she rubbed that over her skin, hoping to disguise any gunpowder residue. She grabbed her boots and then ran to hide behind a rack of dresses, deep inside the shop.

She laced her boots and then sat perfectly still, listening to the gun battle play itself out as her heart thumped madly in her chest. Would they catch her? Would they know she was part of the attack?

It was a full ten minutes before she spotted the shadow moving across the front of the shop window. The quiet punch of footsteps reverberated up her spine. Then voices and she heard a group of people scurry out of the storeroom. She moved quickly and joined them when the cop had his back turned. A saleswoman looked at her and Pilah burst into tears. "I thought I was going to die," she sobbed.

The woman wrapped her arm around Pilah's shoulders and hugged her tight. Made her part of the group. "We all did, honey. We all did."

They followed the cop back into the mall as he led the way out. The other women gasped at the blood and carnage. Pilah covered her face with her hands. Jamal had made the ultimate sacrifice and his battle was over. Razur too. They'd be revered as martyrs the same way her husband was revered. But his ghost made a cold companion in their bed and a poor substitute as a father for their girls.

The image of her eldest daughter, Sabreena, flashed through her mind. Murdered by government troops simply because she had been in the wrong place and the wrong time. That's why Adad had taken up arms in the first place— revenge. But their other children were now stuck in Syria, a country torn apart by civil war while the West refused to act.

Sargon said they needed to demonstrate that the instability in Syria could overflow even as far as the heartland of America and then the Americans would intervene. Breadcrumbs of evidence would point to the Syrian Government, and maybe then the West would arm the rebels and help expel the vicious tyrant from power.

Sargon had requested her help, told her that her children would be raised as his own if anything happened to her. Promised to help get them to safety if she succeeded.

Well, she *had* succeeded. She'd worked at the mall for several months and supplied all the information they'd needed to stage the assault. Her stomach clenched. Many of the people she'd worked with had been killed today.

She sobbed loudly and someone patted her back. The faces of the people who had died flashed through her mind and her sobs became louder. Then she saw her own daughters. Her beloved husband.

It wasn't supposed to be like this. They'd been such normal people leading such ordinary lives. Now she had to get her daughters out of Syria, out of danger. Save her babies before the real war started.

———————

SARGON AL SAHAD sat in his villa in Rabieh on the outskirts of Greater Beirut and chuckled at the events unwinding on his satellite TV. He'd already checked his bank account and then transferred the first half of the payment into a Swiss numbered account. He was now a very wealthy man.

Of course, he'd already been a wealthy man. And he wanted the second half of his payment, along with the luxury of time to enjoy his riches.

He popped a fresh, succulent fig in his mouth and savored the sweetness that flooded his senses. The phone beside him on the couch rang. He'd been expecting the call.

"You've done well," the voice said with no introduction.

Sargon preened. "Did I not tell you I could do it?"

"Do your people suspect?" The man's voice was deep and full of undercurrents of immense power.

Sargon craved that sort of power. "They believe we are setting up the regime so the West will step in, which I suppose is true. No one suspects anything else. Our secret is exactly that. As promised." A Syrian by birth, Sargon was sick of watching his country being systematically torn apart from the inside. For good or bad his homeland would be rid of the old regime and ready to rebuild. And when the fighting died down, he intended to be at the forefront of that political revolution. Until then he was biding his time in Lebanon— although the people he'd recruited in the US believed he was still fighting on the frontlines. A necessary subterfuge.

"As long as the American people never suspect where the terrorist plot truly originated."

The enemy of my enemy is my friend. "That would be a death sentence for us both," Sargon agreed.

The man gave a heavy sigh. "Is the next part of the plan in place?"

A film of sweat bloomed on his back and made the thin cotton of his shirt stick there. This was the part that made him nervous. It was a tightly balanced plot that had many potential downfalls. He prayed it would work.

"Do not worry, my friend." If his part in it was ever revealed it would make him the most hunted man on the planet. He didn't want Bin Laden's fame or his fate. "We both have too much to lose for this to fail. No one will link either of us to the attack. The evidence will point elsewhere." Nothing could connect back to him or his powerful ally.

"I won't contact you again," the man said.

Sargon put the handset back in the cradle and climbed slowly to his feet. Time to move on. People who got sloppy didn't live to get old. Sargon intended to grow very, very old.

SNOW OBSCURED ELAN'S vision, making it hard to see from his position on the roof of an insurance building a half kilometer east of the Minneapolis Mall. The mall itself was surrounded by emergency vehicles; people were running through the streets, heading away from the chaos and violence. In his homeland this was where the danger was greatest, but these people seemed oblivious.

Helicopters buzzed in the air above, risking much as the weather ramped up to a bitter, arctic storm.

Ambulances streaked through the streets below him, lights flashing, sirens screaming with a compelling sense of urgency as they swept through intersections.

Right now everything was going to plan, but he wasn't foolish enough to trust blind luck. A helicopter turned and headed toward him, back to the airport. He withdrew into the shadows.

His breath condensed on his binoculars and he wiped the lenses clean. His heart was heavy. Life was precious. But stakes were too high to lose his nerve. He had his orders, to watch, to oversee, to clean up any mess that might lead back to them. He was very good at cleaning up other people's messes.

CHAPTER FOUR

VIVI SAT BESIDE Michael as he lay in a hospital bed. The relief of seeing him safely out of the mall had quickly morphed into panic when he'd passed out in the parking lot. The ambulance had sped through traffic, sirens blazing even though the medic figured it was just a combination of low blood sugar and stress. Vitals had been stable, but his blood pressure had dropped dangerously low. The other patient riding with them had been a fifty-year-old woman with a shrapnel wound in her leg. The woman had worked hard at reassuring her that Michael would be OK.

Such bravery humbled her.

Vivi couldn't believe how close they'd all come to death today. The fact they were still breathing was a miracle—knock on wood.

The doctors had assured her that Michael was basically fine, but his face was waxy pale against the white sheets, and worry gnawed at her insides with a physical grind.

She held his hand, but he'd withdrawn from her, and every time he focused inward she had to fight her instinct to hold on to him even tighter because smothering him only exacerbated his need to escape. David—her ex—always said she fussed too much. Whereas he had ignored or belittled their son. Treated Michael like a failed military recruit, barking orders, yelling insults—worse. That was before he'd ditched them for some hot NSA agent with 36 DD boobs and a Ph.D. in Astrophysics.

The woman had done them both a favor.

Vivi had married a jerk, but at least she'd received this precious gift of a child. So even though she wished David a serious case of erectile dysfunction she never regretted having fallen for him in the first place. He was the price she'd paid for the best thing that had ever happened to her.

Michael.

She clasped his warm hand in her cold one and tried not to squeeze too tight. It was natural to be introspective after what had happened today. She hadn't even begun to process everything, and she was an adult.

A small, persistent tug on her conscience told her she needed to call Michael's father, even though the idea of talking to him right now made her ill. Still, he could make things hard for her if he chose. Better to head him off with a dose of cold, clinical information and an invitation to come visit if he had any concerns. That should keep him far, far away.

The hospital was abuzz with activity. They'd set in motion an emergency response contingency plan and every bed they could spare had been cleared and assigned to patients injured in the mall attack. Michael was in the orthopedics ward, along with many other people who'd received minor wounds. Vivi had closed the curtain around the bed to try and create the illusion of privacy, but it was noisy, and tension snapped through the air, putting everyone on edge.

The attack was over, thank God. The terrorists were presumed dead; law enforcement were clearing the mall and searching for terrified civilians and booby trap bombs.

The curtain swished open, and the nurse came in dragging

an IV pole.

"How's our boy doing?" The nurse was a muscular guy with a round, smiley face and a booming voice. Michael turned his face away.

"He's exhausted." Vivi wanted to hold him close to her chest.

Don't baby him.

"No wonder. You said he hid in a cupboard in the toy store when terrorists were nearby, and they never suspected a thing?"

Vivi could barely stand to think about it, but Michael's lips turned up slightly at the corners; he was obviously pleased people knew how heroic he'd been.

She went with it. Tried to engage him and draw him out. "He was incredibly brave. You stayed there until the police could get to you and the bad guys didn't even know you were under their noses, right Michael?"

He nodded weakly. The tiny spark of interest in the conversation bolstered her.

"You are one brave kid. I would have peed my pants." The nurse started an IV to rehydrate Michael and get his blood sugar levels up. His lips looked dry and cracked. He licked them pathetically.

"Can I give him some water?" she asked the nurse as he filled in a chart at the end of the bed.

He nodded. "Sure, but just a sip or two every so often. It shouldn't take long for him to feel better now that he's getting some fluids inside him. Wouldn't be surprised if he isn't discharged in a couple of hours." *Because they needed as many beds freed up as possible...*

She gave the guy a sad smile and he patted her on the

shoulder. "It's going to be OK. It's over now."

She'd tried not to think about all the suffering, but images kept rushing back in horrific detail. The mother being shot and falling on her young son, probably saving his life by shielding him with her body. The unnatural angle of the cooks' bodies in the restaurant kitchen. The drops of crimson blood on white tile…

Nausea threatened but she forced it down. She needed to be strong for Michael. How would he be able to deal with something he couldn't talk about? She didn't know. She was going to have to get back in contact with Dr. Hinkle. If he'd agree to counsel Michael she might agree to a longer term study, but no more MRIs. Michael had panicked in the machine that morning and no way was she putting her son through more trauma.

Diagnosis was complicated. The doctors couldn't even agree on whether Michael was autistic or not. The lack of definitive answers made decisions about treatment and schooling even more torturous, but they were muddling through. Coping. Just.

Or, at least, they had been.

She didn't want to lie to her son about what had happened today. It was important he knew exactly what he'd faced and overcome. The world could be a dangerous place. But she didn't want to freak him out either.

"Were there many injured?" she asked.

The light in the nurse's eyes turned bleak and he nodded. "Hundreds of people with minor injuries. About thirty in life-threatening condition."

She placed a light hand on the nurse's elbow and leaned closer so Michael wouldn't overhear. "A woman was brought in. She'd been shot and lost a lot of blood. She had two children with her, a toddler and a baby girl. Do you know if she…?"

The nurse's brows slid together. "I think I know who you're talking about. She was in surgery last I heard. I'll try and find out how she's doing."

"Thank you." She hoped the woman lived. The idea of children growing up without a mother was awful…still, it beat not growing up at all.

The nurse moved on to another patient. Vivi gave Michael another sip of water. He squeezed her fingers tighter for a moment but then his grip gradually slackened. His eyes drifted closed, chest rising and falling steadily. He was asleep.

She closed her eyes and said a silent prayer. Then she carefully disengaged his fingers and stood. She wore blue, paper slippers which looked ridiculous. The soles of her feet were covered in small lacerations which had been cleaned and disinfected, but they were starting to throb in reaction to the battering they'd taken and no way could she wear her heels. She stretched out her spine and heard a click as the vertebrae realigned.

She needed to use the facilities and she wanted to see if she could find out any news on the children she'd rescued. She also had to call her ex.

Leaning over Michael, she kissed his cheek and touched the cleft in his jaw, the only thing he'd inherited from his father.

Special Agent Jed Brennan had the same dent in his chin. For a moment, she recalled the burning intensity of his eyes just before he'd gone back inside the mall to rescue Michael. Some of her tension leeched out. She'd been furious with him but he'd kept his promise and gotten Michael out unharmed. The chance of ever seeing him again was slim, but if she did she owed him an apology.

She went over to the nurse and asked him to watch Michael for five minutes. That's all she'd need because her ex never picked up when she called, so she'd leave a brief message and save them both some angst. Straightening clothes that had looked so smart that morning and were now bloody and rumpled, she limped out of the ward. She had to be back before Michael woke.

———

PILAH LAY IN bed listening intently. She'd been admitted to the hospital after she'd feigned a swoon in the parking garage and hit her head on the concrete, giving herself a bloody nose. Aside from a slight headache she felt OK. She could walk. She could run if she had to.

The kid in the next bed had been hiding in the toy store? Had he overheard them saying her name? Or Sargon's? That could blow the whole point of them trying to set up the Syrian Government. She tried to remember what they'd been talking about then but the operation was a blur of gut-wrenching action and deafening gunfire.

They'd been assigned code-names, but Bazal wasn't the smartest knife in the block and slipped up more than once during the day. Even the fact she was a woman was information *she* didn't want out there. Had they mentioned the fact there'd be a second attack?

Sargon Al Sahad had guaranteed her children's safety if she helped them stage this attack on the mall, but if she was captured? They had never discussed that scenario. Her fingers gripped the cool sheets and her jaw clenched so hard she could feel it click. He would kill her daughters slowly and painfully if he thought she'd betrayed him.

She had to get rid of the boy. She wouldn't risk the safety of her own children for that of someone else's.

Her heart pumped rapidly at the thought of what she needed to do. She didn't have a gun or a bomb. It was much easier to end a life when you didn't have to look someone in the eye or hold their warm body in your arms as they struggled for breath.

The image of Sabreena, broken and twisted, flashed through her mind and hardened her resolve. Children died all the time. No one cared.

The mother in the cubicle next door asked the nurse to watch the boy for a few minutes, then Pilah heard her leave. This might be her only chance to get him without the eagle eyes of his mother watching over him. *You should never leave your babies alone.* She'd learned that the hard way.

If she pulled the curtain completely around her bed and smothered the child with a pillow it would be quiet and look like natural causes—at least in the short-term. She'd walk out of here as if nothing had happened.

They'd suspect her eventually of course...

She bit her lip. She didn't want anyone to suspect her, but what could she do?

The nurse checked a pager and strode out of the ward in a hurry.

Sweat dampened her skin as she swung her legs over the side of the bed. Her feet hit the floor and a bolt of cold shot through her. A gentle wave of dizziness made her pause to find her balance. They would have no idea the boy had been smothered until the autopsy, which could take some time given today's events. She dragged the curtain all the way around her bed. The only person who'd had a view of her was a woman who'd been sedated because she was screaming so much. Only the nurse had paid her any real attention and he must have seen a hundred patients today. Given the general confusion, she bet no one would remember exactly what she looked like or even suspect her as long as she didn't panic. She'd have to risk it.

She needed to be brave. Her children's survival depended on her. Her hand was on the curtain that separated her from the child when the nurse strode into her cubicle.

"I-I thought I heard the boy cry out…" Her voice crackled. Guilt radiated from her in waves that made her cheeks burn.

The man didn't seem to notice. "That would make a lot of people very happy."

She frowned. "I don't understand."

The nurse came closer and lowered his voice. "He's mute. Has been for years. The poor little guy can't speak."

The heavy darkness that had fallen over her lifted and dissipated with a blast of relief that made her sway. "Poor little guy," she echoed.

The nurse pursed his lips. "You can sign your release papers at the desk. Any lingering headaches or vision problems and you come back here or go see your GP, OK? You have someone at home?"

She nodded. "My mother."

"Rest up." He smiled and moved away.

She groped for her shoes beside the bed. She did not live with her mother. Her mother had died shortly after Pilah came to the US to visit her after she became ill. Adad had made her stay in the US where she was a dual citizen, and apply for visas to get their girls out of danger. But Syrian government forces bombed her home and killed her eldest child before the application came through.

She pulled on her new coat. That's why she'd helped Sargon do such awful things today, but she wasn't part of the rebel movement. She wasn't a terrorist. She'd kept her part of the bargain. No way was she going to lose her two remaining children.

As she left the ward, she didn't look at the child she would have killed to keep silent. She refused to empathize with someone else's kin when no one gave a damn about hers. She didn't think he knew anything of real importance, and she was grateful she hadn't had to harm him. "All praise be to Allah," she whispered soundlessly as she walked away, keeping her head down in case of security cameras. Her part in this was almost over.

Another thought took over. Maybe she could enter Syria through Turkey and figure out a way to get her children to safety overland. The idea of a refugee camp was daunting, but it would be better than sitting at home waiting for a letter that never came.

Determined, she walked away. The police wouldn't find her. Her part in this was done.

JED SQUATTED DOWN beside the terrorist Wright had shot, who had then fallen from the upper balcony. Wasn't much left of his face but his DNA was everywhere. Wearing latex gloves so he didn't contaminate evidence, he searched the guy's pockets. He pulled out a cell phone and turned it on. It looked like a burner but Jed would bet the tech guys would get a ton of information off this sucker. They needed as much actionable data as possible, as quickly as possible, in case more attacks were imminent or more terrorists were sitting home in front of their TV high-fiving each other for a job well done. Disgust twisted his stomach.

He dug into another pocket.

Men, women and children were among the dead. Indiscriminate slaughter in the US's heartland. Most of the mall's security had been taken out at the beginning of the attack—a highly sophisticated and targeted assault. It obviously wasn't the first time terrorists had hit mainland USA and probably wouldn't be the last, but this struck too close to home. This wasn't Iraq or Afghanistan. It was Minnesota for Christ's sake.

He found another cell phone in the man's pocket and frowned. It was exactly like the first. Maybe one didn't work? He turned them on and they both fired up.

Why carry two cells?

Had someone not turned up for the party? Was it a spare? Had he taken it from a dead colleague?

"Hey," he shouted to the Evidence Response Team tech shadowing him. Her name was Cindy. She was petite, dark-haired, and had that intense focus and attention to detail that, he suspected, made her damn good at her job. He held up both cells. "Need to photograph and bag these ASAP."

Cindy pulled out some bags, then fast-tracked the evidence by handing them to another cop who was delivering anything that needed expedited straight to people from the state lab where FBI and local forensics people were working in close collaboration. Deciphering communication and biometrics data would give them the fastest way of discovering who these people were and making sure the whole crew was dead or captured. He walked over to where an AK-47 lay discarded on the floor. He looked back at the dead guy, and over to another dead terrorist nearby. Both of them had assault rifles slung over their shoulders. Both had handguns strapped to their belts. Why was that rifle just lying there?

Jed didn't know but he intended to find out. They bagged that too.

The air stank of smoke, blood, and burnt gunpowder. It stuck to the back of his throat and made him nauseous, but he had a job to finish and time was against him. He looked up and saw the hunting shop and remembered he hadn't paid for the knife that had saved his life, and the life of Vivi Vincent and those two kids. He walked down to the store, still checking every crevice for anyone who'd been injured or was hiding. Inside the store, bullet holes riddled the back wall. A feeling of unreality hit him as he assessed the damage. He'd been within inches of death today. It had taken him by surprise and he'd let his guard down. Maybe his boss had been right about him needing a break, but the chances of him getting one now were a thousand-to-one against.

He left a hundred dollars on top of the register, and stuck a yellow sticky-note to the monitor of the register to say what the cash was for. He grabbed the plastic shopping bag that he'd left here a few hours ago. The toy was for Bobby's son. Bobby had been his and his twin brother's best friend growing up. They'd all joined the Army together. His brother, Liam, was now the Chief of Police in their small hometown. Jed had joined the FBI. Bobby had stepped on an IED and been blown to kingdom-come.

Emotion punched his throat. He still missed his friend every single day.

The tendons in his neck were strung so tight his jaw ached. He tried to loosen up his shoulders, but gave up. Walking around in a knot of tension was a permanent state of being these days. At least he was alive. He needed to stop whining and get on with the job.

He walked back to the toy store. The idea that gunmen would fire on a place where children gathered pissed him off. Those bastards had traumatized kids for life.

Michael Vincent's russet hair and big, blue eyes flashed into his head. Brave kid.

He frowned. Why the hell didn't he talk? Was it physical? Psychological? Had he been abused?

It happened.

He saw it almost every day.

His mother didn't seem the type though. In their brief encounter her love and devotion to her son, combined with a level of courage normally associated with those serving their country didn't jive with some asshole who abused those weaker than themselves. Her fiery temperament sure as hell matched her hair. He smiled for the first time in what felt like eternity. Maybe he would track her down after all this was over and invite her for coffee. He rubbed the back of his neck. Yeah, like she'd go for coffee with a guy who'd left her son in a store with armed gunmen.

The word struck him in the solar plexus.

Gunmen.

Gun-*men*.

What about the female terrorist he'd seen?

He tried to call the head of the local FBI field office but couldn't get through. He called his boss instead. Lincoln Frazer answered on the first ring.

"Enjoying your vacation so far?"

"Yeah, it's been a blast. Question. Any females found among the bodies of the tangos yet?"

"No. All male. Why?"

Jed squinted up at the pockmarked roof. "Not sure." He hung up, which would piss off his boss but he needed to think. Had he really seen a woman? The individual had been shorter than most guys, not slim but not fat either. Damn. He suddenly wasn't one-hundred percent sure and didn't want to start a shit-storm for nothing. He wandered into the clothing store next to the restaurant. They'd cleared the backrooms and storage areas but nothing had been assessed in terms of potential evidence yet. That was part of his job. Cindy shadowed his every move, taking photos of everything.

"This is odd…" She sounded puzzled.

"What is?"

The flash of her camera bulb dazzled him for a moment. He blinked away the glare and crouched beside her behind the sales counter. There was a bunch of wadded up material, but they weren't new clothes, or the kind of clothes this store sold for that matter. Personal items? Something dark and sticky stained them. Blood? He pulled the items carefully, aware they could be booby-trapped. He inched out the material and thankfully there were no wires visible. Just clothes. He spread the dark sweater and black canvas pants across the counter. Pulled out a long black headscarf. His heart pounded. Cindy took more shots. He called his boss.

"What?"

"I think one of the terrorists is a woman, and I think she escaped."

"Are you sure?"

"We just found wadded up clothing identical to what I thought I saw on a female perpetrator earlier. They were under the cash register in a women's clothes store. Fuck!" He was furious with himself for not mentioning it earlier. He knew better than anyone to always share every detail no matter how insignificant you thought it might be. He jammed his hand in his hair. They needed to figure out who this woman was. "If only the kid in the store could tell us something."

"Which kid?"

"A little boy named Michael Vincent. He was hiding in a toy store during the attack. I saw at least three terrorists in there with him, but his mother insists he can't speak or communicate in any way."

"Is his mother the hot redhead?"

Jed held his phone away from his ear and blinked. Was the guy a mind-reader now? He moved it back. "Pardon me?" he asked.

"You need to find a TV and turn on the local news right now. Actually forget local. This thing is going national and international."

"What is?" Jed strode down to an electronics store just along the corridor. He avoided looking at all the bodies that the ME's department was trying to get out of there. People he hadn't been able to save.

"The press is telling his story to the world," Frazer said.

There was a bank of TVs on the wall. On every one of them a serious, polished and beautiful Vivi Vincent was being interviewed. But it must have been recorded earlier that day, before the attack, when her stockings hadn't been shredded and her skirt and blouse were unstained by blood and grime. Then the scene cut to a view of Michael sitting behind a screen, drawing a picture of the reporter with astounding detail and accuracy even though he couldn't see her.

Eidetic memory.

"They're calling the kid a prodigious savant when it comes to seeing something for a brief instant and then recreating it on paper. He has a photographic memory...so even though he can't talk—"

"He might still be able to help us identify the bad guys." *Oh, hell.* Jed didn't know how the press had gotten hold of the kid's story, but it didn't matter. "If any of the terrorists did survive, that report just put a giant bull's-eye on the kid. Find out where they are, Frazer." Jed hung up on the man. He went back to the clothes store and searched through the trashcan by the counter. Still wearing his latex gloves, he pulled out tags and tossed them beside the register. Cindy eyed him with interest. She knew they were onto something big. "We need to find out what clothes these are for." If his hunch was correct they'd have a description of size and shape of the woman, the clothes she was wearing, and with luck her DNA, maybe even her prints.

He called one of the local FBI field agents who he knew was working somewhere in the mall, caught him up to speed and told him to get his ass there right now.

"Gotta go," he told the tech, ignoring her shocked protest.

Then Jed started jogging back to his SUV. Terrorists who attacked innocent shoppers a few weeks before Christmas weren't going to baulk at eliminating one young boy. Vivi Vincent and her son were in danger. He needed to find them fast.

CHAPTER FIVE

Michael wouldn't eat. Didn't matter if she offered him candy or soda, he still wouldn't eat.

Vivi needed a way to bring him back from whatever head-space he'd floated off to, and she had to do it now, before he was set back months, if not years, in progress.

The hotel where they were staying contained a huge indoor water park. That and the proximity to the mall was the main reason she'd chosen it.

"Here."

He flicked a listless eyelid.

She thrust a pair of swim shorts and towel at him. "We're going to the pool."

Michael turned to face her. *Finally.* His expression contained both wary interest and banked fear. He loved the water. She hoped that love would be enough to kick-start the recovery process so she could get him back into his normal routine. The most important part of that was eating regular meals and getting plenty of sleep, so she planned to exhaust him, feed him and then let him rest.

She'd already pulled on her bathing suit beneath yoga pants and t-shirt, and wore a pair of red crocs Michael had bought for her birthday last summer. "Come on. I'm going for a swim and I'm not leaving you here alone."

He moved reluctantly, knowing she wouldn't be budged now that her mind was made up—a stubborn streak they both shared—and went into the bathroom to change.

Two minutes later they headed downstairs, the hotel buzzing despite the terrorist attack that was so close-by. Life went on. Police presence in the city was massive. It was dinnertime so groups of people were headed to the restaurant. Some of them looked clearly traumatized. Several sported cuts and bandages. One woman gave them a weird glance that Vivi put down to her general walking-dead appearance.

She was limping but trying to hide it. The cuts on her feet were more painful than she'd anticipated and throbbed unmercifully. They were heavily bandaged and she hoped she could get Michael onto one of the slides before he realized she couldn't enter the pool with her wounds.

Duplicitous parenting. Something she usually disapproved of, but tough times called for tough measures.

They entered the pool area and were hit by a wall of heat and the stench of chlorine. The heavy rush of the water from the many interlocking slides was deafening, but also strangely soothing—enough white noise to block out even the memories of gunfire and screams. The place was almost empty of people. The idea of being in a crowded space, any crowded space, freaked her out now. It was something she was going to have to deal with eventually.

A small group of children rushed past them in a short, shivering line. The odd parent was dotted around, staking out lounge chairs while they acted as spotters to make sure the kids were OK.

Michael took one look at the slides, handed her his towel and ran off to play. A wave of relief rushed her and her knees went weak. She dropped onto a nearby lounger, so shattered and terrified all her energy fled.

Her son flew out the end of one of the slides and erupted from the water grinning.

A starburst of relief filled her chest. *It was going to be OK.* Everything was going to be OK. He'd latched onto another boy about his own age and they took off to do the slide again. He was a good swimmer and she allowed herself to relax just a little. After discovering autistic children were particularly drawn to water she'd had him take lessons three times a week, and now he swam competitively. Autistic or not, he was a great swimmer. Lifeguards kept eagle eyes on the slides, so she allowed herself to mentally unwind.

Just breathe.

It was over.

They'd been through hell.

But they'd survived.

Some unknown instinct had her turning to look through the glass windows toward the main lobby of the hotel. A man stood there staring at her. He was about 5'8", dark hair, dark eyes, beard, swarthy skin. When she caught his gaze he looked away. She turned back to the pool, then glanced at the window again, but he'd wandered away toward the coffee bar.

Great. Now she was going to racially stereotype everyone she met. She detested prejudice. It was one of the things she'd fought hardest against when getting Michael into mainstream school and not special ed.

Her eyes frantically sought out Michael again, panicked after having taken her gaze off him for more than a few seconds.

She knew she was obsessing and it wasn't healthy, but she

couldn't help it. She'd almost lost him today. There was no one to lean on—just her. She had no family. David was too busy being important to even think of helping with Michael and she'd rather eat raw liver than subject her sensitive and struggling son to his hard-core parenting methods. She hadn't even kept his name, and he hadn't objected when she'd changed Michael's last name to Vincent too.

He was ashamed of his son, and she was ashamed of him.

She stood and caught sight of Michael's red hair—darkened to auburn by the water—plastered to his skull. He was running toward the next slide with a big grin on his face.

"Don't run," she muttered, too far away to be heard over the rushing water even if she'd yelled.

Loosen the damn reins, Vivi, you're going to strangle the kid.

Fuck off, David.

Great, she even argued with her ex inside her head, as if reality hadn't been bad enough. She rolled her eyes and sat back down. She tried to relax, breathed deep, opened a book she'd pulled from her purse, and read the first line. Twice. Images of blood and death kept intruding and she put the book away.

Today had been hell, but it was over now. Tomorrow they'd head home to Fargo.

Fargo. Not where she'd thought she'd end up living. After her divorce, an old friend had offered her a partnership in her translation business. While Vivi didn't need to live there for them to work together, frankly she had no reason to live anywhere else.

Plus, she liked the isolation. The excuse not to keep up with her old life in DC and NYC. Winters were hellish.

Summers were buggy as all get out. Every January she contemplated moving somewhere more temperate but Michael loved it in North Dakota. His school, his teachers, his friends. She'd put up with almost anything as long as her son was happy. Hell, she'd sell her soul to figure out a way to get his voice back.

He hadn't always been mute.

He *had* always exhibited behaviors on the edge of the autistic spectrum, maybe Asperger's. He craved routine, liked his things in the exact right place and excelled at repetitive tasks. But he had no truly obvious disabilities except when stressed he zoned out and would often crawl into small, cramped spaces and stay there for hours.

It was exhausting. The search for answers. The constant worry.

She hunched up and watched Michael blast out of the biggest slide the pool had. Fearless. Brave. The grin that wreathed his face more than made up for the effort of having to drag him down here. She smiled back. Agent Brennan had praised Michael's bravery earlier today. It had touched her deeply that he'd instinctively understood what her son needed, something she'd been too terrified to give him.

She spotted the guy who'd been staring at her through the window. He now wore neon green shorts that looked way too big for him. Reminding herself to breathe and that the world was full of good people just trying to get by, she closed her eyes and counted to ten. It wasn't some movie where everyone was out to get her. This wasn't some conspiracy plot to destroy her. He'd obviously been scoping out the pool and not her. He dropped a towel on a lounger, half-hidden behind a huge palm tree and headed toward the nearest slide.

Michael ran past and gave her a wave. His buddy looked perturbed, probably because Michael wasn't actually talking to him, but he sent her a shy smile too and a little wave. She waved back, then checked her watch. She'd give him another half hour and then they'd go eat.

A shadow fell over her. She looked up and her mouth fell open when she saw Special Agent Jed Brennan looming over her. Her lack of make-up and limp hair tied back in a severe ponytail made her feel self-conscious, which was ridiculous. He hardly cared what she looked like.

"Where's Michael?" he asked.

She pointed to where he was racing halfway up the steps of yet another slide. "Why?"

Brennan's shoulders drew back and down as he looked up at the ceiling in relief. She turned sideways on the lounger. What was going on? Why was he here? He wore a thick, wool coat and it was so hot in the pool, perspiration already dampened his brow. A five o'clock shadow darkened his jaw. He shrugged out of the coat and sat on the lounger opposite. Their knees brushed. Vivi jumped.

"How did you know where to find us?"

He slanted her a look. "FBI, remember?"

"But *here*," she insisted, "at the pool?"

"Reception rang your room. When you didn't answer I decided to search the public areas. Michael's eight so I figured this was a good place to start." Agent Brennan nodded toward the viewing window. "I saw you through the window from the lobby. That hair of yours is hard to miss."

She smoothed it self-consciously, but he wasn't here to talk about her hair. He held her gaze, those eyes of his so dark brown that she couldn't tell where pupil met iris. But there was something in his gaze that made her uneasy, some unspoken tension. A shiver of fear moved over her. "What is it?"

He pressed his lips together as if considering what to tell her.

"Don't you dare lie to me," she warned.

The light in his eyes dimmed. "I'd like to know which guy treated you so badly that your first thought is always that someone is going to lie to you." He leaned forward. "Right now I'll tell you why I'm here—which is probably because I'm a paranoid, federal officer who's seen too much of the bad stuff, and this is probably a massive overreaction on my part."

She gripped her knees. She'd thought this was over but from the tight cast of Brennan's mouth she was wrong. "Tell me."

"Did you see the news on the TV?"

She shook her head.

"They showed a clip of Michael drawing a likeness of some TV reporter from memory?"

"We filmed the piece this morning." She didn't understand. "They showed that? Even with everything that happened in the mall today?"

"Yeah." Brennan nodded. "Then they linked his photographic drawing ability to the fact he was trapped inside that store with those terrorists today."

The blood leeched from her brain. *Oh, God.* She turned toward where she'd last seen her son. Stood. Started scanning the pool, searching the slides, but didn't see any trace of him. Where the hell was her son? Where was Michael?

JED TOUCHED VIVI'S arm. "Hey, he's probably at the top of a slide waiting his turn." But he couldn't see the kid and after everything that had happened today he was starting to worry. "Stay here."

He strode around the poolside. He may as well have told the sun not to shine because Vivi ignored his order and started jogging around the other side of the pool. It was a big area, lots of little alcoves and interlocking slides. He looked around for a lifeguard and noticed three of them bending over a guy wearing a red t-shirt. He jogged over. One of the girls was crying, another was calling for an ambulance.

"What happened?" he asked.

"I don't know. I found Ray unconscious."

"Blow the whistle," Jed ordered. He had a bad feeling about this. When they hesitated, he flashed his badge. "Empty the god damned pool!"

One of the young women blew the whistle about a second before he was about to grab it out of her hands and do it himself. They started getting the kids out. But he still didn't see Michael. A horrible feeling descended. That he'd messed up. He'd been so busy chatting up the pretty mother he'd forgot to protect the kid. Amateur. Asshole. He spotted a flash of green at the bottom of the pool and his heart stopped. But it was too big to be the body of a kid. Then he realized exactly what he was looking at. He threw off his suit jacket and handed the nearest lifeguard his weapon, toeing off his shoes and socks at the same time. He took a running dive into the water, cold flashing over his skin as he arrowed into the deep end of the pool.

It took an eternity to reach the man holding the little boy beneath the water. Jed punched the man in the head and then grabbed him around the neck and yanked him off Michael. The kid didn't swim to safety, he just floated lifelessly away from them. The would-be child killer wheeled and slithered around him until Jed was the one being choked. Jed shoved him hard backwards into the wall, desperate to break away and reach Michael and get him to the surface.

A tsunami of bubbles erupted around the boy and a flash of long, red hair. Vivi was there, dragging her son out of the water.

He turned his attention back to the dirt bag who'd sunk low enough to try and drown an eight-year-old boy. Spots danced in front of Jed's vision, but this guy had been under for much longer and was hurting for oxygen a hell of a lot more than he was. Grimly he held onto the fucker. Tighter when the guy finally started to panic and tried to head for the surface. Jed could hear his own heartbeat pounding in his ears and deliberately calmed his mind, slowed his pulse. Sniper training took over and his body relaxed despite the adrenaline and testosterone that cruised through his bloodstream. The look in the other guy's eyes was worth every second of dealing with his own discomfort. He waited and waited until the guy finally inhaled and started choking. *Suck it back, asshole.* Then Jed dragged him to the surface and let the lifeguard haul him out onto the side. He got himself out of the pool and fished handcuffs out of his saturated pants pocket. Snapped them onto the terrorist scumbag even though the lifeguard protested as he tried to perform mouth-to-mouth.

Jed retrieved his weapon. He wasn't worried about this guy. You couldn't drown a cockroach. On cue the bastard started coughing and spewing up water. Jed strode over the where Michael Vincent lay pale in his mother's arms. He was conscious and shivering uncontrollably. Her eyes were red-rimmed, from chlorine or crying he couldn't tell.

What a fucking day.

He crouched down and put his hand over hers, squeezing her fingers, wishing he didn't feel personally responsible for this whole damn mess. "He OK?"

She swallowed and nodded, looking fragile and exhausted and battle-ready all at the same time. Admiration for this woman kept growing—forget the fact she was beautiful, she had a backbone of steel; she'd been through hell but she didn't wallow in tears. She was a fighter.

He grabbed a large, thick towel from a pile stacked on a nearby table and wrapped it around her shoulders, feeling her stiffen at the contact. "It's OK, Vivi." He ran his hand up and down her back wanting to reassure her and make her feel safe even though he knew better than to make promises. "Everything is going to be OK."

Jed looked at the lifeguard who'd been knocked out. He seemed to be coming around. Jed retrieved his jacket and shoes from the damp floor and pulled out his phone. He was cold, wet, but damned happy he'd reached Michael in time. He called the local office. "I got one of them attempting to drown the Vincent boy in the hotel pool." He gave some details over the phone, just enough for them to know exactly where he was and what to do.

The hotel was only a few miles from the Minneapolis Mall and it took less than three minutes for a couple of feds to show up. Vivi and her son sat clinging to one another, shivering uncontrollably. Michael was crying soundlessly. Something about that mute grief twisted a knife in Jed's heart.

He handed the terrorist suspect into custody while one of

the other agents picked up the guy's belongings from the locker room. The would-be killer wasn't allowed to get dried or dressed. Jed hoped the guy's balls snapped off on the way to interrogation.

Jed grabbed his coat and Vivi's bag from the lounge chair. Turned to find her watching him. There were questions in her frank blue gaze. Big questions about what happened next. Questions he didn't want to answer.

"Come on." He herded them out the door, through the lounge and into the elevator. Inside, he slipped his gun out of his holster. "Which floor?"

"Eight."

"Which room?"

She reached into the side pocket of her purse and handed him a key card. He looked at it. 801.

He led the way, made her stay back while he did a rapid search of the room. It was empty. He figured these guys had people scouring all the local hotels and had gotten lucky. Chances were the guy under arrest had notified his cronies and they'd be on their way over, but they had feds and cops covering every floor and exit. His colleagues were staked out on all the nearby roads, watching and waiting for a bunch of bad guys to arrive on the scene. Even so he didn't intend for Vivi or her son to be here if anyone slipped through the net. "Get dressed. Quick as you can."

"What about you?" she eyed his wet clothes.

Thankfully his overcoat and feet were dry. That would have to do. "I'll be fine until we can get to the local field office. I have other clothes in the car I can change into there."

She started drying her son's hair, but he put his hand on her waist and nudged her aside. "I'll help Michael. You get dressed."

Her pupils flared in an instinctive reaction to his touch, something animalistic that no one could control. He felt it too and it pissed him off. He did not want to get his job tangled up with emotions. Not this time. They all had far too much to lose if he didn't bring his A-game to the field.

Then her expression shifted to surprise—which pissed him off even more. As if no one had ever offered to help her before. She nodded, suddenly as mute as her son, grabbed a handful of clothes and went into the bathroom. Jed stripped the kid, dried him, and pulled dry clothes on him. He rubbed himself down as best he could with a towel, ignoring the discomfort of his own wet skin. He wasn't about to wander into work wearing a robe. He'd never live it down.

Next he packed the Vincents' belongings. Stuffed everything he found in the drawers and wardrobe into the medium-sized suitcase—pausing for a second over the scraps of silken underwear in the top drawer. A knot of something uncomfortable tugged inside him. These bits of colored satin reminded him she wasn't just a victim, she was a strong, beautiful woman whose life was about to take another nosedive after a seriously shitty day. There was nothing he could do about it. He didn't like it. And he really didn't like knowing it was this particular redhead who'd been caught up in this web of hatred and cowardice that put her and her son in danger, and that he'd played a part in it. Because now it was personal and he didn't like that either.

This was what his boss was always warning him about. Personal was when you let people get too close, and it ended up screwing with your perspective and objectivity.

Not gonna happen this time.

Michael lay curled up in a ball on the floor. Jed threw everything he could find in the case without folding it. They had to get out of there fast.

Vivi came out of the bathroom looking more like her former poised, assured self. Her hair was slicked to her skull emphasizing her pale features, and tied back in a braid. She frowned at the case, then went back in the bathroom and came back zipping a toiletries' bag. She tossed it in, then swept a hand under the pillows for night clothes and a stuffy that she pushed into Michael's arms.

"Put his shoes on for me, will you?" she asked him.

Jed nodded.

Out of the corner of his eye he saw her pack up her laptop and charger, then ease her feet carefully into winter boots— fresh spots of blood stained the thick socks she wore, but she didn't slow down to deal with it. "Where are we going?" she asked.

"I don't know yet."

She eyed him distrustfully. It seemed to be her default mode. They had that in common, but he was law enforcement. What was her excuse?

"Is there a Mr. Vincent I should contact?" Shit, he hadn't even thought about it earlier. There hadn't been any need. She didn't wear a ring but it didn't mean she wasn't married.

"No Mr. Vincent."

The fact he was glad about that was a really bad sign. *Emotional distance—remember?*

"You're going to freeze outside in this snowstorm." She eyed him like he was an idiot. So much for lusting after his manly body.

"Not a lot I can do about that right now. I'll be fine until we get to HQ." He closed the suitcase and tugged Michael to his feet. Bent down and looked the boy in the eye. "I know you're wiped, kid. You've beaten bad guys twice today and no one deserves a break more than you do." He searched the kid's face but he was zoned out. Jed didn't blame him. "All I need you to do is get to the car, then I'll do the rest. OK, buddy?"

Michael didn't answer but he did take a few steps toward the door. Good enough. Vivi put her coat on while Jed helped Michael. She took the boy's hand and grabbed the handle of her suitcase, her laptop bag already slung over her shoulder. Self-sufficient. Efficient. Alone. Even holding her son's hand Vivi Vincent looked very much alone.

That thing tugged inside his chest again.

Terrorists. Danger. Focus.

Jed pulled out his handgun, placing his hand on Michael's shoulder before carefully opening the door. Waiting for the elevator was one more pulse pounding moment in a day full of adrenaline rushes. They got out at the second floor and walked to the end of the corridor and down the stairs, heading to a side entrance nearest where he'd parked his car. Vivi stalled. "I need to check out."

Jed shook his head, hand on her lower back urging her forward. "Don't worry about it. We're hoping to trap anyone who might be after you."

Her eyes bulged and her throat rippled as she swallowed repeatedly. *Shit*, he hadn't meant to spook her more than she already was.

"How did you find me?"

"Tracked your credit card activity."

"Can the bad guys do that too?" Her eyes narrowed.

"I doubt it, but possibly." Depended on who they had on

the inside and Jed was betting they'd had someone on the inside at the Minneapolis Mall. Hopefully they didn't have anyone inside the police department.

She fished her cell out of her pocket. "Can they track this?"

He flashed his badge at the uniform who stood at the outside door, then covered Vivi's hand with his. She was freezing but it didn't stop the skin-on-skin connection zapping along his nerves with a jolt of something hot and ill-timed.

"Turn it off but leave it in your pocket for now. Let's get to headquarters where they can figure out a plan and I can get changed." Because walking around Minneapolis in wet clothes in December was asking for frostbite. "Maybe the feds can use your cell to set another trap for the bad guys and end this thing."

"And if they don't?"

He didn't want to think about that.

Her lips pinched. Blue eyes piercing in their intensity. "You won't be staying with us, will you?"

Michael's eyes shifted toward him, just enough for Jed to know the kid was listening to every word and that his answer mattered. "I don't know where I'll be yet, but I won't just abandon you." He'd thought he was way too experienced to make promises he might not be able to keep—obviously not. He gave Michael's shoulder a squeeze and opened the door and walked into the frigid winter chill of the first major snowstorm of the season. *Hello, Minnesota.*

"We're going to be stuck in protective custody, aren't we?" she shouted over the howling wind.

"For now." Christ, he was going to freeze to death before he reached the frickin' car. He took the case from Vivi's fingers and tried to shield her and Michael both from view and the wind. He scanned the parking lot, searching for the bad guys, knowing they could be anywhere. Goddamn it. This was the USA. None of this stuff was supposed to happen here.

Yeah. Which was the point these fuckers were trying to make. Welcome to the rest of the world.

———————

PILAH'S HEART RACED as she sat in her little, blue Ford Focus in the hotel's huge parking lot, engine running to try and keep warm as the thickening snowstorm turned the whole world white. The heater blasted out hot air but her hands and feet were numb with cold. She wasn't used to such harsh weather. Her mother—a beautiful, blond American—had lived in Florida. Her parents had divorced when she was ten and her father had taken her back to the Eastern plateau of Syria without any objections from her mother.

She knew what it was like to grow up without a mother and didn't want her daughters to go through the same experience.

After leaving the hospital, Pilah had gone home to find a man called Abdullah Mulhadre camped out in her living room. She'd surprised him. The cold light in his eyes had scared the crap out of her. At first she'd thought he was there to kill her, to tidy up any loose ends, but as time wore on she'd relaxed her guard. They'd spent the afternoon watching news of the attack, monitoring the growing swell of outrage. Then the feature on the boy had aired and she'd rushed to the bathroom to throw up.

She couldn't believe she'd made such a terrible miscalculation and let the child live. She'd been blindsided by the scale of her mistake. Abdullah had followed her to the bathroom and she'd had to confess she couldn't remember exactly what they'd discussed in the toy store and the boy *might* have overheard something.

He'd struck her.

Her cheek still stung, and she touched it gently. She hadn't told him she'd seen the child at the hospital. The man would have killed her on the spot for not eliminating the problem. Abdullah gave her the creeps. She shivered. Most of the men she'd been involved with recently gave her the creeps.

"Why did you get involved with these people, Adad?" she asked her dead husband angrily, wiping the condensation of her breath from the windshield. Of course he didn't answer, too busy hanging out with vestal virgins while she tried to figure out a way to save their children. "You always were a damn fool." Her eyes dampened. Fool or not, she'd loved him.

Now it was only a matter of time until the boy gave the authorities a detailed sketch of her face or enough information for the Americans to realize the Syrian Government wasn't responsible, it was the rebels who'd attacked the mall, and they weren't finished yet.

The Syrian president would crush those who'd tried to implicate him in international terrorism and the US wouldn't stop him. Her children would be caught up in the fighting and probably die.

She checked her phone, waiting for a text from Abdullah. Where was he? Out of the corner of her eye she saw a tall, dark-haired man shepherd a woman and child through the snow, past her car toward a black 4X4. The man's hair and pants were damp, snow clinging to him as he moved swiftly through the frigid air. It was *them*, she realized, sucking in a shocked breath. She was glad for the accumulation of snow on the windshield obscuring her from view.

What had happened? Had Abdullah not found them in time? Where was he?

She thought about the pistol in the glove box, but the man was obviously law enforcement and the harshness of his features caused a little shiver of trepidation to flicker over her skin. Before she could decide whether or not to attempt to take care of the problem herself, the black SUV pulled away. She memorized the license plate.

Abdullah had obviously failed in his mission.

Had he been captured? Should she leave? Sargon favored the arrogant man and she didn't dare cross either of them. If he came out in a few minutes, walking into a snowstorm without the jacket he'd left on her back seat, he'd be angry. Her face still throbbed from his earlier outrage. Her head pounded, a mixture of injury, cold and fear.

Squad cars sped along the nearby roads. If she didn't leave soon she'd be trapped. Obviously, the cops were waiting for the terrorists to turn up to kill the woman and child, but the boy was gone. Whisked away.

She had to leave.

The phone rang and she checked the number.

The twinge of unease mingled with the hope of hearing her children's voices.

"Hello?" she said.

"Has the errand been completed?"

How had he heard about the boy? Had Abdullah called him without telling her? Probably.

"Not yet." They were both careful with their choice of words in case someone was listening in. The fact he'd called

70

her on yet another disposable cell that Abdullah had given her should be enough to protect her identity, but she'd rather he hadn't called at all. The sudden need to hear her children's voices made her reckless. "Can I speak to Dahlia or Corinne?" she asked.

"No." The word was snapped out. "Complete the rest of the *errand*, then you can speak to them."

She shriveled on the inside.

Finding the boy now was going to be next to impossible. She ached to talk to her girls just for a brief moment of time. "Please?" she begged.

She heard girls' laughter and then shouts of "Mommy!" before they were gone again.

Sargon's voice gentled. "They are too busy playing to stop and talk. What can you tell me?"

"We were too late." Emotion squeezed her throat. Sargon hated failure. She didn't want him taking out her failure on her children. "But I do have the license plate of the vehicle they used to take him away." It was probably useless but she reeled it off anyway.

"They'll put him in the Witness Protection Program." There was a long silence while he mulled over her information. "All is not lost. I have someone who might be able to find out where they take him next. I have another task for you. Go home and wait for instruction."

What the hell? No. No! She was done. Finished. She opened her mouth to tell him so—

"Girls, girls, come talk to your mother…"

Hope surged for a moment only to be doused when the line went dead. She let out a sob then rested her head on the steering wheel as hot tears welled in her eyes. Cell connections to that part of the world were notoriously unreliable. Or had he done it on purpose to remind her he had control of her babies?

She flung the cell on the seat. "Adad, if you weren't dead, I'd kill you myself." She wiped away the tears and put the car in drive. Abdullah had either been arrested or he'd escaped another way. She left the parking lot, keeping an eye out for the man, then turned in the opposite direction that the SUV had taken.

Her mouth went dry. What would Sargon make her do next? He'd never mentioned details of what would happen after the mall. Of course, she probably wasn't supposed to have survived the attack. She turned left and got lost in a tangle of roads, traffic being streamed away from the mall.

Abdullah hadn't expected her to come home at all, she realized. The apartment was rented under a false name that couldn't be linked to her real identity. He'd assumed he could use it as a safe house because she'd be dead. Betrayal at the way her life was so callously disregarded cut deep—except what had she really expected from these people?

Her tires slid on the slick road and she almost spun out.

It felt like a reflection of her life—at the mercy of things she couldn't control. She managed to keep the car pointed in the right direction and tried again. Needing to get home. Needing to find a moment of quiet in a day that had exploded into hell. It shocked her how alone she was right now. No friends. No family. No one who would claim her if her part in this came to light. She should have died today. It would have been easier than facing the future.

ELAN WATCHED FROM a distance.

This particular loose-end threatened everything. He'd thought the former soldier would be able to deal with it, but the boy and his mother had been taken into federal custody and the Syrian arrested. This was bad.

The second phase of this operation was by far the most delicate and critical. There was no room for error. Hopefully the boy knew nothing, but regardless the threat had to be eliminated.

He swore.

He did not like to kill children, but children grew up to be warriors and sometimes they were a necessary sacrifice. Did he take care of this himself? He didn't want to step in unless he had to. Sargon had to be aware of the problem otherwise he wouldn't have sent the woman and his puppet to deal with it. The old Syrian would be panicking in his Lebanese bolt-hole, fearful he wouldn't get the rest of his money, wouldn't get his chance at power.

Elan narrowed his eyes. He'd watch and wait. Give Sargon a chance to fulfill his promises without his intervention. The woman in the blue car was another loose-end though Sargon had her on a tight leash. She might be useful now that the soldier had been detained.

Elan loved his family, but he was glad he'd never had children. Too easy to exploit. Too easy to kill. He disappeared into the thickening storm, nothing but a ghost of a man.

CHAPTER SIX

S TARS SHONE BRIGHTLY in a deep navy sky, reflected by the fresh drape of bone-white snow as they drove down a long, curved driveway. Six inches had fallen since they'd left the hotel. An added burden on a city's resources already stretched to the limit as it struggled to deal with the devastating effects of a terrorist attack.

Vivi was exhausted, but fury gave her the energy to do what she needed to do. How dare someone decide her child had to die? How dare some stranger walk into a swimming pool and hold her son underwater until he was nearly unconscious?

The terrorist attack on the mall hadn't felt personal, but *that*? That had felt personal.

For the first time, she regretted ignoring her ex-husband's demands that she learn to use a firearm. She wished she'd paid more attention when he'd discussed security concerns. Not that she'd run to him for help. The cold-hearted bastard had tried to stuff Michael into an institution years ago. Forget Michael was an innocent child who needed his family. Forget Michael was his son. *He'd* been jealous. David hadn't liked the amount of time she put into Michael's care. He hadn't liked the fact she didn't dress up to the nines in designer dresses or hang on his arm at work functions anymore. He hadn't liked the fact she was too tired and worried to screw his brains out whenever the hell he wanted it.

Well screw him and screw the bastards trying to kill her baby. She wasn't going to let any of them near him.

Vivi stared out the car window at the house that was to be her prison for some indeterminate amount of time. It was set along the banks of the Mississippi near a jagged ravine. Picturesque and attractive, but a jail nonetheless. She pushed open her car door before Brennan reached the handle to open it for her. She hadn't expected him to accompany them but he had, and she was damn sure he had more important things to do than babysit her and Michael.

She climbed out, boots crunching in the thick snow. Her injured feet throbbed. She'd replaced the bandages while they'd waited at the FBI field office, but they still hurt. Minor injuries considering what others had suffered, just enough to remind her how lucky they had been. She turned to get her son out of the car. Hands clamped on her hips a moment before someone physically lifted her aside. Brennan. He let her go, the impressions of his fingers branded on her skin. The man was always touching her. She wasn't used to it—didn't know why she didn't tell him to stop.

He reached inside the vehicle, coming out with Michael cradled in his arms. He raised a quizzical brow at her standing there open-mouthed.

Words dried up on her tongue. The guy bowled her over. Not with words. With actions. Actions that had saved her son's life twice today and he was still putting himself in the line of fire for a little boy he didn't know. She knew he was just doing his job but it was hard to separate all her emotions from that simple fact.

Feelings of attraction seemed foolish and juvenile when they were running for their lives, but it had been a long time since she'd felt any of those things and it unsettled her.

Another agent grabbed her suitcase and laptop. The feds had scrambled the latter in some way so she could still use it but it didn't reveal her location except to them. They had a decoy set up somewhere they could monitor and hopefully use to lure out the bad guys.

Traps.

They were setting traps left, right, and center because some mystery terror organization wanted to kill her son.

She inhaled a massive rib-straining breath of cold air. She wanted to yell her anger at the world, but noise traveled far in this sort of terrain so she remained quiet as she followed the two feds to the front door, holding every particle of fear and frustration inside.

"Is it safe here?" she asked instead.

They'd driven for forty minutes but she knew they'd traveled in circles to circumvent anyone trying to follow them. They were probably only fifteen minutes outside the city limits of Minneapolis. Close enough for a rapid response team to reach them in an emergency, but remote enough to ensure their privacy. Hopefully.

Brennan had changed into dry clothes at the field office and looked a lot more approachable and a damn sight warmer than he had earlier, wearing a down vest, worn jeans, blue, plaid shirt and a pair of heavy winter boots. The tall, lean frame and the handsome face kept tricking her brain into thinking how attractive he was, when she should have been paying attention to all the effort being put into their safety—except when she thought about that she wanted to scream with fear and frustration.

This was all so crazy.

"It's a safe house used by the US Marshal Service and should be secure for now." He gave her a patient look. His patience made her anger drain. Some of her desperation ebbed.

A bald man with a handlebar mustache opened the door and she, Brennan and Michael, quickly slipped inside. The other fed stayed with the car.

The first marshal indicated Brennan follow another marshal, a tall blond woman with some serious curves, up the stairs. Vivi went too. The marshals had prepared a room with a double bed for them. Brennan slipped Michael's boots off and dropped them gently on the floor. He pulled back the covers and very carefully laid Michael on the bed, unzipped his jacket and eased it from his lax body.

Vivi stared in fascination.

This is what David should have been doing. *This* was what her son was missing. How pathetic that it took multiple attempts on his life to get a man to tuck him in at night. Tears that she'd held back all day suddenly wanted to flow but she blinked them away, then swiveled to find the pretty marshal watching her.

The woman held out her hand and whispered. "Deputy US Marshal Keene—or you can call me Penny. Cute kid you've got there."

"Thank you." Vivi shook her hand. It didn't escape her notice that the other woman's eyes skimmed down Brennan in a way that suggested she thought he was cute too. It was none of Vivi's business. *He* was none of her business.

"How long will we need to be here?" she asked just as

Brennan came out of the room and eased the door closed behind him, leaving it open just an inch.

"Let's go downstairs and discuss it," he said.

DUSM Keene led the way. Brennan sticking to Vivi's shoulder like a shadow.

An awareness sizzled between them. Or maybe it was just her—an exaggerated case of hero worship. Or maybe he had this effect on every female he met. Maybe he wasn't cognizant of the fact his handsome face combined with that protective demeanor was a hell of a draw to women—especially frazzled, terrified, single moms on the verge of a nervous breakdown. And surely she must be about to lose her mind if she was thinking about being attracted to a guy when her child's life was in danger.

Her head was going to explode.

She touched her forehead and took a deep, calming breath. He put his hand on her lower back and it grounded her in a way she didn't expect. As if he knew she was going crazy on the inside and was trying to help. Maybe she should just give herself a break for being human and wanting to think about something other than bloodshed and death.

They got to the kitchen where she was introduced to the guy with the mustache, DUSM Bob Townsend.

Vivi didn't want to appear ungrateful but all she really wanted was to go home and forget any of this had ever happened. "How long will we need to be here?" she asked again.

The marshals looked at Brennan probably because the FBI was in charge of this operation. *God.* Her stomach hurt just thinking about it.

"It depends," he said.

She crossed her arms and faced him. "On?"

"Us rounding up all the people involved in today's attack, or..."

"Or?"

"Or Michael being able to draw the faces of everyone he saw inside that store and therefore neutralizing the threat."

Silence boomed in the quiet of the house.

"You don't understand." How many times had she said that in relation to her son over the years? Because no one did understand. Not even her. "After everything that happened I don't know when or even *if* he'll start drawing again."

"You have to make him try."

She shook her head. "Trying to force him will make him withdraw even more. I can't *make* him do anything."

She jolted when Brennan picked up one of her hands that was clenched into a tight fist. He massaged her fingers as if he understood she was so uptight she was about to implode.

"Vivi." His voice was deep and soft and caressed her ragged nerves. But she wouldn't be played. She wouldn't let Michael be played. "There is no handbook for this situation. I'm just saying that the fastest way to neutralize the threat to Michael is to make sure we have access to all the information he has locked up inside his head. Then he ceases to be a threat to their organization.

"In the meantime we'll be working our asses off trying to catch these bastards and end the threat that way. And on that note I need to head back to the office and see where we're at." But he didn't let go of her hand. He stroked and massaged until slowly the tension loosened and she unclenched her fingers and her jaw, and let out a slow breath. It was a long time since someone had touched her in comfort. Even longer in desire.

Heat rose in her cheeks and she pulled her hand away. It was her own fault, she knew that. She pushed people away. Everyone except her son.

Both marshals watched the exchange with interest. She didn't know what they thought or what was normal in this sort of situation. Maybe *this* was normal? This instant attachment to someone who'd saved her child's life. How could it not be?

"Write out a list of things you or Michael need and I'll try and bring them by in the morning." His dark eyes were warm and full of patient concern.

She stepped away. She didn't want to respond to him this way. She didn't want to respond to anyone. All she wanted was to go home.

Quickly, she wrote a short list while their protectors discussed how long it would take backup to arrive and the firepower capability on site. Every word made her insides shrivel a little. How foolish to think her life was complicated enough when she'd gotten up that morning. Or even after they'd dragged a panicked little boy from an MRI machine. Her life had been rosy. She'd just been too stupid to understand.

As much as she liked Brennan, as much as she was attracted to him—had been from the moment he'd pulled her to her feet in the crowded mall that morning—she was not about to let him manipulate her into doing something she didn't want to do.

She turned away without a word. Left them to huddle and plot like the security experts they purported to be. The simple fact was she didn't trust anyone. Especially not when it came to her son. She went upstairs and crawled into bed beside

Michael, hugging his slight body to hers. His heartbeat reverberated fiercely against her palm, that small vital organ the noisiest part of his body.

EIGHTEEN HOURS AFTER the attack, Jed was at the FBI field office on Freeway Boulevard waiting for the briefing to start. It was dark outside but the snow cast an eerie light over the city to the south.

Every alphabet agency in the country from Homeland to ICE had descended on Minneapolis to confront the current terror threat, which was still considered severe. The whole country was on high alert. Commercial flights grounded until further notice.

More than fifty bodies had been recovered from the mall, including thirteen children, the youngest just three years old. It was sickening, and could easily have been worse. Vivi Vincent's face flashed through his mind. When he'd left the safe house a few hours ago she'd looked like a hollowed out version of the woman he'd first met in the mall. Washed out and exhausted. Wary of everyone and everything. Foolishly he wanted to make her smile again. A simple thing under normal circumstances. A damn sight harder when she and her son had been marked for death by some shadowy terror organization with an unknown agenda.

He leaned against a wall in the bullpen. The FBI's Rapid Deployment & Technology Unit were in charge of creating a local Joint Terrorism Task Force, which pissed off Homeland, DOD and the National JTTF because they all liked to be in charge. BAU's terrorism experts were headed up on the next military transport available.

He hadn't mentioned that technically he was supposed to be on leave.

Jed knew the guy running the show; they both worked at the BAU's National Center for the Analysis of Violent Crime at Quantico. Supervisory Special Agent (SSA) Steve McKenzie was a solid agent with an excellent rep for getting the job done. Jed wanted in on the task force even though it would take him away from Virginia for a few months—his boss would probably think it was a good idea. He wanted this terrorist cell shut down so they never hurt another living soul, especially not a redheaded little boy he was starting to like.

The fact he'd been boots on the ground when an attack occurred might give them an advantage and he'd use it. He just wished he'd been properly armed. More civilians might have been saved—although a SIG versus an assault rifle wasn't much of a match and in reality he'd probably be dead.

It was time for the meeting to start. The bullpen was crowded with personnel but the room was as silent as a freshly dug grave. Shocked and tired, everyone listened attentively. McKenzie began by outlining everything they'd learned so far.

"Seven dead terrorists. One in the ICU under armed guard—"

"Is he going to make it?" This from a guy in jeans and a faded University of Minnesota t-shirt who'd walked in late. He looked like a hippie. Jed didn't know the guy or which agency he was with.

"Doctors are saying 50:50 chance. Bullet went through his lung, did a lot of damage."

"Make sure someone has eyes on him at all times, and search him for suicide pills. No one talks to him except me."

Spook—Jed recognized the type from his days in Kandahar.

The guy continued, "Not the doctors, not the nurses, not the guard. Just me. Take away the clock, TV, any form of communication, be it radio or internet. I want him completely isolated with no idea what time of day it is and no access to outside information, and I want to know the moment he wakes up." The gleam in his eyes told Jed the guy was experienced at getting information out of these guys. *Good.* He wanted these guys put through the wringer until they were bled dry of information and then left to rot in some stinking prison for the rest of their natural lives.

"We're holding the guy Brennan nabbed from the pool at the federal facility—he refuses to give his name and so far his biometric profile isn't popping any databases. That joker is claiming he saw the boy drowning and tried to save him. Wants his lawyer so he can sue Brennan for assault," SSA McKenzie told the group.

"Good luck with that from Git-mo," muttered Jed.

The intelligence officer shot him an amused glance.

"We've ID'd four of the dead terrorists." McKenzie reeled off names that meant nothing to Jed. He hadn't worked terrorism since his probationary period at the BAU and things moved fast on the international scene with so many willing and enthusiastic recruits constantly blowing themselves up. The spook wrote down all the names. "We are running them through every database but from what I can tell none of them were on any US watch-list." Which was unusual and disturbing. "They were all Muslims. Two of them were American citizens."

That was a blow. The Muslim community had been rebuilding relationships and this would put their efforts back a decade and probably radicalize a whole new generation with the blow-back.

"What about the female tango?" Responsibility for her escape scraped Jed's nerves.

McKenzie looked irritated by the constant interruptions, but Jed was more worried about Vivi and her son. He didn't intend to let their safety fall through the cracks of such a massive operation. Plus this guy wasn't technically his boss so pissing him off probably wouldn't get him fired, but it wouldn't get him on the task force. He reeled in his frustration.

"Thanks to your smart thinking in the clothing store we know she left wearing black pants, burgundy shirt, gray wool coat. She's approximately five-six, one-hundred thirty pounds and they are running her DNA as we speak."

The ERT deserved the credit and Jed had put that in his report. "Get anything from photographs of people leaving the mall?"

McKenzie shook his head. "We're canvassing the media and crowd-sourcing social media for images but it may take some time. We don't want a screw up like we had in Boston, or any vigilante nonsense."

"All the security cameras inside the mall were down?" someone from the back of the room asked.

McKenzie nodded. "From the time of the explosion onward. Whoever these guys were they had some sophisticated help planning this attack. We'll have analysts going through all today's footage from before the explosion and then they'll run previous days' and weeks' tapes through image recognition software to see if we can find the bad guys scoping out the joint." He rubbed his forehead. "We are asking for anyone who took footage at the mall over the last few weeks to submit that to us online. It's a slow process and we want to make sure we get this terror threat contained ASAP."

The trouble in today's world wasn't a lack of information. It was an abundance. By the time they'd plowed through everything the perps could be long gone.

No one intended to let that happen.

McKenzie continued. "Weapons were all smuggled in illegally and we're tracing serial numbers. Ammo was bought legally. The anti-gun lobby and NRA are both going to be all over this thing saying it supports their cause." Like they needed added political pressure while investigating this thing. "No comments to the media either way from this side of the investigation—got it?" He eyed them sternly.

"I'm all for gun control as long as I get to keep mine," one agent joked.

Jed didn't say anything. Fewer guns on the street would probably make his life safer but people were plenty capable of killing with crowbars, vehicles, screwdrivers, knives, fire, electricity and all manner of other household items. Guns were tools, but they sure as hell were effective when the job was killing as many people as possible in the shortest amount of time.

Changing gun laws in the States was going to take an act of God. His whole family was licensed to carry concealed, including his mother. They'd have to pry those weapons from his family's cold, dead hands, and considering his twin brother was the local police chief he didn't think it was going to happen any time soon.

"What about the kid?" asked the spook. "What can he tell

us?"

Fifty pairs of eyes swung toward Jed. Shit. "He's a mute, autistic eight-year-old boy. Yeah, he can draw but I'm not convinced he even saw anything." Jed shrugged. "He's been traumatized and didn't look like he was capable of remembering his own name when I saw him last."

"He's in a safe house?" The spook scribbled something in his notepad.

Jed was not discussing the Vincents' exact whereabouts in front of fifty people. He stood straighter, held the man's gaze in a direct challenge. "You're not interrogating the kid, CIA."

The guy's lip curled into a lopsided smile. "Never crossed my mind."

"Sure it didn't." Tension knotted Jed's muscles and his jaw ached from being clamped shut.

"The mother?" The spook's smile was a thin slice of cunning. He had too long, dirty blond hair and a surfer laid back attitude that didn't fool Jed one bit.

"She didn't see anything."

"You sure?"

"I'm sure."

"OK then, if you're *sure*..." The guy's lip tightened a fraction. "She's an interpreter?"

"Used to work for the UN." Jed had done a little superficial digging but nothing stuck out. She'd had good security clearance up until a few years ago.

"Any chance she was the original target of the attack?"

"Nope. None." Jed shook his head, remembering how the big guy had knocked her over without a backward glance. If she had been the target he'd have started shooting the moment he saw her.

"Good thing you were there, otherwise we might have to do some actual investigating." The intelligence officer's tone was mocking and someone laughed.

"But I *was* there." Jed straightened away from the wall. "If she'd been the original target she'd be dead." He held the man's gaze. "The last thing we need is for this investigation to go off on a wrong tangent." There was something. "She did speak to the guy in Arabic when she was cornered in the restaurant kitchen. Whatever she said made him hesitate for all of two seconds before he started shooting. She was damned lucky to have got out of there alive but I don't think the guy was after her specifically. He was trigger happy and hunting anyone still breathing."

"Like I said, good thing you were there," the spook said, watching him impassively.

Christ. Jed knew when he was being riled. He was half-tempted to let this guy question Vivi Vincent as long as he got to watch. She'd never let him near her son. He wasn't fooled by the guy's demeanor. He was an interrogator and after 9/11 they all knew what that could entail. The guy *would* try to talk to Vivi and her son. Ah, shit. The guy probably *should* talk to them but Jed did not like it one bit. The Vincents had been through hell already.

They moved on to discussing the list of mall employees— hundreds of people long. Forensics were backed up because of the sheer volume of information.

"Cell phones were bought in a couple of different locations in Madison. Buyer used cash and even the stores where we got him on surveillance show the perp concealed by hats and glasses. It could be the guy Brennan caught in the pool though. He's the right size and shape, we just need something solid to hang it on him," said McKenzie.

"His DNA might be on those cell phones or the SIM cards," Brennan suggested.

McKenzie agreed. "We're on it. We'll cross reference ASAP." He checked his watch. "But it'll be a couple more hours until we get the preliminary DNA profiles to compare."

Brennan quashed his impatience. Compared to how slowly things usually moved this was lightning-speed. And he knew the guy in the pool was part of the group. He didn't need proof.

"The phones were only used to communicate with each other. The same ten numbers were logged into each cell." McKenzie continued. "Data says the phones were activated and programmed yesterday morning."

Just for the attack. "Any corresponding phone activity on the pool guy's cell?" Jed asked.

"We didn't find a cell phone or a wallet with his belongings."

That didn't make sense. Very few people traveled without cells and the guy certainly hadn't planned on getting caught—but he was definitely a pro. Jed tried to remember if he'd seen a cell phone anywhere at the pool but came up blank.

The spook raised his voice to be heard over the muttering crowd. "It's imperative we identify the unknown female. This wasn't a lone wolf act of terrorism. This was a terror cell and cells are always connected to someone, through training, ideology and cash. We need to find the female and we need to figure out who sent them and shut them down before they target another mall or fucking Disney World."

"Thanks for pointing that out, we'd never have figured it out on our own." McKenzie's eye-roll was understated. He flipped the cover over the tablet he was holding. "We're pouring resources into it but there are the hundreds of witness statements to sort through, piles of forensics to examine, and more images than Hollywood. I suggest you—Intelligence Officer Killion—start with the suspected terrorists we already have in custody. I was told that was your specialty when the Director of National Intelligence volunteered your services." The raised brow questioned the spook's abilities but the guy wasn't fazed. Jed eyed him more carefully. It wasn't often the DNI got personally involved, although it wasn't often terrorists attacked an American mall—thank God.

"That's all for now folks. We'll meet again at noon. Keep me apprised of any developments no matter how small." The SSA left the room with the boss. The spook stared after him before turning to unerringly meet Jed's gaze. The guy grinned then scooped up his belongings and headed out the door.

Jed didn't trust the guy as far as he could throw him, but if he'd been sent specially for this purpose by the DNI it suggested he wasn't all big-mouthed bullshit.

Everyone started moving in different directions. They were all about to pull some long hours. But before he dug into paperwork he had something to check out first, something his gut told him didn't sit quite right.

———————

PILAH SAT INSIDE her apartment staring at the floor. Abdullah hadn't returned and she was glad. She'd been here for hours uselessly awaiting instructions. Waiting for word. What she really wanted to do was get on a plane to Damascus and find her children and never let them go. But Sargon would know the moment she went to the airport and he'd told her to wait. She was too scared to disobey.

Had her husband considered any of this when he'd taken up arms?

Oh, she understood the fury that accompanied grief. She'd tasted the hunger for revenge—but eventually vengeance became a vortex of hate that no one ever escaped. The images of the people she'd seen killed kept flashing through her mind, even when she'd tried to sleep, their screams wouldn't let her.

What had she done? What had she done? She wept and rocked and prayed, but nothing could change the past. Nothing could bring her daughter or husband back.

The realization came way too late.

She paced. If she could just get her girls out of Syria they could start over somewhere. Rebuild their lives. They could go somewhere far away—Indonesia or Australia, somewhere no one would know her. She could forget all the things she'd done. Become someone else.

The phone rang. She jumped and stared at it, dread expanding in her chest. It rang again and she snatched up the handset. "Hello?"

"There is a man in the hospital. His name is William Green."

"I-I don't understand."

"He was injured during the attack."

Did he want her to finish the job? The idea made her recoil.

She waited. She didn't want to say the wrong thing and make Sargon angry.

"He is in a coma and has no registered next-of-kin. I need you to visit him."

"Why?"

"It would be a kindness."

She could hear his impatience. Did he *want* her to get caught? She rubbed her forehead and paced. "I really don't understand."

"You do not need to understand. You just need to visit a sick man in the hospital—as his niece perhaps." The voice was full of cold purpose under the guise of compassion.

"Look, I said I'd help you at the mall, but that was it. I never agreed to do more." Her fingers were rigid against the hard plastic of the phone. "I'm coming to get my children—"

"Enough! Do not think to question me again." Fury resonated through the air.

"I won't do it." Her voice cracked. "I can't do it."

"Then say goodbye to your daughters and know that it is your fault they suffered," he hissed.

Dizziness made her stumble. "You promised—"

"Do not dare to question me!" She heard his ragged breathing but his voice was much quieter when he continued. "I have given you a task. It is easy enough to visit a sick man, is it not?" His voice gentled further, wheedled and cajoled. "Do as I ask and nothing will change. Your daughters will continue to be raised alongside my own. You will see them just as soon as we obtain our objective."

But Pilah had a sudden flash of insight that she didn't know what his objective was, and probably never would. Her resolve crumbled to bitter dust. Her fingers hurt from their grip on the phone. "I need you to *promise* that no harm will come to them, ever."

"That is up to you. What is it to be?"

But there was no choice and he knew it.

"Which hospital?" she asked.

CHAPTER SEVEN

A FTER WHAT MUST be the longest night of his life it was
still dark outside, blowing snow sweeping across desolate
highways and the roads quiet after a shocking day of mass
murder. Jed strode into the hotel and headed toward the men's
changing room for the pool. No way in hell would the
operative who'd tried to drown Michael Vincent *not* have a
cell phone. He eyed the area. Climbed on top of the bench that
ran between the row of lockers to see if there was anything on
top. Nada. Nyet. Too easy. Too obvious.

Agents had checked inside every locker, so they were all
clear.

Where would he hide something he might need to pick up
again in a hurry? There was a cupboard with a blue door to the
left of the entrance to the shower area. Jed tried the handle but
it was locked. A massive fake palm tree sat in one corner. Jed
walked over and donned a pair of latex gloves, delving into the
mulch. He dug around, immediately touched something solid.
Gotcha. He tugged out a black wallet, holding it by the corner
of the leather.

Inside was cash—several thousand dollars' worth—credit
cards in three different names, driver licenses and more false
identities. The forgeries were good. Excellent even. But no
goddamn cell phone. He slipped the wallet into an evidence

bag and placed it in his vest pocket.

He dug deeper into the blue ceramic pot but nothing else was hidden. He brushed off his hands. Tried to think like he was on a military op. So the guy had hidden his wallet because if things went wrong he didn't want whatever was in it to be found.

The guy had known going in that this was a high risk operation. It was unplanned because Michael Vincent was an unforeseen complication. Jed thought for a moment. The fact this guy had stayed outside the fray during the attack on the mall suggested he was high value. Worth more to the organization alive than martyred to the cause.

So why risk revealing his identity for the kid?

Jed was missing something.

Give him a series of mutilated bodies and he could predict all sorts of salient details about the killer. But terrorists killed for different reasons—they murdered out of conviction. Now, with the attempt on Michael Vincent's life, the motivation had switched to one of murder for elimination. Michael was an inconvenience or a danger to them. Jed just didn't know why.

They were organized offenders. Highly organized in this case. The fact they'd taken such risks to go after the boy... Maybe the female terrorist who'd escaped was personally involved with this pool guy and he hadn't wanted her exposed because they were lovers. Maybe they were plotting further attacks? The latter seemed much more likely considering the female tango could easily have died during the mall attack. Her escape was both bold and daring.

Was she the brains behind the organization? Were they simply trying to protect the mastermind's identity?

What might be locked up inside Michael's mind?

He walked into the pool area, feeling the heat and humidity cling to his skin, the slight sting of chlorine in his eyes. Sweat ran down his temple. He slipped out of his down vest and scanned the poolside. It was early but already filling with people. Kids were laughing and splashing like nothing had happened yesterday—and why not? Better than these sadistic morons disrupting people's lives with their hatred and bitterness, which was exactly what they wanted. A pair of navy-blue eyes and red hair flashed through his mind. The sooner he could wrap this thing up, the sooner Vivi Vincent and her son could go home.

OK then.

Think.

The injured lifeguard had sported a goose egg from where the guy had hit him over the head. What did he hit him with? Jed walked over to the secluded alcove where the lifeguard had been stationed yesterday, not far from where he'd seen Michael underwater.

A heater blasted against the window, condensation forming a dense mist on the huge panes of glass. A first aid kit was attached to the wall. Jed checked inside but nothing jumped out at him. Another fake palm sat nearby. It couldn't be that simple, could it? He ran his hand inside the lip and touched something smooth and hard, not hidden just propped out of sight.

A gun. Holy hell. He pulled it out, recognized a Browning Hi-Power pistol. Crap. The lifeguard was damn lucky he'd just been knocked unconscious, rather than shot. Jed was assuming the terrorist hadn't wanted to cause a ruckus and risk losing Michael Vincent in the chaos. Instead he'd been patient and pounced like a crocodile.

Jed swept his hand further inside the rim and came up with pay dirt. Cell phone. *Ding ding ding*. Grinning, he bagged it and headed out the way he'd come. This guy was important, Jed could *feel* it. These items were going to provide valuable intel and help them round up the dregs of this particular terrorist cell.

Slipping into his vest on the way out of the changing room door, he stopped dead when he saw the spook from the briefing on his hands and knees digging out a potted fern in the hotel corridor. A trail of debris circled each piece of foliage in the foyer. Jed leaned against the wall and watched the guy for a full ten seconds before he spoke up.

"Pretty good instincts you've got there, CIA."

The man sat back on his heels. "Why don't you say it louder? I don't think they heard you in Canada."

Jed grinned. There was no one close enough to overhear them talking and the guy knew it. The spook looked up at him. "You find it?"

Jed held back a smirk. No one liked a bragger. "Yup."

The spook narrowed his gaze. "Gonna share?"

"I think the question is, are *you* going to share?"

"Feebs are in charge." The spook climbed to his feet, brushed his hands on his thighs. "How about I look at it while you drive me?"

"Drive you? Drive you where?" The guy was too cocky and too confident. Frankly, he didn't trust him.

"To visit the Vincent woman and her kid." Jed opened his mouth to argue but the intelligence officer cut him off. "Look, I like you Brennan. I like how you think. I like the results you've gotten so far. She trusts you. Work with me and I promise not to break out the plastic wrap and buckets of water."

"Not funny, asshole."

"Agency humor. C'mon, Brennan, work with me here." The spook trailed after him, leaving the dirt scattered for someone else to deal with—a sure reminder of how the Agency usually operated, always leaving someone else to clean up their mess.

The spook didn't shut up. "It'll go smoother if you're there too. I need to talk to her. To assess her and the kid. Hey, maybe she'll like me." The grin was practiced and smooth and made Jed want to knock his gleaming white teeth out of alignment.

The pressure in his jaw ramped up a notch and he rubbed his neck. Sooner they figured this out the sooner Vivi and Michael would be free to carry on their normal lives. This guy *was* supposed to be on their side.

"Fine, but I want in on your intel." He carried on walking, figuring someone from the CIA could probably manage to follow him to the car without getting lost. He climbed in his SUV and started the engine. Blew on his hands as the spook jogged through the snow to catch up. "Where's your ride?" he asked the guy.

"I caught a cab."

Because he hadn't wanted to tell anyone where he was going or what he was planning.

"Where do you live?" asked Jed.

"Wherever they send me."

"Not much of a life."

The spook shrugged. "I'm used to it."

"What do I call you?" Jed asked. "Aside from the obvious." He gave him a grim smile. He didn't want this guy thinking he didn't understand what his agenda was—and that the agenda was thousands of miles away tracing the source of the problem. Jed got that, admired it even, but he didn't want to be anyone's stooge. Vivi and Michael were not pawns in his game.

"Patrick Killion. Everyone calls me Killion."

"Right, Killion, we've got a couple stops to make first." He handed the guy some latex gloves out of the box he kept in the dash, then dug out the wallet and cell he'd found hidden, saving the pistol until last. "Knock yourself out."

Killion turned on the cell just as they were leaving the parking lot. "And we have a name—Abdullah Mulhadre." He pulled out his own cell phone and spoke to someone presumably at Langley.

"Anything?" Jed asked impatiently after a minute of silence on this end and the other guy busy scrolling.

Killion's expression grew forbidding as he hung up. "Yeah, there's a record of one Abdullah Mulhadre being assigned to the Syrian Embassy—they're checking his immunity status although no one is immune from terrorism charges." Killion's eyes gleamed. "If it's the same guy he's a member of the Syrian Republican Guard."

A wave of dread crashed over Jed's body. "Are you saying this attack came from Syria itself?" He'd seen the cost of war up close. Hell, he'd lost his best friend to it and didn't want more of it here.

Killion's lips thinned. "Not a word about this, Brennan. Not a fucking word until I hear back from Langley."

He blew out a frustrated breath. Dammit. Was he supposed to lie to his colleagues? But sharing with everyone at the field office could mean this information could leak, and a leak could precipitate a series of events that might morph into full-scale war. No way did he want to risk thousands of lives. And what about the Vincents? If it was the whole Syrian Government they were facing their lives would never be safe—or maybe, if this was the big secret the terrorists were trying to protect, then publically revealing that the Syrian Government had attacked US citizens on US soil meant the boy's safety would no longer be an issue.

War would be declared.

It was too big to screw up.

"We tell McKenzie but no one else—that way we can control the flow of information and he can take it higher." Jed didn't want to be responsible for the investigation missing a solid lead or veering in the wrong direction, but he didn't want to be responsible for starting a war either. He didn't trust spooks. And spooks didn't trust the FBI. *Damn.* They were in for a hell of a ride.

———————

VIVI WOKE WITH a start. A door slammed downstairs and her heart hammered. Then she heard the murmur of conversation and subdued laughter. The US Marshals going about their normal day.

OK. It wasn't bad guys. They were safe.

She pushed up onto her elbow and stared down at Michael. He had his eyes pressed tightly closed. Faking it.

"OK, sleepy head. Time to get up and eat some breakfast." He squeezed his lids even tighter. *Crap.* Although this was better than the trance-like state he'd arrived in, it wasn't exactly business as usual. "How about I bring you breakfast in bed? Special treat?"

He didn't answer and a little drum of panic fluttered just beneath her ribs. The attack in the pool last night had undermined any progress they'd made after the mall shooting. She'd promised no one would hurt him but a stranger had held him under the water until he'd almost drowned.

What sort of parent did that make her?

Flawed.

Inadequate.

Struggling.

Normal.

Time. He just needed a little time and space from what had happened. They'd be OK.

She eased out of bed, wincing as her injured feet hit the ground. She showered, ignoring the slight throb of discomfort, and put on fresh salve and bandages. She pulled a pair of jeans, a green blouse and thick socks from her case. One look in the mirror had her dragging out her make-up case—she'd seen zombies with more color. Subtle eye shadow, mascara, and a light coating of lip gloss made her look almost human. With another glance at Michael's sleeping form—he'd drifted off again—she went downstairs to see if she could rustle up something good for him to eat.

Two strangers stood in the kitchen, both wearing dark suits and shoulder holsters. It was an unwelcome slap of reality. They both looked up as she entered.

"I was wondering when we'd get to meet you." One guy, not tall, but blond and nice looking in a rough and rugged way came toward her with an outstretched hand. He shook hers vigorously. "We're the day shift. I'm Inspector Patton and this here is DUSM Rogers."

She nodded at Rogers who appeared a little older—in his fifties with graying hair and a hard edge to his face that made him look both capable and dangerous.

"How's your son doing?" Patton asked. He wore a wedding ring and seemed easy going. The title "Inspector" suggested that Patton was the boss.

She cleared her throat. "Not great actually. I was hoping to take some warm milk and a bowl of cereal up to the room to try and get some fuel inside him."

"You sit and have coffee. I'll make his breakfast." Patton was already in the fridge getting the milk. He was either a family man or had lots of siblings growing up. "Does he like Cheerios?"

"Yes. Thank you." Not all men were as good with children or as comfortable doing for others.

FBI Agent Brennan had been good with Michael too, she thought with a pang. Perhaps they were the norm and her expectations of the male of the species had been skewed unfairly because of Michael's father. Sad that she'd found more caring in the presence of strangers than she'd ever experienced with her ex.

The other marshal, Rogers, handed her coffee and joked. "Thank God you're awake. This guy can't sit still. The next phase was to redecorate the living room in soft, pastel colors that feel more 'homey' and then sew new drapes." He winked at her. "He's heading toward retirement at lightning speed and, personally, I can't wait for him to get there."

"Yeah, well wait until Dr. Phil is on TV this afternoon and see who the little homemaker is then," Patton taunted him back. Rogers winked at her. They were obviously people who'd worked together for many years, both easy with their authority and, in turn, trying to put her at ease. She smiled back. She'd forgotten how much she enjoyed the company of men. Nowadays her world was filled with Michael, his friends, and a couple of other moms she knew from school. She worked over the internet. Had no close male friends. Certainly no dates and absolutely no lovers.

Her mood dropped.

The guilt of motherhood was prodding her not to enjoy anything about this terrible situation. People had *died* yesterday. Michael had almost died twice. But everything that had happened also made her realize how lonely her life had become. She had no one who cared if she never went home. It was a sobering thought.

She edged up onto a tall stool. Patton slid a plate of toast and marmalade across the kitchen island toward her. It tasted delicious and she was ravenous.

Rogers's cell phone rang and he checked the window that overlooked the long, winding driveway. "Just make sure you both have your ID out and hands outside your pockets until I verify the new guy." Rogers hung up and dialed someone else. "Visitors," he told her and Patton, who left cook duty and went to check the back door.

"Who is it?" she asked nervously.

"Jed Brennan and some intelligence officer."

Her stomach somersaulted. Had they figured out who Michael's father was? What would she do if they tried to take Michael away from her, or lock him up? She'd scream bloody murder, that's what. No. David hadn't even returned her call from yesterday. He'd lost interest in them years ago, but he did like wielding power just to prove he could. She stood rigid with indecision and told herself she was being stupid. Every counter-terrorism agency in the world would want to see what they could get out of Michael. They'd see him as an asset, a tool.

Even if Michael had been a normal kid this would have been a traumatic time, but with his brain so delicately balanced between this world and some unknown place, it was even more difficult. She would not let them push him.

Rogers waved to get her to move out of sight behind the kitchen counter. She crouched, knowing these guys had a job to do and she could make that job harder or easier. Michael's safety and well-being were all that truly mattered. Not David. Not the CIA. Not Jed Brennan. Just Michael.

She heard voices at the door. Footsteps. When she looked up she found herself staring at a very tall Special Agent Brennan. There was some distance in his expression which helped her see him as a federal agent again, rather than an attractive male. It settled her. Made her think that maybe they could do this. She climbed to her feet, feeling slightly foolish. Another man spoke to the marshals in the hallway. She couldn't see him.

"Everything OK?" He sounded tired. Eyes red-rimmed from fatigue, the shadow of a dark beard sweeping his jaw. He still wore the jeans and plaid shirt he'd changed into yesterday, but the whole outdoorsy thing looked even better on him than the tailored suit. As a woman who'd always preferred tailored suits that was troubling.

"Michael's asleep." She grimaced as she realized she was once again hiding behind her son.

"What about you? Sleep OK?" Brennan watched her with something akin to pity. The fact he saw straight through her, made her want to hunch her shoulders and turn away.

Instead she straightened her spine and went with honesty. "Hanging in there. What about you?"

"A little too busy for sleep." His dark hair was ruffled as if he'd run his hands through it countless times. His ears were pink from the cold.

"Have you made any arrests yet?"

Brennan shook his head. "We're working on it. I called the hospital like you asked. The woman whose kids you saved woke up in the ICU. Looks like she'll make it."

"Thank goodness."

He grinned, and that wave of attraction hit her again, harder this time.

He was the same tall, dark and handsome that had been her undoing ten years earlier. He had the same broad-shouldered, lean frame, the same confident-competent manner. But there the resemblance to her ex ended. Brennan's eyes were warm, his grin easy. His voice was calm and non-threatening, even though power radiated from the way he held himself and the way he commanded attention. Even when she'd met the take-charge version of the guy yesterday he hadn't yelled or gotten angry. He hadn't lost his temper or lashed out.

It could all be an act though—she'd been fooled before. She couldn't afford to forget that the FBI had an agenda when it came to her and her son.

A stark reminder of that fact appeared behind Brennan's shoulder.

Everything inside her went quiet and still, the way a mouse froze when a buzzard hovered above. The newcomer's eyes were pale blue; his gaze dissecting her like a surgeon's scalpel. The long, sun-bleached hair softened the overall effect but she knew exactly the sort of man he was. Cold. Hard. Ruthless. No way in hell was he getting anywhere near her son.

Jed introduced them. "Vivi, this is Intelligence Officer Patrick Killion. He's hoping to speak with you and Michael about what you experienced yesterday." There was something in his voice that she didn't know how to interpret. Almost humor.

The two marshals stood close by and watched the exchange.

"Nice to meet you, ma'am. I was just hoping to ask Michael a few questions." Killion held out his hand and she took it.

Despite the firm handshake his touch made her skin crawl. A shiver climbed up her spine but she didn't give herself away. "Did no one tell you my son is mute, Mr. Killion?"

Something in the intelligence officer's eyes sharpened further.

"It was mentioned, Ms. Vincent. I was hoping to take a look at him and see how close he might be to trying to help us."

"*Trying* to help you?" With that one word he ramped up her pissed level by a factor of a thousand. "Are you suggesting he might be willfully *not* trying?" She stood tall, facing off with the man. Oh, she had met this type before. Hell, she'd married it. "He's eight years old and on his best day he doesn't speak. Are you telling me you think he does that on purpose? Or do you think you can magically *cure* him when the experts can't?"

"Hey, lady." Killion held up his hands, palm out. "Chill. From what I hear there's nothing physically wrong with his vocal cords." *How the hell did he know that?* "It's not out of the realm of possibility that the trauma from yesterday might be

104

the impetus that gets your son speaking again."

She put her face right next to Killion's. "How dare you dangle that carrot in front of my eyes so that I'll let you go up there and *interrogate* my son? He hasn't eaten since yesterday. He's barely opened his eyes but you come in here as if you have the right to doubt him?" Fire burned through her, hot and furious. She shoved him back a step. An arm wrapped around her middle and Brennan pulled her away.

"But I *do* have that right, ma'am. A threat to National Security gives me that right." Killion was getting angry too. She could see it in the tightening of his jaw and the narrowing of his gaze. Good. She went to take another step forward but Brennan anchored her around the waist. And the sudden awareness of his hand spanning her stomach made her lose her train of thought.

Some of the fire died, but not the resolve to protect her child. "Not today you don't. Not today. And not someone like you."

Killion looked at the floor, his chest expanding slowly as if seeking patience. "If not me, then who, Ms. Vincent? And when? When all the terrorists have fled back to their bolt holes? Or when you and Michael are both dead?" Killion's gaze turned from pissed to cynically amused. But he'd lost his veneer of cool and Vivi didn't intend to let him get it back.

He was a chameleon and she didn't trust people who worked in the shadows. She needed truth and honesty. Her husband had taught her that too. As an interpreter she'd worked some highly classified cases and knew how these guys operated. Sure, he was a patriot, but he was also playing a game that was much bigger than Michael's safety. Pawns were easily sacrificed when people concentrated on the 'big picture' and she wasn't about to let that happen to her son. But she also knew that when it came to terrorism the US Government did not pull its punches.

He proved it to her the next moment. "Maybe I should contact Michael's father?"

The intelligence officer looked at where Brennan's arm was wrapped around her waist and gave her a mocking smile. Now she really wanted to shove him. *Does he know or is he fishing?*

Even though her blood beat to the rhythm of fear she kept her face implacable. "He hasn't seen or spoken to Michael in four years. You think a judge will let *him* determine what's best for my son? I have full custody. I'm the one you need to convince." Threatening to go the legal route would tie this guy up in so much red tape he'd strangle on it. And speed was the most important factor in a case like this. Any idiot could figure that out. The silence crashed down on them. "Look, I want these people caught just as much as you do." *Maybe more.* "But Michael isn't like other children. He hasn't made a single sound since his accident. Not when he's hurt or mad or crying." It broke her heart to think about it.

She became aware that her back was still pressed against the very warm, very solid heat of Special Agent Brennan. He must have realized he was still holding her at the exact same moment. He let her go and stepped quickly away. She immediately missed the connection.

Such an attractive image, the sex-starved divorcee.

She continued. "There's a well-respected psychiatric neuroscientist based in Minneapolis called Dr. Hinkle. He's the reason we're visiting the state in the first place." Michael had liked the doctor, but she hadn't wanted her son forced to do anything that freaked him out.

The terror attack meant she was desperate for advice as to how to move forward from an expert, not some jumped-up Agency man. "Bring him out here to talk to Michael. Depending on what he says I'll consider letting you speak to my son afterward, here." She nodded through to the open-plan living area. "*If* Dr. Hinkle approves." She glanced at Brennan. "And I want Special Agent Brennan there, too."

His pupils flared in shock but apart from that he didn't give away his thoughts. Despite everything that had happened, she trusted him. How the heck had that happened?

The CIA agent surprised her. "Deal. What did you say to the man who tried to shoot you yesterday in the restaurant kitchen?"

"Pardon?" She frowned in confusion.

"You said something to him in a foreign language just before I, er...turned up," said Brennan.

"Oh. *That*." A vision of blood droplets spinning off a blade flashed through her mind. She swallowed the lump of residual terror the memory resurrected. "I asked him in Arabic why he was doing it—shooting people."

"Did he understand you?" Killion asked.

She nodded. "He didn't say anything but I could tell from the way his eyes widened that he understood what I was saying to him and he was surprised I spoke the language."

"Did he say anything back to you?" Killion's pale, blue eyes bored into hers.

"All he did was pull the trigger of his very big gun, and try to wipe me and two little children off the face of the earth."

"Does Michael understand Arabic?" Killion prodded.

Every cell inside her body froze. When he was a baby she'd

often played language CDs. It helped with her fluency and, yes, she'd hoped it might rub off on Michael, but she didn't know for sure if any of it had stuck. "No, he does not."

Killion stared at her for a long moment and then gave her a curt nod. "You're lucky to have made it through yesterday alive. I'm going to walk the perimeter of the property if it's all right with you guys?" The dramatic change in subject stunned her. Classic approach when you wanted people to be constantly off balance. She blew out a breath wondering if he'd believed her or not. "I'll check the security and layout while you speak to Agent Brennan? See if he can persuade you I'm not going to eat the kid alive."

"I'll show you 'round," said Rogers. "Snow's at least a foot deep so you might want to borrow some boots."

The intelligence officer turned his back on her and Brennan. She didn't get the guy. Did he really not understand Michael was a troubled little boy? Or did he think it was all some kind of trick? One thing she knew about those guys was they trusted no one. Ever. So maybe they had more in common than she thought.

CHAPTER EIGHT

JED PICKED UP the plastic bag he'd placed on the island and held it out to her. "The stuff you wanted for Michael."

There was something so honest and earnest about this guy that he was burrowing beneath all her defenses. Her brain screamed danger because as cynical and jaded as she was, she trusted this guy and she should know better. She cleared her throat. "I appreciate that. Thanks."

"Can I go say 'hi' to Michael?" he asked.

"Only if you don't mention Killion." She still hadn't fed her son breakfast and grabbed the milk and cereal and toast that the marshal had started to prepare, then searched the cupboards for a tray. "He was asleep when I came down. We can go take a peek and see if he's awake yet."

He stopped her with a hand on her elbow. "How long has it been like this?"

Her brain scrambled at the simple question. There had been a time when she'd been considered sophisticated and composed. She didn't know if it was motherhood, divorce, or Michael's uncertain diagnosis that had stripped her of those attributes. "I don't understand the question…?"

"Michael. How come he stopped talking?"

Ah. She put down the tray and rested her hands on the counter top. Closed her eyes. This would be a good time to spell out exactly what her life was like rather than fuel some stupid fantasy that only existed in her mind. Hysterical, divorced, single moms were not attractive to hot *I-can-have-any-woman-I-want* FBI special agents. She needed to lay her craziness on the table and back away from the nice man. "It's tied to the breakup between me and Michael's father four years ago."

He stared at her intently, so she carried on. "Which was all my fault apparently."

"Naturally."

"David said I was cold and distant. Controlling."

Brennan's eyes suggested he disagreed, but he didn't know her very well.

"He was right." She didn't need platitudes. She didn't need lies. "Michael was a normal baby. Cute and vocal." How his father had hated his colicky cries. She pushed the man out of her thoughts. He'd infected her with cynicism and bitterness and she was sick of it. "He was a normal baby. He exhibited a minor degree of autism as a toddler, right on the edge of the spectrum, he liked his things to go in the exact right place and was absorbed by patterns and symmetry. He still likes routine—I mean *really* likes routine. He goes to bed at the same time every night, and he doesn't even need a clock to do it, another reason yesterday was hard on him. As a baby he had no obvious disabilities and was considered 'normal' right up until the day he was pushed off a play structure at daycare and hit his head. He suffered a severe concussion. Needless to say I freaked out."

She looked at Brennan then. Let him see that beneath her exterior she was a raving lunatic when it came to her son—although he'd already seen her at her worst, handcuffed by the cops and screaming at him from a concrete floor. She probably still owed him an apology for that. "I couldn't get hold of Michael's father after the accident. He had a history of ignoring my calls,"—some things never changed—"Michael and I got home from the hospital and I still hadn't heard from him. At nine PM he comes home complaining that I called the office too much and was constantly bothering him and his staff. I told him about Michael's accident, and he told me that kids got hurt in the playground all the time. It was *good* for them. Then I told him Michael had a concussion and hadn't spoken since the accident. Rather than acting like a concerned parent, David went all hard-core military on him. He yelled and screamed, but Michael still didn't speak and frankly seemed pretty pleased about it—it was as if he'd suddenly found something his father couldn't control."

"You think he deliberately stopped talking?"

She raised both hands, palm out. "I don't know. Did shock turn to anger and then into a defense mechanism against a man who abused him?" Brennan stiffened but didn't say anything. "Or did the bump on the head somehow damage the part of his brain that controls speech? I don't know." Agitation swirled inside her. "All I do know is that when Michael didn't speak, David hit him, twice." She clamped her jaw shut. She'd never forgive him for that. Or herself for letting it happen. "I told him to leave and never come back. Turned out *that* wasn't a problem because he'd already found a beautiful woman called 'Julie' who was neither cold, distant, nor controlling." Her eyes turned diamond hard. "So maybe it wasn't *all* my fault, after all. Just most of it."

He took her hand, gripping her fingers tight, as if he had no intention of letting her go, but that was a foolish thought. It made her realize that underneath all the hurt and heartbreak she was still a romantic. Kind of pathetic really.

"You should have kicked his ass."

"Honestly, if I'd had a gun, I'd have shot the bastard." At the time she'd wanted to hurt David even a fraction of how much he'd hurt her and Michael, but then she'd just wanted rid of him. Some of the remnant anger dissolved on a ragged exhale. "We're better off without him, trust me." She rubbed her forehead with her free hand. Raking up the past always made her feel slightly ill. Seeing all the mistakes she'd made in glorious Technicolor hindsight was humbling. "The point I'm trying to make is no one can tell me which of those events stole Michael's voice, or if it's a result of the autism that the experts aren't even positive Michael suffers from." Uncertainty was one of the things that constantly ate at her. Hard to fix a problem when you didn't know the cause.

"And I suppose your ex is also the same guy who taught you that men lie?" Brennan watched her carefully.

"He's one of them." She gave him a direct stare.

Brennan nodded as if acknowledging the lies he'd told her. But they were different. And to balance the lies, he'd kept every promise he'd made. She knew the difference.

She heard footsteps and then watched Inspector Patton walk to the front door whistling. She'd bet a thousand dollars he'd eavesdropped on every word. Not that it really mattered.

She picked up the tray and Brennan followed her up the stairs. For a big man he moved like a ghost. She got tingles from him being so close, but ignored it. It was just a long time since she'd spent time in the company of a man she found to be the slightest bit attractive; it whispered to the echo of the woman she'd once been.

Brennan moved ahead of her to get the bedroom door. He waved her through and then held up the bag of supplies he'd bought. "Hey, bud! Rise and shine!"

So much for seeing if Michael was awake...

She rolled her eyes as Brennan strode into the room and she tried not to wince as she saw her case open, lingerie on full display. She set down the tray on the bedside table. Stroked her son's hair off his forehead and used her foot to shut the lid of the case. Michael's gaze glanced off her and away. That single action made all thoughts of clothes and Special Agent Brennan fade into insignificance. The idea of her son just drifting away terrified her.

The fed sat on the bed, making the mattress dip. "Whatcha doing, sport? Caught any bad guys today?"

There was a flicker of a smile and then an infinitesimal shake of Michael's head. She blinked. For whatever reason her son connected with this man. She was right to include him in the meeting with the cold, calculating CIA agent.

"I've got some good stuff for you in here, but first you've got to eat breakfast. Come on." Brennan plumped pillows and then hoisted Michael upright in bed. He handed him the milk first and Vivi held her breath as she watched her son take a sip. Finally. "Now eat this." Brennan bit into a slice of toast. "And I'll show you what I brought you."

Brennan started pulling things out of the bag while Michael took a bite of toast. The man's easy manner and lack of fussing really worked. Vivi didn't even care about crumbs in the bed as long as her son was eating.

He presented Michael with one of his favorite types of books. An encyclopedia. And an almanac. Michael loved non-fiction but Brennan had also included some Pokémon sticker annuals and cards. He held out an advanced Sudoku book to her. She shook her head quickly and nodded toward Michael. He didn't miss a beat. "Any good with these things, Mikey? They drive me 'round the bend."

Her eyes widened at the nickname. His buddies called him that at school. Michael took the book and smoothed his hand over the cover. There was more than a spark in his eyes now. He loved math puzzles. He grinned up at her for the first time in twenty-four hours and she smiled back. Emotions clutched at her heart until it threatened to tear itself apart. Brennan's dark gaze found hers and then he grinned too. It transformed his face from good-looking to ridiculously handsome.

The effect was so overwhelming. The butterflies fluttering in her stomach started to Kamikaze dive parts of her body that had been dormant for years. She already felt such a wealth of gratitude toward this guy but now it was morphing into something stronger, something deeper that manifested itself in an intense attraction she wasn't prepared for.

His eyes searched hers as if he felt it too.

She looked away.

She couldn't afford to fall for this guy. Michael could not afford to fall for this guy. Because if he did and Jed left…she didn't want to think about how that would make her son feel. She didn't want to think about how it would make her feel either. She'd been there and wasn't keen to repeat the experience.

Noises from downstairs alerted them that both the marshal and intelligence officer had returned.

"Brennan?" Killion yelled up the stairs.

"On my way." Brennan stood. "Bye, Mikey. See you later, OK?" He ruffled his carrot-colored hair and got another tiny smile in response. More than she'd got in the last eight hours. She could kiss the guy for that alone.

Outside the bedroom door, he turned and almost bumped into her. "I promise I won't let Killion hound Michael or push him beyond the mildest coaxing—that's assuming the doc gives permission." He picked at a stray down feather on his shirt. "But having him ask the hard questions might be easier than you doing it."

Reality washed over her and she crossed her arms over her chest. He was right about that. "But he doesn't speak, Jed." His given name slipped easily on her tongue. Too easily. She wanted to keep him at a distance and think of him as a federal agent—just a federal agent. "How can he answer that man's questions if he doesn't speak?"

"Can he write or type?" Brennan was being patient with her, not *handling* her—which had always driven her insane—but trying to help her figure this out.

Agitation swirled inside her. She shook her head. "Last time he used a tablet at school he dropped it and it broke. After that he wouldn't touch them." Scared of getting into trouble because he'd spent the first four years of his life being yelled at whenever he made a mistake.

Why had she stayed with David for so long? *Because you believed in the sanctity of marriage and, dammit, he'd been gone most of the time.* She squeezed her eyes closed. Old memories weren't helping today's situation. "I hope I can get him to start drawing again soon, but he doesn't always draw what I ask him to. Sometimes he draws whatever is in his head in no particular order."

"We'll figure it out." Brennan shrugged like it was no big deal, but Michael's life might depend on this.

She started to shake.

"Hey." He gently gripped her upper arms and some of his strength seeped into her own tired muscles. "If we can't keep two people safe from a known threat then we shouldn't bother turning up for work every morning. We will catch these people, with or without Michael's assistance. You're both safe here. I swear on my life you're safe."

"O-k-kay," she stuttered. "I'm just not very good at relying on others or…"

One side of his mouth turned up. "Or trusting men."

She blew out a tense breath. "Or that."

His gaze dropped to her lips. She froze. The pull of attraction zinged between them and he didn't look any happier about it than she was.

"Some of us have work to do!" Killion shouted up the stairs. Impatient and pushy. Snapping them both back to the moment and why they were here.

"I didn't realize I was your damn chauffeur." Brennan gave her arm a last squeeze, then turned and jogged down the stairs.

A wave of loneliness stole over her. It was stupid to miss the man's presence before he'd even left. It was stupid to trust him on such short acquaintance. He was just doing his job and would have done the exact same for anyone in their situation. But she believed in him. He made her feel safe.

If it weren't for Michael she'd have run and disappeared until the threat was over, but she couldn't risk it. Not with her son. She was trapped and she was in big trouble.

———————————

"SO SHE'S LATCHED onto you as her knight protector?" Killion

116

planted his feet on Jed's walnut dash. "She's hot. I wouldn't mind protecting some of that myself."

Jed had two brothers. He was old enough and ugly enough to know when someone was trying to get a rise out of him. Didn't mean they didn't get a fat lip when they pushed it too far.

"Maybe it was saving her kid's life that did it." He maneuvered the SUV carefully up the slick driveway. "Or the fact I look like someone she can trust."

Killion snorted. "Shows what she knows about the feds."

Jed grimaced. Maybe he *was* using Vivi—using the red-hot attraction that simmered between them. He'd thought about kissing her on the landing upstairs—*idiot*—but he did not intend to cross that line. This case was complicated enough without getting involved with a witness. Hell, his life was complicated enough. But they needed to know what Michael had seen and heard. Jed wouldn't let anyone harm the kid to get that information, but they *really* needed to know. And so did the Vincents.

"Shouldn't you be driving nails through terrorist palms or something?" he asked the spook.

Killion checked his watch. "Right about now."

"You're letting them sweat?"

"It's a tactic that works." There was an edge to Killion's voice. Vivi had managed to shake his cool back at the safe house. The guy wasn't as impervious as he tried to let on. "I don't have a choice with the guy in ICU; he still hasn't woken up. Abdullah Mulhadre is another matter entirely. He doesn't know that we know who he is. The Agency is trying to get me as much intel as possible before I go in there." Killion's expression grew hard. "We're struggling to figure out who's behind this or if there are more attacks planned. Mulhadre could play the diplomatic immunity card, but hasn't. And that makes him look even more guilty of working for his own government. However, we can't just accuse the Syrians of staging the attack without risking all-out war in the Arabian peninsula, which would draw in Israel, Iran, Russia and China, and basically fuck the planet. So, yeah, I'm waiting for more intel while Abdullah 'sweats'." Killion's eyes were glassy from fatigue. Neither of them had slept. Jed watched him squeeze his temples between a thumb and index finger. "This whole thing sucks. It's one thing when it happens thousands of miles away in Kabul—"

"Another when it happens at home." Jed got it. "I doubt the victims feel any different though."

"We're all human beneath the skin."

"Even the CIA?"

Killion grunted. "Except the CIA."

"DOD?"

"DOD are human. Unfortunately they're also a bunch of fucking morons." *Inter-agency politics were alive and well.* "At least we have the FBI to bring everyone together under the white flag of truce." Killion's mouth twisted. Politics had gotten more than one person on the ground killed and they all knew it. "I'm not a monster you know. I'm not going to hurt the kid. I just need to figure out if he knows anything. Even the smallest clue might help. The mother isn't telling me everything." Killion grunted. "No surprise there."

"You really going to get in touch with the father?" asked Jed. That wouldn't win the guy any points with Vivi but he had a job to do, even if Jed didn't like it.

"Only as a last resort." Killion's grin returned. "She's fiery.

I can see why you like her."

Jed refused to be drawn.

"What have you got lined up for the rest of the day?" The CIA agent seemed to be way too interested in what he was up to. But information was king to these guys. "Shouldn't you be constructing some sort of profile?"

Jed shook his head. "Not me. BAU sent people from the counter-terrorism unit to do that—I'm just another grunt chasing the evidence. You're gonna give that cell phone to McKenzie as soon as we get to HQ, right?"

"Of course." Killion tilted his seat back and closed his eyes. "Why are you even here? Don't you work out of Quantico?"

"I'm on vacation."

Killion opened one eyelid. "Seriously?"

"Yeah. What are the chances, huh?" Jed turned onto the main highway toward the city. "I'll call Dr. Hinkle and see if I can get him out to the safe house today. Then I'm planning to go through witness statements, look for anyone who might have seen our mystery Black Widow. See if I can get enough description to build a sketch artist's impression to circulate to the media."

"Thus possibly eliminating the need to get the information locked up inside the boy's mind," Killion stated quietly.

"Hopefully eliminating the threat, yeah. He might not have even seen their faces. The cupboard door was almost fully closed. He might not have any actionable intelligence."

"Yeah, but he *might*, and you know what? That could be enough to save lives, and that's all I care about."

A slow anger built inside Jed, dispelling the earlier sense of camaraderie. He got it, he really got it, but Michael wasn't your typical witness.

"He's an eight-year-old boy who doesn't speak. The kid is messed up." Jed's hand tightened on the wheel as he thought about what the father had done to Vivi and her son. Sounded like a piece of work. "And as a minor and American citizen, good luck getting access to him if you piss off his mother or step on his constitutional rights."

And that was it in a nutshell. That's why this guy was shadowing Jed. The CIA's authority lay beyond the borders of the United States. He needed the FBI's jurisdiction, and Jed's influence on Vivi to get access to the boy.

"We both want the same thing," the spook assured him, reading his mind.

Sure. "Except I have a few moral values regarding how I go about things."

"Didn't stop you breaking that killer's nose back in DC."

Jed bared his teeth in a smile. "And don't you forget it." The intelligence officer had known why Jed was here all along. What else did he know that he wasn't sharing?

The look in Killion's eyes turned colder than a Minnesota winter. But Jed had grown up in Wisconsin so winter didn't bother him. The other guy finally shut the hell up as they pulled into headquarters. Small mercies.

———

PILAH WALKED INTO the hospital with a large bunch of pink carnations. She'd called earlier to say she was trying to track down her "uncle" and find out if he was one of the victims of the terrorist attack at the mall. The admin people confirmed he was indeed a patient. Signs directed her to ICU.

There were cops in the corridor, talking to people, taking

statements. Heat grew and expanded in a wave across her shoulders and rushed up her neck. Her fear was a tangible entity and she wondered if they could see it pouring off her like steam. "I'm here to see William Green," she told the nurse.

The nurse's eyes grew wide. "Are you the woman I spoke to who called a couple of hours ago?"

Pilah frowned. "I did call but I don't think I spoke to a nurse. I'm his niece." Damn. Was someone else about to arrive and blow her cover? Sargon would have no qualms about selling her young daughters off to some old, disgusting man if she failed him. Assuming he didn't shoot them or let them starve to death first. Her stomach cramped. "Did they leave a name?"

The nurse checked a sticky note she'd posted on the counter. "Marie Thomas."

"Ah, Marie." Pilah nodded as if she'd heard of her. "I'll give her a call to say I'm here. I was out of town and came as soon as I realized Uncle Will had been caught up in that attack."

The nurse gave an upper-body shudder. "Those people should be ashamed of themselves, although I doubt they have a conscience. What they hoped to accomplish I don't know. Did nothing but murder and maim a bunch of innocent people. I know what I'd do with them if I had the chance."

The nurse was smug and fat. It was easy to sit in judgment when you lived in a democracy where your rights mattered. Where Pilah came from, entire towns had been massacred— men, women and children, tortured and killed on the orders of their own president. Pilah hid her feelings, her cynicism, her contempt. Americans knew little of suffering. She'd known little about it until the civil war had engulfed her nation in a fierce battle for freedom.

She'd expected rumors and speculation about Syria's involvement to be circulating in the media by now, but nothing. Not yet anyway.

Had Sargon lied about their agenda or were the authorities keeping a lid on any information they uncovered? Both, probably.

"Is he still in a coma?" Pilah asked.

"He's in a medically induced coma until the swelling in his brain goes down. It's not as bad as it sounds," she reassured her.

The nurse led the way and they entered a unit which contained three beds. Oh no... Pilah frantically scanned the people lying there. There were two unconscious men but she didn't know which one was the man who was supposed to be her uncle.

Pilah stopped dead. "I forgot I'm not allowed to bring flowers in here." She waved the bunch in front of her, stalling for time. "Let me take them outside and give Marie a call. Then I'll come and sit with him if I may?" Her tactic worked because the nurse kept walking to the bed at the end, then looked up.

"It sounds like a plan. I was feeling sorry for the guy having no visitors. It'll do him good to have some company."

She recognized him. He'd been nearby when they'd detonated the blast that took out the Security Center. Amir had shot him when he'd approached them. She hoped to hell he didn't recognize her if he woke up. Of course she'd changed her appearance. No headscarf, tight-fitting, western clothes. Her hair was naturally dark blond, something she'd inherited from her mother and the reason Sargon thought he could use her. She'd given herself bangs which came low over her eyes, and wore bright colored make-up and pink lipstick.

"He looks terrible." Pilah really looked at the man's face. Gray skin, mouth slack, big white bandage wrapped around his head. He looked as if he was in pain and somehow that was worse than seeing someone dead. She'd helped to do this. She had caused this suffering. For the first time she experienced real remorse for her actions. "Just give me two minutes and I'll be back." She went outside and walked down the corridor toward the main entrance. She dialed a number Sargon had given her, her fingers shaking so badly she misdialed twice.

When someone picked up she said, "This isn't going to work. He has a niece who called earlier."

"Name?"

She frowned. "Marie Thomas."

Her contact was already typing on the computer. He reeled off an address. "Got her. Not married. Appears to live alone as far as I can tell."

"Should I just leave?"

"No. Do exactly what you were told. Then later on you need to deal with this. I have other things that require my attention."

"Me?"

A soft snort echoed through the phone. "Yeah, you. You have proved surprisingly resourceful so far. You know what to do."

But I don't want to do it! Inside she screamed. Outside she kept calm. How could she get out of this mess she had gotten herself into? "Did you find the child?"

"Don't talk about it," the man scolded her. The guy hung up.

The image of the redheaded woman and her son's face had started to haunt Pilah along with all her other ghosts. Were they still out there? Could the boy identify her? Had he overheard anything of importance?

She put the flowers on the closest nurses' station. Then she turned off her cell and entered ICU. She surreptitiously checked the notes at the end of the bed—something every relative did. William Green. Fifty-five years old. She sat beside him and picked up his hand. His skin was cool and dry. She squeezed his fingers and was unsettled to feel a slight pressure squeezing back.

CHAPTER NINE

VIVI PACED. SHE'D gotten Michael up and dressed but he'd spent the whole day lying on the couch unwilling or unable to respond. Her jaw clenched. He was slipping away from her. She could feel it with every lack of reaction, every avoidance of eye contact.

"When is he going to get here?" she asked Inspector Patton for the fifth time in the last hour. Dr. Hinkle had agreed to come as soon as he'd finished his afternoon rounds at the hospital. The marshals had supposedly informed the CIA agent and FBI but she wasn't delaying until they arrived. The wait alone was driving her insane. She felt so helpless.

"On his way."

This whole setup was starting to feel like a massive waste of time and resources. The threat to them seemed ridiculous. The more she thought about it, the more she decided the authorities were overreacting. The news media suggested all the known terrorists were dead and the general furor was dying down. Some parts of the mall had already started clean up.

"I can't believe anyone would go to this much trouble to find us. We don't *know* anything."

"You know what I can't believe?" Patton replied evenly. "Is that so many of my fellow Americans were gunned down in

125

my local mall yesterday. A little caution might be warranted, especially considering the guy at the hotel pool."

Bile hit her throat. *God, yes.* But the whole thing just seemed so surreal.

Patton put a hand on her shoulder. "It's OK to fall apart, you know. No one is grading you on how well you cope."

"It's a good thing they aren't." She gave a strangled laugh and shook her head. "But I can't afford to fall apart. I have a little boy to protect."

Patton rested his hand on his sidearm. He seemed like a good guy. Rogers, too, although he was sterner. "It's my job too, don't forget. Give yourself a break."

Hard to do when she was holed up with nothing to do and Michael was drifting further and further away from her. "I do appreciate your help. I just want everything to go back to normal. Do you have kids?"

"Yup. Two boys. One in college. One just finishing up high school."

"I hope they know how lucky they are to have you."

He opened his mouth to say something, but the sound of a car pulling up outside stopped him. He went to the door, gun drawn. Cell phone to his ear. "It's Hinkle," he said.

Rogers led the doctor inside, the man's glasses fogged up from being in the cold. He gave her a somewhat bemused expression. Yesterday, she'd refused to let him run any more tests on Michael after the MRI procedure had ended badly. Now she'd begged for him to come and see her son. "Dr. Hinkle. Thank you so much for coming."

"Ms. Vincent. I'd say it was a pleasure to see you again so soon but unfortunately the circumstances…"

Vivi nodded. The circumstances were a bitch.

The doctor came inside the kitchen and stared at where her son was lying dejected on the couch. "He's been like this since the attack?"

"Up and down, but basically, yes." She nodded. "He isn't eating unless I force the issue. He isn't interested in much beside sleep. I'm worried—" Her voice cracked. *Worried he'd just fade away and die and no one would care except me...*

The doctor patted her arm. "Of course you're worried. I'll go talk to him but..."

"What?"

"It's possible that this is a perfectly normal reaction to a very traumatic incident."

Normal? "Like Post Traumatic Stress Disorder?"

"I doubt it's even had time to escalate to that yet, but a normal reaction to trauma, certainly. We all take time to process fear, and grief, and even the guilt that we survived when others didn't. Grief is a process. It takes time. Days. Weeks. Sometimes years." Kind blue eyes met hers. "For you too."

Vivi didn't care about herself. She was strong enough to get through this as long as someone helped her with Michael.

"Because of Michael's age and the fact he doesn't speak we'll need to devise some sort of specialized therapy schedule for him so he can appropriately process the events of yesterday and the emotions that go with them."

"OK." She crossed her arms over her chest. Action. She was good taking action. It was letting things slide that bothered her.

"I'm not saying *don't worry*. But I'm saying that this behavior is probably to be expected after the shooting. In fact, his natural reaction to events is rather encouraging."

Encouraging? *Really*?

"Because he's processing what happened exactly the way I'd expect a 'neurotypical' child to process it."

His patient smile was starting to annoy her. Almost as much as when he'd explained using very small words how not all people with prodigious talents—i.e. Michael's drawing ability—were savants. And people with a true savant syndrome always had some underlying developmental or physical disability, and the good doctor wasn't sure whether Michael's lack of speech fit that criteria. The paradox of genius being intertwined with disability, he said. She'd argued that Michael's artistic ability combined with his incredible memory for detail—he only had to see something once to recreate it perfectly—was conclusive proof. Apparently not.

Some people were just *gifted*, the doctor had explained. And some people were *mute*. As far as he knew Michael was the only child who was both. He was reluctant to put a label on Michael without more tests.

It wasn't like she wanted Michael to be autistic or suffer from Asperger's. What she wanted was answers to questions that had hounded her for four long years, and a way of helping her son be everything he could be in life.

She took a deep breath. Hinkle was the expert and the human brain was still largely a mystery, but if anyone could reach Michael it was someone who specialized in this sort of condition. "Not that he has a recognized *condition*," she muttered under her breath.

"Pardon?" The man's eyes twinkled.

"Nothing. Sorry." She swallowed the knot of frustration stuck in her throat. She had asked him here. It was only fair to listen to what the man had to say.

"I'll go talk to him now." He removed his overcoat and handed it to her. "Coffee would be wonderful, milk and two sugars."

The doctor walked away as her mouth dropped open. Rogers waggled his finger at her as if he could read her mind. A reluctant laugh popped out. The marshals were amazing, combining duty with a sense of humor that stopped her from choking to death on the terror of it all.

She put on the coffee.

Hinkle sat on the chair beside Michael and started talking to him softly. Her son turned away, but the doctor kept talking. She stood in the kitchen watching from a distance. It was overcast outside. The snow had finally stopped falling, but winter was just starting. She tapped her nails on the granite counter as she strained to hear what was being said. Maybe one day she'd stop being a control freak when it came to her son, but today wasn't that day. She edged closer but the doctor gave a hefty sigh, closed his folder and stood up. He walked over to where she was pouring out his coffee.

He took the mug, stirring in his own sugar. Three spoonfuls. "I think Michael needs a little more time to come to terms with what happened. I don't want to push him. His brain is simply overwhelmed and over-stimulated and he's withdrawn to protect himself."

"What can I do for him?" she asked.

"Peace. Quiet. Space to just be for a little time."

That's it? That was his expert advice? "O-kaay."

"Do *you* want to talk about what happened?" He eyed her kindly.

She flinched. The image of blood smeared across the mall floor flashed through her brain. The sounds of terrified screams and gunfire. She crossed her arms. "No. I don't want to talk about it. Not yet."

He smiled, patiently.

Maybe he was right. Maybe her son just needed time that she was too impatient to give him. The doctor had come here for nothing. "I'm sorry I wasted your time, Doctor."

"Not at all, Ms. Vincent. Not at all. I think even the reintroduction of a familiar face from before the shooting is proof to Michael that the world didn't end yesterday. Under ordinary circumstances I'd say to go home and recover in his usual surroundings but with this threat to his life you'll need to improvise. Try and recreate all the things that are most important to him. The food he eats. Your daily routines."

Vivi thought about Michael's routine. School, friends, and home were unavailable. But she could paint his room and put some of the posters he had at home on the wall. She knew where to buy them online. "Thank you for your help, Doctor."

"I'm glad I could do something during our city's period of need."

Vivi looked toward Michael but he wasn't there anymore. She blinked in surprise.

"He's probably just in the bathroom," the doctor assured her with a squeeze of her arm. "Give him some space." Every inch of his crinkled brow screamed 'over-protective mother.'

Relax. Calm down. He'll be fine. All mantras from her marriage. Her divorce a testament to her inability to do any of those things when it came to her son.

She gave the doctor a pinched smile. "Of course."

Rogers asked the doc a question about how heavy the traffic had been on the drive out and Vivi edged away and went into the living room. She searched behind the curtains and behind the arm chair. She even checked a small cupboard beneath a shelving unit but there was nothing there except a chess set. Good to know. Michael liked chess.

She went through the other door from the lounge to the corridor that ran to the back door. Nothing. She walked into the laundry room, opening cupboards and bending to look under the sink.

"Michael?" she called. There was a sound from inside the attached garage where the marshals parked their cars. She pulled the door open and was hit by a blast of cold air. She shut the door behind her so the house didn't get more frigid than it already was. Vivi's teeth chattered. "Michael, come on, it's too cold for you to stay in here." She'd discovered the heating was kept low so no one looking at electricity consumption would red flag the property as newly occupied. While she appreciated the thoroughness of the operation she would appreciate a little more heat. The cold penetrated her thick woolen socks. Her cuts were tender but healing fast. She searched around the whole double garage but there was no place to hide. Where was he? She peered inside both vehicles. Then she noticed the trunk of Rogers's silver sedan was open just an inch. There. She released a long, hard breath.

Small dark places.

She opened the lid and found him wrapped in a thick wool blanket, next to a snow shovel. "Oh, Michael." The sadness in his gaze begged her to leave him alone, but she couldn't do it.

Instead, she carefully climbed into the trunk with him. The carpet was clean and it had that new car smell. She sighed, remembering her own car was still at the hotel. She needed to ask Brennan to take care of it for her. She pulled the lid down just enough to plunge them into shadow, then she wrapped herself tight around her son's shivering frame, burrowing beneath the blanket with him. She kissed the top of his head. "I love you, Michael."

He squeezed her arm. It wasn't much, but it was better than nothing. They lay there quietly listening to the sounds of the wind whistling outside. There was no spare flesh on his bones. He shook against her with cold but obviously would rather be here than warmer somewhere else. Right now she had to give him what he needed. After a few minutes their body heat warmed them enough that they both stopped shivering. Her thoughts calmed. Who knew the trunk of a car would prove so relaxing? They both started to drift off to sleep.

The sound of glass shattering broke her reverie. All her muscles tensed. What was that? Had someone dropped a glass?

"Stay here." She edged out of the trunk, carefully opened the door and peered through into the house. She slipped through the laundry room and across the hallway into the lounge. What was happening? Dr. Hinkle crouched behind the kitchen counter. Then the unmistakable pop of gunfire made her want to flee, but she was frozen in place. The front door opened, and she could see Marshal Rogers in a firing stance as he shot at something outside. A bullet cut through the drywall above her head and she ducked. A man cried out in pain. Oh, no! That was Rogers. Had he been hit?

She hugged a wall and almost sobbed in terror. She needed a gun. A weapon. Anything to help protect themselves. Footsteps hammered as someone ran up the stairs, toward where she and Michael slept.

The terrorists *had* found them. They'd tracked them down and the bad guys truly wanted them dead. She scurried into the kitchen on her knees to try and get Dr. Hinkle to come hide with them. But before she could reach him his body jolted and fell.

A masked stranger stood in front of her. Not dark skinned or swarthy; the skin around his blue eyes was pale. She sucked in a breath to scream but the sound of a shot and the red bloom of blood on the front of the man's shirt stopped her. The bad guy crashed to the floor and Rogers caught her eye.

"Run," he mouthed. The light in his eyes dimmed and he slumped to the side. Right in front of her eyes the man who'd sworn to protect them, died.

Gunshots rang out upstairs. The marshals would have called for back-up but how long before it arrived? Fight or flight? Neither option was going to save them today. Nor did she have the car keys or the skills to hot-wire a vehicle. She had to protect Michael and stealth and guile were their best chance. She grabbed the pistol out of the gunman's hand, then ran silently back to the garage, closing the door quietly behind her, listening to more gunfire being exchanged upstairs— Patton must be up there. Oh, please let the troops arrive before he was hurt. She got into the trunk, thankful Michael was still there, unharmed. The sound of sirens started quietly filling the air. *Thank you.*

"Help is coming."

Michael shook in renewed fear.

"I won't let them hurt you." She shielded her son with her body, spread the blanket over them, trying to make sure it covered their entire form from head to toe. Quickly, she reached up and pulled the trunk shut. The metallic click sounded like a prison door clanging shut. If the bad guys caught them here there was nowhere to run.

It was the best she could do. She pointed the gun toward where anyone who opened the trunk was most likely to stand, more than willing to pull the trigger. The metal hull muted the noise outside, muffled the sounds of feet pounding, men shouting, and more gunfire. All she could do was defend her son and hope the bad guys didn't find them before the cops did.

They'd fallen into a nightmare that seemed to be never-ending. Michael's small fingers gripped her shirt, pinching her skin. Vivi relished the sensation with every atom in her being. She would die to protect Michael; she just prayed she didn't have to.

JED FOUND HIMSELF drifting off as he read the thousandth account of where someone had been when the shooting started. Many had barricaded themselves into storerooms or hid inside clothing racks. One guy was found in a deep freeze and had almost suffocated. Frankly it was a miracle more people hadn't died. It was horrific. But he was working on no sleep, his brain was fried and he needed rest.

So far no one mentioned the woman that he knew had been part of the attack. Her DNA was back, no usable prints. No matches in any of their databases. Press photos hadn't revealed anything either. She'd deliberately avoided the cameras.

His cell rang and he saw it was his boss, ASAC Lincoln Frazer. For a moment he was tempted not to answer but, crap… "Brennan."

"I just got a call from the head of US Marshal Service in

Minnesota. Safe house was attacked," Frazer said without preamble.

Even as Jed climbed to his feet he saw other agents lunging for flak jackets and running out of HQ. "Any casualties?"

"It looks bad, Jed."

Jed's vision tunneled. He couldn't even force out the words to ask about Vivi and Michael, especially not to a man who kept telling him not to get involved. If anything happened to them, so help him…

They shouldn't mean so much to him. He shouldn't have let them. He raced to his car and heard a shout. Patrick Killion ran out beside him. "I just heard. Both marshals are down. So is the shrink. No word on Vivi or Michael."

"Hinkle was there?" No one had told him the meeting had been arranged already. Jed got in the car, started her up and peeled away from the curb before Killion pulled the door fully closed.

"Yup. I got a call earlier but I was in chatting with our pal Abdullah. He's in it up to his neck, but he thinks he's stringing me along like I'm some rookie." Killion checked the bullets in his SIG. Intelligence officers didn't usually carry guns but Jed wasn't surprised to see this one did. "The doctor must have led the bad guys straight to the safe house. Fucking smart to keep tabs on the guy."

"Or they have an inside man." Jed didn't look at the spook but it was obvious what he was thinking.

"Not very smart to accuse the guy riding shotgun of being in league with terrorists," Killion replied coolly. "Especially when he just checked his weapon."

Jed tensed.

"Lucky for you I don't hold grudges and I don't collude

with mad fuckers who stage shootouts in packed malls. I may be an asshole but I'm a patriotic asshole."

"Good to know." Not that he necessarily believed the guy but for now he didn't care. Someone somewhere had leaked information, or these guys had eyes and ears in way more places than they should. That suggested powerful allies and oodles of cash, something these organizations never seemed to lack.

"We didn't catch them all," Jed said.

"No fucking kidding."

"They have more attacks planned," Jed continued.

"Because otherwise they'd have scattered like roaches and not worried about the boy."

Exactly. They were worried Michael had overheard their plans.

The roads were icy. He'd thankfully put on snow tires ahead of his trip to Wisconsin. They still skidded like a hockey player going in for a tackle. Jed was forced to slow down. Just this morning he'd promised on his life Vivi would be safe. What the fuck did his promises mean if terrorists could infiltrate law enforcement enough to figure out the location of a US Marshal Service safe house? Why did they even pretend they could combat this?

He was on the highway, tucked in behind an ambulance, all sirens blazing, forging their way through stacked up traffic on the 77. He didn't let himself think about Vivi or Michael. It wouldn't bring them back if they were dead. It wouldn't track them down if they were missing. He shoved the guilt deeper, along with the rage, and pulled out the cold, hard version of himself that got the job done. He would catch these guys. He would shut them down.

He and Killion didn't speak for the next five minutes as Jed concentrated on driving at high speed in difficult conditions. A uniform tried to stop him at the end of the drive but Jed showed him his badge and drove on regardless. Two other ambulances were pulled up in front of the house, but the medics weren't treating anyone. Fuck. Squad cars, sheriff's deputies, city cops were everywhere. Law enforcement swirled around trying to figure out who was in charge and who had jurisdiction. With two marshals dead and a safe house compromised it was going to be between Marshals, DOJ, the FBI and the task force. Jed pulled up around the side of the house, in front of the garage, out of the way of any emergency vehicles. Killion jumped out but waited for him. Jed was probably the most senior FBI agent on the scene right now, that's why the guy stuck close. It wasn't for his winning personality or fragrant cologne.

The front door stood wide open. Wood splintered, glass broken. One marshal lay in the hallway covered in blood. An unfamiliar male, clasping an AK-47, lay on his back at the bottom of the steps. He had three holes in his chest.

They stepped inside, avoiding blood spatter. Hinkle was in a heap on the kitchen floor, brains blown out. Another terrorist lay beside him with a hole in his back. Jed would bet money the marshal had taken him down, even as he'd lain dying.

Good for them. Good for fucking them. He shoved down the heartache for his fellow law enforcement officers and concentrated on his job.

Find Vivi and Michael.

"How many tangos?" Jed asked, taking the stairs two at a time.

"One marshal reported four armed gunmen."

"They have search parties in place?"

"McKenzie instigated roadblocks and put the city back on high alert."

Jed skidded into Vivi's room, bracing himself for what he was about to find. One of the marshals lay on the floor in a pool of blood. A medic stepped away and shook his head. Another tango lay dead with a hole in his face. *Ugh.* The saliva in Jed's mouth dried up. The marshal had defended mother and child to the death. The wardrobe doors were all ajar as if someone had been searching for something. Jed checked the bathroom as Killion scoured the other bedrooms.

They met in the hallway.

"No sign?" Jed asked.

"Nothing," Killion confirmed.

Jed walked back down the stairs. "Find any more bodies on this level?" he asked a deputy.

"No. And there's no basement. I checked."

Despair hit him, and he turned to the spook. "Call McKenzie and tell him we think one of the attackers took Vivi and Michael with them. Hey," he gestured a group of cops toward him. "I want you to search the woods toward the river. Parallel with any tracks—mark them and photograph them to try and preserve evidence. Be careful, there is at least one suspect at large and two witnesses missing. A kid and his mother. Both are redheads."

The cops nodded and organized the search party, glad of something useful to do.

In the kitchen, Killion crouched and checked the psychiatrist's neck for a pulse. "He's still warm. They can't be far away. We'll find them."

Sure they'd find them. Riddled with bullets and dumped on the side of the road.

Jed didn't want useless words. "Call your people. Find out who is orchestrating this shit." He frowned at all the shell casings littering the floor. "The task force needs detailed intel so we can stop this—even if it points to someone above your pay grade." *Syria.* He didn't say it out loud. He wasn't going to be the security leak responsible for causing a war. But he would push for answers, regardless of how difficult those answers might be.

He didn't hold out hope for Vivi or Michael. The most he could ask for was that they died quickly. Grief smashed him in the gut and threatened to bring him to his knees. Despite what his boss thought, Jed had learned to compartmentalize his feelings, to shove the humanity of the victims into a box where they wouldn't invade his dreams. Hell, he dealt with nightmare scenarios on an almost-daily basis so he had to be able to detach to get the job done. He'd tried to stuff Vivi and Michael into one of those boxes. Failed.

This was personal.

He cared about the Vincents.

So maybe his boss was right. Maybe Jed wasn't cut out for this job after all. Maybe some ice cold schmuck would be a better agent than he'd ever be.

Something suspiciously like tears burned the back of his eyes. No way was he breaking down in front of the others. He strode away, going through the back door and standing hands in pockets, inhaling large gulps of frigid air. Footprints led around to the front of the house, and off down toward the woods. Jed drew in a tight breath. Christ, the air was so cold it hurt to breathe, but he didn't care. He felt numb.

He'd been attracted to Vivi, her beauty, her vivid hair, her take-no-bullshit attitude. He'd seen the stark vulnerability she tried so hard to hide. And he really liked her kid. The boy was brave and sweet.

He pressed his lips together, fighting emotions. *Get a hold, Brennan. Do your fucking job.* He'd lost people before—Bobby, Mia. She'd died on base and the Army had been willing to sweep her murder under the carpet until he'd contacted Quantico and persuaded them a serial killer was at work. He hadn't let go of the case until Lincoln Frazer had actually arrested the guy. His tenacity made him a good agent, but his need for results meant he could never let *anything* go—hence his never-ending workload and barren personal life.

He went back inside, glanced into the garage and did a quick walk through. There were two cars parked. An SUV and a sedan. He walked around both vehicles. There were no bullet holes in here. Didn't look like the bad guys had made it inside this area. Pulling on a latex glove he touched the garage door opener and the door rattled open. He checked the snow on the driveway. Although it had been shoveled earlier, a tiny sprinkling of fresh snow was enough to tell him no one had entered or left this way. He went back inside and closed the massive double garage door. He flicked off the light.

A muffled thump made him pause.

Had that come from upstairs?

He shook his head, deciding it was his imagination. Then he heard it again and froze. The noise was coming from the trunk of the silver sedan. He drew his weapon and slipped off his shoes so he could move silently over concrete that was fuck-me freezing.

He stood off to one side, touched the trunk's latch and

squeezed, keeping his gun trained on the center of the space, finger on the trigger.

A pale face dominated by massive blue eyes met his. Big ass Beretta clasped in her shaking hand pointed in his direction. *Vivi.* And behind her a lump of blanket squirmed. *Michael.* They were safe. They were alive.

She lowered the gun. "I think they found us, Jed."

CHAPTER TEN

PUTTING HIS WEAPON back in his holster, he leaned inside, cradled her head in his hands and kissed her full on the mouth. Her lips were icy cold, and tasted of sweet coffee and tears. She clung to him, obviously terrified from her ordeal. The kiss only lasted for a few seconds, just long enough for him to remember she was a witness and this was unprofessional, but she tasted so damn good it was a shame he'd never be able to do it again. He pulled away. Then hugged her, squeezing tight. "Jesus Christ, you scared me."

She shook so violently her bones rattled inside his embrace.

It took a full thirty seconds for him to let go.

"Are the marshals...?" Her voice trembled. The question was left unfinished, her glance cut toward Michael.

Dead?

He nodded.

"How did they find us?"

That question brought Jed up short. How *had* they found them? Had they followed the doctor? Maybe. Or was there a leak inside one of the many law enforcement departments involved in this whole terrorist investigation?

"I don't know." They were both whispering. He heard people talking inside the house and made a quick decision.

One that would probably get him fired from a job he loved. Hell, it might get him arrested, but he didn't see any alternative that would keep Vivi and Michael safe. "I'm going to open the garage door. My car is parked right there. I'm going to leave the rear door open to help block you from sight. You guys throw yourself on the floor of the back seat and keep covered with this blanket. Don't let anyone see you."

Vivi's eyes had dark smudges beneath them. Her forehead furrowed.

"Can you manage him?" Jed pointed to Michael.

"Of course." Like she'd ever admit anything else.

He closed the door into the house, flipped the lock, and slipped his shoes back on. Then he jogged back and helped her climb out of the trunk. It wasn't as easy as it looked and he lifted her carefully, placing her gently onto the floor while she found her feet. She only came up to his chin, her frame as fragile as spun glass beneath his palms. "I'd give you my shoes if it wouldn't raise suspicion."

Her lips formed a heart-breaking smile. She and her son had been through hell the last few days, cold feet were the least of her problems.

"You've done enough."

Hardly. So far he'd failed in his promise and almost gotten her killed.

He tugged Michael out of the trunk and wrapped him up in the blanket, then handed him over to his mom. "Stay in the corner over there while I check that it's clear outside. If anyone's outside I'll try and redirect them. Bottom line is I don't want anyone knowing you guys are alive. Not yet."

She didn't ask why. Maybe she'd already figured it out. He raised the door again, then made a show of getting something

143

out of the rear seat of his SUV, before heading back into the garage and leaving the car door wide open. Vivi hopped quickly into the SUV and disappeared. He came back and slammed the door shut, obliterating her footprints as he went. He headed back inside, closed the garage door and unlatched the door into the house to allay any suspicion. Then he put his cell to his ear and made it sound like he was being ordered back to headquarters. Killion was thankfully upstairs taking photographs.

Jed went out the front door. A team of marshals was unloading from a work van. Keene and Townsend—the marshals from last night—climbed out, both looking shaken and pissed. If the attack had occurred earlier it could have been them cooling on the safe house floor. That knowledge combined with the loss of friends and colleagues was bound to haunt them, not to mention the US Marshal Service hated to lose witnesses. If they found out he'd whisked Michael and Vivi away without telling them they'd lynch him.

But his life expectancy wasn't the issue.

He climbed into the driver's seat of his SUV and gave them a tight-lipped nod.

"Keep low," he muttered as he headed up the driveway through a cavalcade of law enforcement and emergency vehicles. The rear windows were tinted. Still, his heart thudded against his ribs at the thought of someone spotting them. He expected to be exposed every time someone glanced his way, but by the time he reached the main road no one was even looking at him anymore.

He called headquarters and asked for an update on roadblocks, found out exactly where they were all located. Now he could avoid them.

He glanced in the rearview but he couldn't see either Vivi or Michael. "I wish I could tell you to sit up front, but I think until we get where we're going you need to keep out of sight. You could probably lie on the backseat though." He heard the rustle of blankets and Vivi tried to coax Michael off the floor but he wouldn't move. She was getting increasingly agitated.

"Vivi, leave him. He's not hurting down there. You just lie down and try to get comfortable. Drag my parka from the trunk." His cell rang. *Killion.* "I better take this. Don't say anything, OK?"

His eyes met hers in the mirror for a moment. She looked brittle and shaken. White-faced with fear. He'd promised her she'd be safe and look what happened. Two dead marshals and no clue as to who was behind this thing.

Knowing he needed to be on his game to fool Killion he turned his eyes back to the road and imagined Vivi and Michael dead in a pool of blood. Suddenly the thought of lying to the guy wasn't so difficult.

MARIE THOMAS LIVED in the Camden area of Minneapolis in a rundown bungalow that hearkened back to the 1950s. White, wooden siding had long since grayed and started to flake; mint green trim was faded and streaked with grime. The front three steps and sidewalk had been carefully shoveled, though the concrete was pitted and starting to crumble.

There was no one out on the street. Everyone was tucked up inside which suited Pilah's plans perfectly. She carried a clipboard and wore a black, wool coat over a black pant suit, both of which she'd found in a local thrift store. She kept her head down because you never knew where surveillance cameras were although this wasn't the sort of neighborhood where people installed them on their property.

She pressed the buzzer, then wiped the button with her cuff.

Dogs barked inside. Crap. She hadn't planned on dogs. Heavy footsteps. A woman came to the door. She had the worn-out face of someone who'd worked long and hard and knew she wouldn't get a break any time soon. Wrinkles radiated from her eyes as she smiled. "Yes? What can I do for you?"

Music played on the radio in the background.

"Mrs. Thomas?" Pilah asked.

"Ms." The woman corrected firmly.

Good. "My name is Pat Jones. I'm from County Hospital where your uncle was admitted?"

The woman sagged against the door frame. "Poor Uncle Billy." She checked her wristwatch. "I was hoping to get down there after work but I'm too tired now." She wiped her hair out of her eyes. "Come on in out of the cold."

Pilah accepted gratefully.

"Down Rhett. Down Ginger!" Both dogs stopped jumping and stood wagging their tails. "Don't worry about them. They're friendly."

Pilah's stomach clenched. She did not want to do this. Why the hell was she doing this? "What do you do for a living, Ms. Thomas?"

"Oh, God, I'm not going to get hit with all his medical expenses am I?" She dragged a hand through her bleached, blond hair. "I don't make that sort of money."

"No, ma'am. Your uncle had insurance." If he didn't Sargon would probably foot the bill himself. Irony in its highest form. She didn't know what he planned to do to the man but it couldn't be good.

"Thank Christ for that. Come on through to the kitchen. I left the stove on."

Pilah touched the dogs' heads as she followed their mistress into the kitchen. They were sweet pooches. What would happen to them if anything happened to Marie? She couldn't afford to care. Her hands shook and she stuffed them inside her pocket, her right hand clasping the gun Abdullah had left in her glove box.

"I'm going to go down to the hospital tomorrow. I've got a few days off."

Which meant her cover would be blown as soon as Marie spoke to the nurse. "What is it you do?" Pilah asked.

"I work at the Y, running youth programs."

Pilah's palms grew sweaty and she wiped them on her thigh. "Sounds like a lot of work."

The woman's scrawny shoulders shrugged beneath a cheap sweater. "I like it."

"Does Mr. Green have other relatives or close friends we should contact?"

"There's just him left on that side of the family. His wife died and they never had kids. I don't know his friends. Why do you want to know?" The eyes were speculative now.

The hourly news came on the radio. The lead story made her stiffen. The redheaded boy and his mother were missing after an attack on the safe house. Cops were looking for them. The danger was intensifying. The threat of failure increasing with every loose-end.

She snapped herself back to this worn-out woman and her

modest little kitchen. "He's going to need some extra care when he first gets out of the hospital. We are doing a trial program where we try and get input from relatives before release to make sure everything is in place ahead of time." Pilah put her hand back in her pocket. If she allowed herself to think about this she'd never go through with it and her children would be sacrificed. Adad's calming voice tried to soothe her. She shook him out of her head. Stupid man.

Marie Thomas flipped an egg in the pan. "It's just me and frankly, we aren't close. But the guy got shot so I want to be there for him—"

Pilah gripped the pistol in her right hand and squeezed the trigger. The gun fired through her coat pocket and hit the woman in the stomach. The dogs started barking.

"I'm sorry," she said quietly.

Marie dropped to her knees on the kitchen floor. Blood ran through her fingers as she pressed her hands to the wound.

"I am so sorry."

The woman crashed forward and lay still. Pilah closed her eyes and drew out a long breath. The dogs continued to bark in confusion and fear. *Forgive me.*

"Hush now, hush." She crouched and both animals came toward her, uncertain. They didn't understand what had happened. Her stomach churned. She didn't understand it herself. Once they started wagging their tails she petted them for a moment and then stood up. She couldn't linger too long; someone might report the noise.

She saw Marie's purse on the table and took her wallet, slipping it into her pocket.

Pilah used her sleeve to turn off the gas burner, then noted the empty dog bowls. She opened the pantry door and found a big, plastic canister of food. She gave each dog four big scoops of dried kibble, enough to last a few days. Then she pulled the curtains and blinds, wiped her prints off everything she thought she'd touched. The radio played loudly enough to be heard, but not loudly enough to cause complaint. She left the hallway light on.

With any luck it would be a few days before anyone noticed the body and no one would connect this woman to the events at the mall.

Pilah let herself out, keeping her face tucked into her collar as she strode away. She'd never expected to become a killer, but the act got easier with practice. Or maybe she was dying on the inside, slowly and surely every time she took a life, until nothing of worth remained.

There was very little of worth left now. Just the tiny hope she could somehow keep her daughters alive.

———

VIVI PULLED OUT the pistol she'd tucked into her waistband and placed it on the seat beside her. She didn't like guns, especially didn't like them around Michael. He was only eight. He didn't always make the most sensible choices. Or maybe they seemed sensible when you were eight, which didn't necessarily jive with the thoughts of the rest of the population.

She listened to Brennan's side of the conversation with the intelligence officer as he lied his ass off. He should have been an actor.

"Where am *I* going? What are you, my fucking mother?" His words were punchy and disrespectful. Exactly how he should sound if a witness he'd placed in a protective custody went missing, presumed dead. She winced at his crude language in front of Michael but at the same time knew he had to act natural. Plus, cuss words were pretty low on the list of priorities after two days dodging bloodshed and bullets.

"No way, Mr. CIA. I'm done. I'm doing what my boss originally told me to do four days ago. Taking time off so I can keep on doing this job without my head exploding. Is that OK with you or would you like a doctor's note?"

There was another pause. The guy wasn't giving up. "Not my fault? I know it wasn't my fault but I promised them they'd be safe and now they're—" He cut himself off as though he couldn't bear to say anything else.

It was a masterful performance and momentary panic hit her. Could Jed be in league with the terrorists? Then she remembered how he'd saved her when cornered in that restaurant kitchen during the mall attack.

Unknown forces were out to get them and, despite her ingrained reticence, if she didn't allow herself to trust this man, the chances were she and Michael would be dead by morning. If there was one person she believed would keep his word in this whole awful nightmare, it was Jed Brennan. And Vivi would do anything and everything she had to in order to ensure her son was safe.

"Look, Killion, it's been fun, but I'm done. Find someone else to latch on to and chauffeur you 'round the place." His breathing was ragged as if he really believed them to be dead. "If you find them…you can reach me on this number to let me know or email, just…no pictures, all right?"

Killion said something she couldn't hear. Brennan hung up and caught her gaze in the mirror. There was a lot going on in those dark eyes, none of it good. Two marshals were dead.

So was one of the most respected neuroscientists in the country.

"This is all my fault." She slumped back against the seat.

"Because you invited Hinkle out there?"

"Yes." She looked at him then, ready for recriminations. It had all happened at her insistence.

Jed shrugged. "He was mentioned in the news article, so it's possible they put a tail on him on the off-chance you'd want to see him again. Not a bad idea considering Michael's problems."

That's what she should have figured out before she'd asked to see him. Her throat felt as if someone was inside trying to climb out with a grappling hook. Oh, God, how many people were involved in this group? How could they ever be safe?

"Vivi." Brennan's stern tone snapped her out of her panic. "It's also possible there might be a mole somewhere inside law enforcement, feeding the bad guys information. In which case it's my fault." He concentrated on the road for a moment letting the words sink in. "Honestly? I don't know who to trust."

It surprised her that she wasn't more shocked. The way he'd snuck them out of the safe house, the way he'd lied to Killion had clued her in.

"We need to figure out what to do. Right now authorities will assume you're dead and the terrorists might not know for sure either way. We have a small block of time in which to make you disappear."

It had been bad enough hiding from terrorists, now she had to hide from the good guys too?

"If you want me to take you somewhere that you feel safe, I'll do that and figure out a way to protect you there. But I have another suggestion. It means trusting me completely."

She could hear the beat of her heart above the noise of the road. It was too loud and too fast to be reassuring. Emotions sparked from deep within those rich, brown eyes, emotions she couldn't read.

"I *can* hide you. I can take you somewhere you will be safe until this is over. But I don't know how long it will take, and we'll be on our own—you, me and Michael—no marshals, no real backup. And I can't guarantee Michael any specialized help while we're there."

The memory of blood spraying out of Dr. Hinkle's head made her dry heave, and she put her hand over her mouth and swallowed repeatedly. She didn't want anyone else drawn into this mess. Didn't want anyone else to die. The fact he considered her worries about her child significant when they were running for their lives was a little stunning.

She drew in a series of deep breaths and tried to get herself together. "B-before the attack the doctor suggested that perhaps all Michael needed was peace and quiet and time to grieve." She searched for a tissue and blew her nose. "He said that Michael was processing everything that happened in a perfectly normal way."

Perfectly normal.

The doctor had been murdered while they'd hidden in the trunk of a car. Her son was now curled up on the floor of the SUV. How could any reaction to this horror be *normal*?

She looked out the window at the bleak, snow-covered landscape.

Part of her wanted to just vanish, disappear, from everyone, including this man who reminded her constantly of the threat they faced. Slip under the radar so far no one would ever find them. No one would hurt them. But with a child like Michael she couldn't do that without help. She couldn't even leave him in the car by himself without worrying he'd wander off and not know how to ask for help. And they'd be recognized almost immediately if they went into a store together.

She had to assume someone was watching her little house in North Dakota so she couldn't go home. And despite holding the pistol earlier she didn't really know how to use it.

David could probably protect her...he'd rip out her heart and trample her pride in the process, which would be fine, except he'd do worse to Michael. And if there was an insider feeding the bad guys information they might be no safer with David than with anyone else inside the system. Frankly, there was nowhere she felt safer than with Special Agent Jed Brennan. She leaned down and rubbed Michael's shoulder. He seemed to have drifted off to sleep.

"Why would you risk helping us?" Because she knew there was a potential cost to all this. The marshals had paid the price. One of the great psychiatrists in the field of autistic research had paid the price. They all had families. People who cared about them. And they were dead.

The cost was immeasurable. Her eyes were too dry to cry. She was too wrung out to do more than shiver despite the hot air that blasted through the car.

"I already let you down once, Vivi. I promised you you'd be safe and they found you."

She blew out a huge breath. "It wasn't your fault." He was doing everything he could to help them and she knew this could cost him his career. Federal organizations loved bureaucracy and this definitely hadn't been rubber stamped by the powers that be.

He rifled through the glove box. "Here, write a list of everything you're going to need to stay hidden for at least a week. *All* the essentials including clothes sizes. I'll hit the stores and max out my credit card."

"I'll pay you back."

Jed laughed but it was a harsh sound. "The money isn't my concern. I just want to make sure you and Michael are safe."

"I'll pay you back as soon as I can access my accounts safely."

"When this is over."

"ASAP," she insisted.

"Which will be when this is over."

"I don't want to be beholden to you, Agent Brennan."

He gave her a tight smile. "Stubborn."

An unamused snort escaped. "Expensive. At least that's what David always said."

"David is the ex?"

She nodded.

"Well excuse me for saying, but aside from fathering a great kid, your ex is an asshole."

"You won't get any argument from me there, Special Agent Brennan."

"You better start calling me Jed." He half-turned to face her, keeping one eye on the road.

She didn't want to call him Jed. When she did it felt intimate and about *them*, not some big international terrorist threat. It reminded her of the fact he'd kissed her. She'd almost forgotten in the shock of everything that had happened. She touched her lips.

"If we're going to avert suspicion you're going to have to pose as my girlfriend because otherwise I wouldn't have brought you with me." His eyes skimmed her hair. "And you're going to have to dye your hair. Blonde or brunette?"

She smoothed her hair behind her ear. "What do you normally date?"

"Blondes." He laughed.

"Then I better go with brunette."

Their eyes met, and the air between them sizzled. "It's just a front, Vivi. Nothing more."

Yet the memory of that kiss and all the deep, dark, remembered longing that it had stirred refused to go away.

"I'll tell my family the truth."

She froze. "We can't put your family at risk."

"We aren't staying with them directly, they have a rental cottage I'm borrowing for a couple of weeks."

"But—"

His gaze softened. "It's OK. They live in an isolated, remote spot. My family is extremely safety conscious. No one will catch them unaware or unprotected. Hell, my dad has more weapons than Quantico. Plus, my twin is the chief of police in the nearest town so we can trust him to keep a secret. In fact we're gonna need him."

"Twin?"

"Not identical—he's the ugly one," Brennan deadpanned.

The idea of having family, people you trusted at your back. Well, it had been a long time since she'd been part of something like that and it was extraordinary. Most people took it for granted and didn't know how lucky they were. She cleared her throat. "I don't know how to thank you, Special Agent Brennan."

"Jed," he corrected firmly.

OK, if she was going to do this, she was going to have to

do it properly. Her son's life depended on it. Jed's family's lives might depend on it. She flashed back to watching Dr. Hinkle get shot. Pretend to be his girlfriend? Not a problem. She just hoped Michael would be able to deal with the line between pretend and reality. It wasn't as if she had many choices.

"Fine. I don't know how to thank you, *Jed*."

"That's a start." His smile made her want to forget what this was really about, but she couldn't. Not when someone wanted them dead.

CHAPTER ELEVEN

P ILAH LET HERSELF into her apartment and stood for a moment with her back pressed against the door. She'd walked back and it had taken her more than two hours to get here. The smell of gunpowder permeated the old wool of her coat and the stench of death stuck to her nostrils. She couldn't rid herself of the harsh reality that she'd murdered a woman in cold blood. A woman who'd done nothing except show some compassion for a relative she wasn't even close to.

It was dark outside. Pilah didn't bother turning on any lights. She wanted to disappear into the shadows. Her feet were frozen stubs, her entire body numb. Still the awfulness of what she'd done reached out and wrapped its way around her throat like a garrote.

They didn't know her identity yet but it was only a matter of time. The Americans would track her down and lock her up forever. She would rot in a cell for decades while her daughters...

Oh, merciful heavens—what would happen to her daughters? They would never even know her, they barely remembered her now. Sobs rose up and spilled out. Poor innocent little Dahlia, and vibrant, funny Corinne. Her life was a bloody mess. The only things in the world that mattered to her were in danger and she could do nothing to protect them.

She wanted to go to them, but she dared not leave the US, the very place where she was in the most danger.

Hot tears squeezed from between closed lids and rolled in a wide path down her cheeks.

The wail of a police siren brought her away from the door and stumbling to the apartment window. A squad car sped past below, heading downtown. Her heart slowed its panicked beat.

The news had said the cops were still looking for the little boy and his mother. That they'd somehow escaped the attack on the safe house and disappeared. He might be able to identify her...to name her. But the idea of him dying the way Marie Thomas had died clawed at her brain.

It didn't seem right.

He was a *child*! He couldn't even talk. Why did he have to die?

Why did everyone else have to die while Sargon sat in his safe, little idyll far from US soil? *He* was the one who'd orchestrated everything. *He* was the reason Adad was dead. Sargon had gone into their town following the bombing and recruited grieving, angry men still reeling from their loss. And he'd sent them off to fight an unwinnable war.

Adad and many of his friends were dead, but Sargon magically avoided the bombs and bullets of the conflict. Dictated the strategy away from the battlefields.

Her reflection in the window was indistinct, like a ghost of who she used to be. A pawn to be used and discarded like human trash. But maybe she was going about this all wrong. *Maybe* she should offer the Americans insider information as long as they got her children out to safety?

They had SEALS, and spies who could find Sargon and his

people, and they'd be very interested to know he was trying to stir up a war between the US and Syria. That he'd organized this attack with the goal of implicating the Syrian regime. She wanted the regime toppled, but she wanted her daughter safe, more.

She didn't know why she hadn't thought of it before… Except they'd lock her up and throw away the key.

Not if she bargained with them.

Terrified but excited she turned to pick up the telephone, only to stumble back in alarm.

A man sat in the shadows.

"Who are you? What do you want?" Her voice was high pitched. The pounding of her heartbeat unnervingly strong against her ribs. She hated it and she hated him. "Are you here to kill me?"

He unfolded from the chair where he sat. "Why would I want to kill you, Pilah?" His voice was soft, but the edge to it made her want to run. He knew her name.

She went with indignation. "It's a natural question to ask when you find a stranger in your home. Get out before I call the cops."

He came closer, and she backed away. He was tall, and the way he moved was all stealth and darkness; his face remained shadowed.

"I do not think you would call the cops, no matter what I did to you." He stroked her cheek and she fought the urge to cringe. He was right. She was completely powerless. His accent was almost American yet he spoke in her native tongue as fluently as she did. "You have served Sargon far better than all the others even though he underestimated you from the start."

She jerked away, her voice thready and weak. "Who are

you? What do you want?"

He moved away and picked up a box from the couch. It was a box Abdullah had left behind in a bag of his belongings. She hadn't looked inside. He went to the window and the streetlights provided enough illumination to see the shape of a pistol. "Sargon wants you to sneak this into the hospital."

"Why?" She didn't touch the weapon. She couldn't hide the uneasiness in her own voice. "Why would I do anything more until my children are somewhere safe?"

"Where will they ever be safe, Pilah?" Deep laughter mocked her. "Here, with you? Or with a man who is trying to start a war between Syria and the United States? Which of you will keep them *safe*?"

She recoiled.

They would never be safe with her in the US. If the Americans found out it was Sargon who had attacked them while trying to blame the Syrian government, they'd blow him up, along with everyone close to him. She swayed. If she tried to work out a deal with the unbelievers she would sign a death warrant for her own children.

So stupid. So naive!

She licked her lips which were dried and cracked. "If they will never be safe then why should I help any longer? What is the point? I am sick of killing and I am dead anyway."

"It is almost over." His touch was gentle as he smoothed her hair behind her ear. "I will make sure your daughters are taken to safety."

"How do I know I can trust you?"

"Pilah, you don't know you can trust me." His laughter was a warm, soft sound that sliced down to the bone. "But you have *no* other options and I have no need to lie. You will do this for me, otherwise the second phase of the plan will fail and everything you have done will have been for nothing. You have no choice."

Her knees buckled, and she had to catch herself to stop from dropping to the floor. He was right. She had no choice. She would never know for sure if Dahlia and Corinne survived. Perhaps it would be better to condemn them to a swift death with a US bomb... *No*, she couldn't do it. Some hope was better than none, no matter how futile.

She reached out and took the pistol. It was light. Almost like a toy. The man put his hands over hers. His fingers warm and smooth. "You need to reassemble it inside the hospital just before you need to use it."

Her hands shook as he made her practice putting the weapon together.

Finally, when she'd mastered it, he wrapped his hands around hers again. "Place this with the belongings of the man you visit."

"Why?"

"You know why."

Everything inside Pilah froze. Another attack. More death and destruction. She rested the gun back in its case and gave it back to the man. "I can't take any more bloodshed."

"There is no one else, Pilah. Only you." His voice got hard. "Abdullah got himself arrested. All Sargon's men died except for one who escaped the safe house. I found him preparing to barter what he knew in exchange for immunity from prosecution. He should have realized that prosecution was the least of his worries." The threat was more than implied. "Just one last target, Pilah. That is all we ask. Then you will be free." He pressed the box holding the weapon into her hands.

And suddenly she understood who the target was. Knew exactly why details of the plan had never been shared. "It will never work. They will sweep for weapons and explosives."

"This weapon is special." She watched his lips move. Wished she could see the face of the man who sent her to her death. "They won't be able to sense it."

"They will check my background and find out I am not who I say I am," Pilah argued.

"Your background cover will hold, never worry. Just hide the weapon in the bedside cabinet or under the mattress. Anywhere it won't get noticed for a few days. Your 'uncle' was moved to a private room an hour ago so you will have all the privacy you need. Spend as much time with him as you can, just in case something happens unexpectedly."

Fear scratched along her throat. "What if he wakes up?"

The man took a vial of tablets out of his pocket and pressed it into her palm. "If he starts to wake slip one of these on his tongue. Just one. It will keep him under for as long as we need him to be. But the doctors have no plans to wake him from his coma for a few more days. Sleep is the best way for his brain to heal."

He might wish that he never woke up.

Pilah bowed her head, hiding her feelings. "Will you contact me when my daughters are safe?"

"Soon. I have to find the boy."

No. "The child might know nothing."

"Or he might know something." For the first time the stranger sounded tired. Weary.

"The plan won't work," she said, desperately.

A shaft of light caught the man's mouth as he smiled. "Do not fret. The plan will work. The only possible weak link is the child and I will make sure he isn't a problem."

The endgame was never the mall attack; it was what happened after the mall attack. There was no way the US would ignore *this* sort of event, no matter who instigated it. It would mean war. If she failed, Sargon would take it out on her young daughters. And if she succeeded she would be dead. If the US discovered Sargon's involvement…her children would still be dead.

She grabbed a handful of the man's shirt, prepared to beg. "Promise me you will get my daughters safely away from Sargon. Now, before it is too late!"

"I promise that I will try." He replied solemnly.

The ache in her stomach intensified. "I will need proof they are safe before I do this. I won't be used anymore."

He stood watching her for a long moment but she was no longer scared of him. He needed her as much as she needed him.

"I will do what I can, *ghazi*." And then he was gone.

———————

JED STOPPED IN Spooner to grab groceries. He had no doubt his mother had stocked the fridge in anticipation of his earlier arrival but there were going to be three of them now and the longer they could stay out of sight, the better. He'd bought clothes and extra ammunition in another town. Winter boots, jackets, gloves, mittens, toothbrushes, hairbrushes, pajamas, tampons, and hair dye. Paper and drawing supplies for Michael. He'd bought a tablet for Vivi and a mini tablet for Michael. Who knew how long they'd be here? Also he picked up two burner cells that he paid for with cash. At first glance most of his purchases could pass as supplies for a few weeks away in a cabin or Christmas gifts, but not the burners.

Part of him wanted to ditch all his electronics but the bureau—especially Frazer—knew where he was staying and disappearing entirely would send out a red alert which would get the FBI investigating. He didn't want that. He had to do everything exactly as if he'd been telling Killion and Frazer the truth so he didn't raise any suspicion.

In a weird coincidence Frazer had also been born and raised in the great state of Wisconsin. Two cheeseheads at the BAU? What were the chances?

He loaded the groceries into the trunk which was now packed with purchases. He hadn't slept in forty-eight hours and fatigue was starting to slow him down. Not a great head space for making critical decisions. He paused for a moment, wondering if he was doing the right thing. By not sharing the fact that Vivi and Michael were alive he was putting his job on the line. No one liked rogue agents. The fact he'd almost been killed by Miles Brandon—the so-called Rainbow Killer—had been because he'd been digging into the case after hours. He'd started staking out the guy on his own time, without backup. Frazer had been busy helping their new rookie agent nail a serial killer in West Virginia and had missed the signs of what Jed had been up to. To say Frazer had been pissed when he'd found out was an understatement.

This would add fuel to Frazer's warnings that he not only got too emotionally involved, but also wasn't good at following the rules. And at the FBI rules were king.

Did he really want to lose his job?

No, he didn't. And he couldn't risk asking for help from his best buddy, Matt Lazlo, either, because it might cost the other guy his job and the former Navy SEAL was a damn fine FBI agent.

Jed got in the car. Vivi sat in the front seat, a gray cable-knit hat covering her bright, red hair. Bright, red hair that was going to be dark brown by tomorrow. She turned to look at him but didn't say anything. Michael was sleeping in the backseat and she had to be running on fumes.

The idea of calling Frazer and telling him the truth, of placing Vivi and Michael in another vulnerable situation when they didn't know where the threat was coming from…? He just couldn't do it. His stomach clenched. He'd joined the FBI to help protect people, but right now the only way of protecting Vivi and Michael was by lying.

He put the car in gear and pulled away. They drove around the big lake where he'd spent countless summers water-skiing with his brothers and best friend Bobby. It was getting dark. He didn't want anyone in his hometown to see him. Not yet.

Snow was gently falling through a canopy of trees, and lay in a thick unbroken swathe. It was beautiful. It could also kill you if you got lost out here without the right equipment. He was counting on using that in their favor.

He still needed to visit Bobby's widow and his godson, who lived in Sawyerville just a few miles away. He exhaled and fogged up the windshield. He wasn't looking forward to that, but it brought an unexpected blast of nostalgia for simpler times. If only the tangled web of teenage love and lust was the worst of their problems—he'd take it. Although lust could still be a problem, he conceded silently, thinking about the effect Vivi had on him. But it didn't control him.

He drove south, on the west side of the lake toward where

his family had property. The snow tires gripped the road despite another five inches of fresh snow.

"It's lovely out here," Vivi said quietly in the darkness.

He'd thought she'd drifted off but the woman was determined not to give herself a break. "It is the prettiest place in the US, but don't tell anyone. It's a state secret."

It was hard not to admire a woman who tried so damn hard to do everything on her own. But he couldn't quite quash the thought that it was more out of necessity than choice, although trusting people was obviously difficult for her. Had her ex abused her too? The idea had his hands tightening on the steering wheel but he was helpless to do anything about it right now. "I don't get back as often as I'd like."

"Where do you work, normally?" she asked.

"Quantico."

"At the National Academy?"

"No." It took him a moment to realize she knew almost nothing about him and yet she'd trusted him anyway. He cleared his throat. He owed her. "The bureau's Behavioral Analysis Unit—part of the National Center for the Analysis of Violent Crime."

"Catching serial killers." Her voice grew somber.

His work took him to dark places; places single moms tended to avoid. "We assist all sorts of criminal investigations. Serial killers are the ones who get all the press."

Her eyes never left him. Vivi Vincent was no fool. "They've been in the news a lot lately. Were you involved in any of those investigations?"

His unit had helped stop three serial killers in the last month or so—two dead, and one in jail where Jed had put him, hopefully to live out his days rotting in a cell. It went some way to alleviating the pain of losing Mia, but it was never enough. Maybe it would never be enough.

"It's what I do," he said simply.

She turned to stare out of the window. "You're a brave man."

He shook his head in denial. The fact he'd already let her down, twice if he counted lying to get her out of the mall that first time, made him feel like a jerk. But he'd make it up to them both. No way were terrorists finding them here in the Northwoods.

Back in the late eighties, before property prices had exploded, his parents had bought a huge chunk of land that included several private lakes. Then his dad had built ten rental cottages doing most of the physical labor himself. Each cottage was isolated and secluded. The cottage Jed always used was on a little island connected to the mainland via a small bridge tucked out of sight. It was one of the few cottages with an internet connection which was both a blessing and a curse. Having internet meant he never really escaped work, but as he also carried paper files maybe he never escaped anyway. Taking a vacation was a state of mind he'd never really mastered, not since he'd graduated the FBI training academy.

His parents' place was tucked away in a well-hidden gully and both his mom and dad were pretty reclusive. Jed used to wonder if his parents were on the run, they took such great care with their anonymity and personal security. He'd actually run them through the system once, and found nothing. Nearing his family's property he noted there were no fresh tire marks. Good. Snow was a great way to track people's movements.

"You grew up around here?" Vivi asked.

"You sound surprised." He didn't take his eyes off the road. He had no desire to skid into the embankment because he was busy looking at an attractive woman. And her being attractive was something he was working hard to ignore. He'd become her bodyguard. Her protector. He wouldn't betray that position of trust. Nor would he get involved with a woman who deserved more than a short-term fling, especially not one with trust issues the size of the San Andreas Fault, and a kid who needed every bit of nurturing the world could provide.

"Just curious." Her eyes scanned him. She was still waiting for more information. "And you didn't answer the question."

That pulled a reluctant laugh out of him. Exhausted and weary as he was, it felt good to laugh. "Sure you're not a lawyer? You're not like most women I know."

She flinched and crossed her arms, staring determinedly out of the window.

"Hey, it wasn't an insult. Most women treat my word as gospel, just on account of my FBI badge. You don't. Why is that?"

Her brows rose up. "Gospel?"

"Yup." He was watching the road, but out of the corner of his eye he saw her arms release before her fingers clenched in her lap. "And this time *you* didn't answer the question."

There was a sigh. The sort that screamed bone-tired weariness with no chance of rest. "I guess my parents taught me to question everything when I was growing up, and I mean everything. It's a hard habit to break."

"Are they still alive?"

She shook her head. "Plane crash."

"They traveled a lot?"

"Yes," she hugged herself again. "They were academics. I spent a lot of time in Africa and South America as a kid."

He wanted to ask more about her family, about *her*. He needed to know who she really was, and how she was going to hold up during this ordeal. "Is that where you discovered you had a flair for languages?"

"Ah, so you did check me out." She crossed her legs and he couldn't help checking her out in a totally different way. He'd bought her the black boots. They just hadn't looked that sexy in the store. Dammit.

He turned his eyes straight forward and told himself to watch for the turn rather than crash the SUV into a tree. "Just the basics to verify you were who you said you are. Got something to hide?" He hadn't had time to look at the detailed background check Frazer had emailed to him earlier that day, beyond the fact that until a couple of years ago she'd had high level security clearance. He'd been too busy looking for the female terrorist and then racing to the safe house like a demented, mad man.

"Doesn't everyone have something to hide?"

The evasion made the hair on his nape prickle.

She was deflecting. But then there were things in his past he wouldn't want everyone to know either, including the fact his best friend's wife had tried to seduce him while his buddy was busy risking his life in Afghanistan. No way in hell would he want anyone to know *that*.

Another reason he didn't get home much.

But this wasn't about him. They needed to trust one another, which wasn't going to gel well with his need to keep a little distance between the two of them. And he couldn't mess it up. Vivi's trust issues had been apparent from the very beginning, and yet she'd followed him when he'd asked her to, and what's more she'd also trusted him with her most treasured possession, Michael. This was a big deal.

"How many languages do you speak?" Get her to relax and open up. Establish some common ground.

"I'm fluent in French, Spanish, Arabic, Farsi, and Pashto. I've got a good understanding of Italian and German. I tried to learn Mandarin but it turns out my brain just refuses to go there."

"Wow. You just made me feel like an uneducated hick."

She laughed. "You need me to stroke your ego, Special Agent Brennan?"

A shock of heat spread over his shoulders, down his spine and straight to his dick. *Shit.* He knew she hadn't meant to make it sound so sexual, but when her voice got low his IQ dropped to meet it.

Her cheeks flamed even in the dimness of the cab. "I didn't mean that the way it came out."

"I know how you meant it." This woman had been involved in two recent gun battles and someone had tried to drown her son. She wasn't in a place to flirt. She was just trying to make it through the week without going insane, and without dying. This was his job—that's why he needed to remember his training. It wasn't her fault she turned him on. The vibrant hair, the slender body, the vivid eyes, even her devotion to her child seemed to short-circuit the part of his brain that controlled desire. He was not going to compromise the situation when she was so vulnerable and relying on him for protection. They needed to stop this terrorist organization so they could all get on with their lives.

End of story.

Problem was the more time he spent with her, the more attractive he found her. Hell, he couldn't even remember the last time he'd gone on a date, let alone been more than fleetingly interested in anyone. For the last nine months, he'd been working his ass off tracking the Rainbow Killer every spare moment. He'd even begun hanging out in gay bars in the hopes of hearing something that would lead him to the UNSUB—and eventually it had. He rubbed the back of his neck. Hell, no wonder he hadn't had a date.

So he was just a little horny that's all. He could cope with that. He'd been a soldier for three years and knew how to abstain—wasn't that what cold showers were for?

He cleared his throat. "You worked at the UN. Is that where you learned that having a badge is no guarantee of a man's veracity?"

"A woman's actually."

"Ah."

"My ex's new wife—" She checked Michael in the back seat, but the kid was snoring like a puppy "—works for the NSA. Let's just say I didn't need the Agency to figure out they'd been intimate while he was still married to me. I know even the important jobs are done by humans—flawed, difficult, temperamental humans. Trust has to be earned, I don't give it freely."

Her spine straightened, on the defensive again.

He mulled over the words and ignored the warning. She'd already given him her trust when she'd snuck away from the safe house with him. If he pointed that out she'd probably rethink her actions so he changed direction instead. "Isn't that the definition of a human being? Flawed, difficult, temperamental?"

"Most of them." She smiled, letting go of her earlier embarrassment. "So *did* you grow up here?"

Back to her original question. She would make a good lawyer.

He was wearing the dark wool suit he'd changed into at the office before the noon briefing. It didn't fit into the Northwoods lifestyle but it didn't mean this land hadn't forged the bones of the man he'd become.

"Yeah, I did. Never thought I'd leave and then 9/11 happened and I ended up joining the Army after I graduated college. I guess that day changed the course of many American lives." For good or bad? Sometimes he wondered. It was good to want to protect your country but he thought of his eldest brother Max who he hadn't seen in almost a year, doing God knew what, God knew where. And he thought of Bobby... and his throat grew tight.

A snowshoe hare bobbed along beside them and three white-tailed deer watched them cautiously from between spindly branches in the forest. He'd gone to war to protect this vision of America, but the terrorists were still out there, multiplying like the damn rabbits and killing people way too close to home. That wasn't winning the war on terror. He didn't know what the hell that was.

"I think I might love to live in a place like this."

He blinked, surprised. From the sophisticated way she dressed and carried herself he'd never have guessed she would have embraced country life, although, hell, she lived in Fargo where they had a wood chipper as a major tourist attraction.

He had to drag his gaze back to the road again because not only was she beautiful, she seemed to draw comfort from this world to which he'd transported her. A world that he loved.

Many would find even the idea of this kind of isolation overwhelming, but after what she'd been through maybe isolation was exactly what she and Michael needed.

They went over a rise and started to skid on the other side. She grabbed the door.

"It's fine. Roads out this way are also difficult and flawed. I'm hoping it keeps the bad guys away." He turned the wheel into the skid and they straightened. "Nearly there."

Up ahead the road forked. Left would take him down to his parents' house. He turned right, slowing to a crawl. A fox in winter garb stood illuminated by the headlights for a split second before it ran into the forest.

He'd missed the wildlife. He'd grown up surrounded by things that lived in parallel to humans. It had made him see the world as an ecosystem, whereas his condo in Virginia made him view the world as a bubble of humanity—a cruel, vicious bubble of humanity.

He really did need time to unscrew his head. As long as no one found them here this was a win-win situation.

Snow crunched under the tires as he followed the gentle dips and curves of the track before rumbling over the narrow bridge. He spotted footprints in the snow and unclipped his holster. Then they turned the last corner and the headlights lit up a large log cabin.

On the front porch stood a man with his feet firmly planted apart, shotgun in hand.

"A friend of yours?" Vivi asked with remarkable self-restraint under the circumstances.

"Not exactly." Jed left the engine running, got out and walked over to the older man, wrapped him in a bear hug and lifted him off his feet. The man hugged him back. Even though they were the same height, the other man seemed smaller somehow. Still fit and strong, but noticeably thinner. No longer the giant from childhood that Jed still held in his mind.

It had been way too long since he'd been home. "Good to see you, Pop."

His father stood back with a twinkle in his eye. "Had an inkling you'd turn up tonight."

"An inkling or a phone call?"

The older man twisted his lips. "Your boss thought you might be upset on account of losing two witnesses." His dad's down jacket rustled in the almost silent forest. "Looks like you picked up a couple of strays." He squinted at Vivi through the windshield. "And I think you've got some explainin' to do, son…"

If it had been anyone else he'd have told them to butt out, but this was his father. "Didn't feel like I had a lot of choice, Pop."

"Worth losing your job over?"

His dad knew how important his career was to him—how important catching killers and putting them behind bars was. It didn't bring back the people you loved, but it helped. Jed covered his discomfort with a grin. "They'd never fire me. The FBI would be lost without me."

His dad snorted. "Pretty sure they'd cope."

Better to lose his job than Vivi or Michael losing their lives. "Think you can find me a few chores to keep me busy if they do fire me?"

His old man laughed. "I'll get Liam to hire you on as his deputy."

His brother for a boss? *Shoot me now.* "Let's hope it doesn't come to that. Mom wouldn't want to attend his funeral."

His father grinned. "You two have been scrapping since you were in the womb. One of these days you're gonna figure out there are other ways of expressing brotherly love."

"Where's the fun in that?"

Vivi climbed out of her side of the vehicle and stood there watching them, her breath freezing into a cloud of vapor. His father raised one wiry brow. "Pretty thing, fragile looking though. Hope you know what you're doing, son."

"So do I, Pop. So do I."

———————————

IT WAS WARM inside the log cabin. Jed's dad had turned up the central heating and started a fire in the wood stove so a tinge of smoke tainted the air. Vivi followed Jed into a bedroom on the ground floor level and watched him lay Michael on a fresh sheet that his father had just stretched over the mattress. She went to grab the top sheet but the two men beat her to it in what looked like a well-rehearsed routine. She comforted herself by dragging a fresh pillowcase over a puffy, down pillow.

Jed held out his hand and she passed across the pillow which he placed gently beneath Michael's head.

Then the two men left without a word.

Michael was fast asleep so she didn't bother undressing him. His boots and coat had been removed at the door; the sweatpants and t-shirt loose enough for him to sleep in comfortably. The dark circles under his eyes were pronounced against his pale skin and his forehead crinkled as if in pain. She placed a kiss on his brow. "Sleep well, baby."

She followed Jed and his father out into the main room knowing they needed to talk about what was going on and the implications for their safety.

The cabin was stunning, she realized, looking around for the first time. No rustic hidey-hole but a comfy, luxurious getaway. The front of the cabin was a two-story open-plan area containing the kitchen, dining, living area, divided up by a long wide granite island. A huge stone chimney covered one entire wall. Lots of windows looked out over the lake—a great spot to watch the snow fall, bringing with it a sense of seclusion and safety. A shiver rippled over her skin. The peace was an illusion but she appreciated it anyway. Jed was closing all the blinds although she doubted there was anyone out there for miles. The idea that the bad guys could find them so fast seemed ludicrous. There were stairs against the wall behind her, presumably to more bedrooms. A couple of lamps bathed the cabin in a warm amber glow that begged her to sink to the nearest flat surface and pass out from sheer exhaustion, but she had to keep going.

Jed's father turned to face her. The expression in his eyes was kind but contained a *spare-the-bullshit* gleam. "Want to tell me exactly what's going on?"

"Mr. Brennan, my name is Vivi Vincent and you just met the sleeping version of my son, Michael."

"I saw a picture of you guys on the news. There's a full-scale manhunt out there searching for you—led by the US Marshal Service and the FBI." His eyes cut back to his son.

They looked remarkably alike, father and son, except the older man's hair was silver-white which made the dark brown of his eyes and tanned skin stand out in contrast.

"Your boss thinks you came up here to drown your sorrows over these two being killed, but you really came to hide them, didn't you?"

"The bad guys found the safe house, Dad." Jed's voice reflected the full gravity of the situation. She'd forgotten for a little while exactly why they were here. "And I don't know if they followed the shrink who'd come to treat Michael, or if someone on the inside let the information leak."

Keen brown eyes swept back to her and nailed her in place. "How did you escape the gunmen who attacked the safe house?"

A sudden flashback to seeing Dr. Hinkle shot dead made her stomach twist. She sank down to the sofa and wished she could turn back the clock. Wished she'd chosen a different day to visit Minneapolis, wished she hadn't gone to the mall, or hadn't taped that stupid TV interview.

But she had to deal with the here and now and sticking her head in the sand would get them nowhere. She cleared her throat. "After Dr. Hinkle examined my son, Michael ran away and hid. I found him in the trunk of Marshal Rogers's car," she stumbled over the name of the man who'd saved her life while bleeding to death from a gunshot wound. She'd done nothing to help him and the guilt ate at her. If she'd tried to save him she'd be dead too and Michael would be alone, but it didn't matter. She hadn't tried to save him. *God.* She breathed heavily through her mouth, wishing she was brave and calm and able to deal with this craziness without feeling so utterly useless. "Small dark places are my son's comfort zone. It's where he goes when he's stressed and trying to escape the world. I couldn't stand to move him, but didn't want to leave him alone either. So I got in the trunk and just held him tight, praying they wouldn't find us." It sounded nuts. She was nuts.

Not exactly a newsflash.

Jed flicked on a lamp, then put water on the stove to boil. She watched the way he moved, so calm and confident even though he'd just broken about a million rules that could cost him his job. Why would he take that risk for them?

Finished with his preparations, Jed leaned against the kitchen island and took over the story. "When I got to the scene, I assumed the cops had cleared the place. Then I heard something in the garage, found them hiding in the trunk."

"I was too scared to move." Vivi confessed. "I didn't know if the bad guys were still in the house or not. I just stayed where I was, in shock." How could so many bad things happen to them and yet they still lived?

Jed nodded. "I managed to sneak them into my car without anyone seeing." He stood in the middle of the room, filling the large space with his presence. Everything about him screamed safety and promise. "The marshals and feds are going to bust my balls when they find out, but if I had to do it again?" His eyes said he would.

"News says the child is autistic?" Jed's dad asked her.

"Honestly?" The weight of a thousand uncertainties beat at her. "No one knows for sure." She explained Michael's condition. It was complicated and she was tired. She didn't know if she was making any sense.

Jed stepped in. Saving her again when she'd always prided herself on her strength and ability to save herself.

"The way I figure it the bad guys attacked and shot their way inside. But Vivi and Michael weren't where they expected them to be and the remaining attacker took off when they heard the sirens going off."

The sofa beside her gave as someone sat down. She opened

her eyes expecting to see Jed but it was his father.

His eyes searched her face. "Forgive me for asking, son, but how do you know Vivi didn't kill all those people and then hide in the trunk of that car?"

CHAPTER TWELVE

VIVI FLINCHED AND pulled away from the older man. She felt like he'd just punched her in the stomach. How could he think like that?

"Well the fact that there were three dead terrorists on the ground when we got there, and one of the marshals reported being attacked by four armed men prior to him being shot dead." Jed sat on the arm of the couch beside her and placed his hand on her shoulder in reassurance. "I forgot to mention my family are conspiracy theorists and don't take anything at face value. It's made my time in the FBI...interesting."

Jed's dad's eyes softened. "Just need to be sure you are what you say you are before I leave you alone with my son."

"Pretty sure I can handle it, Pop." Jed touched the gold shield on his belt. "Federal agent, remember?"

Vivi's laugh came out like a sob. "I admire your paternal instincts, Mr. Brennan, I really do." She looked up and caught Jed's gaze. "Without your son I don't know where we'd be—dead probably. I'm not a danger to him, but the people after my son could be and I don't want to put any of you in danger." The idea made her start to shake. "I should probably leave. Go to a hotel."

The old man's expression softened. "Drag that poor little boy from pillar to post? It's safe here. I'm sorry I made you uncomfortable but Jed's right, I don't take things at face value. But I do trust my son, and despite what I might think of the FBI in general, he's damned good at his job." He held out his hand to her. "Jeremiah Brennan at your service, ma'am."

Bemused, she shook his hand. Either she was frozen or he had lava in his veins.

"You feel like ice." He rubbed her hand between his. "Get the lady a hot drink, son."

"On it. Want something for yourself?" Jed filled a mug with steaming water and stirred in sugar. She didn't bother telling him she didn't take anything in hers. She could do with the energy boost even though Jed was the one who hadn't slept in a couple of days.

"So what's the plan?" Jed's father asked, suddenly onboard with everything.

It knocked Vivi off kilter again—as if she hadn't been totally out of her depth enough over the last few days.

Jed handed her a cup of steaming tea, and went to stand in front of the fireplace. He looked as solid and immovable as the rock behind him. "We're going to hole up here for a few days—hopefully give the feds enough time to chase down and lock up the remaining terrorists. Vivi is going to dye her hair brown and avoid as many people as possible. If anyone asks you can tell them I'm visiting with a girlfriend and don't want to be disturbed."

Vivi's cheeks heated. Oh, the joys of a pale complexion. She hid behind her mug and inhaled the steam.

"Like the idea of you bringing a woman home won't have everyone abuzz?" The older man snorted. "You going to tell Liam or shall I?"

"I'll tell him."

"Angela?"

Who was *Angela*, she wondered. She took a sip of the tea and was hit by a wall of sweetness. She took another drink. It tasted good.

"I'll drop by and see her at some point too."

"What are the chances of these people figuring out this young lady and her child are here with you?"

Jed pursed his lips, thinking. "Slim, but nothing is impossible."

"You disable the GPS in the SUV?"

Jed nodded. "In Spooner. Frazer knows where I am, but I trust him. I turned the GPS off on my phone and laptop too. If it is someone in law enforcement and they suspect Vivi and Michael are with me then they will find us, but it will take them time. I don't intend to make it easy for them."

Jeremiah wagged his finger at her. "No checking your email or using any online stores for anything through your own name or credit card. If you need anything tell Jed. Or Mary can order it for you. That's Jed's mother."

"He watches a lot of TV." Jed read her bemused expression and gave her a wink.

The man eyed his son. "There'll be no keeping your mother out of this, you know that?"

Jed nodded. Sober now. "I figured the easiest way to do this was go with Plan A, my planned visit to see family before Christmas. The fewer people who know about Vivi and Michael the better, but there'll be some who'll ask questions. Then we give them the shy girlfriend story."

"It's a workable plan as long as you stick to the rules. Your mom and I and Liam aren't going to give you away." His gaze rested heavy on Vivi as if she were the weak link.

"These people are trying to murder my little boy." She leaned forward, unable to subdue the fierceness in her voice. "There's nothing I won't do to keep him safe. That includes lying to people, hiding out from the world and avoiding online *shopping*. Nothing matters except Michael."

"You matter," Jed interrupted quietly.

She shook her head and placed her empty mug on a coaster on the oak side table. "You protect Michael, don't worry about me. If anything happened to him…"

Jed's dad's face filled with empathy and he patted her hand. "Nothing's going to happen to either of you. You've come to the right place. We may be quaint and a little rustic up here in the Northwoods, but we know how to protect what's ours."

She'd gone from murder suspect to acceptance in five short minutes. "I don't know how to thank you, Mr. Brennan. Most people would run screaming in the other direction."

He pushed himself to his feet. "My family aren't most people, Miss Vincent, I raised 'em better than that. And thank me by looking after that boy of yours. I bet he's a live wire when he's awake."

"He sure is." Aside from the fact he didn't speak. That conversation was for another day. Maybe tomorrow she could get Michael drawing and he'd give the feds the information they needed to catch the bad guys and then it'd be safe for them to go home.

"I better get back to your mother. Oh, the breaker keeps tripping, I need to pick up a different fuse," Jeremiah said to Jed, who nodded. Then Jed's father got up and pulled his boots and jacket back on. "Keep the shotgun. It's loaded. I'll bring by more stuff tomorrow."

"Won't he need that?" Vivi asked, but the man had already disappeared into the darkness. Jed closed the door on the still falling snow.

"Trust me, he has others." Jed went over and placed the gun in the tall cupboard beside the door. Then he locked it and slid the key onto the top of the door jamb.

She went to the window and edged the blind aside. Snow was falling in large, heavy flakes, surrounding them, cutting them off from the world. She just wanted to disappear. To stay here forever and never have to worry about anyone trying to hurt her baby. "You learned to shoot before you learned to walk, didn't you?"

"Pretty much." He faced her. "I'd like to teach you and Michael, starting tomorrow."

A shiver ran over her flesh. The idea of her sweet little boy firing a weapon… "I hate guns."

"I understand that, but there's a good chance Michael's going to be exposed to guns, one way or another over the next little while. How about we start with some safety lessons and maybe a little bit of empowerment. If ever a kid deserved it, it's Michael."

She thought of all the times David had tried to get her on the gun range. This was different. This was pure survival, which in many ways made it worse. The idea of taking a human life was abhorrent, but the idea of someone executing her baby because she was too dumb or idealistic to pick up a firearm was worse. She drew in a breath and agreed to something that just a few days ago would have been unimaginable. "I'd appreciate that. Thank you."

Dark brown eyes swept over her, glancing over her lips. A shiver of awareness uncurled low in her belly because despite everything that was going on she was still very much aware of him as a man. A very attractive man. And the heat she spotted in his gaze whenever he didn't carefully shut it down told her he thought she was attractive too. Talk about bad timing.

"You look dead on your feet." He winced at his choice of words, but carried on. "You take the master bedroom upstairs. I'll take the other room downstairs."

That stopped her short. "But I-I assumed I'd sleep with Michael." The stutter pissed her off. She thought she'd lost it back in high school.

Those dark eyes watched her solemnly. "Do you sleep with him at home?"

She shook her head. "No, but—"

"How about we try getting him back into a place of routine. You said that's what he needed. Why not start right now?"

"But this is a strange place, and after what happened…"

"Michael's been through hell, but he's smart, tough and resilient. Give him the chance to prove that." He caught her by the upper arms, and she remembered how he'd kissed her when he'd found her alive in the trunk of that car. A ping of awareness shot along every nerve.

She thought of all the ways David would have tried to convince her to do the same thing. That she was smothering Michael, ruining him, turning him into a mommy's boy that all the other kids would tease. All this guy did was use a little of her own logic and some natural compassion.

She needed to stop thinking about her ex and start living in the here-and-now.

Jed's eyes softened, as if he knew he'd won. "I'll hear him if he wakes and I want to be on the main floor in case of trouble.

There are only two bedrooms down here so you get the luxury suite upstairs—you look like you need it."

She wasn't insulted. She was so tired she literally swayed on her feet as if she had a bad case of vertigo.

"I'll make sure he's OK and come get you if he needs anything."

After everything that had happened it was odd that Jed's kindness and understanding pushed her over the edge and almost brought tears to her eyes.

"OK." She was too exhausted to argue. "I'll check on him first and leave both doors ajar in case he wakes."

He nodded.

Without planning to, she smoothed a hand over his jaw. He stilled and she froze. His dark eyes were hooded and impossible to read as she stretched up on tiptoes and kissed him quickly on the cheek. She liked the feel of the subtle scrape of stubble beneath her lips. "Thank you for everything."

He held her still, his gaze intent on her lips. Sexual awareness swirled between them, made her breath catch as arousal stirred low and hot in her belly. The air around them crackled, and she shivered as she stared up into his face, mesmerized.

Jed slanted his mouth over hers like he had to taste her—just the way he had when he'd found them at the safe house. It was an open-mouthed, full-on assault and she willingly met him halfway. Her tongue tangled with his in a silky slick slide, the taste of him hot and very, very male. Something inside her ignited with long forgotten need. She tried to move closer but he tore his mouth away, eyes glittering.

They were both breathing heavily, chests pumping. Wood popped in the fire, breaking the spell.

He let go of her and stepped away. "That was a mistake. I

shouldn't have done it." He ran a hand through his short hair. "I'm sorry. Get some rest. I promise I'll call you if Michael needs you."

She nodded, more than a little shell-shocked by what had just happened. That she'd kissed a man when her son's life was in danger made self-disgust rise up inside her. She backed away, wishing things were different. Wishing she'd never met Jed, or that he'd never reminded her that there had once been another part to her life, something that involved naked skin and the hard thrust of pleasure.

That pleasure had once given her a precious child, but it had also ripped her heart to shreds.

"I'm sorry too." She was such a fool. She needed to remind herself Jed was here because of his job, not because they were involved, or he was attracted.

Jed needed the information Michael might know, and the best way of finding it out was by keeping them safe and becoming an integral part of Michael's life. She needed to regroup when it came to Jed Brennan. Keep him at arm's length, not just physically but mentally too. No matter how tempting the man was, this wasn't some romantic getaway or excuse for a quickie to sate a few basic, human needs. It was a race for survival and Michael was the prize.

UNTIL VIVI KISSED him, Jed had managed to put out of his mind the fact he'd laid one on her when he'd found her in the trunk of that car. When her lips had connected with his cheek, the memory had exploded into his mind and he'd had to kiss her again—the need no doubt heightened by the life and death adrenaline rushes of the last few days. There was no other reason it had felt that incredible.

Now he couldn't get the taste of her out of his mind. He wanted to follow her up the stairs and press her into the mattress and kiss her all night long. Everywhere.

He paced the floor in front of the fire.

Not how he usually responded to witnesses.

Especially not single moms with issues and responsibilities—not to mention on the run from terrorists. What the hell was he thinking, taking advantage like that?

Since losing Mia in Afghanistan he'd avoided getting in too deep on the relationship front. He kept things light, reserved his focus and commitment to solving the murders that crossed his desk in an unending stream of violence. Every time he put a killer away it was as if he was scoring a victory for the young soldier he'd loved and lost to another monster. But Vivi called to that part of him that he'd been denying for almost a decade. The timing sucked. The situation sucked. And he couldn't afford to fuck it all up just for a few hours of physical relief that would turn into mental anguish and self-recrimination as soon as their skin cooled.

He blew out a long breath. The visual of Vivi naked, in the throes of passion, got his blood pumping a little too enthusiastically through his veins. She deserved more than a quick fuck, but that was all he had in him, and he couldn't afford to get involved again.

So stop thinking about her, asshole.

He poured himself a stiff drink and put another log in the wood stove. Opened his laptop and checked his email. Fifty-seven new messages. *Hell.* You'd think he'd been gone for two days rather than a few hours. He replied to his boss who told him there was no news on Vivi or Michael, so to turn the computer off and take a break.

Sure.

A thread of guilt wove along his nerves. Should he tell Frazer?

Despite the fact that his boss had benched him, he still considered the man a friend. The guy was dedicated and smart and took his job very seriously.

He could trust him.

So why didn't he confide in the man?

He knew why.

The best way for Vivi and Michael to stay alive was to tell no one, not even his boss. Not a soul outside his parents and twin brother who were helping him here on the ground.

One basic tenet of human behavior was that reactions and actions changed according to what someone knew. Jed used this knowledge on a daily basis and so did Frazer. That's how they caught a lot of criminals. Hopefully it was how they'd catch these terrorist assholes. He emailed his boss asking if any progress had been made as to how the bad guys had tracked down the safe house. Frazer emailed back immediately that they were still looking into it, although they'd checked surveillance images from the parking lot where Hinkle kept his car and various traffic cams. No sign of a tail.

Jed thought about how he'd do it if he didn't want to be seen. The bad guys could have put a tracking device on Hinkle's car...

A second email appeared: *No tracking device found on Hinkle's car although they could have removed it before they started shooting.*

Jed grinned. They were usually on the same wavelength.

Then he emailed back and asked if there was any evidence of a leak.

I have Alex Parker consulting with us on it, Frazer replied.

Alex Parker co-owned a private cyber-security firm with a first-rate reputation in DC. He was also the boyfriend of the newest member of BAU-4, Special Agent Mallory Rooney. Jed figured he was about to find out if Parker was as good as his reputation suggested. He'd take all the help he could get.

Another email popped up in his inbox. Killion. *No sign of Vivi or Michael yet.*

He emailed the guy back. *What did you get out of the interrogations today?*

Jed's cell rang. He sighed. Killion. He didn't really want to answer, but he didn't want this guy's spidey senses tingling either. Given who and what Killion did, he could probably find him easily. Plus, Jed wanted information.

"Brennan."

"You missing me yet?" asked Killion.

"I hate to break it to you, but you're not my type."

"I think your type has long red hair and a sharp tongue."

Jed waited a shocked beat and choked out, "That's a little insensitive even for you."

"Yeah, well, I don't think she or the boy are dead. I think they got away and are hiding somewhere."

Shit. "I hope to hell you're right, but it's a little unlikely, don't you think?" His tone told the other guy to convince him.

"These guys wouldn't have gone to the effort of taking the bodies with them. They'd have tap-tapped and gone."

They'd been so close to doing that that nausea gripped his stomach. "Jesus Christ." He used the imagery to his advantage—his own form of dissociation. "I hope they're alive."

"One of the attackers is missing his weapon. We found 9-mm casings, but ballistics couldn't match them to a gun on the premises."

Jed had bagged the weapon Vivi had taken for evidence and put it on a high shelf in the cupboard so Michael didn't have access. "If there was a fourth attacker he could have picked up the weapon."

"Maybe… Why are you so convinced they're dead, anyway?" asked Killion.

"Look. As far as we can tell these people are Islamists and she's a beautiful woman. Even if they didn't kill her they might have taken her to…" Sell her. Rape her. Behead her on Youtube, and play it for the world to see. Fuck. Sweat broke out over his brow. All of that could have happened. It could *still* happen if he didn't play this properly. "And if she's alive why the hell hasn't she come forward?" He was getting loud and obnoxious.

"After the way the safe house got attacked? I'd definitely go it alone without the so-called help of the government."

Jed grunted. This guy was a master manipulator, no doubt. He wasn't falling for it. "What did you get out of the interrogations?"

"Apart from the fact Abdullah is a stone-cold killer?"

"I could have told you that when I pried his fingers from around an eight-year-old's throat."

"Yeah, well, I showed this guy some pictures of how his comrades ended up and there wasn't an iota of emotion."

"Blame the vestal virgins."

"Who'd want to spend eternity with a virgin anyway? I mean seriously, give me an experienced—"

"Killion," Jed snapped. The guy was going off topic big

time.

"Right. Two things of interest came up aside from the fact the guy is a sociopathic creep. First, Abdullah is still officially a member of the Syrian Republican Guard."

That wasn't good for world peace.

"But he could be working for the rebels and stirring up trouble for the government forces. There are many rival factions fighting there from al-Qaeda, the Free Syrian Army, even Hezbollah for the regime. It's hard to get any solid information on who is linked to whom. Politics and religion are mixed up and Iran has a hand in most of it. It's also possible the Syria connection is a decoy. So many groups in the Middle East want America to eat shit and die. The Arab Spring is turning into a fucking nightmare for our interests abroad. Let's face it, democracy is only great as long as they do what the US wants."

Fighting for democracy and freedom was one of the most important things he'd done in the Army, but in some societies it wasn't stable or sustainable, and in others it turned around and bit you on the ass. Still, free and fair elections should be a human right. "What's the second thing?"

"Ah. This is kind of cool, actually. MI6 contacted us with a hit on one of our dead safe house attackers in their database. So I've got one of Her Majesty's finest wending his way across the pond with a bunch of files they refused to email. Not sure what to make of that except perhaps we caught a break or they have someone on the inside somewhere. He gets in tomorrow morning."

So the cell had a connection to the UK. Not unusual. Terrorists tended to scatter like roaches and had pockets all over the world. But it meant they were probably getting training and funding from somewhere. Jed wanted the backer.

"Any internet chatter about another attack being imminent?"

Killion exhaled audibly. "Nothing. According to our analysts they aren't communicating via chat rooms or email or cell phones."

"They're either evolving in sophistication or the plan was in effect from the start."

Killion was silent for a few long beats. "Are you really taking a vacation in the middle of an investigation this huge?"

"I sure am. Look I have two choices. Burn out and destroy what has been up until now a promising career. Or just stop and take a breath. I'm choosing the latter."

Killion grunted. The guy probably hadn't taken a break since joining the Agency.

Jed forced himself to talk about Vivi and Michael. "Look, if the Vincents turn up…"

"Don't worry, I'll call if I hear anything. Hey, maybe I'll join you for a vacation when this is all over."

A thought flashed inside Jed's head. Shit. Had he completely misread the situation? He cleared his throat. "You know I'm straight, right? I mean it's OK if you're not, but I—"

"What the…are you serious?" The guy started laughing. "Don't flatter yourself, Brennan. I don't mind playing with my own dick, but I'm not touching yours."

"Thank fuck for that." Jed was glad he wasn't totally losing his ability to read people.

"I like 'em young, pretty, and female. Less brainpower the better." Killion sounded tired. Not just from staying up too long, but from something more. Intelligence officers burned out even faster than FBI agents.

Jed kept it light. Don't get drawn in. "The less brainpower they have, the more chance you have of getting laid, right?"

"Hey, don't get nasty." Killion laughed again. "You can relax, I'm not after your body though I'll happily fuck with your mind." The hint of self-loathing in his tone brought Jed up short again. He opened his mouth to ask if the other man was all right, although he knew he was probably being played. Killion cut him off before he got the chance. "OK, I killed some time, amused myself. Now I'm off to take another stab at Abdu-madfucker. We're trying to confuse his body clock and speed up any confessions. The guy is lost without his Rolex."

"My heart bleeds."

"Yeah, but I don't think he's falling for it. OK. Later."

Jed grunted and hung up and tried to remember what he knew about terrorists. State terrorism differed from religious terrorism. Assigning motive to this attack was probably the best way of figuring out what the next one might be.

The public had trouble understanding how seemingly normal people could kill innocent civilians in the name of their cause. Psychiatric research suggested a phenomena called doubling, first observed amongst the Nazis. They often started off with a desire to fix something that they saw as broken, but after a certain amount of indoctrination, they became two people—their former seemingly benign self, and a morally disengaged killer capable of horrific acts of murder.

State sponsored terrorism was a different beast, with horns and claws and tentacles.

Ironically, doubling was encouraged in certain professions—hell, most law enforcement personnel were masters. How else did they confront evil and death on an almost-daily basis and then go home to the family?

But how could an internal conflict in Syria be related to a terrorist attack on the Minneapolis Mall? He pressed his fingers into his temples to try and relieve the pressure. He knew nothing about Syria, but figured it was time to get educated. He started surfing and pulled up Brown Moses.

An hour later, he was about to fall asleep when headlights swept through the thickening veil of the snow. He pulled his weapon and headed to the door. A police car flashed its lights and then sat idling out front. Jed pulled on his boots and headed into the night to one of the few people he trusted to have his back, no questions asked.

CHAPTER THIRTEEN

V IVI AWOKE, DISORIENTED and groggy, heart pounding from a nightmare. Glaring digits on the alarm clock told her it was only two a.m. Damn. Her throat was dry. She inched out of bed and went downstairs to make herself a drink.

She put a glass of milk to heat in the microwave and then noticed the fire was dying so went to put on another log.

When she turned she realized the room wasn't empty. Jed Brennan lay sprawled on the couch. His shirt was creased, unbuttoned at the neck, sleeves rolled to just below the elbows. His tie was tossed on the floor next to his suit jacket.

His arm was stretched over his head. Long legs stuck over the other end of the sofa, too tall to fit comfortably. His mouth was slightly open and the guy looked absolutely dead to the world. This was probably the first time he'd slept since the attack, and as much as she'd like to stand and stare at his handsome face, she really should give him some space.

She couldn't believe she'd kissed him earlier. Foolish wasn't a good feeling.

She shivered. It was cold in here. The microwave dinged but Jed didn't stir. Determined not to wake him, she took an afghan off the chair. She held it aloft and then draped it slowly over his body. The action reminded her of doing the same thing for her son. He didn't stir. A pen was grasped in one hand. She knelt, leaning close so as to try and remove it before he got ink on his shirt or the couch. She eased it out of his grasp, but found herself staring into the dark depths of his eyes and froze.

Wow. She blinked. This wasn't like tucking in Michael at all.

He smelled all male, warm and rumpled. The race of her heart got faster and faster. A tingle of electricity shooting from the tips of her breasts to the apex of her thighs, reminding her what sex had felt like.

Back away.

His eyes searched her face, obviously trying to wake up and catch his bearings. His gaze lingered on her lips and the look in his eyes turned molten for a brief moment.

She swallowed nervously. She couldn't afford to do anything stupid like kiss him again. She could only take so much rejection.

"Hi." The sound of her voice snapped him out of his stupor.

He groaned. "Sorry, for a moment I was back in some Army tent in Bagram." His voice was rough with sleep.

"Was it bad?" she asked.

"Hell no, I was dreaming one of my greatest fantasies was about to come true."

"That's not what I meant," she said softly.

"Yeah, but it's all the information you're getting right now." He flashed her a grin, taking away the sting.

She edged away, reluctant to go back to bed when she was so wide awake and yet not wanting to disturb him. "I'm sorry I woke you. You must be exhausted."

He nodded, still lying down, but blinking hard as if that

would help. "I was. Am." He shook his head and then sat up in a fluid motion.

"Has there been any break in the case?"

He shook his head.

She shoved down her disappointment. "I'll just check on Michael before I go back to bed."

"You're a great mom, you know."

She snorted. "I'm obsessive." They both kept their voices to a murmur.

"Give yourself a break. Being a single parent is tough." His eyes held a kindness and a patience that calmed her raging fear of being overwhelmed by this entire situation.

She was doing the best she could under difficult circumstances, but delegating was tough. Trusting anyone else with her son's welfare was extremely tough.

"You remind me of my own mother."

"Neurotic?" She tried to make a joke but failed. He saw her weakness and insecurity.

"Fierce—like a lioness." In the light of the fire his face was all harsh hollows and shadows.

"How did it feel to have a fierce mother?" It worried her that Michael would one day resent her for caring so much.

"I could never get anything past the woman, still can't, but..." he paused, thinking. "I have never doubted her love for me. Michael will never doubt yours for him either."

Her heart gave a tumble. Her throat squeezed closed. He had no idea how much that meant to her. Or maybe he did. Maybe he knew how desperately she needed something positive to cling to. "Thank you."

She checked Michael, who was fast asleep. Then she took her milk and walked up the stairs, even though she'd rather have sat with Jed.

"Goodnight," she called out quietly.

The problem with Jed wasn't that she didn't like him. He'd saved Michael twice and frankly she'd never be able to thank him for that. But she also liked everything about him. And after the emotional agony she'd been through with her ex, that made her uneasy. As soon as this thing was over he'd be gone, and she had too much to lose by letting her guard down. She hadn't just been burned by her ex. She'd been incinerated.

The risk wasn't worth the heartbreak.

———————

VIVI STOOD ON the deck the next morning, well-rested and wide awake as she looked out at the lake that steamed slightly in the startlingly bright light of dawn. Everything was so dazzling it hurt the eyes. She was wrapped up, wearing a pair of new jeans which were a little stiff and loose at the waist, a thick, cream, cable sweater, good wool socks, winter boots and a down vest. Jed had thought of everything, even buying her lingerie and a nightshirt to sleep in. It felt weird dressing in clothes someone else had picked out for her, like stepping into a part in a play. But without his help she didn't know where she'd be. Struggling, that was for damned sure. Scared, that was a given. Dead was a high probability.

The fact she'd kissed him—twice now—the fact she'd dreamed about doing more than kissing him after she'd gone back to bed last night and had woken feeling dissatisfied and empty made her hyper-aware of every facet of him.

That kiss had most definitely been a mistake, but probably not for the reasons Jed thought.

It had reawakened inside her the need to feel again. To be a woman again. She had nailed the mother thing but somehow in doing so she'd lost the part of herself that made her so essentially female. The desire for sex, the desire to feel desired, had lain dormant since well before her husband left her. David had started acting differently not long after Michael was born, resentful, harsh with his judgment and his censure. In response she'd put up emotional barriers and much of the physicality of their relationship had disappeared right along with it. When relationships went south, sex was often the first thing to go.

The door opened behind her and Jed stepped out onto the deck. She tensed and turned to face him, forcing a friendly—but not too friendly—smile.

He wore similar clothes to her, but his shirt was deep blue and looked good against the darkness of his jet black hair. He hadn't shaved. It made him look rugged and perfectly suited for the outdoorsy scene.

Or just perfect.

Crap.

She met his gaze and experienced that inexplicable pull that you only got with certain people. That weird mutual desire that happened less and less as you got older, became rarer and more special. She'd thought she'd outgrown the feeling altogether. Obviously she'd been mistaken. Still, they had bigger things to deal with.

One side of his mouth kicked up. "The hair suits you." He reached out to touch a strand of the newly dyed dark hair that escaped the cable-knit hat he'd bought her yesterday. Her hair was almost as dark as his and she thought it made her look like a witch. She brushed it under the hat, self-conscious and annoyed that she cared.

"I don't think Michael's going to suffer through getting his hair dyed quite so easily."

Jed laughed. "Maybe we should just give him a buzz cut and paint his head brown."

Vivi laughed. "He'd probably go for that."

Jed made her forget the reality that surrounded them, and she didn't know if that was a good thing or not. "I should have asked you to buy me some make-up so my lashes and brows match."

"I'm hoping no one gets close enough to see your lashes, but I can pick up something from the store if it makes you feel better."

A man buying her make-up; now that was a miracle.

"You think Michael and I should just stay here and hide?" A kernel of guilt was starting to grow inside her that she hadn't told Jed who Michael's father was. But if she told him now, he might change his mind about them staying, and she really wanted to stay. Wanted to hide out here in the woods for as long as she possibly could.

Had David realized they were the ones attacked in the safe house? Would he even care? He'd severed all ties with her and Michael years ago. Was it possible no one had linked them yet?

"Given the manpower being poured into this investigation I can't see it taking too long to find these guys and take them into custody. I think the safest thing is to lay low, even though it's tough." He'd misunderstood her.

"Oh no, I don't mind staying here, I love it. It's beautiful." She huddled into her thick sweater and looked out at the mist over the lake. "It's good to have the chance to finally breathe again—I can't believe I took it all for granted before."

He moved a little closer, dipped his head. "What do you mean?"

"Life seemed so hard before with Michael's problems. And yet I actually had it pretty easy." She smiled at him over her shoulder. "The last few days have been like stepping into Hell. But all this makes it seem so far away…makes me appreciate everything I've got." She indicated the gleaming beauty of the snow-covered woods.

He stood behind her, close enough she could feel his heat. "You can relax for just a little while." He rubbed her upper arms, almost as if he couldn't stop himself from touching her. It felt so natural, so calming that she closed her eyes and released some of the built up tension.

She wanted him to pull her against him and hold her.

He didn't.

"It won't be forever, Vivi." His warm breath brushed her ear. She didn't think he was necessarily talking about being on the run. He was talking about them.

Obviously he thought she was the hearts and flowers type, not the realist that life had made her. She placed her hand over his, staring out at the gleaming ice that sparkled like a thousand diamonds as the sun rose. In her experience happiness was fleeting, even when someone wasn't trying to kill you.

"I don't need forever. Maybe I just want something for right now." And if that didn't tell him she wanted to be with him without any long-term strings, she didn't know what would.

The sound of a car engine had them both tensing.

"Inside, now." Immediately back in bodyguard mode, his

hand went under his jacket, and he urged her toward the door. She stumbled inside and quickly hid behind the curtain of the window near the front door to see who'd arrived. Michael was still asleep. Had the bad guys tracked them down? Jed had seemed so confident they wouldn't.

She was about to grab the shotgun when a beat-up truck pulled in front of the cabin belching out a cloud of black smoke. A slender woman with a long, blond ponytail jumped out of the cab and threw herself into Jed's arms.

Vivi blinked. Oh good lord, she'd just offered herself to a man who was involved with someone else.

Jed returned the hug and then pulled quickly away. A line of disappointment marred the brow of the all-American beauty as he stepped back. She looked all tall and slender, the cheerleader type. Vivi's inner class nerd shrank back. She recovered and snorted—because cheerleading was such a life skill? But every teenager who'd survived high school knew it was so much more than that.

Sheesh. Who the heck was she to judge this woman like some jealous girlfriend meeting the ex? She was nothing to Jed Brennan. No one. *Work.* Annoying work who kept throwing herself at the man.

Embarrassment rose up her neck and into her cheeks. *Ugh.* Well no one said being a woman was easy, and at least she wasn't being shot at.

The blonde said something and then hitched her thumb over her left shoulder with a questioning smile on her cherry gloss lips. Jed glanced at the cabin, but he didn't appear to see Vivi. Harsh lines cut down around his mouth. A grimace twisted his lips. He did not look happy. He turned back toward the woman, shaking his head. He didn't want the woman to come in even though she clearly expected to.

Who exactly was she? A girlfriend? The mysterious *Angela*?

There was a small child in a booster seat in the back of the truck. Vivi backed up a step. Was the child his? It would explain why he was so great with kids. Was this woman an ex-wife or significant other he hadn't mentioned?

Suddenly she felt foolish, the same kind of foolish as when she'd realized her husband had been doing more than paperwork when he stayed late for work. But she had no right to feel like that. Jed Brennan owed her nothing. They didn't have a relationship outside the threat to her son's life. How could watching this tableau hurt even a little bit after everything she'd been through?

All it had taken was a spark of chemistry and a few kind words to slip past her guard. She turned away and saw Michael standing in the hallway between the bedroom and kitchen and stiffened her spine. "Hey, sweetheart." She walked toward her son. "Come on. Let's get you fed."

She heard the truck start up again and rumble away. Jed came in a few seconds later, but she avoided looking at him and he went straight to his room, closing the door with a soft snick.

———————————

SHAME WASHED OVER Jed's entire body. He dragged a hand over his face and wanted to sink into the ground. Nausea swirled inside him, doing tricks in his stomach.

It had been obvious to him each time he came back since Bobby died—hell, since even before he died—that Angela wanted to renew their old relationship. They'd dated on and off all through high school, but like most jocks, he'd been casually indifferent and certainly never intended anything permanent. He'd broken off the relationship when he'd gone to Michigan State, assuming she'd just move on.

But apparently she'd been more upset than he'd expected—and Bobby had been there to pick up the pieces. What he hadn't realized was Bobby had been in love with her the entire time she and Jed had been dating.

Jed was such an ass. If he'd known his friend had feelings for Angela, he would have stepped aside. Bobby was like a brother to him, and he'd known even back then that, although he liked and admired Angela, he didn't love her.

Considering his day job, you'd think he'd be able to get over the guilt of something so minor, but Bobby's death had hit him hard, hit his family and the whole community hard. Angela had seemed almost relieved. They'd been having troubles with their marriage; being deployed was hard on anyone. At the back of his mind Jed couldn't help wondering if she'd told Bobby about the fact she'd kissed him, maybe lied about his response. Was that why Bobby hadn't written to him during the entire month before he died?

Was *Jed* the reason his best friend was dead?

Christ. He didn't need this angst. He was a federal agent. He was looking for killers. Hiding from terrorists. Protecting Vivi and Michael from people who wanted to shoot them. This was real and vital and important. It wasn't frickin' high school which was how Angela made him feel.

He pulled himself together. He wasn't here to figure out women troubles, although they were multiplying all of a sudden. Vivi had pretty much given him the green light for a quick fling, not seeming to understand that she might not be in the right mindset to make that sort of decision.

The desire to wrap her up in a giant hug on the deck earlier had almost gotten the better of him. Yeah, *hug*, that's what he wanted to do to the hot redhead with the sharp mind and vulnerable eyes—not something that involved a wall and a pair of legs wrapped tight around his waist. And seducing a woman he was supposed to be protecting was *such* a great idea. Even if she thought she was fine with it, she wouldn't be fine with it. Shit, he knew women.

He was all too aware of how flawed a human he really was. He looked in the mirror and tried not to hate himself because, honestly, he wanted to go for it. Spend their nights hot and naked with him buried deep inside her. But it would be a massive mistake in the long run, and he didn't want her or Michael to get hurt.

He went out of the room and plastered a smile on his face. He had work to do.

Keeping these two safe and seeing if they could pry the lid off Michael's memories was his top priority. He had an idea that might work, but it required no pressure and lots of patience, which was hard when the clock was ticking.

"Hey, Mikey. How's breakfast?"

The kid gave him a tentative smile. His lips going back to droopy and sad afterward, but that *was* a smile. Vivi passed Jed a coffee, then put milk and sugar on the table.

"Thanks." His voice was gruff, emotions still close to the surface.

"Old friend?" The seemingly innocuous question made him pause and take a good look at her.

Was she jealous? Or just naturally curious?

He didn't play games. Not with people's emotions. He'd lost the only woman he'd truly loved to a sadistic killer. Games had always seemed ridiculous after that. Probably why Angela's antics pissed him off so much. *Mia would have liked Vivi*—that thought came out of nowhere.

So he held those piercing, blue eyes and gave it to her straight. "Angela and I dated in high school. She married my best friend from high school, but he died a couple of years ago in Afghanistan. She's struggling to cope, and I think she wants to fall back into old habits."

She blinked. He saw immediately that she hadn't expected him to be that open with her. Her trust issues were showing. She surprised him then by revealing another little bit of herself. "I think I had *one* date in high school—it was awful, a total disaster. No one wanted to date the class nerd except the male equivalent, and I scared the poor guy half to death when I demanded a kiss." Her eyes were amused. The woman could probably take her pick of the male species now, but she chose to see herself as the reject, rather than a beautiful and intelligent woman. Her ex had done a real number on her.

"High school is a zoo. Some people have it, some people don't." He winked and she snorted—it made her seem more approachable, less nerd-turned-goddess. "Just wait until Michael is in high school, the girls will be flocking."

Michael choked on his cereal and milk splattered on the counter. Jed slapped him on the back, threw a paper towel at the boy, and let him clean up while he got out his own bowl of cereal. Vivi hovered. "And just because you don't say much, kid, don't think that'll stop them." Jed gave an exaggerated shudder and leaned closer to Michael's ear. "Girls like the strong, silent type."

Michael pulled a gross face and showed a mouthful of cereal. Vivi looked like she was doing her best not to berate him for his manners, but she made herself turn away and wash the dishes. Jed was hard to gross out. Two brothers and too many serial killers to mention.

"They also like guns."

Michael's eyes gleamed as they locked onto the weapon Jed flashed in his shoulder holster.

"So you probably wouldn't want to know how to fire one of these, huh?"

Michael's eyes bugged, big and round, begging him as plainly as words.

Vivi looked between them and let out a ragged breath. She threw the dish towel down on the counter. "Fine, but only if I get to learn too."

Jed shared a look with the kid. Michael blinked in surprise. "What d'you think, Mikey? Should we let her?"

The grin that broke out on the little guy's face actually caused a stab of pain just below Jed's sternum. The smile lit up the whole room. Despite everything he'd been through, despite being scared down to his marrow, he could still smile.

No way was he letting anyone hurt this boy, or his mother. He tapped the kid's knuckles and they finished their breakfast in easy silence. When he caught Vivi's gaze, it showed a mixture of hope and defeat; hope that they could actually fight the people who were after them, defeat that her world had irrevocably changed and there was no going back to what it had been before. There was something else in her gaze that looked suspiciously like admiration. He swallowed and concentrated on his cereal. She obviously had terrible taste in men.

———————

PILAH WALKED INTO the hospital. The weapon was in her tote, concealed in a lunch bag. There were a high number of police officers walking the halls. People were still clearly on edge. One officer's gaze raked over her and came back for a second look, but it wasn't suspicion. The man's eyes lingered on her tight jeans and small waist, drifting higher in a way that would have made her husband rant and rave. She stuck her chest out just a little and lifted her chin. *There, Adad, that's what you get for dying.*

She walked to where William Green had been yesterday and frowned when she got to the ward only to find he wasn't there. She retraced her steps to the nurses' station.

"Oh, he's been moved to a private room. I thought you'd have known."

Pilah shook her head.

The nurse led her along the corridor. Police officers and some sort of security people came out of the room that the nurse stopped beside.

Pilah looked up at the wall of solid muscle and testosterone that stalked down the halls. Ice-cold fear swept down her spine. The group went into the room across the hall.

"Who are they?" she whispered. She knew. She knew exactly who they were and what they were doing. She gripped her bag tighter.

The nurse pursed her lips and shrugged, waving her inside the private room.

William Green lay hooked up to a machine that measured his heartbeat and various other monitors. The bandage around his head was pale against the warm, pink flush of his face.

"Will they come back in here?" Pilah was worried she was overreacting, but the men had certainly seemed intimidating. Did Sargon really think she could ever get the drop on someone like that? Surely not. But she had more to lose than they did. A lot more.

"Some bigwig is visiting soon. They're doing security checks everywhere. I couldn't even park today without one of them checking my little car for explosives."

"Why would they search in here?" Pilah asked.

The nurse avoided her gaze. "I couldn't say."

It was actually going to happen. Pilah didn't know how she felt about that but maybe, just maybe, the man in the shadows would keep his promise and rescue her daughters and if so, she would keep hers.

"Do you mind if I just sit with him?" Pilah asked the nurse.

"Not at all, just make sure you talk to him, or read to him. It's good for him to hear a familiar voice."

Pilah took the man's hand. It was warm and dry. She squeezed his fingers but got no response. She was sorry he'd been hurt. It had seemed so much easier during the planning stages, so simple to "take out" an imaginary foe. Pilah regretted everything she'd done, but it didn't even matter anymore. She had no choice.

THE PLATES FROM the SUV that had whisked Vivi and Michael to safety from the hotel belonged to one FBI Special Agent Jed Brennan. The interesting thing about that was the GPS signal had since been turned off. The BAU agent had been heavily involved with the Vincents before they'd disappeared, but he was now supposedly on leave and had left immediately following the safe house shooting.

Elan *might* have believed the man's cover story, except he knew the gunmen hadn't taken the woman and the boy. He'd had someone pull Brennan's credit card purchases and either the guy went all out for Christmas, or he'd been outfitting two people who'd needed to buy everything from scratch.

His instincts told him Brennan had the woman and the boy.

The fed had been heading in the direction of Sawyerville when he'd gone off the grid. Brennan's twin brother was the Chief of Police there. Parents ran a cabin rental company on a lake about six miles southwest—that's where he'd start looking. The other brother was thankfully overseas, so he didn't need to deal with him.

He'd bet money Brennan had come home.

It was still a gamble that the boy was with him, but there were no other leads or sightings, and time was running out. They'd have one shot at this. If the boy started communicating any of their plans, the opportunity would be blown and people would have died for nothing.

Pilah Rasheed was the best chance of this second attack working. Elan intended to be there in the background, making sure she either pulled it off or died trying. She could never be allowed to talk. Too much was at stake. Too much to lose if any of the pieces failed to fit the expected picture.

He parked off the main street and went into the local bar, taking in the stink of stale beer, and the dead animal decor. Stuffed fish in glass museum cases, along with furry woodland creatures contorted into bizarre human parodies.

Hunting, shooting, fishing. That was what this area was all about.

Hunting.

That's all he was interested in. And not getting caught.

Wood gleamed like honey, the bar, the walls, the ceiling. The sticky, white, tile floor needed a sweep and the lick of a warm, wet mop. He walked over to a burgundy, vinyl stool and sat, waiting patiently to be served.

"What can I get you?" The barkeep's reddened eyes kept being dragged back to the TV screen over on the far wall.

Good. He wouldn't remember him. "Beer. Whatever is on tap is fine."

They were still showing coverage of the mall attack and brief flashes of the interview Vivi Vincent had done with the media about her son's amazing artistic ability. Bet she wished she'd never gone near Minneapolis. He definitely wished she'd stayed home.

The barkeep slid a tall glass of frothy liquid across the bar to him. Elan gave him a ten dollar bill and told him to keep the change.

"I'm looking for a place to stay for a few days. And a decent place to eat."

"You up here hunting?"

He nodded. "Deer." He'd dressed the part. Thick warm boots. Lined camo pants. Beige shirt. Hunting jacket. Orange hat. His rifle out in the truck was a Springfield M1A with a Nightforce scope, good quality but nothing to raise eyebrows. He pointed at the screen. "Wanted to get out of the city so figured I'd come up early." There was a short window to hunt antlerless deer opening tomorrow. He was lucky. He got to hide in plain sight.

"Got everything you need around here. DNR office can give you maps and sell you a license. I can give you the name of some locals who'll butcher anything you shoot." The barkeep's eyes were assessing despite the red glow.

Elan would do well to remember these people were generally more in tune with their environment, and most of them owned shotguns. He'd need to be careful. A lot depended on him tracking down the boy and eliminating any potential threat. An entire nation depended on him. He couldn't afford compassion or pity. If the plan went wrong, war would loom between enemies and allies alike.

His people were tracking Sargon, who'd slipped out of his villa immediately after the mall shooting. Sargon had traveled to a small village in the hills where one of his daughters had relocated after her marriage to a tribal leader. She was fourteen years old.

Later that same day, Pilah's daughters had been brought to him also. Leverage. To make sure Pilah did as she was told when the time came. If Abdullah hadn't been captured, she would probably have already been dead, but too many of Sargon's pawns had fallen, and the man needed everyone he could get.

Elan had promised Pilah he'd try and get her children to safety, and he kept most of his promises. Forces near the Lebanese village would rescue the children before the house where Sargon stayed was razed to the ground. The fact the children would end up in a refugee camp or orphanage was regrettable. He took no pleasure in children dying, but his loyalty to his country was paramount. Hence the capacity to eliminate any potential threat Michael Vincent represented.

Elan checked his watch and finished his beer. The barkeep

told him of a motel along the highway. He thanked him and left the bar, driving past the police station to the DNR offices. Time to get himself a ticket to go hunting. Time to take care of the problem once and for all.

CHAPTER FOURTEEN

I T TURNED OUT they weren't just going into the woods to shoot a few beer cans. Jed's father had created a permanent gun range on his land, cut through the thicket of dense forest about two-hundred meters long, and a few meters wide. The older man had hauled out an entire arsenal of weapons that would have looked right at home inside the lair of a Mexican drug cartel.

Vivi drew in a cold breath and watched Jeremiah coach Michael on how to hold the gun, where to point it when not shooting at something, to keep his finger off the trigger until he was ready to fire.

Despite her dislike of guns there was no doubt her son was enjoying his lesson. Michael had been much more alert since coming to the cabin. He'd slept well, eaten. The fear and trauma from yesterday and the day before were still in his eyes, but they were more a shadow than the shroud they'd been yesterday. Maybe poor Dr. Hinkle had been right, all Michael needed was peace and quiet and a sense of normalcy. Plus, a shooting lesson from a man who seemed to live and breathe weapons…

"He's fine."

Vivi looked up at Jed who stood beside her. "Easy for you to say."

His eyes sparkled. "Trust me. I might not know much about Michael as an individual, but I do have firsthand experience with being an eight-year-old boy. Shooting targets is a surefire hit."

Jed Brennan did seem to know how to appeal to her child. Michael had never appeared more 'normal.' He was watching Jeremiah intently, doing exactly as he was told. The fact guns were involved made her nervous, but something about them drew him. They obviously drew a lot of kids, and at least this way he had a chance to learn about them in a safe environment.

Her eyes cut to the man beside her and traced the stubble on Jed's jaw which she'd kissed last night. She looked away before he caught her staring and gave her another warning about them not making a mistake. She got it. She totally got it. But she liked looking at him. She liked that he tried to make her and Michael smile. Despite the awful things he must deal with on a regular basis Jed had retained a keen sense of humor and, more importantly, his humanity. It showed the heart of a good man.

They were rarer than they should be.

She wanted to ask him about his work, but had the horrible feeling that if she did their situation would get a little too real, a little too scary, and she'd had enough of real and scary to last a lifetime. So she kept it light instead.

"This must have come in handy when going through new agent training."

"Sure did. My dad used to trek me and my brothers up here after every Sunday lunch, and we'd spend hours on the range. Heaven for boys."

Her gaze cut to his holster. "Looks like some little boys

never grew up."

He rubbed his hands together in the cold air trying to keep them warm. "Little, huh?" The light in his eyes grew more amused as he towered over her 5' 9" frame. He leaned closer to her ear. "And if you think me being in the FBI is bad, you should have seen me in the military when we had ordinance."

"Oh, please, no bombs. I don't think my 'mom' gene would survive the experience."

"Better cover your ears," Jed told her as his father and her son walked toward the target.

He slipped a pair of ear protectors over her head, and a shiver ran all over her body just from the feel of his fingers in her hair. Damn, he shouldn't affect her like this—she wasn't fifteen. She adjusted the earpieces and then winced as Michael emptied an entire clip rapid-fire into a red circular target.

Holy crap.

Michael turned and grinned with such pride and excitement her heart gave a little trip. He repeated the process with several different pistols and then a BB gun. Finally Jeremiah looked up with a proud smile.

She pulled off the ear protectors and Jed's father waved them over.

"You ready to give it a go, Vivi?" he asked.

"I don't know, Michael looks like he's getting cold."

Jeremiah placed the last handgun they'd used on a table they'd set up. "Don't worry about Michael. I'll take him back to the house. Mary will have hot chocolate on the stove to warm us both up. You two take a few minutes to run through some basic drills." He pinned her with a narrow gaze. "You do believe in equality, don't you?"

Vivi's mouth fell open. He was challenging her on a different level. Telling her that her responsibilities now included being able to protect her son, and his, with deadly force if necessary.

Could she do it?

A week ago she'd have said no. But Vivi wasn't feeling like she had much of a choice anymore. All she had to do was remember the mall shooting, or Dr. Hinkle getting shot, or the marshal bleeding to death on the floor of the so-called *safe* house. The idea that that could be Michael or Jed made her insides feel like tangled skeins of wool.

She would pull her weight. She would learn how to load a gun, how to fire one.

"Let's do it," she said.

Jeremiah touched one of the pistols on the table. "Try out the Glock and the 1911, then the shotgun last. Recoil could knock you over if you're not used to it, but it's the most effective thing for scaring the crap out of people."

She nodded. The idea of her holding a gun should scare the crap out of anyone.

Jed helped his father pack up most of the weaponry and put it in the back of the ATV.

"See you back at the house. No rush." Jeremiah tipped his head at her and helped Michael jump on the four-wheeler for the short journey down the plowed road back to the cabin set above the bank of the lake. She'd thought Michael would cling to her in this strange environment, but being with the Brennans seemed to come naturally. He didn't even wave goodbye. He trusted them. The weird thing was, she did too.

The engine of the ATV faded out of earshot, and the total silence of a snow covered forest settled around them.

It was just her and Jed, and a few hundred rounds of ammunition.

———————————

"OK, CHANGE YOUR stance."

Jed had taught people to shoot before. The main thing was making sure the person holding the gun remembered that the metal object they held in their hands needed to be treated with absolute caution and respect, otherwise someone could die. It wasn't exactly a problem with Vivi. If she were any more cautious around weapons, she'd have her hands in the air, walking backward toward the road.

She held the gun in a two-handed grip pointed at the ground in front of her. She shifted her foot slightly to the side.

"Try to relax your shoulders."

She sagged like someone cut her strings.

He hid a smile. "Nervous?"

"As a cat in a room full of rocking chairs."

"That's it." He adjusted her grip so her skin didn't get shredded on the slide, or get in the way of the spent case ejecting. "Now move your finger onto the trigger and aim at the target. Squeeze slowly."

She started tightening her finger on the trigger, her arms shaking so much he feared she was going to drop the gun. Not a good option.

"Nothing is happening," she gritted out.

"Relax," he repeated. He stepped up behind her and supported her left arm with his just to keep her steady. Her scent whispered with a hint of lavender soap that his mother had put out for them. He wished she'd stuck to Ivory, because right now he wanted to inhale Vivi. To lean closer. Taste her.

Not the time or the place to be thinking about anything but guns and bullets and the reality of their situation. They were together through necessity, not choice.

But did that mean they couldn't enjoy the quiet moments?

He supported her arm so she stopped shaking. Spoke loudly so she could hear him over the ear muffs. "The Glock 21 has a five and a half pound trigger." He kept his voice and expression stern so she wouldn't misread the situation as anything but a practical lesson in survival. The gun went off, and he steadied her stance again. "You just need to get a feel for it." She squeezed again, and this time the gun fired much more easily. She hit center target with the last two shots. Then she fired the rest of the thirteen rounds and never missed the target once. A natural. Figured. Women were often the better shots. When she was finished she grinned at him, looking a hell of a lot like her son.

She handed him the weapon with a sigh of relief, their faces only inches apart.

Being a brunette didn't decrease her appeal one bit. Wearing not a speck of make-up just made her look younger and fresher. She had freckles on her nose and full pink lips. Pretty lips. Damn she looked like a schoolgirl rather than a grown woman. But there was something in her eyes. Not just sadness. Not just fear. Not even just the flicker of attraction they were both fighting. Wisdom? Courage? That core of inner strength and intelligence that shone through her gaze? Whatever it was, she affected him differently than any woman he'd met since Mia.

Christ.

Good thing Liam couldn't see him now. When his brother had come over last night, Liam had told him to watch his back and maintain his objectivity.

Sure. No problem.

He cleared his throat. "How did you like that one?"

She grimaced. He checked the weapon was empty, and they repeated the lesson with the SW1911 and he taught her how to load it.

"I think I like this one better." She tried the grip in both hands, adjusting her fingers to find the best position. She'd hit the target repeatedly, dead center.

"The Glock packs a bit of a punch. At least now you know what to expect if you have to fire one…"

Her exhilaration seemed to evaporate as if she'd recalled why they were having shooting lessons. He touched her shoulder. "Hey, this is a last resort. They shouldn't find us here, but if they do, we need to be ready."

"I understand. I do. It just doesn't make me feel any better about it."

Because shooting a target was one thing. Putting a bullet in another human being was something else entirely. He picked up the shotgun and cracked it open. He showed her how to load it, where the safety was. Then he positioned her in front of a different target, this one further away. He moved behind her and wedged the butt of the shotgun into her shoulder. "Line up the sights like before. The shot scatters so it should be easier to hit something—anything—even at a distance."

She cradled the shotgun and he stood behind her, ready to catch her if she fell. She aimed the gun and settled into the calm of the woods. The sky was a soft, bruised purple that promised more snow. She gently squeezed the trigger, and even the trees seemed to shake with the boom. She took a step back, but didn't fall. He rested his hands against her back. He liked putting his hands on her. He wasn't even thinking about sex—OK, *now* he was thinking about sex, but generally he just liked touching her. After a few seconds she drew in a deep breath and then raised the gun back to her shoulder. She fired a second time, and this time her stance didn't waver.

She lowered the twelve gauge, and he caught it up in his hands, checked that the barrels were empty. They both removed their ear protection and stood staring at one another, their breath misting in the subzero temps. "You did great."

"Thanks." She opened her mouth to say something else, but hesitated.

"What is it?"

"I wanted to ask you a question."

Warily, he said, "Go on."

A shadow moved across her eyes. "Is it easy to kill someone?"

Not what he was expecting. The memory of him slitting the guy's throat in the mall rushed over him. It wasn't pretty, but he didn't have any regrets. "Easy? No. Not hard either when the person is trying to kill innocent civilians." He began putting the pistols and ammunition in a small backpack his father had left.

A hand touched his arm. "I'm not judging you. I'd be dead if it wasn't for you. I just don't know if I'll be able to do it if I have to."

He turned and took her cold fingers in his and rubbed some warmth into them. She was freezing, but hadn't complained once. He enclosed her hands in his and blew on them.

"Shooting someone from a distance is easier than killing

someone in hand-to-hand combat, but I don't recommend either except in extraordinary circumstances." He let her go and concentrated on getting the ammo packed up.

"You're a profiler, right? You spend most of your time in your office and yet you overpowered that man using only a knife? He was massive."

The guy had been slow and stupid and full of blood lust which had left him wide open. "I'm a federal agent who works at the Behavioral Analysis Unit—there's no such job as a profiler. I was in the Army for a few years, and I'm trained in combat. I do a lot of martial arts to keep fit," *to keep sane,* "and I had a hell of an incentive to take out that guy in the mall." One side of his mouth kicked up. "My boss wishes I spent all my time in the office, because I have a habit of getting too involved in cases." Obviously his boss was right.

Her eyes flashed with surprise, and she crossed her arms over her chest defensively.

"Not with women, Vivi. Just with catching the bad guys." He hardened his tone. This was a good time to make sure she didn't think he was going to make a serious pass at her, even though he'd kissed her, and it was obvious he found her attractive. He wanted her to relax and trust him on every level, but it was hard with this unsettling energy swirling between them. "I don't get personally involved with women on cases. I don't want you to get the wrong idea because I made a mistake and kissed you."

So many thoughts flitted over her features, he couldn't read her. Probably a good thing.

"So, to answer your question, some people find it easy to kill. Others enjoy it. If they didn't, I'd be chasing bank robbers through city streets. Even though I've had to take a life on more than one occasion, I don't enjoy it." He let some of his experience into his eyes. "I can't tell you if you'll be able to kill someone if it comes down to it, not even in self-defense. There are plenty of cases where men faced with imminent death during combat have refused to fire a shot." He held her lightly by the elbows. "It doesn't make them weak or cowards, it just makes them human. I *do* think you will do whatever it takes to protect Michael, even if that means shooting someone until they are dead."

She flinched but squared her shoulders. That fierce maternal passion that he'd seen in her right from the start blazed through.

"I would do anything to protect my child." She grabbed a handful of his vest and pulled him closer, surprising the hell out of him. "But what I hadn't realized before now is I'd do it to protect you too. And you need to know that." Her eyes narrowed. "You need to be able to trust me to have your back the same way I need to trust you."

Christ. He'd told her he didn't get involved with women on a case, and she told him she'd kill for him.

One of them was lying, and he didn't think it was Vivi.

Guilt ate at him, along with the relentless pull of temptation.

Something rustled in the bushes, and she whirled around and backed into him.

"It's just a squirrel," he reassured her. When she turned around with a self-deprecating laugh, she was right next to him, and despite everything he'd said, he wanted to kiss her. Her lips parted, and she stared up at him with an expression that surely mirrored his. She wanted him, but knew they shouldn't.

Then he was kissing her, and she leaned into him, grabbing the collar of his vest to pull him closer. She licked inside his mouth, and a furnace exploded inside him. He backed her up a few paces to the shelter they'd built years ago. Hunger filled him, and even though he didn't release her mouth, his hand was pulling her shirt from her jeans, his hand cupping her breast, finding her nipple a taut, firm pebble against his palm.

How did she do this to him? Reduce him to nothing but want.

Her hands touched his bare skin as they burrowed beneath the layers he wore, they were cold but felt amazing against his too hot flesh. His fingers slipped inside the stretchy waistband of her jeans, and she opened her legs, allowing him access to her slick, hidden folds.

His limbs shook. This was a bad idea, but his fingers eased inside her anyway. She gasped, but didn't let go of his mouth. Instead she put her hands on his zipper and stroked him through his jeans until he thought he'd burst.

He drove his fingers into her, keeping a rhythm that made her writhe against him and lose her ability to do anything except react—and God help him he liked that. He liked giving her pleasure. His thumb found her clit and then he pressed his palm hard against the throbbing nub of flesh. He drove deeper, wishing it wasn't so damn cold, and he could strip her naked right here in the woods.

She stiffened against him and shuddered, inner muscles clenching and spasming against his hand. He drew back to see her expression, but her eyes were closed, lips rosy from his kisses. She clutched his jacket, holding on as if she'd fall over if she let go.

Goddamn it. What the hell was wrong with him?

He withdrew his hand and tucked in her shirt. She opened her eyes, which looked so dazed with passion he almost wept. "Jesus, you make me stupid."

"Oh, God. I'm so sorry…" Vivi quickly scanned his face. The uncertainty on hers reminded him her ex had done a real number on her, and he probably wasn't helping.

"It isn't your fault; stupid comes naturally." He clamped down hard on the need to apologize. His body ached and his blood ran hot, wanting to finish what it had started. Because he was a guy, and an asshole to boot. But what he really wanted was to be a good FBI agent.

And he was failing.

He needed to unlock the secrets in Michael's mind before the bad guys found them, because they couldn't stay here forever. And the longer they were here, the greater the chance of him fucking up and making this even more personal—as if her coming around his fingers wasn't personal enough? *Shit.* His body begged him to forget the rules, but he didn't think he could live with himself if he compromised this situation.

Isn't it already compromised?

It was messed up, that was for damn sure. He turned away, unwilling to let her see his conflicted emotions, unwilling to let her see the fact he wanted to yank down her panties and do her against the nearest tree. Yeah, great work Special Agent Brennan, go polish your badge and prepare a report on that.

"We better get back," he said instead.

AFTER THEIR TARGET practice that morning, they'd shared hot

chocolate with his parents, Jed trying to pretend he hadn't crossed a line and wasn't furious with himself for losing control.

The three of them had snowshoed back to the cabin via the woods, and his dad had dropped the SUV off later. The walk in the quiet of the forest with Vivi and Michael had finally cooled his brain, forced him to relax. Almost like a real vacation. It was obvious his parents liked Vivi and Michael, which added a whole surreal aspect to this fake relationship. It was going much better than any of his real ones ever had.

Now they were back at the cabin. The fire roaring. Radio playing softly in the background.

Vivi had made soup for lunch, and he'd had to force any regrets from his head. He needed to focus all his faculties on keeping them safe and getting Michael to start drawing again.

She sat with her feet on the couch, pretending to read a novel. All very relaxed, except the air between them crackled with ever increasing sexual awareness, and killers were out there somewhere, trying to hunt them down.

He rubbed the back of his neck. None of this was easing his tension.

They needed a break in the case. He was betting that once Michael finally felt safe and secure, he'd turn to his go-to method of mentally dealing with things. Vivi said that was drawing.

He didn't know the status of the investigation and that irked him. Killion and Frazer would probably both call later, though he couldn't afford to act too interested, even though he was interested as hell.

Jed grabbed a mirror from the bedroom and set it up on the dining table. He took one of the sketch pads he'd bought for Michael, picked up a pencil, and started sketching his reflection in the mirror. He'd taken art throughout high school because band conflicted with his football schedule. Ironically he'd turned out to be pretty good at it. He scratched his chin. He needed a shave, but never usually bothered when he came home. Still, he looked like a Neanderthal. His gaze glanced off Vivi.

He angled the mirror and started putting in pencil lines where the eyes, nose, lips would be, his too wide forehead. Where had those lines between his brows come from? He stared hard at the man he saw in the mirror. There were shadows under his eyes, evidence of too many sleepless nights and guilt-ridden insomnia, lending an age to his face he hadn't noticed before.

Time moved on.

He looked every one of his thirty-four years. Hardly old, but not young anymore either.

Michael sat at the table drinking milk and eating a cookie. Every so often he'd reach out a finger and touch the screen of the tablet Jed had given him. He seemed to be figuring out what it could do, although he didn't attempt to pick it up or even move it closer to him. The kid was definitely scared of what would happen if he broke it, even though Jed had told him twenty times it didn't matter. Accidents happened.

"H," said a small text-to-talk electronic voice.

Vivi's head jerked up.

"Hey, buddy, that's awesome." Jed grinned at the boy, who grinned back.

The next letter was a 'C' which deflated Jed slightly. He was hoping for a whole word, maybe a detailed account of what had gone down in the toy store. He shook his head at himself and went back to his self-portrait. Patience was the key.

Jed had no doubt Michael was a smart kid. He understood why the doctors refused to label Michael autistic, because he was so high-functioning. But there was also no doubt the kid didn't make a sound, not even when terrified, and that wasn't normal.

It was heartbreaking, but it was also frustrating when they were trying to capture terrorists who were in all likelihood planning another attack. Jed also knew that the moment he let his frustration show he'd lose the rapport he'd built with Michael. He couldn't afford to do that, so he needed to step back. To ignore. And to hope.

He sketched in his nose, lips, the shape of his eyes.

The news came on the radio, and the newscaster started talking about the FBI investigation into the mall attack. Jed put down the pad and stood up. It seemed unbelievable that it had only been two days since the shooting. Two days since the awful events that had changed their lives forever. He went over to the radio to turn it down, because he didn't want Michael to be reminded of that bad stuff, but he did want to hear what the media had to say. There was no satellite or cable at the cabin. Just a TV hooked up to a DVD player, and the internet.

Vivi came up beside him, arms crossed over her chest, biting her bottom lip, as she listened in too.

"...an unofficial source today leaked the fact that the weapons used during the mall attack were issued by the Syrian government to its armed forces..."

A cold sweat broke out on his brow.

"What does that mean?" Vivi whispered at him urgently. "The Syrian government attacked the Minneapolis Mall?"

"Not necessarily." But that would be the general consensus. "A lot of government troops defected to the opposition at the start of the conflict, and they would have taken what weapons they could with them." But Abdullah was Syrian Republican Guard. If the media discovered that, there would be a frenzy demanding action.

She pressed closer to his side, both of them huddling over the kitchen counter where the radio sat. He tried not to be aware of the shape of her beside him, the points of contact. He wasn't a teenager with hormones to match. Theoretically he had some control.

Yup. Not.

"…Funerals for the dead are due to begin tomorrow, and a memorial service will be held for all the victims…People still in hospital…Missing woman and child…Hunt continues for a mystery female terrorist…"

Jed placed a finger on her lips before she repeated that information out loud. Her irises dilated, and a jolt of heat shot through him. He'd never told her one of the tangos was female. He didn't want Michael influenced. He dropped his hand when it was clear she'd gotten the message and ignored the fact his finger felt like it had been branded.

"…Rumors suggest President Hague might attend the memorial service…White House officials say no details have been finalized…"

"I used to work in the White House many years ago," Vivi said contemplatively. "That's where I met Michael's father."

A tingle of unease crawled down his spine. "Your ex works in the White House?"

She pulled a face. "No. The Pentagon." She put her hand to her head as if she had a headache. "He coordinates military attaché appointments around the world."

The slight dread turned into a rush of ice that swept over Jed's body. "Your ex works for the Defense Intelligence Agency, and you didn't tell me?"

The expression on her face was misery stacked with guilt. "I know I should have, but I didn't think it mattered when we were at the safe house and then after the attack." She pursed her lips for a moment. "I forgot for a while."

DIA? *Holy shit.* The woman had probably just sunk his career without even knowing it.

"...the search continues for Veronica Vincent and her son, Michael, who were abducted from federal protective custody yesterday and are feared dead..."

Fuck. Fuck. Fuck!

He jammed his hand through his short hair. "Should we call him? Inform him you're safe?"

Icy distance entered her entire demeanor—expression, posture, voice. "I called him when we were at the hospital after the attack." Even though she held herself rigidly under control, Jed spotted the sheen of tears in her eyes. "He never called back. Am I really supposed to think he gives a damn about us now?"

Jed held onto his anger for half a second and then dragged her against him, not understanding how much what she thought of him mattered until she relaxed in his arms. *Damn.* Her ex was a prick. He squeezed her so hard it had to hurt, but he didn't let go. Her hair was soft against his lips. The scent of her shampoo fragrant and sweet. Then he looked up and froze.

He shifted them both slightly and leaned down to whisper in her ear. "*Look.* Look at what Michael is doing..."

CHAPTER FIFTEEN

MICHAEL DREW WITH absolute determined concentration. He'd been at it for hours.

Vivi stood as if to go to him, but Jed caught her arm.

"He needs to eat." She tried to pull away, but he held onto her as gently as possibly.

"Put a sandwich and a drink beside him. I'll do it." He stood and went to the fridge. She followed.

Her eyes narrowed. "He also needs to rest."

"He needs this more."

Protectiveness flared. "You do, you mean."

He sighed. Patient. "We all do, remember?"

She flinched and pulled away. He let her go, wishing he could recapture some of that earlier connection and trust, but her child was under pressure, and she was worried about him. Jed was fine with that. But their opinions on what was best for Michael differed. He thought Michael needed to get this out of his system and dammit, yes, Jed needed to find a way to save a career that was probably already shot. If that made him an asshole, he was a fucking asshole. Nothing new there.

Defense Intelligence Agency. Shit. Why couldn't the guy be a used car salesman?

It didn't matter. Even if he'd known, he wouldn't have done anything differently, except maybe tell Frazer what was going on.

After another thirty minutes, Jed couldn't take sitting still any longer. He left the cabin, checking the perimeter for footprints in an effort to work off some of his energy. He didn't know what was wrong with him, but his skin felt itchy, and he couldn't settle. Maybe the fact he was on the verge of a massive breakthrough with the case? He called his brother Liam, the police chief, who'd agreed to keep an eye out for any strangers coming into town and do regular drive-bys of all the local routes, running vehicle checks on anything suspicious. Nothing untoward as yet.

When he got back to the cabin, Michael was still drawing, Vivi was still pacing, and he was still on edge.

He waited.

And waited.

Every forty minutes or so, Michael would set aside a finished drawing, and now Jed had a bunch of images, some of which touched him unexpectedly. The first one was of him holding Vivi in his arms earlier in the kitchen. Something about the moment had motivated the kid to pick up the pencil and draw. Jed didn't know what it was, but he was damn glad. The picture was so skillfully drawn, Jed could see all the emotions he was trying to hide as he tucked Vivi against his chest. Anxiety, anger, lust.

She remained silent as he slipped the drawing into the back of his own art pad.

His father was next, the likeness so incredible, the image so detailed Jed wouldn't have believed the phenomena if he wasn't witnessing it with his own eyes. His dad had a scar on his left eyebrow and a tiny mole on his nose. The kid had drawn both perfectly. To see these drawings come from an eight-year-old's pencil was a little unnerving, like the kid had been possessed by Picasso or Michael Angelo with a camera-like memory. No wonder Vivi was convinced his talent was savant-like.

"Who's this?" Jed asked Vivi, holding up an image of a broad-faced black man.

"The nurse from the hospital." She avoided looking at the likenesses of Dr. Hinkle and both marshals.

"Michael really is incredibly talented."

"I know." Those navy blue eyes of hers held a seriousness now. A reserve. He knew he'd put it there.

"I'm sorry for being angry about your ex, earlier. I had no right." He should have found out for himself on day one, but he'd been too busy chasing his tail.

A brief frown crinkled her brow. "I should have told you."

He stilled and really looked at her. "When we left the safe house I gave you the chance to go to him for help. Why didn't you?" He took a step closer, a subtle sort of anger stirring inside him, one he was familiar with. One that came from the thought of people hurting others just because they could. "Did he hit you too?" DIA or not he'd put his fist in the man's face if he'd touched her.

She shook her head. "He never lifted a finger against me." The spark in her eyes suggested he wouldn't dare. "But he mocked and belittled me, often in front of others. It seems like such a small thing looking back on it, but it corroded everything I thought we had together." She paused, clearly weighing her words. "Have you ever had a relationship that turned so sour that every memory you have is tainted by what happened at the end?"

Angela. "Yeah."

234

"It's as if the fact we ever loved one another has been buried beneath a mountain of pain. I can't forgive him for what he did to Michael, or to *me*." Her voice cracked. Her fingers gripped her arms so tight the knuckles shone white. "I don't want anything to do with him ever again."

"Not even to save yourselves from terrorists?"

She flicked a look at him, and her smile grew sad. "I actually trust you more than I'd trust David to keep us safe."

Every bit of anger or resentment he might have harbored evaporated. Trust was a big thing for Vivi, and this was the biggest endorsement of faith she could give him. He had to do his best not to screw it up.

She crossed the room and put a log on the fire.

Killion called, and Jed took it into the bedroom to answer.

"How's the vacation?"

"Sipping mai tai's on the beach. Saw the folks. Did some snowshoeing." Jed stared out the window, examining the gloom for any activity. "How's the investigation going?"

"It's a nightmare. Presidential visit is making all the bosses figure out how to cover their asses about why we haven't caught the female tango yet." He sounded like he hadn't slept in days.

"Why haven't you caught her? Thumbscrews not working?"

"Heh. Believe me I wouldn't mind turning a few screws on our friend in detention, but we're playing by the book, fucking feds."

"Goddamn Geneva Convention."

"Pity the asshole terrorists don't sign up. The other guy in ICU died."

"Bastard."

Killion's laughter was strained. "No kidding."

"What did your guy from MI6 tell you?"

"He was a she."

"Sweet and curvy?"

"As a rattlesnake."

Jed waited.

"MI6 had a file on one of the guys from the safe house. Guy was a merc."

"What?" That was not what he'd been expecting to hear.

"A German called Klaus Schmidt."

What was a mercenary doing attacking a US Marshal safe house? "And the others?"

"With the exception of Klaus, the others all originate from Arab countries, although IDs aren't conclusive for all of them."

Had Klaus been a convert, or had he just enjoyed killing people? Maybe he'd been doing a favor for a jihadist buddy, but that's not how they usually operated. "Any luck finding the one who got away?"

"Vanished without a trace. They seem to be a bunch of highly-trained professionals. If you hadn't found Michael Vincent at the hotel when you did, Abdullah would have killed the boy and walked away without a qualm. Something tells me you fucked up their plans big time when you caught him."

"I live to serve."

Killion grunted. "Doesn't get me any closer to figuring out who was behind this attack. VP is putting pressure on the president to start an offensive against Syria."

The vice president did not support President Hague's no-war-policy. Shit. This thing was already escalating, and they didn't even know for sure who was responsible yet.

Jed had another question he wanted to ask Killion. "Did you contact Vivi's ex?"

The silence at the end of the line crackled with sudden hyper-awareness.

"I spoke to him."

"Had he heard from them?"

"Not a dicky bird."

"Did you believe him?"

Killion didn't answer him directly. "I have to go. McKenzie is yelling at one of the marshals about whose fault the safe house shooting was…oh, and the marshal just tried to deck his ass."

"I would have liked to see that."

"I suspect you have much prettier things to look at." He hung up.

Damn. What did that mean? Did he know Vivi was here? The guy was fishing. Maybe. Fuck.

Jed headed back into the living room. Michael was still drawing. He appeared to be working backward through time, oblivious to Jed and his mother, and everything except the images that poured from his pencil.

Vivi slipped a banana into her son's hand, and he started eating without even looking up.

"He needs to rest," she said quietly, but insistently after another hour.

"It's only ten PM." Jed knew he had to let the kid sleep, no matter how desperately he needed to not stem the flow of information pouring out of his brain. "Let him finish the next one, then see how he is." He'd beg if he had to. "We need this information, Vivi. He might hold the key to averting a full scale war."

The blood drained from her face at that. "Fine, but if he doesn't rest he won't be able to get up in the morning, let alone draw anything."

Jed held onto his patience. She knew Michael better than anyone and was trying. He was already pushing her way past her comfort zone.

Funny that she did the same for him, but in a totally different way. He shifted, finally recognizing the irritable itch for what it was. Unabated sexual frustration. He still wanted her. A wave of anger rose inside him. Anger at himself. This wasn't the type of federal agent he wanted to be. He wanted to be honorable and focused. The weakness reminded him of Angela and what that mistake may have cost him.

Suck it up.

He was stuck here until they finished this and that was that. But it was torture to be near her, because he couldn't stop remembering the softness of her lips, or imagining those mile-long legs wrapped around his hips—

He blew out a breath and forced himself to stare at his computer screen. No more thinking about sex. No more remembering those kisses or her explosive orgasm. Better tell the snow not to fall while he was at it.

"As soon as he starts drawing someone you can't identify, I'll need to tell my boss you guys are alive and share the images with him."

Her expression grew somber, but she nodded. Their whereabouts might be compromised. He'd have to bring in more security, at least on the perimeter.

"With any luck this will be over soon and you can go home," he reminded her.

Her head shot up, and she met his gaze. Then she looked

away, hiding whatever thoughts had gone through her mind.

He couldn't read her anymore. He thought he could, but the more time he spent with her, the more she backed away—as if she was starting to trust him less, rather than more.

It bruised his pride, which was pretty dumb.

He rubbed his chin, deciding he needed to shave before he sprouted a full beard. So he grabbed a quick shower, glad of the excuse to avoid the woman he was growing more and more attached to.

Despite her words she wasn't the sort to have a quick fling, and he didn't have the sort of job that was a good fit for a family—although others did it, plenty of agents he knew had full family lives.

Dammit, he *liked* the bachelor lifestyle.

Except, for the first time in years, he couldn't think of a single reason why.

———————————

AN HOUR LATER, showered, shaved, and still pacing, Jed had to concede the little guy was toast. Michael's chin rested on the table, and his eyes drooped as his pencil made smaller and smaller scores on the paper. But he'd done several sketches of people Vivi couldn't identify, and Jed figured they were finally getting somewhere. Jed watched as Michael's eyelids closed and the pencil lay flat. Vivi immediately stood, ever the vigilant mother, but Jed was there before her. He eased the kid out of the hard-backed chair and into his arms. A few hours' sleep and hopefully the kid would start up where he'd left off.

"I can do that." Vivi offered.

The self-sufficient look in her eyes tied him in knots. "Did no one *ever* help you with Michael before?"

Her mouth fell open, and then her face crumpled.

Shit. "I didn't mean to—"

She held up her hand. "No. No, I'm just tired. I am grateful for the help." She wiped rapidly at her cheeks, her defenses down, and he could see all the way to her soul. "But the answer is no. No one ever helped. No one. Ever. So seeing you with Michael makes me realize how much he missed out on not having a father to…to do all that other stuff."

To love him, she'd been going to say.

Jed's throat hurt from the emotions that he had to choke back. That a man had walked out on this woman and this child made him want to hurt someone, preferably her poor excuse for a human being ex at the DIA. It took him a moment to find his voice, and when he did, it was low and grim.

"It was his loss, Vivi. Not yours, remember that. Not all men are assholes." And then he walked away, feeling like it was his loss too, because this woman and child weren't his, they could never be his. He just had to make sure they survived long enough to go back to their own lives, which were thousands of miles from his.

ELAN HAD RENTED snowshoes from the man who ran the motel where he was staying. His people had discovered the locations of the properties owned by the Brennan's, but not a lot else about the family. No social media, no press except that regarding their jobs. A website showcasing the cabins and facilities, but not the specific locations. They were more cautious than most modern Americans. He'd checked out several of the cabins and found that while a few were empty, others were occupied by hunters and families. He'd had to watch them for several hours to be sure the redhead wasn't there.

It was so cold his fingers were stiff and uncooperative. Not that a little discomfort mattered, but he didn't want his abilities compromised. He'd gone back to the motel for a hot shower and something warm to eat before venturing out again. Three more places to check before staking out the parents' cabin and that of the brother. He'd left this particular property until after dark, even though he was going to have to cover a lot of rough ground on foot to get eyes on it. It was isolated and remote. Hard to get close to without obviously trespassing, situated on a little island—one road in, one road out, a semi-frozen lake protecting the rest of the approach.

He parked the truck near woods that flanked the property from the west. The two mile hike on snowshoes felt more like ten in the deep powder, and his muscles burned. Even the rifle slung across his back weighed heavy. Considering his training it was pitiful, but they didn't get these bitter temperatures where he was from. Snow occasionally, but not this ravenous cold that hurt when it touched flesh. He was getting old.

Thankfully, the snow made everything bright enough to see where he was going without the risk of breaking his neck. He came to the last rise before he got a clear view of the big log cabin surrounded by trees and approached cautiously. There were lights on, and smoke billowed out of the chimney. He looked through the scope of his rifle, but the blinds and curtains were all drawn. The hairs on the back of his neck rose.

Would you really worry about closing the blinds when you were in a place this remote?

But Brennan was a federal agent. He might not like to sit around as exposed as a big, bare ass in a pair of police headlights.

It was entirely possible Brennan was holed up here alone, taking a break while the rest of the world went to hell. Didn't seem likely though.

Elan couldn't see the vehicle from this angle—might not be Brennan at all. He might be staying with his parents, hell, he might be in Canada by now. Elan was going to have to get closer. Much closer. He ducked down behind the ridge and checked his pistol before he trudged back through the snow. The sweat started to cool on his back and made shivers wrack his body. This whole idea had seemed like such a sure-fire plan two months ago. Now he was hunting children for the sake of his country.

He placed his feet carefully in the snow, unable to be completely quiet with the need for haste nipping at his heels. The silent quality of the woods spoke to him. There was a feel to this world that reminded him of the stakes—survival, pure and simple. It didn't get more elemental than that. The old Robert Frost poem echoed in his head. He too had a long way to go before he could rest.

It took another twenty minutes, fighting his way through thick brush and briars that edged the lake. The lake was crusted by thin ice, not strong enough to hold his weight. It made the cottage the perfect defensive position from a ground attack. One way in. One way out.

He rested for a moment and caught his breath, lungs and muscles burning from the exertion. The slight pain felt good. It made him feel alive. Somehow more worthy of the prey.

A low, rumbling noise had him freezing in place. His eyes

searched the dark, and he made out the faint outline of a dark colored vehicle half hidden in the shadows of the trees. Cop car. Elan smiled.

He'd come to the right place.

———————————

SINCE SHE'D FIRST met Jed Brennan her body had been slowly waking up from a long sleep. It was making her short-tempered and angry at herself that she couldn't ask for what she wanted—a chance to make love with a man she trusted. To recover some of her femininity. To give him back what he'd given her that morning. Even just once.

She stood in the shower, warm water cascading over her. She washed her poor abused feet, pleased they were starting to heal. She imagined it was his hands slipping down her body in a soapy glide. His big, strong hands cupping the weight of her breasts, pinching her nipples into taut nubs, sliding lower, over her navel, between her legs to hot, dark, secret places that wanted him so badly. She squeezed her thighs together, and her legs trembled as she remembered what he'd made her feel that morning. It had been so long she'd almost forgotten she had needs and desires only a man could meet.

There had been a time when she'd been confident of herself in bed. Before. Before Michael had needed every scrap of energy and concentration. Before her husband had turned on her and made her feel like a failure as a woman.

She'd withdrawn into such a pathetic ball of hurt she was almost ashamed to think about it. The control she'd let her ex have over her self-worth was staggering. She touched herself then, and her head dropped back, her dark hair plastered to the tile. Her finger slid over herself and inside and it felt wonderful, but it wasn't enough. She wanted a man. She wanted Jed.

She gritted her teeth in frustration. Her son was in danger, and she wanted someone to screw her? What sort of mother did that make her?

Flawed. Weak. Needy. Like the rest of the human race.

The events of this week had obliterated her nice, safe, little world. It had reminded her about a place that existed outside school schedules and specialists' appointments, outside working her butt off to make ends meet. Surviving had become paramount, blowing aside all the reasons and fears she usually had about opening up to a man, about trusting one. Heck, there was now a handgun in her bedside drawer 'just in case'—life didn't get any more surreal than that. So she shouldn't feel guilty for thinking about sex. It was perfectly normal.

It might be the only normal thing about her life right now.

Everything else went against human nature. Blood. Death. Murder. But wanting to feel Jed Brennan's weight pressing her into the mattress, pushing between her legs, was normal and healthy and OK. It was OK.

The water started to cool so she turned off the faucet. Still aching and frustrated and hungry for a man who was determined not to get involved with a woman he was 'protecting'. She climbed out of the shower, dried off, and towel dried her hair. Then she wrapped a fresh towel around her torso and walked out of the bathroom, steam billowing in her wake.

Jed stood in the shadows placing a glass of wine on the nightstand.

"You forgot your… I thought you might like…" He trailed off as he looked up and seemed to become aware she was only wearing a towel.

The light from the bathroom was enough to show his eyes darkening with desire. He wanted her. Even though he'd held her at arm's length since that morning, he wanted her. Even though he'd said he wouldn't get involved. He wanted her. And she wanted him.

Was that selfish? Probably. But their time together was coming to an end.

He started to back out of the room, so Vivi made a decision and let the towel drop.

His jaw clenched. Lust shone clearly in his eyes, almost violently, but he was determined to resist her, and he didn't move from the spot. Still trying to be noble. Still trying not to take advantage of her. Well, she intended to take advantage of him. She wanted to be a woman again. To make love. Have sex.

She didn't need a lifelong commitment, just mutual respect and a whole lot of like.

She walked toward him, and his eyes glittered darkly as he tilted his head to one side, clearly disappointed in her. Because she'd tempted him, and she intended to take it further than temptation, much further, and he knew it.

Her palms found heated muscle through the warm cotton of his shirt, and she smoothed her hands up his abs, over his pecs, and across the broad shoulders that did funny things to her insides when she looked at them.

She reached up on tip-toe and pressed a kiss beside his mouth. "I don't need forever."

"You deserve more than a quick fling." His voice was

rough. He hadn't touched her yet, but she could feel the strain in his body as he fought to hold back.

She reached up further, dragged her teeth over the lobe of his ear. Took a chance. "It might be the only opportunity we get."

He shuddered, then put both hands firmly on her hips. She thought he was going to push her away, but instead his fingers dug in, and he pulled her against him. The length of him shockingly hard against her stomach. Oh, yes. He definitely wanted her. She moved closer. God, she had missed this. It had been years since she'd had sex and was almost embarrassed by how much she wanted to jump this man. His mouth grazed her neck, and she rubbed her aching breasts against his chest.

He groaned and turned them both around so her back was pressed against the door, and she was trapped in his arms. He dipped his head and licked his way down to one nipple, drawing the sensitized bead into his mouth and making pleasure flick along her nerve endings. His other hand slid lower, and he dragged her thigh around his hip and leaned against her hot, wet core, sending sensation shooting through her like sparks.

"It's been so long. I want to feel you inside me." She ran her hands over solid flesh. She found the top button of his shirt and deftly undid it, revealing a sprinkling of dark hair. She undid the next, and the next. His body was beautiful, muscles defined and perfect. He had a newly healed scar and several old ones, but they didn't bother her—they reminded her of what he did every day of his life. Fought to protect people.

The bravery thing was definitely a turn on. The chivalry

thing too.

It was possible he was going to look even better naked than dressed, which was saying something. And she wanted to see him. She wanted him at her mercy if only for twenty minutes of stolen fun, which was probably all they'd manage before the self-recriminations kicked in.

He jerked the shirt out of his waistband, tried to pull it off and was impeded by his shoulder holster. He growled in frustration, and she helped him ease the harness off his shoulders. He placed the gun on the nightstand, and she knew what it represented. She also knew if she let him think about it for too long, he'd change his mind. He closed his eyes and breathed heavily. No longer watching her or kissing her.

Second thoughts.

No doubt he was about to give her the spiel about not crossing that line between protecting her and taking advantage of her. Like she wasn't the one standing here naked.

So she touched him through the denim of his jeans. His hips moved against her fingers as if he couldn't control his body, and that's what she wanted. No thinking it through. No careful contemplation. Hot, wild sex. They were both unattached adults. She wasn't about to ask him for anything more than this.

She throbbed. This is what happened when you went four years without a man and suddenly craved one. She wanted him inside her. She didn't want to be scared anymore, she wanted to feel alive. She unsnapped the button of his jeans, then drew the zipper carefully down, freeing him from his pants. He sprang free into her hand, and she touched the silky, smooth skin stretched taut over rigid flesh. He shook, and it almost made her laugh to think she might have seduced him.

She didn't know the first thing about seduction, but she was pretty sure being naked and willing stacked the cards in her favor.

She wanted to give him pleasure, maybe release some of the tension that had swirled around them for days, and she wanted to get rid of the terrible craving she had for the man. She scraped a finger down his abdomen, watching his body twitch as he continued to keep his eyes closed, jaw clenched so tight it looked like it might break. She went down on her knees before him and used her mouth. He groaned and banged his head sharply against the door. She released him. "Do you want me to stop?"

"Yes. No." He sounded almost pained, but he could figure it out while she played. She'd forgotten the joy of giving pleasure. The give and take of good sex.

His hands sank into her hair, and then the grip changed, holding her just so as he thrust himself into her mouth. Then he pulled away to kick his jeans free. He looked wonderfully aroused and her anticipation grew.

He stared at her then, a predatory stare that made her shiver. Then he bent down to grab something out of his back jeans' pocket and pushed her back onto the mattress, not giving her time to recover as his mouth settled over her wet core. Spirals of pleasure lashed through her, and she grabbed the sheets to stop from writhing uncontrollably. He pushed one thigh high, his tongue inside her, lapping her and then sinking deep back inside her. The rhythm made her rotate her hips and gasp out his name.

"More," she whispered, because Michael was downstairs asleep, and she couldn't scream.

He pushed her other thigh up, spreading her knees wide

and opening her to his gaze. The light in his eyes gleamed. "You are so beautiful."

She didn't care whether she was beautiful or not. She just wanted him inside her. She heard the crinkle of foil and a rip, then watched him slide the condom over his thick length. Did he know he was turning her on? Making her wet, making her throb?

His eyes said he did.

She started to lower her legs, but he caught both knees and spread them wider. "I did not intend to have sex with you, Vivi. I need you to know that."

She bit her lip. Nodded.

"And if I had thought of making love to you, it would have been a slow, romantic seduction when all this other shit was over." His eyes burned into hers. He was angry. She'd taken away some of his choices, and he wanted to punish her.

"I don't need romance. And I don't want slow." She reared up and caught his lips with hers before sinking back to the mattress. "I just want you." And it was true, she realized. It wasn't just that she wanted to get off. If Jed Brennan hadn't been here, if she hadn't started to fall for the dark, good looks and protective demeanor, she wouldn't be feeling this desperate for sex.

She was falling for him, and that realization made her freeze.

Don't fall for anyone.

He positioned himself against her opening, but must have sensed her hesitation. He locked his hand in her hair, raising her head so she met his gaze. "Are you sure about this?" He scraped the side of his chin against her cheek in an intimate caress.

She shuddered in reaction. He felt so good. Warm, strong,

beautiful. She reached up and touched his bottom lip, so soft and full, so gentle and demanding.

She was a quivering bundle of needy desperation. It wasn't pretty. "I'm very sure."

He thrust forward, working himself inside her slowly, an inch at a time, in and out, easing into her flesh and reminding her body how good it felt to be full and squirming. Finally he buried himself to the hilt and rested his head against hers for a moment. "You feel amazing." He held her thighs wide and pressed deep inside her, pulling out almost all the way before sliding back home. Over and over again. Despite her words, he was taking it slowly, agonizingly slow. *Oh my God*. It had been so long, and she was so aroused that a few deep thrusts were all it took for her to shatter into a million pieces. He never changed his rhythm, but now there was a satisfied smile on his face as the seriousness with which they'd begun this began to melt away.

He pulled out and moved her up the bed, came back between her legs and put her knees over his shoulders.

"Did I tell you I loved your shoulders?" she asked on a quiet breath.

"Did I tell you I loved your legs?" He lapped her with his tongue, driving her back up again.

She'd never come twice in one go before, but damned if she wasn't willing to give it a try.

"The taste of you makes me insane."

When she was panting, he pushed her knees against her chest and entered her again, the angle different, the penetration deeper. She gasped as he hit what had to be the mysterious g-spot—she'd always wondered where it was. Jed had found it with unerring accuracy.

"Hard and fast?"

She was about to explode. "Yes."

Instead, he eased her knees down and kissed her, his tongue driving her out of her mind while he filled her with delicious, hard strokes. And then he started to slam into her and she thrust back, hands slipping on his taut, slick skin. She gripped his ass, feet straining against the mattress as she pulled him to her and clung to his movements, not letting him pull out. The friction, the wildness and ferocity, set light to every nerve in her body, and she exploded around him, her inner muscles clenching so strongly it was like nothing she remembered. She felt his orgasm rocket through him, and it triggered another spasm that tore through her and made her tremble so hard they both shook.

They lay hot and sweaty and out of breath while their hearts pounded.

Jed reared up, sending flickers of sensation sparking through her again. He smoothed the hair back from her brow, his dark brown eyes serious.

"It's OK." She caught his wrists and gave him a sad smile. "I don't expect anything from you. I just needed—"

"Shut up." He pressed inside her again. She shut up, and he rewarded her with another hard thrust.

She groaned. "I thought you came."

"I did. You're not the only one who hasn't had sex in a long time."

She didn't think she could bear to feel any more pleasure, and yet he kept the slow relentless pace and her body, so lax and fluid one moment, was straining against his the next, and pretending everything was going to be OK. Pretending this wasn't extraordinary and he wasn't special. Pretending she'd be able to walk away without her heart breaking.

CHAPTER SIXTEEN

PILAH WOKE AND shifted uncomfortably in the hospital chair. Her back hurt. Fatigue dragged at her eyelids. It was dark except for the icy-blue glow of the machines. The constant beep of the heart monitor was like a form of Chinese water torture after listening to it for hours. But something was different. Something had changed. Slowly she became aware that the body under the blankets was stiff with tension. She lifted her gaze and met the wide-open eyes of William Green.

Despite her lack of hijab, recognition flared as his eyes met hers. He reached for the emergency call button, and she seized his hand. He fought hard, writhing in the bed, and she was terrified he was going to pull out some of his tubes. Forcing his hand down to the mattress, she leaned on his arm, grabbed her bag, and searched blindly through the depths. Something rattled, and her fingers chased it, coming up with the pills the shadow-man had given her. William fought harder against her hold. Desperate, she straddled his body and put her knees on his upper arms, weight on his chest, pinning him down. The heartbeat on the machine had gone through the roof and her own pulse matched the crazy rhythm. She used her teeth on the lid of the container to rip open the bottle. She snatched up a tablet, losing a couple in the bed. Didn't matter. She needed him unconscious before any of the staff came to investigate.

She grabbed his jaw, but he seemed to understand what she wanted to do and clamped his mouth shut. Frustrated, she pinched his nostrils closed until he was forced to open his mouth for breath, and she shoved the tablet in. She struggled with both hands, clamping his mouth shut, using all her strength as he bucked beneath her. The monitor was going nuts, as if his heart was about to explode.

Don't die!

Sargon and the shadow-man would not be happy with her if she killed him and ruined all their plans.

Twenty seconds later his muscles grew lax beneath her. She heard footsteps and quickly climbed off him, straightened the sheets, finding two stray tablets and stuffing them into the bottle which she tucked into her pocket. She straightened her hair and sat back down just as the nurse entered.

"You're still here?"

Pilah nodded. "I fell asleep. He seemed to be dreaming a minute ago. I held his hand until he was calm again."

The nurse checked the monitor. "It's a good thing you were here then. Oh, he's pulled out his cannula." She tut-tutted and replaced the tubing and then turned to her. "You should go home for a few hours." She patted her arm. "I'll call if there's any change. He's lucky to have you."

She picked up her coat and bag, blew out a deep breath, hoping the nurse didn't notice she was sweating. Her footsteps echoed off the walls of the corridor, and Pilah couldn't get out of there fast enough. Part of her wished she could swallow all those pills and put herself out of her misery. But being a coward wasn't part of her personality. She'd gone too far to back out now. As long as the shadow-man saved her babies, she was in this until the end.

———————

ELAN CREPT FORWARD in the shadows, pistol in his left hand, suppressor fitted to the barrel. He'd removed his snowshoes and left them, and the rifle, hidden beneath a bush around the bend of the road just out of sight.

He circled into the forest and then approached the cop car from the rear, using the trees for cover. The engine was running, exhaust fumes creating a cloud of fog that cloaked him.

The vehicle was an SUV. Elan could just make out the profile of someone in the front seat. If it weren't for the narrow bridge he had to cross in full view, he would have let this person live, but with the snow brightening the night, he couldn't risk it. Adrenaline flowed through his blood, but it wasn't enough to make him crave the kill the way he had as a younger man. Maybe because these people weren't the enemy—they were collateral damage in a war that never let up.

He walked up to the driver's side door and shot through the metal. A cry of pain came from inside. Elan opened the door and put another two bullets in the man's brain, and the guy slumped to the side. Dead.

Elan's shoulders sagged as he examined the clean-shaven jaw and brown hair now matted with blood. A young face. A handsome face.

Another martyr for the cause.

A wedding ring encircled the third finger of the man's left hand, glinting in the glow of the onboard computer. More lives ruined. Elan pressed his lips together. Heaviness filled his chest. He was tired of this. This would be his last job, although perhaps the most important.

Did he make a difference? *Yes.*

But his enemies would never stop their persecution, and so he and his kind could never rest either. He reminded himself of his family back home. His mother and grandmother, sister and their families. Their safety was worth every sacrifice. His people knew the price of failure. They knew the cost of waiting for the rest of the world to come to their aid.

Never again.

Never again.

Quietly, he shut the car door and walked swiftly up the road, over the bridge veering around the back of the log cabin. There was a loud rustle from the woods. Elan swung toward it—deer, rabbit, wolf? As long as it left him alone he would leave it alone.

He crept along the side of the building, going slowly and silently now. The lock on the door to the basement was solidly made, but Elan was more than capable of breaking and entering. He took a kit out of his back pocket and inserted the metal picks. He worked carefully and diligently, the rustling nearby masking the dull noise of the metal against metal grind. It took longer than usual, because his fingers were stiff with cold. He blew on them and tried again, finally hearing the telltale snick of the lock opening.

He raised his pistol and inched inside. Although the area was dark as charcoal, there was a feeling of open space he hadn't expected. He closed the door silently behind him and risked using his flashlight. Massive beams stretched across a room that was full of lumber and kayaks and life jackets and outdoor furniture. The place was immaculate and smelled like freshly cut wood.

Behind the stairs was a washer and the furnace. Stowing

his appreciation, he steeled himself for the task ahead. Time to end this before the boy reduced their efforts to nothing but the wishful thinking of mad men.

The fuse box was on the wall. He pulled night vision goggles out of one of his pockets and slipped them over his head. Then he flipped the breaker.

JED LAY IN the darkness staring at the ceiling. Vivi lay beside him, eyes closed, breath slowing and becoming more regular.

What the hell had he just done? *Twice*?

Getting involved with a witness was absolutely a no-no. Sure, it had been blow-his-head-off spectacular, but it was still a massive error in judgment. Taking it this far was a sackable offense. Didn't matter that she'd initiated it. The fact that she'd initiated it had shocked the bejesus out of him because he knew she didn't treat sex lightly, no matter what she said.

And he was too busy to get involved with a woman like Vivi who was a single mom for God's sake—it wasn't just her happiness he was screwing around with, it was her son's too, and no way did he want to see either of them hurt. He hunted serial killers for a living. It was not the sort of nine-to-five job women wanted in the men they dated. It was not the sort of realities mothers wanted in their homes.

And what the fuck?—now he was thinking about a *relationship*?

They were stuck in the middle of nowhere hiding out from terrorists, and he was mentally picturing flowers on the table and a woman greeting him at the door after a long day at work?

Idiot.

Juxtaposed against his stark, stale, barren life, the idea held a weird sort of mental appeal. To have something like his parents had. To find the sort of relationship that lasted beyond a few weeks of dinners and dates and mediocre sex. What he and Mia might have had if her life hadn't been cut so brutally short. Something built on a solid foundation of trust and support and slowly, over time, growing into that bone-deep love that seemed so prevalent in movies, but so rare in real life. He hadn't thought he'd ever feel this way again, but it was happening, and he had to figure out a way to make it stop before they all got hurt.

Bobby's unsmiling face came into his head and he groaned.

No one lived forever…

He did not need another complication, even though he was attracted to every aspect of Vivi, from her brains, to her body, to her love and devotion to her son. Why anyone wouldn't love the boy was beyond him. Michael was a great kid. His father was an asshole. How the guy let someone as incredible as her slip through his fingers was beyond Jed. If he ever put a wedding ring on a woman, he'd move Heaven and Earth to keep her happy and keep her his.

But that wasn't what the future held for him.

He loved his job—assuming he still had a job when this was all over—he made a difference and got killers off the street. And she lived in *Fargo*. Christ. He gritted his teeth.

He should be thinking about terrorists. He should be downstairs photographing and emailing those images. As soon as Frazer knew she and Michael were alive, they'd be sent into protective custody. The fact he didn't want that was already affecting the case.

Suddenly the bathroom light went out. Shit. The fuse must have blown again.

He eased away from Vivi's seductive heat, already missing it and knowing he couldn't afford to make this particular mistake again. Forget being worried *she* might get emotionally attached. He was neck-deep in fucking emotional attachment. He was supposed to be making the world safe for them and others, not chilling out, having sex with a beautiful woman. He groped around on the floor and found his jeans, pulled them on. He needed to fix the breaker and start sending the images to Frazer so they could see if any of the people Michael had drawn were involved in the attack.

He pulled on his shirt, then heard a noise and froze. *That* was the basement door.

Had Michael woken up and gone exploring?

Instinct told him it wasn't Michael, and his pulse ramped up. Shit on a stick.

Silently, he grabbed his SIG off the bedside table. Palmed his cell and texted his brother to get over here fast, that someone was in the house. If he was wrong, he'd deal with the ribbing. Better than ending up dead.

It could be Jed's father, although the old man knew better than to turn up in the dark without warning him first. He was the one who'd taught Jed to shoot first, ask questions later. The FBI had spent weeks beating that out of him.

Adrenaline surged through Jed's bloodstream, and he slid quietly across the floor, grateful for the solid craftsmanship of the cabin so that the floorboards didn't creak beneath his shifting weight. He edged onto the landing and peered over the railing to the ground below. The fire burned low in the grate, casting a weak, orange flicker over the room.

He listened hard, but there wasn't even the hum of the refrigerator. After a few long silent seconds, he detected the whisper of feet over carpet, and the shifting of a shadow in the darkness beneath him—a shadow too large to be an eight-year-old boy.

Was there only one of them?

There was no time to worry about it. Michael was down there, alone, vulnerable. All it would take was one bullet. One bullet. He should have been guarding the kid rather than fucking the mother. Goddamn it.

Fury fueled him. He didn't bother with the stairs, he vaulted the rails and landed hard on top of the dense darkness. He aimed for the head with his feet and was pretty sure he connected from the grunt of pain he was rewarded with before the shadow fell to the floor, skull smashing into the kitchen island. Something spun across the floor. The sonofabitch's pistol.

Good. He kicked at the almost indistinguishable figure a split second before the guy launched himself at him. His SIG went flying out of his hand. Dammit. Jed found himself forced back by a series of fast blows to the face and body. He got his brain in the game and remembered his training a moment before a knife flashed toward his gut.

He jumped back just in time. He grabbed a cushion off the sofa and used it to go after the guy's knife hand. He forced him up against the bottom of the stairs, knocking aside a table and lamp, slamming the guy's wrist against the wall as he jammed one elbow into the man's throat and at the same time drove his knee into the guy's balls. It was a street-fighting move, but his honor was not the object here. Survival was.

The assailant dropped the knife and Jed kicked it away.

The man was hurting, probably from the blow to the head, which was pouring so much blood Jed could see it in the firelight.

Jed was a third dan black belt in Taekwondo, but he had a horrible feeling this guy was better. Without that head injury affecting the guy's vision and reflexes, Jed would probably already be dead. Then Michael. Then Vivi.

The realization renewed the focus of Jed's attack. This wasn't over yet. Jed went after the guy's weak spots, kidneys, knees, throat, eyes.

The guy tried to dance out of reach. He was breathing heavily, a flat, unemotional light reflected in his eyes from the glow of the wood stove. His expression was implacable. A man used to killing. There would be no mercy shown just because his target was a small boy.

"You're under arrest, asshole."

The man startled him with a laugh as he wrenched out of his hold.

"I don't think so." An accent but a faint one. So American-ized Jed couldn't place it. The guy attacked again, driving him back, trying to move toward where the pistols had skittered beneath the furniture. Jed did not intend to let him get near his gun or his knife.

The man grabbed Jed's arm and twisted, sending him flying over the man's shoulder to smash into another side table that shattered beneath him. Jed didn't stay down; he rolled and grabbed a broken lamp and slammed it into the guy's temple. The would-be killer swayed as if dazed. A movement on the stairs caught Jed's eye.

Vivi.

Shit. She was carrying the weapon he'd given her earlier.

The guy lunged toward her. Jed didn't hesitate. As much as he didn't want to get shot, he wasn't sure she would actually fire at another human being, and if the bad guy got his hands on her or the gun, it was all over except the grave digging.

The rug slipped under Jed's feet, and he stumbled.

The reverberation of gunfire shattered the silence. The attacker flinched, but didn't stop moving toward her. Vivi fired again, but the shot pinged off the stone fireplace and exited via one of the windows that overlooked the lake. Then she fired one last time. The guy grunted and veered out the front door, running away.

He went after the guy, but she grabbed his arm. Jed hesitated for a nanosecond. Vivi's eyes were massive in the near-darkness, then her hands started to shake, and he removed the gun from her fingers.

"Michael," she whispered, and bolted toward her son's bedroom.

Shit. He was torn. He needed to catch this guy and shut this organization down. But there was also the overwhelming need to make sure Michael was OK.

Jed locked the front door, grabbed his weapon from the floor just in case there were more bad guys, and followed Vivi to Michael's bedroom. In the dim light he could just make out the boy fast asleep, covers thrown off, chest rising and falling gently as if he didn't have a care in the world.

Vivi swallowed noisily and then turned to him, gripping a handful of his shirt. She buried her face against his chest and whispered, "I just shot a man and my baby slept right through it."

Jed hugged her tight and kissed the top of her head. "You

saved our lives."

He should be out there chasing this guy, but her hoarse breath told of her internal struggle and he couldn't bring himself to leave her. Another mistake to add to the list.

"I don't know how much longer I can go on like this, Jed."

He said nothing, just squeezed her tighter.

ELAN STUMBLED IN the snow. His vision swam, blood pouring from a scalp wound where his head had split open when the man had landed on him from above. *Amateur*. He staggered into a snowdrift, his shoulder burning where the bullet had smashed into him. It hadn't exited, and he needed to get the metal shards out and not just because they hurt like hell.

The snow felt good on his hot flesh. No one followed him yet, which was a miracle, but if he didn't leave now he'd be trapped.

Off your knees!

He staggered to the police SUV, opened the door, and yanked the body of the dead cop out of the seat into the snow, throwing himself into the driver's seat. Forcing himself to use his injured arm, he shoved the car in drive and locked the steering wheel hard right to turn the SUV around along the narrow lane. He fought back the blackness that tried to swamp his mind.

Everything had gone wrong.

A laugh hurt his chest. To think he'd never contemplated failure, certainly hadn't planned on getting shot. Dying, maybe, but not this pathetic wounded escape.

Tires slipped, and he eased up on the accelerator. His

vision faded in and out. Damn. He slapped himself in the face, spotted a water bottle on the passenger seat beside him. He opened the lid after jamming it between his thighs, tipped his head over the passenger seat, and poured the water over his face despite the fact it was freezing. The temperature shocked him enough to get his brain focused back on the road and not in the ditch.

He went left at the intersection and drove for a mile or so before he pulled up a roadmap of the area on the onboard computer. He stopped and got his bearings, trying to ignore the blood trickling down his face. He studied the landscape, struggling to remember the direction he'd walked to get to the cabin. Finally he figured it out and carried on driving. Another mile and there was a turn to the left that he recognized from earlier that day. Five hundred yards along, he pulled into a small parking area hidden from the road, finding his truck exactly where he'd left it.

He stopped the cop car beside it. Shoved against the door, barely strong enough to push it open. He searched for his keys in one of his vest pockets, pulled them out, and turned on the ignition of his truck and let the engine warm for a minute. He dragged the first aid kit from the middle console and taped some gauze to his scalp, wiped the blood off his face and pulled a ball cap tight over the dressing. He sucked in a breath at the pain, but after a few moments the increased pressure stemmed the flow of blood.

He slapped another gauze pad against the entry wound on his shoulder. It had stopped bleeding except for the occasional, ugly dribble.

He forced himself out of his car and back into the bitter midnight cold. He found the GPS locator on the SUV and ripped it off. Then he used bolt cutters—which hurt like hell—to remove the onboard computer before he tossed it in the snow. It wouldn't last five minutes at these temperatures. Back in the truck, he dug into his gym bag and pulled out a thick, black hoodie, put it on, zipping it up to the neck. Hopefully, to the casual eye, he appeared uninjured. He swallowed some extra-strength painkillers with a swig of water to wash them down. His shoulder was numb now. His cell rang and he checked it. A text.

"It's a GO. Forget boy. Get back to city. ASAP."

Elan swore, reversed, and drove away. If only they'd sent him *that* message an hour ago. Dammit. His hands shook. He'd been so close to killing the child. So close. A curious burst of relief surged through him. Thank God.

The endgame was in play. He needed to find out exactly what the situation was. Figure out how long he had to get into position. He needed to remove this bullet and sew himself up. A lot to do in just a few hours, but he had to be careful. Everything had to be perfect. It could not go wrong. He'd rest when he was dead.

———

Leaving Vivi standing guard over Michael, Jed ran outside to see if the bastard was dead in the snow. There were enough dark stains on the ground to know Vivi had clipped him at least once. A blood trail led down the road, across the narrow bridge. *Shit!* A body lay in the snow. The sight of a cop uniform made his own heart stop beating. *Liam!* He ran, skidded to a halt on his knees, turned the guy over to check for a pulse and start CPR.

It wasn't Liam. And CPR wasn't going to help.

He called his brother who answered on the first ring.

"Shit. I missed your text. What happened?"

From the guilt and breathlessness in his brother's voice, Jed had interrupted him with a woman. If there had been any way of delaying or changing the truth, Jed would have done it. Unfortunately, this was gonna hurt and no one understood that better than Jed.

"We had a visitor," Jed ground out. There was no way to negate the pain.

"Shit." Jed heard a rustle that sounded like clothes being pulled on. "I sent T-Bone to watch over the place. Did he fall asleep? I told him I'd be there in another hour. Dammit."

There was a female voice in the background, and Jed frowned because she sounded a hell of a lot like Angela—but right now it didn't matter.

"He didn't fall asleep, Liam."

"Oh, fuck, no. No, no, *no.*"

He heard a door slam and an engine start, the whoop-whoop of a police siren start up.

"Tell me he's OK, Jed."

But T-Bone—who Jed now recognized as being the younger brother of another of his high school friends—wasn't OK. He was never going to be OK again.

"He's dead, Liam. The guy who killed him was the real deal. I doubt he even saw him coming." Jed closed his eyes. Christ, if his brother hadn't had a hot date the chances were it would be Liam's body he was staring at. His assumption and faith that they could deal with this themselves had got an innocent man killed. "Vivi shot the guy, but he ran off and stole your officer's SUV. You need to get a BOLO out on the vehicle and you need to call in the feds. I'm sorry." Jed hung up and called his father. "I need you to come over here and pick up Vivi and Michael. Take them home and guard them with your life."

How had they found them? He eyed his SUV. Until he had someone go over his car for a tracking device he wasn't taking Vivi anywhere in it. But how had they known *he'd* taken her? Someone had sure as hell put the pieces together fast. Or they'd gotten very, very lucky. Killion had probably figured it out. That should have alerted him to the danger earlier. His complacency had put the Vincents at risk and got a cop killed.

He strode back to the house and put more wood on the fire to warm the place up. He used his cell to quickly photograph all the pictures Michael had drawn and sent them to Frazer back at Quantico.

His phone rang thirty seconds later.

"Tell me this isn't what I think it is."

"It's worse. I thought I was doing the right thing, but I screwed up. Vivi and Michael are both with me, and still alive, no thanks to me. I need ERT to process a crime scene." He hung up on his boss, frozen from the inside out. His career was totally fucked, but worse was the self-reproof creeping through his skull. How could he have imagined he could keep Vivi and Michael safe? He'd let them down the way he'd let Mia down all those years ago.

But these terrorists had tentacles everywhere—who the hell could he trust? They had to have someone inside law enforcement.

He gathered up the drawing supplies and the tablet he'd given Michael and put them in a bag to send with them. Then he squeezed his eyes shut. Even now he was trying to use the kid for his knowledge, squeeze that young, vulnerable mind for every piece of information he could find to put these people behind bars where they belonged.

Then Michael and Vivi would be safe.

He spotted a pair of night vision goggles on the kitchen floor beneath the dishwasher. Shit. The guy had certainly been prepared. Jed frowned at the weapon lying beside the island. A twinge of unease shifted through him. Tanfoglio were damn good gunsmiths. They were also the chief supplier of hand-guns to the Mossad.

Could this get any more complicated?

It could certainly get worse if anything happened to Vivi or Michael or anyone else he cared about. Right now he was ill-prepared to stop it. They needed better protection than he could provide alone.

He went through to the bedroom and touched Vivi on the shoulder. She was as cold as a corpse. Eyes shocked and glassy. The woman he'd made love to earlier had disappeared deep inside.

"Liam will be here in a minute. Run upstairs. Get dressed"—she was clad in only a t-shirt and panties, which further reminded him how far he'd crossed the line with her earlier—"and grab your stuff because we have to get out of here fast."

There was a noise at the front door. "Only me," Jed's father called out as Jed reached for his weapon.

Vivi obviously didn't want to leave Michael. He put both hands on her shoulders and pushed her toward the door. "I'll watch him. Go quickly. Dad will take you both to his place. Hopefully Michael won't even wake up until morning."

Her lip wobbled. "Won't I need to make a statement?"

"Yes," Jed said. "But I want you out of here first so we can process the scene and make sure there aren't any other shooters nearby."

She laid a hand on his chest, and he flinched away. She blinked at him then as if finally understanding that what happened between them earlier had been a massive mistake. She dropped her hand and moved away faster than if he'd bitten her. And he had bitten her several times when he should have been guarding Michael.

"I don't want to bring danger to your parents," she said quietly. "Maybe we should go to the police station?"

He tried to soften his features, but it was impossible. Inside he was so angry, with the situation, with himself, he could barely speak. He shook off the emotions that were clouding his ability to function, finally getting what his boss kept trying to ram into his brain. It was time to step back. Detach. He couldn't hunt these people and guard Vivi at the same time.

"Dad will keep you safe for the next few hours. They even have a panic room in the basement of the cottage." Her eyes flared. "And we'll have people guarding the area. You need to hurry though, I have work to do." He made his voice impersonal and implacable. It would be easier this way in the long run.

She firmed her mouth and nodded. Strode out of the bedroom door and past his dad who Jed heard ask if she was all right. He didn't hear the answer, just the punch of feet on the stairs. Then above him, the thumping of belongings once again being thrown into a bag with little regard for packing—they were way past that logistical nicety. On the run again from people who would stop at nothing to kill them.

Who the hell *was* this? And why did they want Michael

dead so badly?

His cell phone rang. Frazer. Jed straightened and answered, wondering if he even had a career left worth saving anymore.

CHAPTER SEVENTEEN

V IVI RAN UPSTAIRS, not even caring she was barely dressed as she passed Jed's father. The fear and anger and distress of the last thirty minutes had made her immune to such minor considerations. The bedroom still smelled of sweat and sex which seemed to carry the price of letting down your guard.

So stupid. So naive.

She heard a police car arrive, sirens blazing. Her life had become a series of disastrous events that involved guns, death, and sirens.

For a brief time today she'd escaped it. Being here, in this beautiful snowbound cabin with a man she'd thought…

Her hands shook. Downstairs she'd wanted Jed to wrap her up like a little girl and take care of her, but she was the one with a child to look after. She was the one who needed to pull herself together. Yes, she'd shot a man, a man who no doubt would have killed her if Jed hadn't disarmed him. A man who'd come here with the express purpose of putting a bullet in her son's head.

The thought had anger pushing away the numbness and shock. She'd shoot him again, happily. She'd spend a lifetime in prison for murder as long as Michael survived this ordeal. And he'd slept through the whole thing.

She gulped back a sob, forced down the shock, and pulled on socks and jeans.

Jed was angry with her for seducing him, and maybe he was right.

She'd known these people wouldn't give up easily. She never should have believed Jed when he'd said they were safe. She had a terrible feeling they'd never be safe again. She ran into the bathroom and grabbed all their supplies, including the soap—as if she might never enter a shop again and these stupid items, however unimportant, were all she'd ever have. She flung them into a plastic bag.

She tossed aside the shirt she'd been wearing, pulled on a bra, shirt, sweater. Everything else was shoved into more plastic bags, and she gathered them all together and ran back downstairs without glancing at the bloodstains on the floor.

A voice from the doorway stopped her dead. "Hello, Veronica."

Bile squeezed up her throat as she recognized the voice. She looked up. David Pentecost, her ex-husband, stood in the doorway wearing a uniform that fit snugly to a thickening chest. His face had gained lines around the mouth that made him look permanently angry, and his super short hair revealed touches of gray that hadn't been there the last time she'd seen him. He was still a handsome man, but there was no vestige of attraction left between them.

His cold, disparaging gaze traveled over her unbrushed hair and flicked over the bite mark on her neck.

The guy had been screwing around during their marriage, and he dared to judge her? Fire smoldered through her marrow, anger igniting in its wake. She narrowed her gaze and lifted her chin. To think they'd once vowed to love each other until death—they hadn't even come close. "What are you doing here?"

"I've come to protect my son."

Her brows rose with incredulity. "Protect *your* son?" She didn't raise her voice. In fact, she was proud of how soft and level it sounded. How *reasonable,* because inside she was screaming. "In the last four years you never even sent him a birthday card and now you've come to *protect* him?" There was enough blood on the floor to prove she could take care of Michael herself.

She spotted another man behind David, the blond spook she'd met at the safe house and mistrusted on sight. Killion came inside, looking at the bloodstain with a critical eye.

"I hear you clipped him. Nice work, Ms. Vincent."

David sneered. "No way did you do that. You would never touch a gun, let alone shoot anyone."

Vivi could feel the feralness of her smile touch the brittleness of her lips. "Oh, trust me. I did it. And I'll do it again to *anyone* who threatens my son."

"Our son," David corrected.

She set her teeth. David wanted something, but it wasn't a relationship with Michael. Vivi didn't know what was going on, but David wasn't going to hurt them just because he had some agenda. Jed came out of the bedroom carrying her sleeping child and more plastic bags filled with their meager belongings. She touched Jed's arm and looked at Michael's slack features. He was sleeping like he was drugged, and although she was glad, she was inversely worried.

"Is he OK?"

"Just exhausted." Jed's gaze raked her from head to toe as if assuring himself she was unharmed. Then it flicked to the men at the door.

"Still mollycoddling the boy, Veronica?"

"You should try it sometime, asshole," Jed told David. Vivi wanted to cheer.

David's expression grew mean. "Considering you're about to lose your job for lying to federal authorities and possible kidnap charges—"

"He didn't kidnap anyone, David, he brought us here for safety."

Supercilious brows rose as he flicked a glance at the floor. "And look how well that turned out."

Jed's expression went blank, and Vivi could tell he was blaming himself.

"Want me to kill him for you, son?" Jed's dad asked from behind David on the porch.

Vivi blinked. David puffed out his chest in indignation. Killion tried to hide a grin.

"I can dump the body in one of the back lakes. No one will find him. Bodyguards too." Jed's father's tone of voice was so flat Vivi half-wondered if he was serious. David obviously did too.

Vivi couldn't help being moved by the offer.

"I can have you arrested for threatening behavior," David said, turning his back to the wall in a defensive position.

Jed's father laughed, clearly unfazed. "Not if you're dead you can't."

Killion's face gave nothing away now. He was watching everything play out. Vivi decided she disliked *him* most of all.

David shifted uneasily.

"What do you want, David?" she asked tiredly.

"I've come to take Michael to safety."

"No." She kept her voice down so as not to wake her child, but panic was starting to swell. "Tell him, Jed."

But a weird expression came over Jed's features. "Actually, it might be the best thing."

Her knees buckled.

"What?" How could he say that? She'd told him what had happened before. He knew what sort of parent—or lack of parent—David had been. Betrayal whipped through her as she stared up at those flat, expressionless eyes. Eyes she'd made glitter with lust less than an hour ago. Maybe that was the problem.

Jed spoke quietly. "My boss told me they think they've identified the faction behind the attack. We should be able to use that information to round these people up pretty quickly, which means the threat to Michael's life should soon be null and void."

Elation rushed through Vivi. "So we can go home?"

Jed shook his head. He avoided her gaze, but his voice was tight. "You need to stay in protective custody for another few days. *He* can get you out of here to somewhere safe." He pointed to David.

She grabbed Jed's sleeve. He stiffened infinitesimally beneath her fingers. And then she got it. It hit her with a solid wave of shame that slammed into her.

Jed didn't need Michael anymore. He certainly didn't need her throwing herself at him and almost getting him killed. God, she was such a fool. She was messing up his life and his career just because he'd been kind enough to try and help them. As for having sex—who wouldn't sleep with a naked woman who offered a quick no-strings shag?

Heat burned across her cheekbones.

Had he been the one to call David? It seemed like a heck of a coincidence that the day he found out her ex worked for DIA was the same day the man arrived at the door. Maybe that's why he'd been so hard to seduce, because he'd known David could arrive at any moment. God, how could she have been so dumb? How could she have thought he actually cared about them? How could she have let herself start to fall for this guy?

Start?

If the pain that sliced through her heart at his rejection was anything to go by, she was way past the "starting to fall for him" stage.

It didn't mean she had to do what he said though. He didn't own her. "I don't want to go with this man. There must be some other alternative?"

"We just added another crime scene to the mix. And another dead cop." Jed's voice was like ice.

Vivi flinched and blood drained from her head. *Oh, God.* She hadn't known anyone had died here tonight. She banded her arms across her stomach.

"Resources are stretched thin, so it makes sense for DIA to get involved from this end." He slanted David a look. "I assume you brought security?"

David nodded.

"Maybe the organizations can work together for a change and actually catch these bastards?"

Vivi's mouth dropped as Jed walked up to David and placed her son in his arms. David looked taken aback for a moment, and then he hefted Michael higher and nodded at the other man. David turned and strode out through the door, leaving her standing there like a fool. Jed turned to face her with a look of apology, but she felt as if he'd slid a blade into her heart. She slapped him hard across the cheek. Then she ran after the man who carried her son. She had no doubt he'd drive off without her and make her beg to find out where he'd taken Michael.

It hurt to breathe. Why had she believed Jed was different than any other man? What a fool. What a stupid fool. She got into the backseat of David's car and pulled her son tight into her arms. She never looked back at the man who stood watching them leave.

———————

JED WAS RELIEVED that Vivi was no longer his responsibility. They'd receive better protection from the Defense Intelligence Agency than he'd been able to provide. He hung onto that belief for about as long as it took for her to ride out of sight. Then his stomach twisted and he threw up.

Heat rushed over his skin. The ex was an asshole, how could he trust him to look after Vivi and Michael? Christ, she'd never forgive him for what he'd just done. Although he'd done it to protect her and Michael, he'd also done it to try and save his career, and get away from the effect she had on him— his inability to do his job properly when she was involved.

Fuck.

He was totally fucked.

A hand rested on his upper back as he retched into the snow beside the cabin. Tonight hadn't gone quite according to plan.

His cheek stung from her slap. No less than he deserved.

"You'll be all right, son."

An affirmation. His dad. The anchor of his life. Jed had no

doubt that if he'd wanted David Pentecost dead, his father would have fetched the ski-doo and some very large rocks.

Jed spat the bitter taste of bile out of his mouth and straightened. He wasn't all right, but he had a job to do, a job that would eventually resolve all of Vivi and Michael's problems—the ones that threatened them with imminent death at least.

They could try and sort out the other ones later. The fact he wanted to sort them out at all made him the biggest kind of fool, because he'd just fried his chances of making anything work with Vivi when he'd put Michael into David's arms.

A father *should* look after his son—his own father had taught him that. So why the fuck did he feel like Judas?

Liam had arrived on scene with some of his deputies and the County Sheriff. The look of pissed-off-grim he shot Jed as he dealt with his fallen officer made the nausea return, but Jed forced it down. He had work to do. The guilt over the officer's loss was made heavier by the relief that his brother, not to mention Vivi and Michael, were still alive. Liam understood. They didn't need to say the words.

He went back inside the cabin and found Killion scouring through Michael's drawings.

"No trotting after your master?" Jed asked bitterly. He should have expected the betrayal, but he'd been naive, assuming they were now friends. Spooks didn't have friends. Backstabbing was their MO.

"He's nothing to do with me." Killion shrugged. "I needed a favor from the military attaché's office and found a way to get it. In return I told him I'd lead him to his wife if I found her alive."

"You knew who her husband was when you met her,

didn't you?"

"Langley figured it out."

"And used it." Jed glared at the man. He vibrated with rage. "The only reason I don't shoot you is because I don't need the paperwork."

"Hey," Killion raised both hands up, palms out, "I'm not the one who bundled her into the car with the guy faster than you could say spit. *That* was all on you. I was expecting a slap-down for the prick, not a Hail Mary free pass. What'd you do so wrong that you had to get rid of her so fast, anyway?"

It was obvious what Jed had done wrong.

"If it's any consolation, I'd have fucked her too," said Killion callously.

Rage singed every nerve. He narrowed his gaze and clenched his fists. If he'd been standing closer he might have decked the guy anyway. Or strangled him and dumped *him* in the lake. The only thing that stopped him was the fact the guy *wanted* to rile him. Wanted him to punch him. Jed needed to regain his equilibrium and sort out this mess with a clear head—hence the reason he'd got rid of Vivi.

Fuck.

She was going to skewer him. Still, she was better off in DC and well out of this nutfuck. He could grovel when this was all over, but first he had to put these people away. He had to do his job.

"You look like you got the snot beat out of you. I take it the guy was a pro or were you weak from too much…exercise?" Killion moved further away, as if he knew baiting Jed was about to get dangerous. Although no doubt about it, rage was an improvement on self-pity.

"The guy was a professional. Came in through the basement, turned off the breaker. I jumped him from up there." Jed indicated the upper floor balcony with his chin. "Only reason I'm standing here now is when I hit him he fell and cracked his skull." Not easy to admit the other guy was better than him, but the truth. "What did you get out of interrogation?"

Killion narrowed his eyes. He'd heard Jed tell Vivi they knew who was behind the attack, but he was being patient for a change. "Abdullah denied everything and suddenly pulled the *diplomatic immunity* card in a big way—turns out he's not only Republican Guard, he's a distant relative of the president himself. The Syrian Ambassador was called to the White House and now diplomats are being expelled like undocumented immigrants crossing the Rio Grande." Killion turned to look at him, flashed his father a surfer's smile that fooled no one.

"Did you find his DNA on the cell phones?"

Killion shook his head. "But we did find a female's that matched those of the clothes you found. No hits in the databases." Killion pulled a picture of a woman wearing a hajib from Michael's pile. "You think this is her?"

Jed grimaced. "Probably." But the scarf covered everything except her eyes and rendered it useless for facial recognition programs. The FBI could ask for the public's help though. Someone might know her—especially if she'd worked in the mall.

Killion's patience was done. "So who was behind the attacks?"

Jed eyed him narrowly and figured he'd suffered enough. Alex Parker, their new cyber security consultant, had a knack for accessing cell phone data—not necessarily through the proper channels—but right now they were desperate to shut this organization down before anyone else died. "FBI sources traced some phone calls between Abdullah Mulhadre and a man called Sargon Al Sahad. He's been fighting with the rebels but recent intel suggests he's available to the highest bidder."

Something calculating flickered behind Killion's eyes. "Might fit in with the fact we found that German merc dead at the safe house. MI6 is supposed to be reaching out to people, but I haven't heard anything from them yet. The attack could have been from a splinter group or Muslim extremist cell or the government itself."

"Terrorists don't hire mercenaries." Or at least they never had to his knowledge. The irony of being an expert on why people killed and yet being clueless right here, right now, was not lost on him. "And they generally use any opportunity to gain publicity—so why has no one claimed the mall attack?"

"You got me," said Killion.

"Could this Sargon guy and the rebels have conspired to set up the Syrian regime and gain more support from the West for their struggle?"

Killion paused as if thinking about it. "It's possible. Just doesn't fit with how they usually operate. These guys are fighting for their lives. If I was a betting man, I'd say it was more likely the regime could have hired Sargon to paint the rebels in a bad light and cut off the arms supplies and support they've been getting from the West."

Damn. They needed better intel. "There's no internet chatter?"

"Dude, suddenly there's so much chatter we can't verify a damned thing."

Jed scrubbed his face, thinking out loud. "Who else would

benefit from pointing the finger at the Syrian Government?" *Oh fuck.* The answer made his head hurt.

He walked over to where the attempted assassin's weapon lay on the floor. He hadn't touched it because of fingerprints. The man hadn't worn gloves. "You need to take a look at this."

Both his father and Killion came to look at the weapon. It only took them a moment to understand the significance of the make.

"Shit." Killion reached out a hand to take the weapon, but a voice intervened.

"Touch my crime scene, and I will arrest you." Liam stood in the doorway, looking pissed.

"If you want the State Department up your ass, go ahead," Killion retorted.

Liam strode forward, eyes narrowed and cold. He'd lost one of his men tonight. Jed knew his brother. Threatening him wasn't going to get anyone anywhere. "Might take the State Department a little while to figure out where you are, Mr. ...?"

"I have a right to a phone call, don't I?"

"Only if I can find a phone. What is your name?" There was no humor in his brother tonight—his wounds were too raw. Hell, Jed realized that there hadn't been any in him until the spook had started in on him. Killion had totally distracted him from Vivi and the dead cop and got him focused on the real problem. He was good.

"His name is Patrick Killion, Intelligence Officer with the CIA. And if that isn't an oxymoron I don't know what is."

Killion met Jed's gaze. "This would be your twin I take it?"

"How d'you figure that out?"

"Because you share the same quota of pain-in-the-assedness."

"You caught the guy yet?" Jed asked his brother, ignoring the spook.

"I've got every police and sheriffs' officer out hunting him down in this and all adjoining counties." Liam shook his head. "I've got BOLOs out for the SUV and alerts at all the local hospitals. You get a good look at the guy?"

"I never saw his face." The knowledge he was out there, that he might right now be hunting Vivi… He dialed her number, but no one picked up. "Any idea how to reach David Pentecost?" Jed asked Killion. Having Vivi and Michael out of his sight was making his skin itch even though it was his own doing.

Killion pulled a card from his pocket. "That's his private cell. He had additional security out on the highway. Guy doesn't believe in taking chances with his personal safety."

Jed blew out a sigh of relief. He'd messed up, but it was still probably the best choice. Protective custody. Crap. It hadn't worked so well last time, had it? He slipped the card in his pocket.

"We might all be better off if this weapon disappears, at least on paper," said Killion.

"That weapon probably killed my deputy. No one is taking it anywhere except to the evidence lab," said Liam firmly.

Tension buzzed between the four men.

"If the gun is processed something tells me that evidence will disappear before sun-up." Killion spoke quietly, but urgently. "And that doesn't bother me much because I doubt they'll match it to anything in the system. What bothers me is the people who process the evidence might become collateral damage."

"Are you threatening people?" Liam stepped forward, fury

in his bloodshot eyes.

Jed stopped Liam with a hand to his chest.

"Not me." Killion's voice got harder.

"What about all the other evidence lying on the carpet over there?" Jed pointed out.

Killion straightened and shrugged. "Wouldn't be surprised if that didn't disappear too."

"That's a big-assed conspiracy theory you've got going." Liam's eyes focused on the spook.

No way was that evidence disappearing. "You got any sterile vials?" Jed asked his brother. Time was wasting. He had work to do.

"Why?"

"More DNA samples the better."

"I want doubles, too," Killion said. "I'll send it to our lab."

"You have a lab?" Jed asked.

"Maybe," Killion's answer was non-committal, but told him everything. "Vacation over?" the spook quizzed him.

"Vacation's over," Jed agreed.

Liam delved in his pockets and gave them each two bottles. "The weapon stays. You can photograph it, but that's it. I'll call in the State lab to deal with the crime scene. That gives us all time to try and figure out this mess and find this cop killer. You do realize that the person who shot the attacker has officially fled the scene?" Liam stared hard at Jed.

And it hit him all over again. She'd shot someone tonight, after he'd promised her she'd be safe. Jed closed his eyes, barely able to believe what he'd done. Earlier that day, she'd told him that she trusted him more than her ex. He'd repaid her by thrusting her out the door less than an hour after screwing her senseless.

She was never going to talk to him again. But what did he care? He'd already told himself they had no future together, that she deserved better. Well, she'd sure as hell deserved better than that asshole of an ex. He turned away from the other men. Stared at the bullet hole in the glass window like that was their biggest problem. "Sorry about the cabin, Pop. I'll pay for any repairs."

"Gonna be hell getting the stain out of the carpet," Killion piped up, as helpful as ever.

His dad gave the spook a smile that would scare the shit out of most people, then turned back to Jed. "Don't worry about the cabin, son. Just figure out how you're gonna make it up to that young woman of yours and her son."

"She's not mine." That fact made the pressure in his chest build. "Michael's with his father." His tone turned bitter. "I thought you'd approve."

"Takes more than a sperm donor to be a father, and you know it." He turned his back on Jed and touched Liam on the arm. "Your mother will come with you to tell that young man's wife. I'll come, too, and see if there's anything I can do to help."

Liam nodded. "I appreciate it." He pointed a finger at Jed and Killion. "Either of you leaves or touches the crime scene before I'm done, I'll hunt you down and stuff you both in jail regardless of your job title, understand?"

The silence was deafening. Neither of them promised anything.

CHAPTER EIGHTEEN

VIVI UNCLIPPED HER seatbelt and fought to hold onto her nerve. She'd entered a realm where David thought he had more power than God. Considering she'd shot a man tonight who may or may not still be trying to kill her son, she wasn't sure enough of herself or the situation to do anything but go along with his plans. For now.

The fact that Jed had abandoned her cut to the bone, and that was foolish. She'd thrown herself at him, telling herself and him she had no expectations. He had a job to do, a job that was important. Catching killers was vital for their society to operate properly, except nothing was operating normally right now and killers seemed to be everywhere.

She was rationalizing his behavior, which meant she was in even more trouble than she'd thought. She was in love with the man, and he'd cast them aside as easily as David ever had. But he'd never made any promises beyond trying to protect them.

She stared out of the window at the flat, desolate landscape as the loneliness expanded inside her chest. This was why she didn't let people close. It hurt too badly when they didn't love you back.

Michael had woken up in the helicopter and was now pressed close to her side. He hadn't seemed particularly scared

285

at first, but then his father turned to look at them and his entire body tensed in her arms. There'd been no gentle smile of recognition. No parental acknowledgment or bonding. Just a cool nod that seemed more assessing than friendly. Bastard.

She'd thought they'd be flying to DC, but the journey had barely lasted half an hour. He'd brought them back to Minneapolis. Right into the heart of danger.

God, she hated the man.

Perhaps Jed was right, and the danger was almost over. She just hoped the bad guys had all received the memo. The pilot set the chopper down with barely a bump. When David opened the door, it was still too noisy from the rotors to ask him any questions or demand answers. She gathered all their belongings in one hand and held Michael's hand in the other.

David's upper lip curled, but she didn't give a damn what he thought of her mothering skills. If his own mother had been less of an ice queen they wouldn't be in this situation now. A black Lincoln Town Car pulled onto the tarmac, and David caught her elbow and urged her toward it. She gritted her teeth at his touch. Her stomach recoiled at the idea they'd once been intimate.

They slid into the car and the driver immediately pulled away.

"Where are you taking us? Why are we here?" she asked urgently.

"Calm down, Veronica. You'll frighten the boy."

Volcanic rage flashed through her. They'd been attacked repeatedly over the last few days and yet her asking some basic questions would 'frighten the boy.'

But this was classic David, always trying to have the upper hand.

"Pull over," she told the driver.

He looked in the mirror at David.

"I said, pull over!" she yelled.

David grabbed her arm and squeezed so tight she was going to have bruises tomorrow. "Ignore her. Drive to the hotel." He twisted her wrist to a painful angle, and she saw the flare of satisfaction when she winced. "Keep your mouth shut and do what I say for a few hours and you can go crawling back to your low level FBI agent—not that it looked like he wanted you. Not anymore anyway. I could have told him the prize wouldn't be worth his job." His gaze flicked to her neck.

Her fingers itched to slap him the way she'd slapped Jed earlier. Only the fear of becoming hysterical in front of Michael stopped her. How many times had she tried to teach Michael violence wasn't the way to resolve differences? But Jed had handed her over to David as if she meant nothing to him, so what did she care—except she did care, otherwise she wouldn't have slapped him.

A man had died.

A cop watching the house had been murdered, probably while they'd been having sex. The fact Jed had been distracted was her fault. No wonder he was struggling with guilt and thank God it hadn't been his brother else she didn't think he'd ever recover. But a young man had died trying to protect them, and it made her feel humble and regretful and wrong.

Why were these people so desperate to kill them? What did they think Michael knew? Was the danger really over?

David leaned closer to her ear so only she could hear him. "When did you turn into such a slut, Veronica? Took a wedding ring for me to get in your panties, and it certainly wasn't worth the price of admission."

Twisting the knife was his specialty. So she whispered back, softly, "The moment you got out of my life, I climbed onboard any guy who was breathing. And you know what? I liked it."

She sat back against the seat with a smile as David regarded her balefully. He was jealous. Always had been. She could see it in his eyes. Even though he was married to another woman, he was jealous of who she slept with because he'd always seen her as his property. Suddenly she was wonderfully glad she'd had sex with Jed. Hot, sweaty, fabulous sex. She let David see it all in her eyes. Her satisfaction. Her derision for him.

"I can make this very hard for you, Veronica. Don't you forget that."

"Threats, David? And yet earlier you claimed you'd come to protect your son," she said archly, wishing Michael wasn't close enough that he might overhear the whispered sniping.

"Maybe I'll have him committed." His smile was ice cold. "Should be safe enough in a mental institute, don't you think?" David spoke as if he were talking about the traffic.

A tic started in her cheek. She wasn't a violent person, but she really did want to hurt him. Michael had his eyes closed, his forehead touching the car door. He wouldn't meet her gaze, and she could feel his withdrawal. She squeezed his knee, silently telling him everything was going to be OK.

She could do this for him. She would do anything for him. "You said you needed my cooperation for a few hours. I suggest you stop playing games and start telling me what you want. Then I'll think about whether or not I'll agree to help you."

His eyes turned flat as a snake's. "You misunderstood. If

you want to accompany your son, then you may, but Michael's coming with me regardless."

Their son curled into a tight ball on the seat and started rocking. She smoothed a hand over his back, the jut of his spine hard against her hand.

"Stop sniveling, you little brat," David spat. "You're going to have the honor of meeting the president of the United States today and you'll damn well address him, and me, as 'sir'!" He went to grab Michael's shoulder, but Vivi forced herself between them.

"Leave him alone!"

David shoved her so hard she slammed into the seat. Pain radiated through her cheek, but that wasn't the biggest surprise.

Michael screamed. He leaped at his father, hitting him in the face with his small clenched fists. David pushed him away; Vivi sat there open-mouthed, stunned.

It may have been triggered by ugliness and violence, but her son had just made his first sound in four years. She opened her arms, and he flew against her, burying his face in her chest. She hugged him tight and watched her ex-husband try to stem the bleeding of his nose and scratches on his cheek.

"I love you, Michael." She hugged him tighter and he clung to her.

Tears wanted to form, but she wouldn't let them. After everything they'd been through, this was minor. She thrust aside all thoughts of Jed. That was already in the past. A few hours. Just a few hours. And then they'd be free of this man forever.

ELAN WENT BACK to the fancy hotel that he'd barely seen since he arrived. He had a well-stocked first aid kit and a few hours to get ready. The rescue mission for the children was underway, and as soon as he'd secured her daughters, Pilah would do everything he needed her to do. Not that he doubted it, but he liked to hold all the aces. And he liked to keep his promises.

Ironic that their plot relied on the enemy. Or maybe not. What their plot really relied on was the strength of a mother's love. And the love he felt for his country was akin to that emotion.

In the bathroom of his suite, he stripped to his skin and climbed under the powerful jets of the shower. Pain stabbed where the spray pummeled damaged flesh. The water ran bright red as he washed out his matted hair. His shoulder throbbed, and it was about to get worse.

Once clean, he turned off the faucets and pressed a towel against the head wound, which had started to bleed again. When the bleeding stopped, he applied butterfly stitches to help the wound knit.

Next he sat on a towel on the toilet. Elan used a cigarette lighter to sterilize a pair of blunt-ended, stainless steel forceps, then he poured whiskey into the hole in his shoulder.

He gritted his teeth at the fiery pain, and pushed the metal ends of the implement into his damaged flesh. Agony hit and sweat broke out through every pore and ran down his body in rivulets. He drew in a deep breath, wishing he could drink the alcohol, wishing he was home with his family, then he pushed deeper and touched something hard. *There.* It took a few attempts to grasp the object, but he drew out the metal and tossed it in the sink where it landed with a dull clatter. Thankfully it looked to be in one piece.

He pressed another towel to the wound and sat breathing heavily.

Very soon he needed to get ready for work.

Sargon Al Sahad had recruited rebel sympathizers who believed they were setting up the Syrian regime for terrorist attacks on US soil. They wanted the West to step in and had achieved their objective far better than they'd ever imagined possible. A few minutes ago, Sargon had received a substantial sum of money from a corporation owned by a high level official in the Syrian Government. The man had expected payment; he just hadn't expected the payment to come from the people he was trying to destroy, or in such an easily traceable fashion. It wouldn't take the Americans long to put one and one together. And the next part of the plan would ensure the president would respond with overwhelming deadly force—no matter if they were antiwar or pro-Arab.

It was guaranteed.

――――――

THEY CHECKED INTO a lavish hotel suite, downtown Minneapolis. David posted a guard on the door, although she had to wonder if it was to keep them in or bad guys out. Vivi hoped they took the risk seriously, too many people had died for them not to take the threat seriously. But would Jed have really sent them away if he didn't think the danger was almost over? Maybe. She wasn't sure anymore.

David stood near the door. For the first time he looked awkward, probably because it was just the three of them now, no one who didn't know the truth about what had happened in their tragic little family.

Michael pulled out the tablet Jed had given him and sat curled up on a chair hugging it to his chest.

David checked his watch. "You have a few hours to sleep and then get cleaned up." He frowned at her jeans and boots. "I'll go pick up something out for you both to wear. Are you still the same size?"

He'd always liked to dress her. The idea sent a wave of self-disgust through her that she'd acquiesced to so many of his domineering ways. But right now she'd wear a paper bag as long as they could just get this 'meeting' over with.

She nodded, knowing he was going to come back with heels and a pencil skirt even though there was snow on the ground. "Make sure you find something that's warm enough." She was thinking of Michael. "And don't forget some make-up." Because she looked like hell.

"Vivi, I…" His expression was regretful for a moment, but the day he apologized would be the day he choked on his own tongue. He trailed off and stood there with his head hanging with shame. But she felt it, too. They'd both behaved badly and neither knew how to stop.

"Let's just move on, OK?" she said. How sad that they'd come to this, two people who'd once purposefully made a baby together could now barely stand the sight of one another.

He left without another word.

She turned to her son who looked so miserable. She closed her eyes. Despite everything, she needed to see if there was a way to fix their relationship enough that she and David could communicate like adults and not further traumatize their child. That Michael might get to know his father—the man she'd fallen in love with, not the jerk she'd divorced. Maybe he was in there still, buried beneath disappointment and resentment and ambition.

Michael was still in his pajamas. His red hair was getting long enough to start to curl. His blue-eyed gaze held hers, looking for reassurance. She was so grateful he hadn't disappeared inside his head from the stress he'd suffered. She was beginning to think Dr. Hinkle was right, Michael wasn't autistic, and he was dealing with everything really well under the circumstances.

She remembered the joy that had shone on his face when they stared at that roller coaster just a few short days ago.

It seemed like a lifetime ago. A whole love affair ago.

If it took a roller coaster—if it took a thousand roller coasters—to make her son happy again, she'd do it. They'd go to Disney as soon as this mess was over, and they'd go on every ride twice.

It wouldn't be so easy to ease the ache in her heart, but that was life. She should be used to it by now. She wouldn't let it break her. She had a child to look after and a president to meet.

God—how unattractive was self-pity?

Where was her fighting spirit?

It struck her then, that being afraid to love was like being trapped inside your own mind, only it was a self-imposed exile.

She was a coward.

A pain clamped across her stomach. She was a damned coward. Knowing how short life could be, she was still too scared to tell a good man she was interested in a relationship with him. And he was a good man. He'd been trying to help her since this disaster started—from helping her up off the floor when she was knocked over in the mall, to taking her to his parents' and trying to protect her there. He'd been trying to do his job, and she kept making it hard for him. No wonder he resented her.

Her brain was fuzzy, and she was almost faint with fatigue. That's what you got living on the run with so little sleep. She'd get some rest and figure it all out. Soon.

"Hey, kiddo. You go get in the shower and then you can get some more sleep, 'kay?"

Michael put the tablet on the table and scurried off to the bathroom. She turned on the shower and made sure the temperature was good. "Don't forget the soap and shampoo." She gave him a kiss and was rewarded with a small hug and a twitch of his lips. She gave him a big squeeze back, careful not to hurt him because she wanted to hold him so tight. He'd tried to protect her earlier, and she knew the fact he'd made a sound had shocked him as much as the rest of them. It gave her hope, though. Made her think *maybe…*

She went back into the sitting room and laid out the drawing supplies next to the tablet Jed had given them, because drawing helped Michael cope with life, and that's what he needed most, a way of coping. A page slipped onto the floor. She leaned down and picked it up. It was the picture of Jed hugging her in the kitchen, yesterday afternoon.

Reaction hit so hard she dropped to the nearest chair. It wasn't quite the moment she'd fallen in love with him, but encapsulated everything she felt. She'd actually fallen head-over-heels when he'd first carried Michael out of the car and tucked him in bed at the safe house.

She touched Jed's hair as if it were real, but it was just smooth graphite on paper. The expression in his eyes suggested he might care about her more than he'd let on—but that might be wishful thinking on Michael's part. It was obvious he idolized Jed and his family. She slipped the drawing carefully into the back of the sketchpad and a huge breath slipped out of her chest. No matter how hurt her feelings, she needed to repay Jed for all he'd done for them and to apologize. She was sick to her stomach that she'd struck him, and that Michael had witnessed the fight she and David had in the car. What had happened to her? Vivi pulled her cell phone out of her pocket and saw Jed had tried to call her earlier. She hadn't heard it ring. She'd probably been in the helicopter.

It gave her a ridiculous sense of relief even though it shouldn't. She dialed the number.

"Vivi?"

His voice jolted her, reminded her of the first time they'd met in the mall before this whole mess had begun.

"Vivi, is that you?"

She cleared her throat. "Yes. I just wanted to apologize for earlier. It was quite wrong of me to do what I did and I regret it more than I can say."

She heard the shock in the silence.

Then he started speaking quickly. "Hey. It was my fault. I should have known better. You were in a terrifying situation and I was in a position of authority. We get warned against this sort of thing during training and I took advantage of you—"

Vivi blinked and gave a bemused laugh. "You think I'm apologizing for seducing you? While I'm sorry for everything that happened afterwards, I'm *not* actually sorry for that. Although I am sorry you regret it." He tried to cut in, but she wouldn't let him. "I'm apologizing for slapping you."

"Oh."

God. Really? *Oh*? That was all he had to say? Enough already. He was obviously not interested in her, and she was embarrassing them both by bringing it all up again. This is why she had withheld herself from people all these years. She didn't know how to put herself out there without getting eviscerated. No one liked getting hurt. She was far better off alone.

She was much more of a coward than she'd ever realized.

"Did you catch the guy who broke into the cabin?" She needed to know how much danger they were still in.

"We haven't found him yet, but I'm sure you'll be safe in DC."

"Ha." She was ashamed the sound came out so bitter. "We're not in DC. We've been invited to meet the president in Minneapolis. How exciting." Her forced enthusiasm fooled neither of them.

"What?" The signal was crappy, and he was obviously in a moving vehicle. Oh, damn, she bet he was on speaker. Shame rose in her cheeks at the idea his colleagues might be listening in—the idea Killion might be listening when he'd probably been the one to sell her out to her ex.

"The president is visiting the site of the attack and the injured in the hospital this morning. David is keen to use the event to present his son to POTUS."

"What?" The same word kept coming out louder. Harder.

"We're in Minneapolis." Her shoulders sagged. Absently, she picked up the tablet and turned on the screen. Her heart leaped when she saw that Michael had been writing. The words and letters were jumbled—still even the idea he might be able to communicate this way eventually... Her heart gave a little squeeze. "Jed, Michael's been trying to write something on the tablet you gave him. It looks like he's trying to say something."

"Send it to me."

"It's gibberish. It doesn't make any sense—"

"Vivi…" His soft admonishment was a reminder they had little to go on, and Michael might truly know something, which still seemed nuts.

"Tell me your email address," she said. Something she'd need to forget, else she'd be stalking him online. Not gonna happen. A couple of days and she'd be over Jed Brennan. She'd probably never see him again. The thought drove a nail through her heart.

Jed gave her the address and she forwarded the note.

"Got it. Thanks. I thought you'd be safer with him. Shit, I can't believe he took you back there…"

There was a commotion in the background of Jed's side of the conversation—the spook was definitely with him and seemed to be excited about something. Jed was about to hang up, she could tell. She forestalled him. "I wanted to tell you something quickly."

"Now isn't a good time." He clearly expected some undying declaration of love but she wasn't into sadomasochism.

"Michael made a sound in the car."

"What? Fuck, if I say 'what' again, shoot me. Michael spoke?"

The idea of telling him it had been a bone-chilling rip of fury wasn't going to go over well. Regardless of his feelings, or lack of them, he would freak if he discovered David had hurt her. Still, she didn't need him to defend her.

"It wasn't an actual word, but *he made a sound*. It-it's the first time I've heard him say anything since…well. Anyway, that's all I wanted to tell you. Thanks for everything. I'll let you get on." Tears started to fall then. The weight of all the years of Michael's silence pressed down on her. Finally her prayers had been answered but she didn't know what it meant or where it might lead, and the man she wanted to share it with clearly wasn't interested—which was fine. He was an FBI agent, and he'd done everything he could to help them. She appreciated it. She really did. But she had the horrible feeling this love thing was going to be harder to deal with than she'd originally thought.

Then she got furious with herself. What was the point in having a voice if you didn't say the most important things? "I love you, Jed."

There was a long shocked silence on the other end, and it was enough to tell her everything she needed to know. Floods of tears blurred her vision. She didn't want to hear the excuses or deflections so she hung up on him. When he called back, she ignored it and then turned off the phone.

Was it cowardice?

No, cowardice would have been never telling him how she felt. She wasn't a child. She understood how the real world worked and she was proud of herself for putting her feelings out there. For a woman who lived in a self-contained world that revolved around her child this was a big step. His excuses for not loving her back didn't matter. He made it clear he wasn't going to be part of her life, and she was fine with that. But the sobs wouldn't stop, no matter how hard she tried, and her heart seemed to crack into a thousand pieces inside her chest. Then the shower stopped running and she pulled herself together.

No one else had to know she was heartbroken.

Especially a little boy who'd suffered enough. She grabbed a tissue and blew her nose.

She knew who and what she was. A mother first and foremost. She'd had a little fun and now it was time to get on with her life.

Her lonely, barren life.

———————

HOLY FUCK. HOW could she say she loved him out of the blue like that and then hang up on him?

Because you blew it, dick head. You let her hear your inner freak-out before you got your head out of your ass and told her you wanted to see her again. Like that was even possible when he lived in Virginia and she lived in Fargo—but that was just geography. *Shit.*

He really did want to see her again, preferably when terrorists weren't trying to kill her son.

He punched the steering wheel of his SUV in frustration. "The asshole ex took them back to Minneapolis where apparently they get to meet the president today." He checked his watch.

Naturally, Killion had overheard every word. "Ah."

They were driving back to Minneapolis which took a couple of hours, he just hoped Liam didn't try and have them arrested for not following his orders. His brother would forgive them if they found the guy who'd killed his officer, but not until. The fact Liam had been in bed with Angela when he'd called him meant his brother had all the same demons chasing him as Jed did, but probably bigger and uglier with talons that ripped you apart.

Had they been seeing each other while Bobby was still alive?

No. No way. Liam would never disrespect their friend, and Angela wouldn't have come on to him if they had been, because she knew how close they all were. He wanted to slap himself on the forehead, because that's how she'd known he was at the cabin, and she'd probably wanted to tell him about dating Liam when he'd more or less thrown her off the property. Moron. Still, right now it was a problem that paled into insignificance compared to what he was up against with Vivi and Michael.

Killion fiddled with the radio.

Jed shot the guy a look. "Why are you even here?"

Killion shrugged. "I needed a ride."

Jed shook his head. "You're such a dick. I just can't figure out why you decided to pick on me." The spook was too good a liar to get anything out of him unless he decided to come clean. "What did you find from Michael's tablet?"

Killion had been checking the scribbles Michael had made and was almost vibrating with excitement. "First of all, considering he's a genius artist, his cursive needs a lot of work."

"I'll let his mother know." Jed blew out a breath of annoyance.

"I think he wrote the names of the terrorists phonetically. I think it says 'Razor', here, and 'Amer.' We ID'd two of the guys who we think were likely to have been in the toy store with Michael as Razur and Amir."

Jed's excitement matched Killion's. Michael really had known something, although probably a lot less than the bad guys thought. If only he could talk, this information would have taken thirty seconds to deliver, tops. "What about the female terrorist?"

"This scribble might be Tira, Tila, or Pila?"

"Get the info to Langley and to the feds running the investigation. Check it against mall employees, lists of the injured, and cross-reference with any foreign nationals. Different spellings."

"Thank God you're here, I'd never have thought to do any of that." Killion rolled his eyes.

"Just do it."

"Yessir," said Killion.

"Prick."

"Jerk."

Killion called it in and Jed dialed his boss, Lincoln Frazer.

"You caused quite the shit storm hiding the Vincents away like that." Jed waited for Frazer to finish reaming him out. "But you also gave us a great way to figure out who might have been trying to find them. Parker traced an electronic trail back to a source in the local police department. We're monitoring the individual until we figure out the next target. Needless to say, US security is tighter than a duck's ass until we figure this out."

Jed passed on the names they'd gotten from Michael's tablet. "It might be nothing."

"But it might be something. Good work. Do you still have the woman and child with you?" Frazer asked quickly.

"Negative. They left with the kid's father. Apparently they have a hot date with a VIP later today."

"David Pentecost is an ass."

"You know him?" Jed wasn't surprised. Frazer was a bit of

a celebrity in FBI circles and got invited to all the big diplomatic 'dos.'

"Well enough to wonder what Veronica Vincent ever saw in him. But maybe she has lousy taste in men." Lincoln Frazer had looked between the lines and seen a bit more than Jed was comfortable with, but considering he was on the verge of losing his job, he kept his mouth shut.

"The real irony is the president just sent a message to my office via the director requesting your presence during his visit. He wants to meet all the 'heroes' of the attack."

Jed wasn't a hero and Frazer knew it. A sour taste coated his mouth. "Does this mean I don't get fired until next week?"

"I guess it all depends on whether or not you make a good impression." Frazer laughed, but he sounded strained. The BAU-4 had had a hell of a month.

"Can Pentecost protect them?" Jed asked.

"Yes. He'll have arranged good security, if only for his own sake." There was a long pause which put Jed on edge. "Parker traced more calls made to the US from this guy, Sargon Al Sahad. All we've found so far is an endless array of burners, but a couple of those burners look like they might still be active. He's got alerts for any further activity."

Alex Parker was turning out to be a good guy to have around in a crisis.

"Keep me posted," said Jed.

"I don't like this business with a professional hit man coming to your cabin—it was a man, right?"

Jed rubbed his jaw. "They don't make females that big." At least he hoped not. "You have a female assassin out there?"

No answer.

Interesting. "This was a big, hairy guy, and we have his

DNA. If he's in the system we'll find him. There was one thing though." Jed told him about the weapon the man had carried.

Frazer grew very quiet. "It seems a little obvious for the most respected intelligence agency in the world, don't you think?"

"Maybe arrogance got in the way. They weren't expecting me, certainly not Vivi, to shoot back. You should make some inquiries."

Killion had also gone quiet. Jed figured his people were already making inquiries—as to the whereabouts of every Mossad and Aman agent the Israelis had.

Frazer finally spoke. "Keep your head down. Meet and greet the man in charge and get the hell back here before I regret not already firing you."

"Ask him for a transfer to Fargo," Killion quipped.

Jed raised his middle finger.

Frazer rang off.

Killion made another of his million phone calls, put his hand over the receiver. "Precision drone strike just wiped out the house where Sargon was staying. Killed at least twenty people."

"President Hague ordered that?" Already? A military op on foreign soil? Jed was shocked. The guy usually avoided violence at all costs.

"The White House held a press conference and said that this was what happened to terrorists who attacked Americans—wherever they might be. Sent quite the message. Needless to say, the whole area is now on the edge of war."

Great. They weren't even certain Sargon was the man behind this yet. Maybe someone had just made sure they never would. "It's getting worse, not better," Jed said.

"Ain't that the fucked up truth," Killion said. "How is Lincoln Frazer?"

Ding. "You know my boss?"

Killion shrugged nonchalantly. "We're acquainted."

"And you owed him a favor." *Ding. Ding. Ding.*

"Not anymore." Killion adjusted his chair and settled back, closing his eyes.

Jed didn't know whether to be pissed or grateful Frazer had sent backup. But it didn't matter now.

His mood dropped as he thought about his earlier conversation with Vivi. She'd told him she loved him, but from her tone of voice it hadn't been a happy or optimistic revelation.

There was so much he hadn't told her—about Mia, about his work—and yet he was starting to think none of it mattered. He wasn't some hormonal teenager. He was a grown man and he'd begun to fall for this strong, yet vulnerable woman.

That redheaded temperament of hers was going to give him trouble. They hadn't even started dating yet—although they had lived together and had sex. He wanted to take her out to dinner and make her feel special. But she was stubborn enough to never want to see him again, especially as he'd not only abandoned her, but also Michael, to his shit-head father.

His mouth went dry, and his fingers tightened on the steering wheel. Deal with the terrorist threat first. Then figure out the woman.

CHAPTER NINETEEN

P ILAH HAD DRESSED with extreme care that morning in her best black dress pants and a pretty fuchsia top with a beaded hem. She hadn't watched the news or turned on the radio. She didn't want anything to intrude on her calm or disturb her resolute state of mind.

Her stomach was too unsettled to eat, but she drank some of her favorite Turkish coffee. Then she pulled on her coat and climbed into her small car and drove to the hospital. She parked a few blocks away, walked through the gray piles of shoveled snow, wishing she'd worn warmer boots because her toes were frozen. She had the pills in her handbag to keep William Green asleep, along with a book she would probably never finish. A buzz of apprehension shot through her when she got to the entrance of the hospital. There were two lines of people and a metal detector to walk through. Her heart fluttered in her chest. It was really going to happen.

She smiled nervously as a man checked her name on the list of expected visitors and another patted her down. This had all been set up with such precision. Considering she wasn't supposed to live past the mall shooting, they must have scrambled to reorganize.

Abdullah was supposed to have carried out this part of the plan, she realized. The redheaded boy had wreaked havoc on this part of the scheme and she had to wonder if he was still alive. She hoped so, but it didn't matter. Not now. Not as long as the shadow-man kept his promise and saved her children.

After she cleared security she hurried onward, using the stairs rather than the guarded elevator. The president was coming. All praise be to Allah. Her heart beat faster, pulse tripping. This was the man who'd had the power to intervene in her country and stop the civil war months ago—*years* ago. This was the man who'd refused her children entry to the US in time to save them. Even though she was a US citizen she hated him, the same way she hated the government in Syria and all the organizations who treated people like commodities to be traded and sacrificed.

Her actions would cause war and turmoil, but they deserved it. Not the civilians though. Not the poor, hapless souls caught in the crossfire.

She shivered.

Many people would die…

Tears filled her eyes. Many had already died. She needed to be selfish and think only of Dahlia and Corinne.

She forced a smile at the nurse and ducked into William Green's room. She dug into her purse and broke a tablet in half, opened his mouth, and placed the pill on his tongue, watching it dissolve. His part in this would be over soon, and she was sorry he'd suffered, but no way would she risk him waking up in the next few hours.

She glanced at the news playing on the TV in the corner of the room. The scene showed a drone strike and an explosion. Then she read the ticker tape. "Mastermind behind mall terrorist attack killed."

Sargon Al Sahad's name flashed across the screen and grief

hit her like a brick. Her knees dissolved, and she stumbled to the floor. Corinne and Dahlia? Dead? Tears streamed down her face as she watched the missile strike over and over again.

Her phone pinged. She ignored it, but then she remembered who it might be. She climbed up from her knees. She had no reason to carry out their plans now. Threats would make no difference. She was too numb for fear.

She pulled out her cell and opened an image someone had sent her, and there were her girls smiling at the camera. Pilah's heart squeezed. They were at a beach with palm trees in the background. Dahlia had lost her front teeth. A woman Pilah didn't know held their hands. She couldn't see the top half of her face, but her hair was long and blond, uncovered. She wore western clothes. Had she taken them from Sargon herself?

She looked strong and confident. A soldier.

Another text came through. "I kept my promise. Now it is your turn."

Pilah nodded even though he couldn't see her. She reached inside the cabinet that held William Green's belongings and started assembling the weapon.

A BEEPING NOISE woke Alex Parker from where he slumped over his computer.

He grabbed the laptop and strode down the hall to Frazer's lair. He didn't bother knocking on the door, just walked right in. "One of the burner cells has been activated."

Frazer rolled off the couch and scrubbed sleep out of his eyes. "Can you trace it?"

"No GPS. I can try signal triangulation and give you a

rough location." Alex waited impatiently for the signal to come through and give him a fix.

Frazer paced. "I don't know whether to hope this is Syria, Iran, or some independent terrorist group. If it is the Israelis…" He trailed off. "Regardless, shit is about to hit the fan."

Alex knew all too intimately the cost of war and political backstabbing.

He pulled up a map of the area. "Cell phone is in downtown Minneapolis." He held Frazer's cool blue gaze. "Tell me again they wouldn't be bold or stupid enough to go after the Commander in Chief?"

Frazer was calling someone, probably the Secret Service.

Alex tapped away on his keyboard.

It had only been just over a week since Frazer had shut down a clandestine organization called The Gateway Project where Alex had worked. He wouldn't say they trusted each other exactly, but they both knew where the skeletons were buried. They'd bypassed the usual getting to know your co-worker etiquette and moved straight to effective strategizing.

Frazer covered his mouthpiece. "What're you doing?"

"Finding a satellite feed over the area. Let's see if we can figure out what the hell is going on up there." A better idea occurred. "Hey, can you get us a drone?"

Frazer carried on with his conversation but nodded.

FBI Special Agent Mallory Rooney tapped on the door and walked in. She'd slept on the couch in the conference room after insisting on coming back to work to help neutralize this terror threat. "What's going on?"

It had only been a few days since Alex's world had shifted on its axis and irrevocably changed. Mallory was still a little pale from her near-death ordeal, but the shock of confronting her sister's killer was beginning to wear off. The knowledge that she'd beaten the evil sonofabitch was getting her through the aftermath of finding her twin sister's remains after eighteen longer years.

She was the most important person in his world—her and the baby she carried. The idea of being a father was still freaking him out—not that he didn't want a baby or a chance of a normal life—just that he wasn't sure he was worthy.

He still owed her a first date, but as long as Mallory was happy, Alex was happy. He pulled a chair out for her while he explained.

Frazer put the phone down. "Secret Service says the president refuses to cancel the trip. Won't bow to terrorism."

"Great." Mallory rolled her eyes.

Alex frowned at the screen. He had a satellite feed, but it was hard to get a clean enough image and it wouldn't be in position for long.

"Get me that drone, Frazer. And get every cop out on the street in case they're planning another shoot-fest to coincide with the memorial service." Despite his dark past, Alex had always been a patriot. The idea of the president being in danger, of innocents dying when they could prevent it...

Another attack would completely undermine people's confidence in whoever was supposed to be in charge. An attack on the president would be a declaration of war. He took another online look at the cell phone in question and hacked into the messages received. He pulled up a photograph, then read the message. A woman holding the hands of two little girls who smiled at him from the picture. He turned the screen toward Frazer. "You need to see this."

Frazer swore. "Find out where that message originated and figure out anything you can about who is talking to whom. Rooney, see if you can link those children to anyone involved in the mall attack."

She nodded.

Frazer picked up his phone again. "I need the plane ready to leave in thirty minutes."

Alex was typing. "It's encrypted. Hell, this is top quality, military grade stuff. I'm going to need some time. It might go faster if I call in people from my company." Alex co-owned a firm that dealt with state-of-the-art cyber-security.

Frazer's eyes bored into his, but eventually he shook his head. "Can't risk it. If our suspicions leak…"

Alex released a pent-up breath. "Fine. I'll do my best. No promises."

Frazer stood and grabbed his coat. "It's only the life of the American president at stake."

Alex swore and typed faster.

"And a third World War."

Alex twisted his lips. "No pressure then."

———————

VIVI SMOOTHED A hand down the scarlet suit David had presented her with. *Scarlet* for a memorial? What was he thinking? Maybe he was hoping the terrorists would have a better target than if she wore black.

Michael was tugging at his tie as if it was something de-signed to kill him. She caught his hand and smoothed his hair out of his face.

"It's OK, Michael. We're going to meet the president of

the United States and your father wants you to look smart."

The face turned belligerent and his hands went back to his tie.

She caught his hand and squeezed. "You've been so amazing, sweetheart. I wouldn't ask you to do this if I didn't think it would be the least painful way of getting through this, OK?"

Michael's eyes grew huge and sad. He opened his mouth, desperately wanting to say something. She held her breath. A small sound came out. It wasn't a word, but it was a sound.

Tears threatened, but Vivi held them back. She hugged him hard to her chest, even though he looked so frustrated with himself.

"You're going to get your voice back, Michael. You are. But it won't happen in one day." She spotted the tablet Jed had given him. "Here, can you spell out what you want to say?"

Michael frowned as he took the tablet. They only had a few seconds before David returned to fetch them.

She didn't want to push him. She wished she had Jed's fun-loving way and could just ease him into using it.

Don't think about Jed.

But when Michael typed, "Ware is Jed?" she realized they were both thinking about the man.

She cleared her throat. Her son had just made a giant leap in communication, but she figured it was best to be low key about the whole thing. *Don't freak him out.* "He had to work. He has to catch the bad guys."

Michael held her gaze with blue eyes so like her own. Then he typed, "I miss him."

The door handle turned and David entered the room, sweeping them both with an assessing gaze. Vivi smoothed Michael's hair again and straightened his tie. Then she bent and whispered in his ear. "So do I, baby. So do I."

———————

JED STOOD IN a line of other suits waiting to be presented to the president in the atrium of County Hospital.

SSA McKenzie was on his right. "I'm going to whip your ass when we're back in Quantico for that stunt you pulled."

"It kept them alive," Jed retorted, although maybe it had been a mistake. Frazer was right about getting too involved, it definitely affected his decision-making abilities, but it was too late to undo things now. He wasn't sure he would anyway. Vivi and Michael were alive, and that time at the lake was something he'd treasure.

McKenzie grunted. "Still gonna kick your ass."

"Better than paperwork."

"Oh, there will be paperwork. Count on it. Mountains of paperwork." The man grew quiet as the president approached.

Jed shook President Hague's hand.

"I hear you were the agent on the ground when the attack happened?"

"Yes, sir, Mr. President." Jed would add it to the list of reasons not to go shopping in the future.

"You saved lives that day, son." The man was tall and slightly stooped. A respected economist, but less respected as a military commander. He'd just lost his virginity when it came to ordering deadly air strikes on foreign soil. "I know Ms. Vincent and her son are particularly grateful for your presence that day."

Jed's eyes widened slightly. Especially when he spotted Vivi in the crowd, skin pale against the red of her suit. Even with her dark hair she appeared very much the poised, confident woman he'd first met just a few short days ago. She caught his eye then looked away. David Pentecost seemed pissed that Jed was talking to the president. Jed searched for Michael, but the Secret Service detail was too thick.

"I'd give my life to protect either of them, sir," he said loudly enough for them to hear.

The leader of his country smiled. "Join us." And then he moved on to McKenzie. Jed eased through the crowd toward Vivi. She tried to edge away, but she had nowhere to go.

He ignored Pentecost and took her hand and gave her fingers a squeeze. She looked up at him then. Wariness outcompeting hope.

He leaned down and whispered in her ear. "I was a jerk. I'm sorry."

Her lips trembled, but then someone pushed between them before he could lean down and kiss her.

Michael.

He picked the kid up and gave him a squeeze. The little boy hugged him back so hard a ball of emotion threatened to choke him. He put the kid down. "Stay with your mom a moment, I need to talk to your dad."

Jed worked his way to the outside of the group and beckoned Pentecost toward him. He leaned close to the man's ear, and whispered quietly, "If you ever lay a hand on either of them again, I will make you scream like a girl. Do we understand each other?"

David's gaze flicked to Vivi with a flush of guilt.

Jed wanted to smack the guy, but he doubted Vivi would appreciate him brawling with her ex during a presidential visit. She was a private person.

Later.

His cell buzzed in his pocket, and he used the call to walk away from the group. The president and his entourage had kept moving. David Pentecost was right next to the president, now dragging Michael close beside him, determined to make an impression while he had the chance. Vivi followed after them, glancing back at him in question. Jed followed more slowly.

He glanced at the phone screen. Frazer. "What do you know?"

At the elevator, the president and Vivi headed to the third floor, so Jed took the stairs with a few of the Secret Service agents.

"We have an ID on the female terrorist. Pilah Rasheed. I'm sending you a photograph."

"Great. Know where she is?"

"No. But we tracked a cell phone that we believe she is using within a quarter-mile radius of the hospital."

Crap. Not good, although if there were any more law enforcement personnel around here you could rob a bank anywhere else in the US and stroll away without a worry.

He and the Secret Service agents piled out at the third floor and Jed saw the entourage walking into a ward. The president paused and started talking to patients, moving slowly through the room. The Secret Service knew trouble was possible. They were twitchy and nervous. Hell, so was he.

A doctor was introduced to President Hague. Vivi shot Jed a glance and he winked at her, trying to put her at ease. A faint blush touched her cheeks. His thoughts turned to what he wanted to say to her when he got her alone. They shouldn't move too fast. He didn't want to scare her but frankly, once

Michael was asleep, he was going to show her exactly what she meant to him. He'd like to—

His cell went off again, jerking him back to the here and now. He scrubbed his hand through his hair. This is what she did to him.

Frazer said, "I want you up on the roof scanning for snipers."

An ominous chill entered his body. Sniping wasn't the kill method of choice by most terrorist organizations, but for presidential assassinations… "OK."

He didn't want to leave without telling Vivi though. He headed over to tell her to wait for him after the big wigs left.

The president and doctor stopped in front of a private room. The Secret Service entered the room first, checked it, then the president entered. Jed overheard the doctor saying that this was a man who'd been in a coma since the attack, and that his niece had been with him ever since.

Jed couldn't exactly shove his way past the Secret Service, but he edged along the wall and got to the doorway. The room was small. Everyone hovered in the entrance as the president went inside. Michael slipped out of his father's grip and followed the president into the room and started tugging urgently on the man's jacket. Jed held back a grin as David looked like he was about to blow his stack, but couldn't without looking like an asshole.

And then his heart stopped beating as three things happened at once. Vivi went further into the room to get Michael. The niece, a tired blonde with a sad-looking mouth, leaned down out of sight. And Michael started making a high-pitched, keening noise that stabbed his eardrum like a needle.

Jed pushed his way into the room to help Michael just as the niece came up holding something that looked suspiciously like a weapon. *Oh, fuck.* He launched himself in front of Vivi and Michael as the woman started firing. A fierce rush of pain took his breath, and then another. He wrapped his arms around the three people in front of him and took them to the floor, crumpled into a heap in the corner. Loud gunfire shook the room and glass shattered.

Goddamn. How had she fooled security?

The shooting stopped. "Are you all right?" His voice sounded pathetic, but he needed to catch his breath.

"I'm fine, son," said the president.

"Vivi? Michael?" he asked. It wasn't the Commander in Chief he was worried about.

Michael scrambled out of the jumble of arms and legs and stood there shaking. His father came into the room and touched his shoulder. Jed swallowed tightly as he watched the man give his son a tentative hug.

Vivi lay stunned and winded. Jed was lying on top of both her and the president.

Secret Service men waded in. One of them trod on Vivi and Jed shoved him aside. "Watch the lady, asshole."

President Hague waved them away. "I'm fine. Ms. Vincent? Are you OK?"

A wall of bodies stood at their back.

Vivi blinked, then her eyes rolled back and she passed out. What the hell? He pushed her hair off her face. "I love you, Vivi. Don't you dare die on me."

Hell of a time to have that realization.

Then Jed saw a stain of darker crimson on her red suit. *Oh fuck, oh, fuck.* He'd failed. He pulled up her shirt, uncaring of all the other male eyes, but there was no bullet hole. Jed blinked in confusion and then someone was dragging him backwards.

"Let me go." He tried to shout, to break away, but his voice was weak. What the hell? Then he looked down at his own shirt and saw a huge patch of blood. He was the one who'd been shot. His blood on her suit. Not hers. Good.

Then the pain started drilling into his back. *Holy motherfucker.*

A doctor was in his face and he was on a gurney, racing through the corridors, lights glaring, people shouting. Mayhem.

He should call Frazer. He tried to reach into his pocket for his phone but his hands wouldn't cooperate. The edges of his vision started to fade. Crap, he was not about to die. He'd just found another woman to love and he wasn't putting her through the hell he'd endured when he'd lost Mia.

"Tell her I love her," he said to the man who loomed over him. He found a last vestige of strength and gripped the man's sleeve. "Tell her."

The stranger nodded, then Jed's vision tunneled gray and turned black.

VIVI WOKE TO a throbbing skull and the sense that something was seriously wrong.

"Michael? Jed!" Where were they?

Her head spun as she climbed to her hands and knees. She'd lost the stupid heels David had bought her. She was going to start wearing sneakers wherever she went, regardless of the occasion.

"Ms. Vincent?" President Hague was on his knees beside her. "Easy. You hit your head." He gave a chuckle but seemed genuinely concerned. "You better wait for a gurney before you try and stand..." But she was already on her feet, wobbling, leaning against the wall for support.

The president snorted. "Yet another woman who won't listen to me. I can't wait to introduce you to my wife."

Two big, burly men came and hooked hands under President Hague's armpits and raised him to his feet. Another watched her hawk-like from the corner. "I want to know how your young man is..." The president was still talking as he was whisked away.

Her brain was thick with a painful fog. Where was Jed? Where was Michael? She took a step toward the woman who'd shot at them. Her pretty pink top was riddled with bullets. It was a garish sight. Such an ordinary looking woman and now she was dead. Vivi's stomach roiled. She glanced at the bed. The poor man in the coma had slept through the whole thing. What was he going to think when he woke up?

"Jed. Michael." She needed to find them. Where were they? She swayed and someone caught her elbow.

"I've got you."

It was the CIA guy she didn't like. She tried to pull away.

"Come on, Vivi. We're on the same team, I promise. Michael's just outside the door. I'm going to take you to him and then we're going to get you checked out."

She looked down at her crimson suit and saw a large smear of blood. But aside from a pounding skull she wasn't hurt. Panic hit. "Where's Jed?"

Killion looked pale and shaken. "He's on his way to the OR." His voice was tight.

"Take me to him."

"As soon as the doc clears you."

She tried to pull away, but he held onto her and forced her to look at him.

"He loves you, and if I don't get you checked out by the doctor before he comes out of surgery, he will kick my ass."

She frowned. "He doesn't love me."

Killion's expression was incredulous. "You didn't hear him declare his undying love seconds after he took a bullet for you?"

She looked around, confused. There was maybe a vague memory of his voice saying *I love you*. "I-I don't… maybe. I didn't want him to *die* for me." Her stomach churned and she put her hand over her mouth, Killion got her to the bathroom in record time. As he held her hair back she decided he wasn't so terrible after all. Suddenly her son was beside her and she hugged him close to her side as soon as she could sit up. "I'm all right, Mikey. Don't fret, baby. But it looks like today is my day to get scanned and poked. You need to be brave for me."

David spoke awkwardly from the doorway. "I'll sit with him."

She turned to look at him incredulously.

One of the president's Secret Service agents tapped him on the shoulder and whispered something in his ear. Nothing like an audience while you vomited.

David shook the guy off. "I can't. I need to stay with my son." He stood there eyeing her with a determined set to his jaw. "I owe him this."

She looked at him dubiously but wasn't in a position to argue. "Don't leave the hospital," she warned.

David nodded.

She tried not to think about Jed as the doctors whisked her off to get a CT scan, but he was all she could think of.

CHAPTER TWENTY

Former Israeli Colonel Elan Gourda walked down the tunnel to his plane and showed the air steward his boarding pass.

His wounds were healing; the gash on his head hidden by his thick black hair and a wool hat. His shoulder was bandaged and not swollen or hurting. He didn't think it was infected.

He was going home for the holidays and had never been more relieved, but the death of the woman weighed heavily on him, even though he'd watched from a building across the street, prepared to kill her if the president's protection detail didn't do the job for him. They had and he'd been grateful.

The plan had been to put the president in real danger, but they hadn't wanted the assassination attempt to actually succeed. Elan's job had been to manage the plot hatched between the former head of the Mossad and a high-level American politician. They'd set up would-be terrorists, led by the mercenary Sargon Al Sahad and given them opportunity. There had been sacrifices, obviously, more people had died than Elan had ever imagined, but these people would have attacked someone, somewhere. At least they were dead now.

His priority had been creating an act of war without killing the US President.

Ironically, he'd almost failed.

Pilah Rasheed had almost gotten to the guy, probably would have clipped him if not for the FBI agent who'd been getting in their way from the start of this op. The bullet probably wouldn't kill the guy, but it might come close.

Pilah's death bothered him. Why, when she'd killed so many innocents, he didn't know. He looked at the picture he'd kept on his cell phone. Two little girls with a female mercenary he'd hired to get them out of Sargon's clutches. They didn't know she was a trained soldier. He could tell by the way they held her hand that the girls liked her.

He hadn't decided what would happen to them yet. At first he'd been going to send them to a refugee camp, but life there would be harsh and cruel. He stared at the screen, a weird understanding flowing over him that he really was retiring. He was tired—no longer the "tip of the spear." It was over. He was done with death and duty, no matter how great his country's need, he could not kill anyone else out of political necessity. He touched the little gap-toothed smile and then deleted the image. He knew what he was going to do when he got home. He knew what his next mission would be.

The girls would have a home. They'd be safe. He'd be keeping his promise to the dead mother and moving on to a new life. The plane taxied along the runway, continued to accelerate. Within seconds they were airborne, his head pressed back against the leather seat.

He closed his eyes and prayed for forgiveness. The image of the little redheaded boy floated through his mind and he sighed. Maybe his God had already forgiven him. Saving the boy meant Elan could live with what he'd done. And he didn't think that would be true if he'd put a bullet in Michael Vincent as originally ordered.

———————

TED BURGER, THE Vice President of the United States of America, stared out the windows of his Kentucky home and smiled. It had all worked perfectly. His telephone rang, but he didn't want to talk to anyone just now. He stood and rifled for the burner cell in his pocket. He pulled out the SIM card and threw it on the fire. Tossed the battery in the wastebasket and the phone casing into the flames after the card.

There was nothing left to link him to the terrorist attack or the staged attempt on the president's life. He allowed himself a quiet chuckle. Hague was a trusting fool. If things had gone wrong and the president had actually died, Ted wouldn't have shed too many tears. He hadn't gone into politics to be second best. And without his wealthy backers, Hague would never have won the election in the first place. But this plan had worked—consolidating Ted's position of power, bolstering his strong support both from and for the State of Israel.

Hague was a fool with his pacifistic ways. But most fools could be manipulated as long as you were tough enough to hold your nerve.

There was a knock on the door.

"Come in."

A maid he didn't recognize pushed in a cart holding coffee and cake. *That time already*? She was a pretty thing. She smiled at him, and he wondered why he hadn't seen her before. He would definitely have noticed.

"Would you like me to pour for you, Mr. Vice President?"

"Sure." He took a wingback chair beside the fire. The smell of burnt plastic permeated the air, but the woman didn't comment. "Where's Nancy?"

Nancy had been with him for years and wasn't so pleasant to look at.

"She came down with the stomach flu."

Ted grunted. Last thing he wanted was stomach flu. "Have the staff disinfect the place before we all catch it."

"Yes, sir."

She carried his coffee across to him. Held his gaze. "Cream, no sugar." She put it on the table beside him. God, she was pretty. Gray eyes and blond hair. Trim figure with long, elegant fingers.

"Thank you. I didn't catch your name?" He watched her ass flex under her uniform as she walked back to the cart.

"Rachel, sir. Would you like some cake? Carrot or chocolate?"

"Carrot cake. Please." He picked up his cup and took a sip. Wondered if he dare make a pass at this female. His wife was away visiting her mother and the rest of the family wasn't yet home for the holidays. He sipped more of his coffee and watched her move. Cutting him a large piece of cake and putting it onto a dainty, porcelain plate. Probably best to bide his time. She might be a gold-digger or a trouble-maker. Best to check her out before he dipped his wick. "How long have you worked here, Rachel?"

"Oh, not long at all, sir."

"Call me Ted."

A wide smile broke out across her features, and she walked over and put the cake next to him on the table.

He drank more coffee, realized he was feeling sleepy. Big day today. He hadn't slept much over the past week.

"Are you OK, Ted?" The maid squatted by his feet.

A sweat broke out on his brow. His hands shook, and she

took the cup from his fingers and placed it on the side table.

"Perhaps I've already got the damned flu." His words slurred. His eyelids got heavier. "Better call the doctor."

She placed her hand on his forehead. "Oh, I think you just need to rest for a little while, Ted."

Audacious chit. But his eyes closed despite his best efforts.

"This is what happens when you start meddling in things you shouldn't, Ted, compliments of The Gateway Project."

The Gateway Project? That was over, finished! Scattered like roaches under a Mexican sun. He'd shut it down himself. Unless… His heart raced. The muscles pounding so hard and fast you'd think he was running. Someone wasn't finished. Someone was still taking vigilante justice. *Against him…* A screaming pain tore through his chest, and his eyes flew open as he clutched at his collar. "Doctor. Get a doctor…" He lunged up out of the chair. The maid sidestepped and he crashed to the floor on the Persian carpet. Rolling onto his back as his breath grew hoarse and thin. His hands clawed the rug. His veins stretched painfully inside him as his blood boiled. "Help. Please help."

Cool, gray eyes assessed him. "Be grateful it was poison and not a bullet, Mr. Vice President. All those people dead just so you could stir up another war."

Not cause a war—protect his people, he wanted to argue. But his tongue wouldn't work. The pain in his chest so intense it was as if his heart was being physically ripped from his chest.

"Sleep now," the woman said calmly. She squeezed his hand, comforting. This lovely assassin with carrot cake and coffee. The last thing he saw was her gray eyes and pretty face. An angel, a beautiful, deadly angel.

JED WOKE SLOWLY, through a mist of fatigue and confusion. But one thing was clear in his mind. "Vivi."

He sensed movement around the bed, indistinguishable as he squinted against the bright light. When his vision finally cleared there was the dark-haired version of the woman he loved. Nothing like a shooter to clarify those emotions.

"Are you OK?" he asked.

She nodded. Jed grabbed her arm as she leaned over him. He didn't give her time to think, he just held her head between his hands and kissed her on the lips with everything he felt for her poured into that connection. She remained stiff for just a moment and still he held her, refusing to stop until she finally kissed him back.

"Looks like the FBI finally managed to get something right."

Jed recognized that voice. *Killion.*

"That's not the FBI, that's Brennan genes." His brother, Liam.

He pulled back from Vivi even though he didn't want to. He was on enough morphine he was feeling no pain. "I guess we have too much of an audience to take this further?" He winked as she shook her head, exasperated.

Someone coughed. "So much for you taking a break." Shit, his boss, Frazer. Great.

"He did throw himself in front of the president." Vivi defended him.

He grimaced. "I threw myself in front of you and Michael, Vivi. The president is just lucky he was in my trajectory."

"Don't tell him that," Frazer raised a brow and came over

to the bed. "I think you're getting a raise, and the chances of me being able to fire you are down to zero." His grin subsided, but the light in his eyes told Jed how worried he'd been.

"I take it I'm going to live?" asked Jed.

They all nodded.

"Until I kick your ass for leaving when you did," Liam muttered darkly.

Jed ignored him. "Lose any vital organs?" His back hurt. Jeez.

"One bullet stuck in your back ribs. The other one passed through your right lung but managed to miss all major organs."

"So your dick's safe." Killion sent Vivi an apologetic grin.

Jed tried to sit up, and they all virtually launched themselves at him. The pain was staggering, but he was more humbled by the fact they cared. Vivi handed him the controls and he raised the bed.

"Is the threat over?"

Frazer pulled out his cell phone and showed him a picture of two little girls. "We believe Pilah Rasheed was pressured into acting by the threat to the well-being of her children."

Crap. She'd been trying to save her children but willing to sacrifice other people's?

"So *this* was always the endgame. Not the attack on the mall itself, but the hit on the president," said Jed.

"Because the president usually comes to visit the victims of a major incident in the hospital." Frazer agreed.

Vivi sat on the bed beside Jed and he held her hand. She wore a black t-shirt and a pair of jeans. Running shoes were on her feet. The terror he'd felt at the thought of losing her had cleared his mind about all sorts of things, and he now knew exactly what he wanted. Her. Them.

"But they failed. The president is still alive," Liam said.

Frazer and Killion exchanged a glance with him. Because maybe the perpetrators hadn't failed. The country was now on high alert and feeling pretty damn hostile toward the Arab nations. Maybe they'd gotten exactly what they wanted.

Frazer took a phone call and then placed his finger over the mic. "Vice President Burger was just found dead in his home. Looks like a heart attack, but the ME is going to conduct an autopsy ASAP." They all exchanged disbelieving glances. "I need to go. I have a briefing with the president."

Jed's pain meds were wearing off and he was anxious to talk to Vivi alone before he needed a fresh dose, which would probably send him right back to sleep.

"Did you catch the man who attacked us in the cottage?" Vivi asked his boss.

Frazer shook his head. "DNA and fingerprints are not in any system we can tap. We did pick up an officer in the local police force who was feeding the terrorists information. Now that Sargon is dead it's going to be harder to figure out his motives and who really hired him." Frazer gathered his coat and sent Jed a smile. "Glad to see you alive, Brennan. Take a few weeks off. For real this time."

Jed looked at his prostrate form. He might not have much choice. "I might take you up on that."

The men all left and Vivi hovered, looking as if she didn't know whether or not she should leave him.

He held out his hand and she slowly reached out to him. "Where's Michael?"

"Your mom and dad took him to the hotel to change. Then they are coming back here to see you again."

He pulled her to him. "I messed up, Vivi. Sending you away, I thought you'd be safer. But I messed up. I'm sorry."

Her serious blue eyes filled with something that looked a lot like love.

"Did you mean what you said on the phone?" he asked. It seemed like a hundred days ago now.

She turned away, head bowed. "I know I said it too fast. It was crazy, but I just wanted to be brave enough to say it out loud—"

"Did you mean it?"

She laughed and blinked rapidly. "I never meant anything as much as I meant that."

"I meant what I said back there after I was shot, Vivi. I found my family. I never even knew I wanted one until I found you and Michael. I love you. I love him. I know I was slow in saying it back to you on the phone, but you shocked me. I never expected you to trust me after all I put you through. After I failed you so badly. You humbled me and made me stupid." He pulled her down so her forehead rested against his. "You think they'll find a spot for me in the Fargo field office?"

"You can't leave your job for us, Jed—"

"My current job doesn't go great with family time."

"You're talking to a single mom and a fatherless boy." Her eyes shone, half sadness, half rueful amusement. "Any time we spend with you will be a bonus, but trust me, we can cope on our own." She pulled her lips into a wry smile. "I don't want you to change your job. It's important and you're good at it."

"I don't know how you know that, considering—"

She placed her finger against his lips, which he liked even though it wasn't her lips. Unfortunately he was really starting to hurt.

"Listen for a moment. I can work anywhere. So if you want to give this thing between us a go and see how we get on, me and Michael will come stay with you for a while. He's starting to communicate." Her eyes sparkled. "He typed out some words and he's making sounds. I'm going to see if I can find some speech therapists who can help him."

"Let's ease him into it." He held her gaze. "I'll stay with you while I recover—or we could all go to the cabin."

She swallowed hard. "I'd like that. Both of those options." Her eyes searched his face, uncertainty making her hesitate. "I don't want to rush into things and make a mistake but..."

"But it doesn't feel like a mistake," Jed finished her sentence for her. "I know."

The door opened and in walked Michael and Jed's parents. The relieved smiles on their faces revealed exactly how worried they'd been. His mother looked like she'd been crying.

For a man who was married to his work and rarely saw his family, he knew life was about to change drastically. He gave Michael's hand a squeeze. "Look after them until I'm out of here, OK, Mikey? Should be tomorrow."

They all snorted but he'd already taken another dose of morphine because the pain burned so bad he thought he was going to start making loud whining noises. Vivi bent to kiss him softly on the lips. She was the most beautiful, most resilient woman he'd ever met. He couldn't wait to get out of this place and start the rest of their lives together. His vision started to fade and Vivi gripped his hand.

"Don't let go," he murmured through the increasing fog.

"I won't let go."

"Promise?"

"I promise." He heard the smile in her voice though his lids were too heavy to lift. At least this time he knew what he'd be waking up to.

EPILOGUE

December 23rd. Eleven days later.

A SSISTANT SPECIAL AGENT in Charge Lincoln Frazer had just watched a man he knew to be a traitor and a murderer buried with full military honors in Arlington Cemetery. Vice President Ted Burger had not only plotted a terrorist attack against his own people on home soil, including an attempt on the president's life, he'd also been a leading figure in The Gateway Project—a high level vigilante organization. The fact that just a few short weeks ago Frazer had agreed to a cover-up based on the Vice President's orders, rather than risk the destruction of the FBI's Behavioral Analysis Unit, made acid churn in his stomach. He had to live with his choices, but it didn't mean he had to like them.

Officially, the VP had died of a coronary. In reality, he'd ingested a tiny amount of batrachotoxin, which had been smeared on the lip of his coffee cup. It had killed him in a matter of minutes. No one had seen a thing.

Frazer stood in the Oval Office at the White House, full of solemnity and not a small amount of unease, surrounded by Christmas cards and decorations that proclaimed Joy and Happiness to the world. Those wishes had never felt more precarious.

"What do we know about the woman who delivered the

poison?" President Hague sat behind his polished desk and eyed him over half-rim glasses. Joshua Hague was a man of economics, not tactical aggression, and had been vital in the recovery of the US economy. He was just now realizing being the president of the United States involved a lot more than balancing the check book.

"She's a professional assassin. We don't know her name or have any good photographs of her face, but I've seen her work before. She's fond of poison dart frogs."

"Any idea who hired her?"

Frazer stood taller. "No, Mr. President. It is possible she was acting alone." He was being granted a rare private interview with the president and what they were discussing was only known to a handful of people. Still, he couldn't reveal the whole truth without putting lives at risk, lives of good people, people who were the best chance they had of catching this woman.

"Am I in danger?" the president asked.

Frazer hesitated. "She only appears to kill people who have also committed murder, sir." He wondered if that put him on her list? She could hardly throw stones under the circumstances.

"As US President, there are many who say I commit murder every day." Hague stared at the papers on his desk, clearly uneasy with some of the recent decisions he'd been forced to make.

"I think after everything that happened you need to be extra-aware of your security, Mr. President. Right now, I don't know who hired her or if she has her own agenda. White House security is excellent, but until she's captured, I think you'd be wise to use caution in all things, but I don't think you're a target."

Hague nodded thoughtfully. "Are you confident the FBI tracked down everyone involved in the terror attacks in Minnesota?"

"All the terrorists directly involved with the mall shooting are dead. So are the men who attacked the safe house—one guy was pulled out of a dumpster with a bullet from his own gun in his brain. We have a local cop who was bribed, but according to our interrogators, doesn't know anything about who was running the show. Abdullah Mulhadre isn't talking and never will." Which raised major issues with Syria as the guy had diplomatic immunity. "We never caught the man who attacked Jed Brennan and Vivi Vincent in the cabin."

"We should release Mulhadre," said Hague. "Something tells me his own people are going to treat him far worse than we ever would."

Frazer agreed. He doubted Mulhadre truly knew who'd instigated the plot. Even they had no *conclusive* proof, just a Tanfoglio handgun, an array of cell phone data Alex Parker had illegally traced between Burger, Al Sahad and Pilah Rasheed, plus the untimely death of Vice President Burger by a known vigilante assassin. It could be a complex setup by unknown malicious entities. Thankfully Frazer had been able to persuade President Hague that, despite the money trail leading from the Syrian regime to the terrorists, he didn't think they were responsible for what had happened.

War had been averted. For now. Everyone was still on high alert though.

Hague slumped back in his chair. "I've spoken to the Israeli Prime Minister. He assured me his country had nothing to do with the attack."

Frazer cocked a brow. "Frankly, he's not likely to say anything else, Mr. President."

The president rolled his shoulders and put his pen down and stood. "I spoke to my Chiefs of Staff." The recent events had stirred up riots similar to the Arab Spring, but this time the anger was directed fiercely against the US. "We are increasing military preparedness at all bases and consulates. With the Russians making moves we're stretched thin at a time we need to be seen as stronger than ever." He looked up. The lines on his face were more marked than they had been eleven days ago, before the attempted assassination. "I can't even point fingers right now without the risk of all-out nuclear war." He turned to look out of the windows as the lights started to come on across the city. "What did they think this would achieve?" He sounded genuinely perplexed.

"Well, someone managed to stir up trouble with every nation in the Middle East, which I think was their main objective." Frazer cleared his throat. "And they never expected to get found out. The fact Jed, Vivi, and Michael survived…"

Miracle.

The president nodded. "I never did like Burger."

"But you chose him as a running-mate?"

A quick grin showed Frazer the sharp mind beneath the laid back persona. "I wanted to win, ASAC Frazer. I needed Burger for that. Now I get to choose someone I admire and can work with." He ran a hand over his thinning hair. "The man did me a favor. That should make him turn in his grave."

"Any idea who you might pick?"

Hague pursed his lips. "I'm going to ask Madeleine Florentine."

The Governor of California was a leading advocate of

developing alternative energy sources to try and break their country's reliance on fossil fuels. Big oil would be pissed, but from a security point of view, Frazer thought it was sensible long-term planning. "She's an excellent choice."

"I want you to check her out before I make a final decision."

He blinked. "Me, sir?"

Hague held Frazer's gaze and nodded. "Your people were the ones who figured out the connection between Burger and the assassination attempt."

"It's all circumstantial, sir," Frazer reminded him. "It might not have stood up in a court of law. And someone else figured it out too—"

"That's exactly my point." President Hague's eyes gleamed. "I would appreciate it if you'd run some background checks just to make sure that I'm not hiring someone who might stab me in the back—literally. I love my job, but I hope to make it to retirement."

"I'll do what I can, sir."

The president nodded sharply and then smiled. "I have a surprise for you. I invited Special Agent Brennan, Vivi Vincent, and her son to dinner tonight. I'd like you to join us."

Frazer checked his watch. He was supposed to go to the Russian Ambassador's Christmas party, but one didn't blow off the US President for the opposition. Plus, he wanted to see Jed.

"Thank you. I need to make a phone call if I may?" Special Agent Matt Lazlo would cover for him. He lived less than an hour away and Frazer would send a car. The guy even had a uniform to throw on for these occasions.

A Christmas party sounded like exactly the sort of thing

they all needed. Then a few days of R&R before they got back to chasing the bad guys. Frazer hoped the bad guys got the memo and everyone took a break. He wondered where the female assassin would spend Christmas. He'd find her eventually. He'd stop her, one way or another.

USEFUL ACRONYM DEFINITIONS FOR TONI'S BOOKS

ADA: Assistant District Attorney
AG: Attorney General
ASAC: Assistant Special Agent in Charge
ASC: Assistant Section Chief
ATF: Alcohol, Tobacco, and Firearms
BAU: Behavioral Analysis Unit
BOLO: Be on the Lookout
BORTAC: US Border Patrol Tactical Unit
BUCAR: Bureau Car
CBP: US Customs and Border Patrol
CBT: Cognitive Behavioral Therapy
CIRG: Critical Incident Response Group
CMU: Crisis Management Unit
CN: Crisis Negotiator
CNU: Crisis Negotiation Unit
CO: Commanding Officer
CODIS: Combined DNA Index System
CP: Command Post
CQB: Close-Quarters Battle
DA: District Attorney
DEA: Drug Enforcement Administration
DEVGRU: Naval Special Warfare Development Group
DIA: Defense Intelligence Agency

DHS: Department of Homeland Security
DOB: Date of Birth
DOD: Department of Defense
DOJ: Department of Justice
DS: Diplomatic Security
DSS: US Diplomatic Security Service
DVI: Disaster Victim Identification
EMDR: Eye Movement Desensitization & Reprocessing
EMT: Emergency Medical Technician
ERT: Evidence Response Team
FOA: First-Office Assignment
FBI: Federal Bureau of Investigation
FNG: Fucking New Guy
FO: Field Office
FWO: Federal Wildlife Officer
IC: Incident Commander
IC: Intelligence Community
ICE: US Immigration and Customs Enforcement
HAHO: High Altitude High Opening (parachute jump)
HRT: Hostage Rescue Team
HT: Hostage-Taker
JEH: J. Edgar Hoover Building (FBI Headquarters)
K&R: Kidnap and Ransom
LAPD: Los Angeles Police Department
LEO: Law Enforcement Officer
LZ: Landing Zone
ME: Medical Examiner
MO: Modus Operandi
NAT: New Agent Trainee
NCAVC: National Center for Analysis of Violent Crime
NCIC: National Crime Information Center
NFT: Non-Fungible Token
NOTS: New Operator Training School

NPS: National Park Service
NYFO: New York Field Office
OC: Organized Crime
OCU: Organized Crime Unit
OPR: Office of Professional Responsibility
POTUS: President of the United States
PT: Physiology Technician
PTSD: Post-Traumatic Stress Disorder
RA: Resident Agency
RCMP: Royal Canadian Mounted Police
RSO: Senior Regional Security Officer from the US
    Diplomatic Service
SA: Special Agent
SAC: Special Agent-in-Charge
SANE: Sexual Assault Nurse Examiners
SAS: Special Air Squadron (British Special Forces unit)
SD: Secure Digital
SIOC: Strategic Information & Operations
SF: Special Forces
SSA: Supervisory Special Agent
SWAT: Special Weapons and Tactics
TC: Tactical Commander
TDY: Temporary Duty Yonder
TEDAC: Terrorist Explosive Device Analytical Center
TOD: Time of Death
UAF: University of Alaska, Fairbanks
UBC: Undocumented Border Crosser
UNSUB: Unknown Subject
USSS: United States Secret Service
ViCAP: Violent Criminal Apprehension Program
VIN: Vehicle Identification Number
WFO: Washington Field Office

COLD JUSTICE WORLD OVERVIEW
All books can be read as standalones

The Cold Justice® series books are also available as **audiobooks** narrated by Eric Dove, and in various box set compilations.

Check out all Toni's books on her website
(www.tonindersonauthor.com/books-2)

ACKNOWLEDGMENTS

As always, biggest thanks go to my amazing critique partner Kathy Altman who's been on this journey with me for more than a decade. Thanks also, for encouragement and beta-reads, to Laurie Wood, and my lovely hubby, Gary, and also for feedback from my early reviewers who rock. Thank you.

Thanks to my editors, especially the patient and gracious Ally Robertson who talked me off the ledge more than once over this book. And Joan at JRT Editing who helped me iron out the kinks and hopefully fix my comma issues.

I'm very grateful to Syd Gill for creating awesome covers for this Cold Justice Series.

And thanks also to my readers and friends on Facebook/online who are there when I need a boost or a kick in the derriere—depending on the day. I appreciate each and every one of you.

ABOUT THE AUTHOR

Toni Anderson writes gritty, sexy, FBI Romantic Thrillers, and is a *New York Times* and a *USA Today* bestselling author. Her books have won the Daphne du Maurier Award for Excellence in Mystery and Suspense, Readers' Choice, Aspen Gold, Book Buyers' Best, Golden Quill, National Excellence in Story Telling Contest, and National Excellence in Romance Fiction awards. She's been a finalist in both the Vivian Contest and the RITA Award from the Romance Writers of America. Toni's books have been translated into five different languages and over three million copies of her books have been downloaded.

Best known for her Cold Justice® books perhaps it's not surprising to discover Toni lives in one of the most extreme climates on earth—Manitoba, Canada. Formerly a Marine Biologist, Toni still misses the ocean, but is lucky enough to travel for research purposes. In late 2015, she visited FBI Headquarters in Washington DC, including a tour of the Strategic Information and Operations Center. She hopes not to get arrested for her Google searches.

Sign up for Toni Anderson's newsletter:
www.toniandersonauthor.com/newsletter-signup

Like Toni Anderson on Facebook:
facebook.com/toniandersonauthor

Follow on Instagram:
instagram.com/toni_anderson_author

64807793R00203